Praise for *Border Crossers*

'The consummate skill with which Bhaskar Roy slips the subcontinent's post-Partition dilemma in, almost as sub-text, is astonishing and reminiscent of Gabriel García Márquez. *Border Crossers* is at heart, like all the very best works, prophetic and optimistic – a fantastic work by a new and accomplished voice.'

– **Paul Pickering**, Booker Prize–longlisted author of *Lucy*

'The characters are strong as is the evocation of locations with writing which is rich and sensual, an extremely good evocation of the sights, sounds and smells of India.'

– **Jad Adams**, author of *Decadent Women: Yellow Book Lives*

'A master of English prose and dialogue, Roy makes one constantly eager, sometimes even desperate, to know what happens next. He trawls the underworld with no skating over its sometimes fetid aspects. He can effortlessly convey loneliness, love, abject poverty, death – the prose never falters. Like Henry Fielding's *Tom Jones*, this is a picaresque novel of supreme quality. Indian history impinges on the narrative – the new scourge of Hindu extremism.'

– **Bevis Hillier**, former editor of *The Connoisseur* and *The Times Saturday Review*

As a journalist, **Bhaskar Roy** worked for some of India's leading publications – *India Today, Indian Express* and the *Times of India* among them. In 2011, Roy quit mainstream journalism and began editing *The Equator Line* quarterly. He was the founding editor of the themed magazine of nonconformist writing. He lives in Delhi with his wife.

ALSO BY THE AUTHOR

FICTION

The Defeat or Distant Drumbeats

An Escape into Silence

NON-FICTION

Fifty Year Road

BORDER CROSSERS

BHASKAR ROY

hachette
INDIA

First published in 2024 by Hachette India
(Registered name: Hachette Book Publishing India Pvt. Ltd)
An Hachette UK company
www.hachetteindia.com

1

Illustration on p. 285 by Bhawani Shankar

Print ISBN 978-93-5731-949-2
Ebook ISBN 978-93-5731-368-1

Hachette Book Publishing India Pvt. Ltd
4th & 5th Floors, Corporate Centre,
Plot No. 94, Sector 44, Gurugram 122003, India

Typeset in Adobe Garamond Pro 11/15.5
by R. Ajith Kumar, New Delhi

Printed and bound in India
by Manipal Technologies Limited

MIX
Paper | Supporting responsible forestry
FSC™ C043100
FSC www.fsc.org

Of course for Manimala

The undiscovered country from whose bourn
No traveller returns

– *Hamlet,* Shakespeare

1
Love in April

Like an obdurate creeper from a crack in the wall, a little bazaar has come up in the middle of the shantytown – unobtrusively, without buzzing like one. The haphazard cluster has grown slowly, one shop at a time, sensing business.

An old man sits on a rough plank, selling groceries – coarse broken rice, cheap pulses, flour, jaggery, sawdust sugar, limp red chillies… In rusty tins, the items look lustreless, waiting for buyers for a very long time. Bugs move inside the flour, causing a mild tremor on the surface. Swollen black ants crawl over the chunk of blackish jaggery. The man grimaces, shooing away flies with an old newspaper and abusing the world.

'Not a single buyer since morning,' he complains to no one in particular. 'Are the fucking fools of the slum eating chow mein?' He raises his voice, swiping the folded paper through the air. 'Maybe the bastards go to the malls to buy salt and grate their balls on the moving stairs, ha.'

'You said it well, Chacha.' The boy from the next stall laughs. The greengrocer. He is splashing the cabbages and cauliflowers with water from a plastic bucket. 'A shop in the new mall actually sells vegetables.'

'What?' The old man looks scandalized.

'Yes, Chacha. There's a fish shop also.'

'Fish! Inside that shiny, cool palace? Chhaa! I tell you, very soon the imbeciles will start selling babies in the mall. Yesss. Babies by the kilo!'

'Something like that is actually happening, Chacha.' On her way back from work, a young woman has stopped by the greengrocer's to buy some vegetables. She was listening to the old man's rantings. 'My madam's sister has come from Germany. Doctors said she cannot make a baby because her heart is damaged. She asked me to hatch her egg with her husband's worm in it. "We will give you a lakh of rupees" – yes, she said that. I died in shame. But the witch laughed, shaking her reedy body. "It's not what you're thinking." She tapped my shoulder. "We take you to the doctor, and she puts the seed from my egg and my husband's worm inside you. Bas. It will grow into a baby in ten months." The cardboard woman coaxed me, pleaded holding my hand. "You will live with us for a year. Good food. Comfort. A visit to the doctor once in a while." She put an arm around me. "If we get our baby all right, why, I can even help you buy a little place of your own somewhere." Scared, I ran away, all the time fearing someone else's baby moving inside me.'

A small crowd has gathered around the woman, hanging on her every word.

'The diseased rich and their moth-eaten balls! Keck…thoo!' The old man's face contorts with revulsion as if he wants to retch. 'You cannot tell their women from frozen fish, huh! And they have the guts to ask our girl to hatch their eggs! Maaro saalon ko!'

The crowd agrees. *Bash up the bastards!* Everyone turns to the woman.

'Putli, you did the right thing by saying no. Why didn't you slap that weedy woman?'

As the old man blusters, others look at her admiringly. A new star.

'I often put a hand on my belly to see if they have already tricked me into something, if a baby is actually kicking.' Looking worried, she taps her navel.

All eyes focus on the woman's stomach, looking for signs of some foul play by her employers.

'Don't worry, Putli.' The old man holds her gaze for a few moments, then turns to the crowd. 'If that witch has already done something to our Putli – some black magic – we will make her pay big money. Yeah, BIG MONEY… one – no – two l-a-a-khh rupees.'

'Ye-e-e-ss, twoo laakkh,' the crowd roars back.

Putli nods, acknowledging her new stature with a broad smile, and walks away. With her, all the excitement too vanishes. The crowd disperses.

Only the man selling mithai and snacks keeps shaking his head. 'What all happens in a city,' he mumbles. Sitting next to a fly-lined rickety showcase, its cracked glass front taped at a few places, he is frying samosas in a gunky cauldron over an open fire. 'It's a strange place.'

Beside him, a woman spreads trays of chewing tobacco pouches, cheap cigarettes, bidi bundles wrapped in coarse paper, FLAG printed on them. Strings of shampoo sachets are tied between two bamboo poles like streamers. The woman slices betel nuts and looks around. 'Here you're citied.' She laughs. Splashes a little water from a plastic bottle over the neatly piled betel on a marble slab. The piece of red cloth covering the yellowish-green leaves turns blood-dark. In a wooden box, she keeps bindi strips. On their way to work, young women stop by to stick a bindi on their foreheads. This is the busiest stall. Business is brisk.

A rickshaw-wallah buys a bundle of Flag bidis, smokes one and waits for a little chat with Mausi. He pulls out a comb from his hip pocket and moves it through his thickly oiled black hair. 'Mausi —' Tentative, he lowers his voice.

'What?' Disgust in her voice.

'Give me… uh…' He fumbles, gropes for words.

She frowns.

'That balloon.'

'Hai!' She screws up her face, taking out a packet of cheap condoms from an old chocolate box. For a moment, she blushes, looking at the copulating couple on the packet, but quickly regains her hold. 'Burnt-faced monkey! You've not earned even ten rupees since morning. And you're going to the pit to smell a mangy bitch!' She throws the little packet at him.

The man laughs. 'Don't be angry, Mausi. I blow up the balloon only in the evening. Now I am going to park my rickshaw outside the mall and wait for the memsahibs with their bulging shopping bags.'

'Go away, you – you shameless langur!'

He giggles, throwing away the half-smoked bidi. 'Honestly, Mausi, when a buxom beauty climbs onto my rickshaw, fair, bobbed hair, something happens inside me. I am thrilled, I pedal fast, with all my might hey… hey…'

'Go to your village, find a good girl and get married. Now clear off.'

Often, the young men and women meet at Mausi's shop for a chat. The migrants are no longer part of the old village society. But the village has somehow caught up with them. The sanction against open free mixing of boys and girls has persisted in the slum of their new life, too. There are unwritten rules, restrictions.

A man cannot enter the shanty of a woman living alone. Nor can a young man and a woman freely move together, frolicking around town. They still need some pretext to meet. This shop is a good excuse. A convenient rendezvous.

At one end of the bazaar is a little temple of the monkey god. The priest, a young man in flowing ochre robes, a long tuft of hair dangling from his crown, doubles as a tutor for schoolgoing children. He cycles through the narrow lanes and stops at every little gathering, talking about Bihar politics, things happening back home.

On the periphery of the slum is a raw, craggy mosque with neither a dome nor a courtyard, only a green flag flying from its top. In its backyard, Akhtar has set up shop. Every morning, he sits there, hunched over a wobbly iron table under a shed, going through the order book in between talking on the phone. He raises his head occasionally to watch the workers making grilles, joining steel plates with oxyacetylene torches. When there are no calls to make, he listens to popular numbers from Bollywood movies on his phone.

This morning, the yard is still quiet, not buzzing with activity. Akhtar sees Jamal stop at Mausi's shop. Leaning against his bicycle, he strikes a match to light a cigarette, puffs on it deeply. He is eagerly talking to the old woman. She must have said something funny; the fart laughs heartily. Blood suddenly rushes to Akhtar's head. The moron's wavy hair, falling to his shoulders, flutters. The cycle shakes. Behnchod Bangladeshi! Akhtar swears, looking hatefully at Jamal. There will be a power cut in an hour, and the fucking fellow is still quizzing Mausi for some news about that darkie whore! The laggard must be lashed and that hooker of his – raped. Nah, gang-raped! Akhtar is surprised at his own anger, the rush of blood, loud words, brutalities unleashed on Jamal for being a *sister-fucker*. Unconcerned, Jamal buys a paan, pushes it into his mouth and chews with relish.

When Jamal pedals leisurely into the yard and finally brakes, Akhtar explodes. 'I have to deliver two hundred feet of balcony grille before lunch. And you were smooching the farting old woman to know about that tart of yours? You Bangladeshi bastard!'

'Akhtar Bhai, talk business,' Jamal shouts back. 'Your work will be done by noon. Who's my love – none of your business. This much I know that you will never love a girl; you'll take home a bride for a fat dowry.'

Jamal sits back on his haunches. The gangly man with his shock of long, unkempt hair puts together two large L-shaped angles as Akhtar watches. The oxy-fuel torch splays, blue flames blossom, the outline of a gate emerges.

'Now hurry. I have ordered tea for both of us.' Akhtar mellows after the sudden outburst. Getting a skilled welder is not easy. Such custom grille workshops are sprouting up every day in this boomtown. Those with big money will naturally pick up the good workers at a premium. The fish-eating Bangladeshi knows his job. A moody fellow with a swirling accent, he, however, has given his business a big push. The chap has skills and ideas, too. Earlier, his grilles had neither perfect finish nor such striking designs. *Let the fool fuck that famished female; that's none of my business really.* Akhtar's head sways to the lilting tune on the phone. A raunchy item number.

He pores over the order book. It's full for the next two months.

He watches the crazy welder. Wearing the dark glass mask, he is busy welding the iron pieces with lead. Blue flames shoot out. Slowly, a design blooms out of the jointed hooks and elbows. The fellow's idea – mixing two or three different patterns. Akhtar unknowingly smiles.

The boy from the tea stall puts down on the ground a cloudy glass from his chai stand. Jamal notices the basket. He made it by twisting iron wire and joining scraps for six slots. Thrilled, the boy instantly became his fan. He now waits, his eyes closely following the blue flames.

Taking out the skin from the surface with his fingers, he sips the sugary brew, spitting out the odd tea leaf. Back in Khulna, he loved black tea with a dash of lemon lightening it gold. He detests the way they boil tea here in milk and water. Too much sugar.

'Ustad.' The boy's face lights up. His eyes glint.

'What?' Jamal fakes annoyance.

'I want to learn this work – dark mask, blue flames, iron strips turning into ivy. Will you take me as your chela?'

'You little devil – clear off. Bhaag, bhaag. If someone works with the flames for a long time, he goes blind – do you know that, buddhu?'

'Ustad…'

'Now what?'

'I met her… your…'

Jamal's ears perk up. Something happens inside him, like a jolt of electric current, his entire being tensing in urgent expectation. Still, he does not drop his guard.

'You're lying, you badmash.'

'Honestly, Ustadji. Rabeya – that's her name? She was buying bindis at Mausi's shop, said she had heard about a job in a big man's house. Is going to meet them today.'

Jamal hangs onto the boy's every word – a new job – in a big man's house in one of those high-rises.

We first met in April
Got close in May
Now rains are coming
I'm nervous, not knowing what'll happen—

The hit song from a Bengali movie always plays on his phone. Memories of a life left behind the border come flooding in; the familiar tune echoes in his mind. In Khulna, they had to wait for months before films from Calcutta were screened in their town.

Rowing his little boat down the Rupsa, he sings the song. The river in the estuary is wild, rushing extravagantly towards the sea. The big waves toss his flimsy boat around; the river widens recklessly, and the banks look hazy. The cargo ships laden with goods from faraway places are heading for Mongla Port. Fancy double-decker launches – packed with tourists, exhausted by the deep darkness of the mangrove forests – send strong eddies, pushing his boat away. Jamal's oar digs deep; the boat pulls for the bank. That way it's safe and easier to catch fish. The last trace of city life soon vanishes: the jute mills, factory sheds, Khulna Shipyard recede. The first hints of the Sundarbans fog up the banks.

Past Katia Nangla village, Jamal sees stunted mangrove palms close to the water. The large, round leaves seem to have sprouted straight out of wet, gooey earth; constantly whipped by marauding waves, their trunks are lost behind the canopies.

That's the end of the human kingdom and the start of dark tides, fish, crocodiles and dense forests. Tiger country. Jamal often rows far looking for the silvery hilsa, on some days drifts to the mangroves where the village women wade into the brackish shallows, push net in hand, to catch prawn seedlings to harvest in hatcheries. In the criss-crossed estuary, he is king. Casting the net for a good catch, he hums:

We first met in April…

Jamal gives the boy a two-rupee coin. 'Chhotu, do one thing. When you see her at lunchtime, tell her to wait for me on the old brick bridge at six on Saturday evening.'

The boy picks up the empty glass and looks at him quizzically.

'Do as I tell you, Chhotu. Tomorrow, you'll get another coin.'

The boy keeps standing there, probing him with his inquisitive eyes.

'What?' Jamal raises his eyebrows.

'Is she then…?' The boy grins.

'Yes – *my love in April*.'

2
Boomtown

Taking long steps through uncertain light and moist darkness, he walks past the new apartment blocks, surveying the vast expanse of farmland. He has no idea that this ambivalence will one day turn his life upside down, testing the limits of his being.

Over the layer of fog, a mellow mix of blue and white, day sloughs off the slumber. In the hesitation of early morning, Arijit Basu takes in the scene of busy activity: women and children pick tomatoes; men briskly bundle dark green spinach; a tractor trundles up and down a field. Soaked up by the fog and exuberant crops, its noise has lost the harshness – now nothing more than the click of a wall gecko's tongue: tik tik pat pat tik…

He sees the child – dark, bright-eyed, barely five – limping around his mother. Not to be left behind, the boy picks up a clump of spring onions and walks towards the cart, dragging his weak foot. Throwing them into a pile of vegetables on the cart, he looks at the unshackled beasts, then turns. 'Ma!' he shouts triumphantly. A smile swamps his face.

A strange smell, actually a clutter of many smells, floats around: sourness from the ruffled tomato plants, earth being ploughed up, the sharp assault of freshly tugged-out spring onions. Yellow mustard flowers quiver in the low wind. Fat white radishes, pulled out of the ground like secret treasure, glisten with a soft dusting of morning dew on ivory.

But the scent of late winter, of primeval earth and its brute fertile instincts, does not actually take Arijit deep into the heart of kisan country. Press of hay. Innocence of the buffalo's unreasoned might.

Walking down the smooth new road, he comes across another construction site. More like a theatre of war. Trucks and rollers and strange-looking Caterpillars have lined up for another day of invasion, incision into virgin territory. Apartment blocks are coming up around a sprawling ground.

He looks at the far side of the ground – an irrigation canal quietly flowing towards the distant villages. On its banks has come up a shantytown of plastic sheets and corrugated tin, of filth and grime. Groups of men and women are coming out of the clusters of zigzag pits. Like rows of ants looking for food. Domestics, rickshaw-wallahs, vegetable vendors… they walk down the dirt to be part of city life. In the daytime.

Arijit sees the women – young, famished – coming across the field in small groups. They chatter and laugh.

One playfully pushes another. 'That hero in the new TV series – he's coming to look for you!' Both of them break into giggles.

'Hey, listen, you *beauty queen*! That TV star will tie the knot with you after walking seven times round the fire, haan.'

The haggard woman – perhaps still a teenage girl looking older than her years – nudges her friend. The other holds her arm.

'Oh, really?'

'Honestly, if the hero really comes down, holds your arms and asks your name, what will you say?'

'Why, Dimple – I'm your Dimple… Simple, isn't it? Hahaha…'

They hug, pat each other's arms, laughing to tears.

Arijit feels awkward on realizing his pace has faltered. He consciously walks faster, not wanting to be caught eavesdropping on frivolous girl chatter.

The giant cranes and menacing earthmovers promise to define life in suburbia. The newspapers are full of ads for apartments on sale. On the outskirts of Delhi, this boomtown is where the professionals want to be: executives, IT engineers, airline pilots, doctors. And the new brahmins – yesterday's expats back from either side of the Atlantic to discover the sobering influence of an ancient civilization.

Arijit hastens his pace further.

He is one of them – the new settlers – discovering life all over again in an improbable place. When he came back to India after decades around the world, he had no idea of such a place, its rules and rituals. For him, it was unfamiliar urban life with hints of cow dung and sugarcane. A mix-up. A new city, and yet, the same Jat farmer, his dream of a good harvest, his sturdy wife with heavy silver anklets shining in the sun – it's a first-rate hodgepodge, this place. Like its name, Noahda – a slow corruption from the original developer's vision of Noah's Dale, whatever that may be. Busy activity on the farm, the newness of the apartments, the lean, chattering women coming out of the warren.

From the street, Arijit turns into a wooded driveway leading to Blue Lotus Grove.

At the entrance of the apartment complex, the Gurkha stands at attention and salutes him. 'Salaam, Sahib.' Ram Bahadur Chhetri smiles. The rigidity of his post melts away. Defying his double-barrel gun and olive uniform, a simple boy from the hills flits out.

Arijit nods. He moves a few steps forward, then stops. A

big Tata truck outside F Block has rumpled the stillness of the foggy morning. The mover's men are in a huddle, working out the unloading plan. The furniture, taped cartons, pot plants – all uneasily wait in the back of the truck, to be taken into the new home. Arijit looks at Chhetri.

'Another family is moving in, Sahib.' The security guard sounds excited. 'A lot of new people are going to home here; I wonder what all is going to happen.' He gets close to the big truck. Laughs not knowing why.

'Right.' Arijit stares at the stationary truck once again and walks down the driveway between the apartment blocks and Chancellor Club. He looks back to the front gate. Chhetri is still watching him.

Waiting for the lift, he looks around. A young woman in a tracksuit and trainers walks up and stands beside him. The smell of sleep, a strange scent of sweat and old perfume wash over him. She is so close he can read the fine beads of perspiration glistening on her forehead. He nods.

She smiles back. 'I think I saw your picture in *India Today* sometime back. You are Mr Arijit Basu, right?'

The lift is taking time, stopping at every floor. He looks awkwardly at the young woman.

'Nice to know a famous man.' Her voice has a familiar ring.

'All that is over; now I am a retired man, a pensioner.' He laughs.

'I am Neha. My husband and I run a small manufacturing unit. We make auto parts.'

'How long have you been living here?'

'We moved in two months ago. We've started liking this place. There is something new about Noahda.' She watches him curiously.

The lift finally arrives, unloading a pack of noisy school children, some with their parents, others herded by maids. They get in; two strangers in a closed lift is uneasiness.

'You run every day?' He surveys her running gear admiringly.

'Oh, yes, three kilometres, five days a week.' She looks at herself to see if her body testifies to the regimen. 'When it's very hot or it rains, I do the treadmill.'

He glances at her healthy, toned body, admiring her extravagant youth.

'I have seen you going out…'

'I take a long walk down the road.'

There's a pause, the uneasiness gone. Neha's smell – that strange mix – has filled the lift.

'We're planning a party, the first in our new home. Rakesh and I will be very happy if you come,' Neha laughs like a schoolgirl, 'so we can tell our friends the big man is our neighbour.'

The lift stops at the seventh floor. 'Bye.' She waves, whizzing out.

The money plant has crept up the wall above the front door. The first plant he raised after moving in. He had filled the clay pot with earth and manure and pushed a moss stick into the middle so the creeper could climb it. Within months, it has grown prodigiously into a rich spread. Life settles down, takes root wherever it can. Arijit smiles, touching a dark green leaf. The plant has tiptoed over the wall, sending roots into every possible pore.

While taking out the key from his pocket, he notices her – a feeble phantom, sitting scared on the step to his door. Dusky, very thin, almost skeletal, she has large eyes and long, black hair.

Slumped, her head sunk between the knees, she looks frightened – an animal hounded to a corner.

It takes her a few moments to realize the house owner is actually here, standing right before her. The man she has come to meet.

'Yes?' Irritation in his voice.

She struggles, trying to say something, then slowly gets up, placing her hand on the wall for support. Frightened, completely unnerved, she gasps.

'Namaste, Sahib. Someone told me… er, I heard you are new here. You might need a maid to cook for you…' She is unsure if there is any point in going on. Her courage gives way.

Arijit looks at her. She's in a salwar kameez, like every other woman here; it's old, frayed but freshly washed. There is an air of cleanliness about her. Her exuberant, rough hair combed and neatly braided.

'Who told you I need a maid?'

Either the question or his booming voice saps her residual confidence. Words get stuck on the tip of her tongue. She waits for a while… one, two, three seconds… a little more.

'Uh… a man, sir, the security guard at the gate.'

Her voice falters. The transparent face reveals no guile or evasion. The eyes hint at happiness before the boils, chilblains of the rough road. She looks up at Arijit again.

'I can cook everything – mutton, chicken, fish, soup, porridge.' Perhaps she has regained a little confidence talking about her skills. 'Whatever you prefer, Sahib – vegetarian, eggs, noodles; I can make everything.'

Her head bent, hands clasped, she pleads with her sad eyes. 'You try me for a month; if you don't like my cooking, I won't come.'

She badly needs this job.

'Do you work anywhere else?'

'I did – for a family. Husband and wife, both doctors, and their little boy. They left for Bangalore last month.'

Arijit notices she is speaking Hindi with an unusual accent. It's familiar, but he cannot grasp it.

'What's your name?'

'Rita – Rita Das.'

'And where are you from?'

'I am from Ranchi.'

'Do you have any ID?'

She gives him a blank look.

'A ration card from the government, a voter identity card?'

She shakes her head. Her eyes mist over – the job slipping away on a technicality. Suddenly she smiles remembering something and hurriedly unzips her purse, rummages inside and pulls out a carefully folded paper. Her face is beaming.

'What's this?'

He unfolds the paper. Dr Stanley Matthews, MD, FRCP, has written on his letterhead that he and his wife Liz had been satisfied with Rita's work in the kitchen and impressed by her punctuality and sense of hygiene. 'We have never had occasion to doubt her honesty.' Clipped to the testimonial is a photograph – the doctor couple sitting on a sofa and the maid standing behind with the child in her arms.

Arijit scrutinizes the picture. The man looks relaxed, in a white cotton shirt and a dhoti wrapped around his waist in the style of his native Kerala. In an off-white sari, his gynaecologist wife seems a happy soul, proud of her long, jasmine-laced hair over the shoulder.

From the balloons and bunting and happiness around

the living room, it's clear the couple is celebrating the child's birthday. That the maid has become part of their household. A big moment in her life before Mr and Mrs Doctor packed and left for Bangalore with their baby boy.

Arijit grunts in grudging approval. 'Where do you live?'

She hesitates; the unease surfaces again.

'Yes?' he grumbles, impatient with her silence.

'In the camp by the canal.'

'Camp? Do you mean the slum?'

She keeps quiet, digging her toes into the floor.

Arijit opens the door and asks her in. Before going out for his walk, he had made a cup of black coffee. The empty cup stands on a side table in the living room. She notices it.

'Let me make you another cup of coffee and – some breakfast?'

She walks into the kitchen.

With the day's *Times of India* in hand, Arijit stands on the balcony. From here, the farm looks remote, very different – a pastoral sketch. The tractor a noiseless toy, the people working the fields all dwarfs. The huge spread of mustard, spinach and other winter crops, a richly patterned green carpet. And the shanties? Very much like children's building blocks without any hint of squalor. From this distance, life over there seems calm, unperturbed – no signs of the gnawing sores, scars visible.

Beyond the farm, the lean, meandering canal is soothing. He wonders where it comes from… where it goes.

Arijit sits in an armchair and flips through the pages. Tries to concentrate on the leader. A mild noise of dishes floats in from the kitchen. The clanging of pots and pans, now scrubbed and washed and arranged on the racks. His ears twitch for more sounds.

The appetizing aroma of freshly toasted bread fills the house.

Rita walks across the living room, wiping a bowl with a kitchen towel, completely transformed in a green apron.

'Sir, will you have an egg with toast?'

'All right.'

'Scrambled eggs?'

He nods. She walks back to the kitchen.

He unmindfully turns the newspaper pages and listens to the sounds of life around the house. For the first time, the kitchen is coming alive, humming with activity. Noise. Busy footsteps. He savours the tempting food smells, relishes the recovery of estranged clinks. Unknowingly, he smiles, waiting for the buzz of the kitchen chimney. The ordinariness of familiar sounds coming back from the past is like lost music.

A complete stranger a while ago, Rita is now part of the household, in charge of the kitchen. The apartment, spooky without conversation, is waking to life, humaning.

Sick of a lifetime of conferencing, dialogue, diplomacy, Arijit came to Blue Lotus Grove looking for silence. For the life of a recluse. Then he discovered loneliness, its affliction, the haunting echoes of his unsaid words, the torture of being all alone in the house, deprived of the lilt and hum of a home.

Above the rich sizzle of frying eggs in the pan floats a soft croon. He has no idea what song it is, from which movie. The apartment feels like home for the first time since he moved in.

'Uncle, breakfast is ready.'

Rita stands leaning against the door frame. No longer the

pathetic thing slumped down to the steps. She is in command now. From *Sir, Sahib,* she has graduated to the informality of *Uncle.*

Rita sees Arijit – relaxed, retired in the armchair. She smiles. 'Let me serve you breakfast here.'

She hurries back, the river song in the air. Her words seem to be coming from another world. For the first time in this house, someone is talking to him, serving him a meal. Despite his protests, she places a low table before him, then artfully arranges the plates, sauce, coffee pot and water jug on it.

He looks at the spread. Orange juice in a glass jug, cornflakes in a bowl, sliced papaya on a platter, scrambled eggs, toast and the butter dish. Fork, knife, spoons – all neatly wrapped in a napkin.

'Where did you learn all this? You seem to have trained.'

She smiles awkwardly without saying anything. Her large, raven-deep eyes do the talking: *Thanks for taking me in your employ, thanks for saving me.*

'I am making dal, sabzi, rice and roti for your lunch,' she says. 'By the side of the canal, they sell fresh fish and chicken in the evening.' Her eyes glitter. 'You buy whatever you like. I'll come around six o'clock to make your dinner.'

3
Jihad

A man comes riding his Bajaj down the dirt towards the grille works. He unhurriedly gets down, puts the scooter on its stand and walks into the shop.

Akhtar gets up respectfully. 'Adaab, Maulana Sahib. When did you return from Lucknow?'

The man sits on a chair, flips through an Urdu magazine and remains immersed in a strange corner of his thoughts. He pushes the magazine away to place his laptop bag on the wobbly table. His intelligent eyes glint through the silver-rimmed glasses. His sharp features, wiry frame, fair complexion, carefully trimmed beard – everything is in disagreement with the foul air and rottenness around the shantytown. He looks more like a firebrand activist than a man of God. He smiles absently as he switches on the laptop.

'I was in Hyderabad for a meeting,' he finally says without addressing anyone. 'My Lucknow trip got cancelled.' Over the computer, he peers at the welder. Briefly. Then closes his eyes as if for a spell of meditation. 'Saw a lot, Akhtar Bhai, learnt a lot.' His voice is anguished, heavy with hints of a pervasive tragedy.

Akhtar busily calls out to the tea stall man. 'Four cups,' he shouts, flashing as many fingers. 'Would you like to eat something, Maulana Sahib? An omelette, toast?'

'No. Thank you, Akhtar Bhai. After what I learnt, I have lost my appetite. I cannot sleep either. Terrible things are happening around us…'

The maulana abruptly stops, looks around suspiciously. Fixes his gaze on Jamal again, watches him weld. The violet-blue flames spark furiously, making an occasional sharp noise – tcharaak, taraak… Jamal's dishevelled, wavy hair flutters in the wind from the canal. Taking a break, he hums:

We first met in April…

The maulana turns to Akhtar quizzically.

'A Bangladeshi – knows his job well but a little cracked.' He lowers his voice further. 'Eats rice and fish and chases a haggard woman from his wretched land. She works in someone's house.'

Perhaps Jamal could guess they are talking about him. 'As-salaam aleikum, Maulana Sahib.' He raises his right hand to his chest, still working with the iron pieces.

The lean, sharp maulana concentrates on his computer screen, ignoring Jamal's greeting. A minute passes. 'Call that chap,' he says without taking his eyes off the screen. Akhtar hurriedly gestures to the welder to come up.

Jamal combs his fingers through his unruly, deep-black hair, slaps the dust off his pyjamas and walks up to the enigmatic man with the strange machine.

'Maulana Sahib is visiting our factory after a long time,' Akhtar says in a flattering voice.

Jamal smiles ingratiatingly, rubbing his hands in submission. 'You're a wise man, Sahib. You go to so many places; we can learn a little from you.'

Moving his index finger over the touchpad, the maulana asks Jamal to sit beside him. The cursor rests on the picture folder like a wily lizard lying in wait before the next hunt. An uneasiness grips the welder. His eyes wide, mouth slightly open, he keeps standing.

The maulana points to an empty chair, then whips out a couple of five-hundred-rupee notes from his buck-leather wallet and turns to Akhtar. 'Send someone to the market to buy good stuff – jalebi, kachori, gulab jamun, samosa and Pepsi.' He flicks a smile. 'Sit next to me, Bangladeshi friend.' He pats Jamal on the back. Clicks twice on a folder on the desktop. 'Look, this is Bosnia – thousands of miles from Delhi.' The picture of bodies lined up on the ground covers the screen.

The long row of corpses draped in white shocks Jamal. It's uneasiness. Perhaps nausea. He is not sure.

'They were brutally gunned down. Their crime? They were Muslim, your brothers.' The maulana's voice drips acid and pain in equal measure. Fire, too. For a moment, he looks at Jamal, then focuses on the screen.

Jamal sees the prone bodies – inert, inconspicuous. Two soldiers on guard. They are looking away. 'Was there any war going on?' he asks, an unruly curiosity overriding his discomfort.

'Yes. War on Islam.' The mystery man looks sharply at him.

Jamal is seared by the toxic glare.

Click.

'This is Chechnya – somewhere in Russia. They killed hundreds of Muslims because they refused to remain slaves of Christians. The brutes attacked them with big guns, tanks and aircraft.'

The man flinches, closes his eyes for a second or two, then slowly turns to Jamal. His icy eyes are burning. 'Wherever you look – Europe, America, Asia – a sinister design is unfolding to wipe us out. Evil Americans and wily Jews have conspired to erase Muslims off the face of the Earth.' He looks pained, deeply distressed. His tortured face has turned crimson. As if he is struggling with turmoil within. 'And this is Kashmir – beautiful Kashmir, paradise on Earth. Now the valley of flowers and lakes and snow-crested peaks drips blood. Its gardens reek of young corpses – Muslims shot like dogs by the Indian Army.'

Pictures come onto the magic screen again – bearded young men lying crumpled at street corners, gateways; soldiers in jungle camouflage and assorted accoutrements aiming their rifles at an unruly stone-pelting mob; armoured vehicles rushing towards a group of violent boys.

'You have heard about the Great Riots? Our men were killed, our women raped. When the Hindu thugs got tired, they pushed sticks into their vaginas and roared in glee.'

'Oh no! Say no more! Stop it!' Jamal breaks down, burying his face in his hands. His head spins. The demonic image of women being brutally lathied in their shame terrifies him. He feels like throwing up. Rabeya's face flashes into his mind – large eyes, sad, expressive. She is breaking into laughter – like the Rupsa at high tide. He shakes his head.

The man, not really a maulana, not yet thirty, works his computer deftly, like Jamal once rowed his little boat. He smiles – a wry, sardonic smile.

'Bangladeshi Bhai, don't you feel like doing something about it? If I kick a dog, it sure will bite me back. Don't you have an obligation to Allah? You will have to give an answer on the day of reckoning.' His voice rises, meandering through many emotions. 'Bangla Bhai,' he grabs Jamal's arm intensely, 'You owe a debt to the dead. Don't you feel like giving it back to the kafirs, the enemies of Islam…' He chokes, his frail frame shakes, eyes hinting at a gathering storm. He looks Jamal in the eye.

A while later, he smiles, regaining his composure. His old self again – cool, unperturbed – after the freak turbulence. He laughs. 'Chalo, I said a lot, more than you could perhaps take. Akhtar, where's the food? Give us something to eat.'

4
L'Hôtel Particulier

'Nan, do you still write in English?' An old friend from London on the line late in the evening.

'Why not?' Mock annoyance in her voice.

'What about your French contempt for the Queen's English?' He titters away on the other end.

'Listen, I had more chai at Stephen's than cigarettes at the Sorbonne, eh?' Both laugh heartily.

He then tells her about a Calcutta newspaper looking for someone who can write regularly from Paris about French cinema, art, new writing and other topics. 'They pay well.' He chuckles. A doctoral candidate, this offer is like a windfall for her.

Working as a journalist in Paris, Nandita has to keep a close watch on Indian affairs, go to the embassy often. The unremarkable building on Rue Alfred Dehodencq has suddenly become important for her. Faint hints of incense and spices greet her as she walks up the steps, looking at the puppets and statuettes in the stairwell windows. The figurines in dhoti and sari are the first flavour of India.

Her first feature was on Syed Haider Raza, the best-known Indian artist living in Paris. His work commands a price many celebrated European artists cannot aspire to. She interviewed the veteran and talked in art circles about his oeuvre, his mystique. The famed dots in his paintings. The full-page feature was well received. Soon, there was demand for more. She began to write regularly. The embassy is the source for a whole lot of information: who's coming from India, new treatises, trade agreements, French projects in the country.

She meets Arijit Basu in his office – a patrician figure with an air of efficiency. Unusually tall for an Indian, his baritone booms around the large room. She becomes a regular at the embassy, begins attending dinners and cocktails he hosts. In her student years, she was part of the university community – students with causes but without borders, left-leaning academics looking for new battles. Her link to India got weakened. She knew about the upcoming writers, artists, filmmakers but could not think of the country as a whole. Nandita rediscovers India through Arijit Basu. He gives her a tour of the country – its dichotomy, distress, diversity; he explains its myriad conflicts and contradictions she has hardly known about. Educated at King's College, Cambridge, his manners are impeccably English. He is a strong candidate for foreign secretary at a later date, she's heard in embassy circles. Scion of a well-known Calcutta family, he is in the good books of the bosses in Delhi.

Arijit should be a happy man; things are going well for him. This is his hour. Yet, a deeply ingrained sadness surfaces in unguarded moments. She has noticed it. His cultivated manners and strong personality cannot always hide it. He regains control quickly, pushing away any trace of distress. But she soon learns about the source of his unhappiness, what troubles him.

His wife Ranjana – a stage actor – is a hardcore alcoholic. In a diplomat's career, the spouse plays a crucial role. At parties and banquets, where she should cast her charm and win over people, she gets drunk, talks incoherently, makes a scene. Worse, picks fights. For Arijit, she is an embarrassment. To prevent such situations, he asks an embassy staffer to play the official hostess. Ranjana stops attending such dos.

The woman official formally hosts the events. However, it's Nandita, vivacious, French-speaking, who sets the evenings rolling. There's no doubt in anyone's mind about the real star of such parties. Though only a guest, she is the centre of gravity, the lady at the ambassador's side, cracking jokes, engaging other guests in small talk. To the Indians, she brings a whiff of Paris life; to the French guests, the tall, broad-shouldered woman with natural auburn hair is a gateway to India, the modern face of the snake charmer's land. Unknowingly, she becomes part of an uneasy triangle, enmeshed in Arijit's life.

Though Ranjana no longer comes to the parties, she hovers around as a constant threat, a source of trouble for her husband. There are calls, complaints from bars about her drunkenness, ugly fights. Often, she is spotted by the police lying unconscious on the pavement after binge drinking. Cabbies call the police when she is in no state to tell them where she wants to go. What has been gossip among the embassy staff now threatens to be the talk of the town. Arijit wonders why his marriage – seen as an act of courage, evidence of his goodness – is turning into a nightmare.

A promising actor, Ranjana breathes the fiery rhetoric of protests, smashing the chains. The tone of theatre is decidedly anti-establishment. Theatre is a match you light to set fire to the decadent values of the reactionary right-wing forces. This is 1992. Bombay in turmoil. The religious right is waging a campaign to capture an ancient mosque in the north. The liberal intelligentsia, students, activists – they are all putting up a stubborn fight against Hindu fundamentalists around the country. Though pathetically outnumbered, they've declared war on the revivalist ideology in the cities. Activists demonstrate, plaster Bombay with their secular posters and stage street plays. Gripped by uncertainty, the city pulsates with tension. The fundamentalists project themselves as the *monkey battalions* of Lord Ram, the mythical warrior-king whose precise place of birth, they claim, lies within that mosque.

Ranjana plays the lead role in *Ek Dhanche Ki Kahani*. A handful of actors with a tom-tom and tabor move around town, performing at Nariman Point, Gateway of India, Marine Drive, Churchgate Station, Chaupatty, Dhobighat. Then they move into the squalid slums. The play about a structure's tale is an instant hit. They often do half a dozen shows during the course of a day. The city streets its protests and voices script insubordination. Newspapers interview her, carry her pictures. She is the face of the liberal challenge to the odious fundamentalists.

When Ranjana walks into the Prithvi Theatre cafeteria to discuss a new play with her troupe, she senses admiration all around. Lalit-ji does a namaste. 'So the star is here.' The friendly manager smiles. The creeper-curtained place with a cerebral air seems so welcoming. Some students have taken a break from their rehearsal. They surround her. 'Your play has turned the street into the most effective stage. Someone has written an article in the *Times of India*: "Theatre as Protest". Have you seen it?'

'A friend told me about it.' Ranjana waves at everyone. Bollywood hero Shashi Kapoor raises his hand from a corner table. The Kapoors run the place started by Shashi's father. Sanjana, Shashi's daughter, has offered her the auditorium free for a show.

A bit of a bohemian, she challenges rules, defies conventions. It is, after all, what the theatre movement is all about. She is there to break stereotypes. Has a name, an image. A radical actor, she rails against all evils – sectarian strife, child labour, dowry, sexual harassment, HIV, feudal decadence. An invitation from Germany to perform in Hamburg comes as further confirmation of her predominant position in the world of protest theatre.

They meet during a theatre festival in Delhi, and Arijit falls for the angry girl. He loves her rebellion, her irreverence, her readiness to take on the world. Everything, to begin with, is sheer rapture.

He's amused by friends' grudging admiration for his *act of courage*. That he has married a theatre personality and not a rich man's daughter for a fat dowry. At cocktails, they raise a toast to the *gutsy guy*.

'So you've married a cause, old boy, not a decked-up beauty? Ha!' The foreign office spokesman warmly shakes his hand when they run into each other in South Block. In the sedate world of diplomacy, Ranjana is West Wind, a new idea. 'Others marry for a big house; you have opted for the stage, ha ha!' The foreign secretary laughs at the wedding reception. Many of his colleagues have married either fellow foreign service officers or the children of powerful people.

But essentially, Ranjana belongs to the crowded street. She is the interpreter of its anger, impulses. Sets the asphalt on fire, acts out its upheavals. An actor who once performed in the steamy Dharavi slums and seedy red-light district of Kamathipura, Ranjana has about her the roughness of raw life, the aggression of the mean street. She soon tires of the effete orderliness of the embassy, the manicured look of the envoy's residence. The rebel in her trashes the trappings of protocol and diplomatic niceties. She slumps into binge drinking.

The birth of their child is a happy interregnum. Arijit hopes she will change, give up her old ways. For a few months after Piu's birth, they become close again. They are in Jakarta. After the rain, when it's cool and pleasant, they go to the beach for a walk or simply look at the ocean from the pier. On the way home, they dine at a Japanese restaurant. But as the pull of maternity weakens, Ranjana sinks into alcohol again. By then, Arijit has been transferred to Paris. It's considered an important posting for any foreign service officer. He gets such a major assignment at a relatively young age. But his career means very little to Ranjana.

In Paris, she meets a few failed Indian artists, lingering on even though their chances of fame and recognition have dimmed. They cling onto her for free booze from the embassy and perhaps, hoping they will be commissioned for some work, for a little patronage. Ranjana goes to seedy pubs with them, and bringing her back is often a problem for Arijit's driver. One night, the poor fellow calls him. He is hesitant, unwilling to say what he has to.

'Madam – er… I think… not well. Sir, will you please, I mean, sir, please come down here… sorry I am troubling you.'

When Arijit reaches L'Hôtel Particulier near Jardins du Luxembourg, he meets the driver at the entrance. The man looks scandalized, a little scared. Past the classical façade and heavy wooden door, he faces the rectangular courtyard with a corridor running on all sides. Antiques in the corners evoke a bygone era – an ancient typewriter, the heavy iron letter box, an old-world gas lamp…

The party has degenerated into vulgarity. Away from the main crowd, in one corner of the courtyard, Ranjana is reclining in an armchair, most of her clothes strewn on the floor around. Two shrivelled-up Indian artists – equally drunk – are fondling her. Arijit kicks one and slaps another, throws his black overcoat over his wife's bare body and carries her out in his arms.

After a few months, she leaves for Bombay. Both of them know this is the end.

Nandita walks into Arijit's office late in the afternoon. He looks unusually dejected. Perhaps struggling to come to terms with the break-up? She's here to know more about a Rodin exhibition in a few Indian cities a couple months later. But the talk rambles around his personal life, the challenge of raising a young daughter all alone. The normally reserved man, impeccably formal, has suddenly dropped his guard.

'The world around me has suddenly begun to crumble.' He pushes his hand through his hair, leaning back on the chair. The dapper diplomat, always in charge of his situation, looks beaten, very vulnerable.

'You must not give in.' Unknowingly, she holds his hand. 'This is a game life plays with all of us.'

In the evening, they go to Le Maharajah, the Indian restaurant on Boulevard St-Germain. She likes the ambience – evocative of India in many ways. They order lamb curry, aubergine and cheese naan. Washing down the spicy food with Bordeaux wine, Arijit looks into her eyes. A peg somewhere has come unstuck.

'Nandita, I'm really clueless, I don't know how to restart. I don't have a grip on things any more.'

'Things will be all right; it's just a matter of time.'

After dinner, they go to the Eiffel Tower and amble around the open esplanade. At some point in the evening, without them knowing it, their hands clasp. They talk – Arijit about the crisis in his life, Nandita about her work.

'In Foreign Service, you build your career brick by brick.' Arijit puts a soft arm around her. 'One misstep and the entire edifice comes tumbling down.' He looks away – forlorn, distraught. A while later, he turns towards her. *'La vie est très dur.'* He tries to laugh.

She looks closely at him, her head leaning against his chest. They do not know when they've actually stopped. 'Life is a tough ballgame.' She laughs, too. 'But setbacks are temporary. Everything will be all right.'

'I wanted to break rules, and chaos caught me.'

'Such things follow no rules.' Nandita turns to him. 'Life is not a straight line. If it were, I would have gone to Oxford, by now been a senior professor at Delhi University or somewhere else. That has been the route for Indians for over a century. Not the Sorbonne.'

Arijit listens, hanging on her every word. Someone else also made mistakes, paid the price for taking the unfamiliar road? He holds her close. Her light-brown hair brushes against his chest, causing a sensation deep inside.

It's an isolated corner behind a statue. He draws her closer, tightens his grip. As their hot, rapid breaths sear each other, they kiss, locked in a deep embrace. For a long, long time. For an eternity.

Then they take a walk along the Seine towards the Boulevard.

She has tastefully done up her studio with a few original canvases by her artist friends. Some of them are now famous. Simple, sparsely furnished, but the studio in the 11th Arrondissement, Boulevard Voltaire, has an unstated refinement. It speaks of her artistic sensibilities.

She pours cognac into two glasses. In the unlit room, they sit on the slender stools at the window, looking at the city below spreading out in waves of light and darkness. They clasp hands. Arijit does not know when his free hand has moved up, caressing the gush of her auburn hair over a long neck. After a few sips of the drink, he kisses her, dips his nose into her bosom. The cognac stirs him into a fever.

By the time the glasses are empty, their clothes are all over the floor. His one hand pressed over her defiant breasts, Arijit tries to tickle her underarm with the other. Her whole body turns crimson. He knows, feels it, without bothering to actually see the flushed skin.

A minute later, she takes charge, lays him flat on his back, pins him down and feels his crotch. Then, rattled by a sudden surge, a new passion consuming her, Nandita takes his phallus in her mouth. Unable to bear it any more, he pushes her away, rummages into her darkness, inhaling the fragrance of rain, soft grass nestling in monsoon.

The bed is too small for their passions to play out. Unleashed in the hungry bodies by an irresistible urge to consume their gloom, the fire is threatening to turn into a conflagration. The two are now like wild animals on a full moon night. The lovers are becoming arsonists. Arijit smells her – the perfume down there, the allure of her hair, the cognac, her sweat, the fire smouldering inside her. She stands there, leaning forward, her arms on the windowsill. He comes from behind, pushing into her, his hands clasped over her bosom.

5
Spinach Soup

IN THE SHADOW OF TERROR: INDIAN SUBCONTINENT – the *TIME* magazine cover grabs Arijit's attention. Against the backdrop of a blast scene – mangled bodies, blood splattered around splintered glass and burning cars in a marketplace – the grim uppercased black letters strike a chill into your heart. From the rocky terrain across the tribal homeland between Afghanistan and Pakistan to deltaic Bangladesh, from the Kashmir Valley to Nepal, the terror outfits are busy setting up sleeper cells, recruiting young men, indoctrinating them to be holy warriors of jihad. In the big cities and small towns, the shadowy gangs with martial names have created modules – Lashkar-e-Taiba, Indian Mujahideen, Harkat-ul-Jihad-al-Islami… Terrorists on a suicide mission are now fedayeen. Fighters who go out knowing they will not come back.

Rita is in the kitchen. The pressure cooker hisses, mustard seeds crackle in the pan. The air thick with pungent nutmeg, roasted cumin and ground cinnamon. Not yet time for lunch, but he is already feeling a little hungry. The girl comes out of the kitchen carrying a bowl on a tray. Puts it on a side table. He looks up at her in surprise.

She smiles.

'I made some soup – spinach.' Her hands clasped. 'Here they

make the soup very thick.' Rita pouts. 'They don't understand soup is soup, it's not curry.' She laughs. There is a mild touch of pride in her voice. The shaky, wraith-like thing that came to his door desperate for a job is now in charge. 'I am making roasted broccoli and grilled fish for lunch.'

Arijit takes one spoon of the soup; it's as good as any trained cook made for him in Europe or America. He watches Rita retreating into the kitchen like a puzzle he cannot crack. Where did she learn such skills? Someone in her situation – a shanty squatter – making dishes like a professional chef? He is intrigued by the rich aroma from the kitchen.

The enigma persists. *The mystery maid,* he quietly laughs. Perhaps the doctor couple had lived abroad, taught her to cook the things they loved to eat? But there are other things, unresolved knots. She said she is from Ranchi, a city in the heart of a mineral-rich tribal belt between Bengal and Bihar. For the first few days, she spoke accented Hindi, then switched over to Bengali. But her language has the swirly murmur of the East Bengal rivers. It's soft, rapid, with a rhythm of its own. Very different from the refined Bengali of the Calcutta elite, Rita's diction is a throwback to the melodious eddy of a mother tongue Bangladeshi diplomats broke into when he met them at receptions or on the sidelines of an international conference.

There are gaps between what she says and what she is. When he first hired her, his only expectation was she would cook the basic dishes – rice, roti, dal, vegetables, chicken curry at most. Now he knows she is well familiar with Western cuisine. It bothers him that someone with such skills should work for so little. What he pays her at month's end is more than what such maids get in Blue Lotus Grove but a pittance for a cook of her calibre.

I don't have to bother, I need not go into her story. Arijit tries to focus on the terrorism story in *Time*. He looks around his life in the apartment. The girl has completely changed the way he thought his days would roll by, alone in an unfamiliar place.

The first few weeks he regretted having moved into an apartment in the new suburb without thinking of his personal needs. Organizing life in a place still in the making was like celebrating chaos. *Don't insist on order when rules have not yet been set,* he kept telling himself. For little-little things – his brand of tea, shaving cream, cheese – he had to hunt around from one market to another, from Atlantic Mall to East End Mall. His favourite biscuits, canned sardine, salami. Life in the suburb was not easy to begin with. He had to learn, research the market. Noahda is gradually coming to life but is not yet zippy.

Rita has made all the difference. Though a boy comes to sweep and mop, do the dishes, clean up the house, she is in control. After finishing her work in the kitchen, she moves from one room to another, doing a little dusting here, rearranging things there. Once in a while, she talks on the phone – sometimes in Hindi, sometimes Bengali. From his distance, Arijit tries to follow the conversation, traces a certain pattern in the calls. The ones prompting her to speak Hindi are normally in the morning when she is in the kitchen.

Rita's Bengali calls come around noon when she moves about the house tidying up things. She hurries to a balcony. Sometimes, her voice falls to a whisper. Still, bits of hushed talk reach him. Her voice takes on a conspiratorial tone: hunh, naah, oh, baah, ki, that, things, man, they – single syllables, cryptic interjections, deliberate pronouns. One moment her face lights up. A smile blooms. The large, black eyes sparkle in happiness. Seconds later, she is angry, arguing, her voice rising. Shouts into the phone.

Arijit can make out it's about money. The caller on the other end is talking about hardship, asking for money. There are cracks, craters in her life she does not want to talk about. A few times he has heard her sob, her voice breaking, eyes misting over. Arijit wants to know why the girl gets angry, why she cries, but has decided not to probe, peer into her haze. He pretends not to have heard anything. After a phone call, she walks into the living room as if nothing has happened. At ease in his presence. She first called him *sahib,* then *sir* and finally settled for *uncle*. Perhaps unknowingly, one day she started calling him *kaku*, Bengali for uncle.

'Kaku, you have been to all the countries in the world?' She scrutinizes a framed photograph of him skiing during a holiday in Chamonix.

'Not all, but quite a few.'

She considers the point for a while. The storm on the phone has blown over. 'In those places, they all live happily…' Her voice trails off.

'Happiness is how you look at life.'

'How beautifully you put it!' She waits, looking around the room. 'Everybody wants to be happy – isn't it, Kaku?' She smiles, pointing to the taped boxes lying here and there – his books and some crockery he had never really used.

'Can I unpack them?'

'Please do that. You will need the crockery. Someone is coming for lunch this Sunday. Will you cook something special?'

'Of course, Kaku. I will make a special dish for your first guest.'

First guest… Indeed, no visitor has walked into his house so far.

Rita still stands there, clasping and unclasping her hands. She keeps staring at the framed photograph on top of a bookshelf. Her eyes narrow in concentration. Seconds later, a smile lights up her face.

'Kaku, she is your daughter, right?'

'Yes. Piu.'

With curious eyes, she scans the photograph.

'Every inch your daughter.'

'She lives in America – she and her husband and their boy, Bubka.'

'They will not come here?'

'Maybe in November.'

She thinks of the date, counts the remaining months on her fingers. 'Falgun, Chaitra, Boishakh, Joishttha… another seven or eight months.' She looks a little thoughtful. Then smiles again. 'Kaku, I'll make special dishes for them – our kind of food and what people eat in America.'

'What do they eat in America?'

'Soup, grilled fish, boiled vegetables and… and lamb roast, lemon pie and of course steaks and sandwiches.' Rita laughs as if there is something funny about all this. 'No spices, no nutmeg, no red chilli. And nothing deep-fried, huh.'

'Where did you learn to make those dishes? Here, ordinary people do not eat such stuff.'

'From my father.'

'Your father?' Arijit stutters, gawking at her. It's difficult to think of this rootless girl as the daughter of an accomplished chef.

'He cooked for Radolf Sahib. Sahib came with his crew, cameras, sketches and books. He filmed what he called *life on the rivers*. For months, we would be on his motorboat, floating down one river, then another. Whenever we saw a big budgerow or steamer waiting at a jetty, we, too, dropped anchor. Sahib got into a smaller boat to reach the double-decker steamboat, his camera panning over the passengers sitting with their little luggage, hawkers selling everything from bangles to rat-killers, quacks offering cures for hair fall and worms in the tummy. Radolf Sahib filmed all that, chatted with them and bought a few things, too. He was making a film about all this – sweetmeat vendors, Bauls and bangle sellers, all on the river. Ha ha – crazy man, wasn't he?'

Arijit looks at her closely. The black eyes, mostly sad, are now gleaming in recollection. Memories of a faraway home, the happiness of being on the boat with an eccentric documentary maker, elaborate cooking in a tent – they now spark a smile. At the moment, she is happy going back to another time, a place very different from this boomtown. But then… that place is not Ranchi; her rivers, boats, busy ghats are somewhere else. He keeps quiet.

With a piece of cloth, she wipes the dust from the side tables and the crockery cabinet, then goes onto the balcony to clean the grilles. This is not her job, nor has he ever told her to do such things. The boy does all that in the morning. But she finds fault with his work, sees dust, cobwebs everywhere.

Another tower has come up across the lawn. Construction is over, some families have moved in. A few more apartments are being readied. From his study, Arijit hears the hoarse crackle of machines. Workers putting finishing touches. They drill into walls, shine tiled floors. Welders fix window grilles. They shout, sing. At times, fights break out.

Rita is listening to the mad mix of noises, her face pressed against the balcony grille. She has stopped dusting. Her eyes travel to the new building across the lawn. A man is busy attaching a grille to the walls around a balcony. Arijit can see him – a haggard face framed by untrimmed, dishevelled hair, the tall, wiry figure seems to have merged into the fluidity of light and shade inside the raw building. The moment the fellow's eyes meet Rita's, he stops. He stands there transfixed, his hands folded over his chest.

Rita smiles. He gestures for her to come over – to meet him. She violently shakes her head; her face clouds over. A while later, she turns to leave, but before turning back, she waves at him – discreetly, softly, the smile back on her face.

Cutting through the fields behind the village, a narrow but sharp stream moves forward, flowing into the Rupsa in the estuary. Looking at the brimming Paankhali Canal through the curtain of long, unruly grass and overgrowth, she walks home after her work in the prawn factory. Tired and hungry after an eight-hour shift.

On the road to Mongla Port, the factory is another world. Tall, red-faced Germans came in the winter to set norms and the standard. With interpreters by their side, the big men in jeans and T-shirts trained them in processing, talked about hygiene and showed them how to do quality control. People from the nearby villages gathered, excited over the icemaker, the contraption to separate the large prawns from the small ones.

'Are they going to make prawns in that factory?' a village elder asked, running his fingers through his flowing grey beard. Others guffawed cheerfully. The factory owner, a local politician, distributed sweets among the villagers.

In the dressing room, women take off their saris, bangles,

hairpins; put on aprons, caps, masks and wellingtons. They look strange to each other. Two hefty women guards glare at them.

You cannot take any metal inside, neither coins nor earrings. The big women in their blue uniforms jab and pinch in the name of frisking. 'Bubu, they are like men,' Ameena whispers to her cousin. Every worker has a locker to keep her things.

Three women work on either side of a table, sizing and labelling prawns, taking off the heads and shells. Every packet is a two-kilo brick: *Sea Water Black Tiger Shrimps, White Chaka Shrimps* – frozen at below eighteen degrees Celsius. Rabeya sticks labels on the hard-paper boxes: *Grey Harina Shrimps, Tail on, Peeled, Undivided.*

She watches the packaged fish and shakes her head: not the robust prawns of the estuary, their black and yellow stripes, sleek whiskers reminding village folk of the big cat in the Sundarbans. Or at least the prancing deer. Peeled, processed and graded, the shrimps are like barley, boiled and congealed. Before the bricks leave the factory in reefer containers for the port on their way to Europe, they are metal-detected. Surely, they do not want a silly village girl's hairpin stuck to an eight-inch lobster's tail!

Collecting two hundred takas from the factory paymaster, she hurries home.

Just for you
Both banks are flooded with love

She turns – Jamal's boat crawling to the bank. He waves at her.

'Let's go to Karamjal. That's where the Sundarbans begin – dark, deep, eerie.' He laughs, pulling the oar.

'I have worked for eight hours since morning. I am hungry.

First, I will go home and eat – rice and whatever else Ma has made.'

'I've got something for you – chom chom and mishti doi from Ghosh Dairy. I'm coming from town.'

A cool, strong wind takes the boat gliding down to the watersmeet. The Rupsa is wider around here, the current sharper. The boat tosses over the big, boisterous waves.

'Give me the other oar.' Rabeya stretches her hand.

'What will you do?' Jamal looks at her, surprised, puzzled.

'Why, I'll row – what else.' She laughs. 'The boat will move faster.' She picks up the oar from the hold, sits in the stern and starts rowing.

Sweep rowing indeed takes the boat faster. She digs the oar into the water and pulls. Her arm muscles tighten up, her chest rises and falls. From the prow, Jamal sees a new girl, partnering, rowing side by side.

All of a sudden, a strong wind from the bay with a dust of rain begins pushing their boat back. Rabeya sees the dark, demonic clouds in a corner of the sky.

'Look!' She nods towards the swollen clouds hanging low over the river. The fierce wind from the sea howls: shooaan… whawoooon… shooooon…

They see the rain-washed big launches returning from the sea, their headlamps on.

'We have to land immediately; can neither go back nor move forward.' The worry in Jamal's voice ends the excitement of boating.

The boat starts pulling for the bank. Jamal shakes his head in despair – there is no ghat to anchor. The jungle has begun. Prawn farmers have dug little ponds in the marshes for shrimps to come in and hatch. They have removed the embankment here and there. The waves – now like mountains – are crashing through the cracks to flood the fields all around. Above the water, the ghostly mangrove palms wink before they are washed away.

It is getting dark, not the usual dark of an ordinary evening – but unforgiving. The reign of the mangroves is not afar and *they* from the deep dark of the forest – fleet-footed, shining stripes, eyes burning, with a certain majesty about them – could *they* be on the prowl, too? The oar seems to be slipping from his hands. Despite the chill and salt in the wind, Jamal starts perspiring.

Suddenly, a stretch of raised land comes into view – Boatiaghata Boatworks. Like an island, the elevated platform of tight white sand has refused to go under. He came to the yard a year ago to get his leaking boat repaired. He moves close to the jetty and ties the boat to an iron pole and jumps onto the ground. The boat sways in the turgid water.

Terrified by the turmoil in the river, exhausted after tough rowing, Rabeya has collapsed in the boat. A storm is breaking. The sky looks ominous. When Jamal calls her, stretching a hand, she staggers to the boat's prow. He takes her into his arms and goes a few yards before seating her on an upturned boat.

It has started raining. The Rupsa is rising in a primeval fury. A malevolent darkness grips everything around – the sky, river, horizon, the whole world. Sharp silver sparks from the sky momentarily unveil the enormity of evil, its obstreperous glee in laying siege to the human kingdom. Thunder crackles as the intimation of an imminent assault.

Jamal holds her tight, her face close to his, a frail, wet bird caught in the whirl of a sinister storm. He lowers his head to take her thin, cold lips between his, determined to save her from the rising river.

6
Old Brick Bridge

Long before the area turned into a boomtown, before the sleek six-lane roads were laid out for the Japanese and Korean cars to glide away, the ancient brick bridge was the only link between the villages on either side of the canal. Buffalo carts laden with the new crop and fodder, bicycles, the odd motorist – everyone waited at one end for the traffic from the other to pass by.

The bridge was that narrow. Built with bare red brick and mortar, without steel and any modern techniques, it did not fit into the design of fancy suburbia. In no time, under pressure from the big developers moving into the area, the city authorities built a wide bridge with a median strip for one-way traffic a little distance away from the old one. In the evening, flooded by neon lights, cars of many sizes and shapes whoosh across the bridge, their headlights sparkling on the still water of the canal.

The discarded brick bridge looks ghostly in the dark. An oddity, a remnant of a time when the kisan's life revolved around the calendar of sowing and harvesting. Since the road has moved away, the bridge is now abandoned, the odd cow or a stray dog its only users. At the height of summer, street children plunge into the cool water of the canal, the disused bridge their springboard.

A loony in grimy tatters relishes the leftovers from some community lunch. He laughs, attacking the food in a plastic bag

– fried rice, potato curry and puri. His eyes pop out of his head seeing a whole delicious gulab jamun in the heap of food. But mostly, the bridge is a desolate place, existing outside the orbit of the new city; it belongs to an unremarkable past. In tomorrow's happening suburb, it has been yesterdayed.

Jamal shoos away the stray dog and spreads an old newspaper below the bruised iron railings. He places two plastic bags on the paper. Smelling the hot snacks in the packets, he fidgets, looking out at the road. Then at the packets again. Like paperweights, they keep the *Hindustan Times* pages in place. A snappy wind is blowing from the fields across the canal with an occasional pinch of winter. His flowing cotton kurta flaps; his carefully brushed, wavy hair gets ruffled.

A disembodied voice echoes from nowhere: '*Hawa… hawa mein pyaar hai… Ha ha ha…*' A face framed in matted hair beams. A subhuman creature crawling out of the water? The flowing beard hangs like aerial roots.

Jamal is stunned by the suddenness of the unearthly outburst. When he recovers, he sees the old madman.

'Bastard! I'll set fire to your beard.' He chases the vagabond with clenched fists.

The loony protests, threatens to fight back, then whimpers. 'Give me a five-rupee coin and there I go – chasing love on the wind.' He dances, snatching something out of the air.

Jamal laughs, throwing him a coin. The madman picks it up and starts jumping. '*Hawa mein pyaar… hawa mein pyaar…*'

Jamal feels good. After a very long time, an unknown happiness sways him. Like when he rowed his little boat down the Rupsa all day long singing his favourite songs. Ah, those magic days! In the slow shadow of the woods, the dinghy being tossed by waves, his heart throbbed, often missed a beat. The wily kingfisher swooped down from nowhere to snap up a perchlet from the shallows. Little boys and girls threw their cast nets for a good catch of shrimps.

And love? Love was a little bulbul singing on a jackfruit branch. He looked for Rabeya everywhere. He knew the clever girl was playing hide and seek; she came close, laughed, let him hold her, then slipped away. That was her way. Like the winter sun traipsing from the window to the courtyard to the glistening garden even before you've soaked in a little warmth. He wondered if he would ever know her, her capricious ways, how much she loved him, if at all.

His runes and lyrics, Jamal sighs, are left on the other side of the border.

The disciples of Baba Bakershah have come from faraway places to his seat in Gallamari to host a lunch. In an adjacent yard, they're cooking rice, dal, fish and beef. Jamal hesitantly walks into the cement courtyard where, seated in a circle, many people are waiting for the meal. Eating over, he follows the others to the place where Baba Bakershah used to meditate for hours under a palmyra tree.

Like the others, he, too, picks up bits of earth from the hallowed ground. Someone watches him from another end of the courtyard.

'Keep this holy earth in a locker, like gold.' The man comes forward, offering him an empty envelope. 'It has healing powers.'

'What does it heal?' Jamal is curious.

'Broken hearts.' The man laughs, moving closer. 'People travel hundreds of miles for a pinch of this earth. They keep it in the safest place at home, spray a little dust over the chest.' He looks Jamal in the face and smiles. 'It gives what you ask for.'

'Really?'

'Try it.'

They sit together on a wooden bench in a corner.

'How often do you come here?' Jamal asks.

'I am here at least once a month. If I did not have to look after so many things at home, I'd have come more often, sat in the shadow of Baba Bakershah – Old Maulvi for the locals.'

Retired from government service years ago, he has nothing to ask for. Still, he makes rounds of such places.

He looks quizzically at Jamal. 'Is something coming close and still slipping away? A clever eel of a girl?'

Jamal laughs. 'Either she is too smart, or I am too slow. Perhaps I cannot meet her idea of a man.'

The sun is sinking in the west. They walk alongside the Mayur River flowing by the dargah. A lean flow surfaced by an overgrowth of hyacinths, the Mayur is in decline. They sit on the bank under a jackfruit tree.

'See.' The mystery man turns to point out a cylindrical fruit hanging from the tree trunk. Jamal looks puzzled – it's a truncated jack, like the top has been eaten off by an animal. And it's still growing on the tree!

'The locals call it the miser's jack.' The man laughs enigmatically.

'How come?'

'A villager, legend has it, prayed to the Baba for his sick child's quick recovery. He promised the first jackfruit of his tree the next summer. The little boy got well in no time, but the miserly man, when the time came, brought to the dargah only half a jackfruit as offering, ha ha.'

'So the Baba had his way…'

'Of course, of course. Did you notice that in this dargah, there's no shrine?' The stranger smiles cryptically.

Jamal somehow feels the enigmatic man is of this Earth and still not.

'If Baba Bakershah lived all his life here, they should have built a shrine to him, right?'

It's already dark. The gentle breeze susurrating through the spooky row of one-legged palmyra trees on the other bank sings to him in an ethereal voice. The bare trees, a sleeping hamlet in the distance – all shimmer under a waxing moon.

'Actually, the Old Maulvi did not die here; he simply disappeared. Like his coming from faraway Persia, his going, too, is a mystery, shrouded in mist. One morning, his followers saw the Baba was no longer there. Gone, vanished.'

The mystery man takes out a tiny silver box from his kurta pocket, pushes a paan in his mouth. The sweet smell of betel fills the air, mingling with the incense floating up from the dargah.

'There are those who give in easily, without much of a fight – the obedient, dutiful type. But your girl is not one of them. She slips away, loves being chased. And you, too, don't enjoy catching an easy fish. And the lassie tricks you, comes close, only to duck out again. You suffer and still chase the mirage. You trip up. That's how life plays games with us. Like Baba Bakershah; he vanished, gossamer floating out of sight before you knew it, leaving his disciples baffled.'

In the soft glow of the moon, the strange man is a haze, a conundrum Jamal cannot decode.

He stands up. Leaning on the rusty railing, he looks at the pallid water below – foul-smelling, lifeless. Yet the long succession of car headlights splashing on the water seems to have set off a wild festival illumination.

Tch, tch! Nothing. Nothing compared to the Padma, Meghna, Rupsa… the mighty rivers of Bangladesh. This canal is a mere caricature, a distortion, not even a pale shadow of the boisterous rivers of his land. The water looks dirty. Still, it wets the fields somewhere. The breeze coming over the canal is cool. He whistles an old song:

O Lolita, tell him to go away –
I'm not coming to the ghat to fill my pitcher.
O Lolita…

The more passionately she loves her man, the more capricious she wants to be. The song travelled from Calcutta, taking time to cross the border and reach Khulna, but it was in the air all the time.

Tell him to go away, he whistles.

A figure emerges in the distance – walking casually, cautiously, both scared and reckless. She is coming to the riverfront for her tryst.

Rabeya silhouetted in the distant street lights.

He recalls her face pressed against the balcony grille, silently saying a thousand things. *If she doesn't love me, why did she do that?* The question eddied, raised a storm within him. And now – now she is here on the old brick bridge for the rendezvous.

In churidar kurta, her hair done stylishly, a large bindi on her forehead, eyes lined with kohl, she is an altogether different girl, not the Rabeya of Paankhali village. He keeps looking at her, spellbound.

'What are you looking at?' Mock annoyance in her voice.

He holds her hands and seats her by his side. The cheap perfume from her body teases him, fills his insides. His nose twitches for more of it. The sweet smell of some flower – gardenia, jasmine, tuberose… whatever. He wants to take it in… more… the whole of her. His hungry gaze laps her up, scans every bit of her.

'Rabee, I keep looking at you, amazed – how you have changed! Honestly, you could be one of those girls on television, no longer Munir Sheikh's daughter – shy, a little shaky.'

'You have always been theatrical. Speak simply, man. I cannot make head or tail of what you say – your roundabout ways, your jalebi talk.'

'When I saw you on the balcony of that house, really! You looked like one of them, as if you have always lived there.'

Rabeya laughs, giving him an indulgent look. 'Will a woman in that rich man's house ever talk to a crazy fellow like you?' She gives him a mild push.

'I saw him a few times from the flat where I put up grilles. The man – tall, fair, like superstar Razzak in *Abujh Mon.* Do you remember the movie?'

'A pukka sahib. Like Radolf. You remember the American my father worked for? Whenever I called him *uncle*, *dada*, *sahib*, he would get angry. "Call me Radolf," he would roar.' Rabeya laughs.

Jamal pushes his hand into a packet, fishes out a couple of samosas, still hot, and offers them to Rabeya. 'They cannot make samosas here like the sweet shops in Khulna. The coating is thick.' He bites into one, chews quietly for a while. He takes some more deep-fried snacks out of the packets. 'Do you remember Ghosh Dairy? What sweets, what taste! These people can neither make hot snacks nor tasty sweets.'

'I am thinking of opening a joint.' Rabeya laughs. 'Fish fries and mutton cutlets.'

'Rabee, I met an interesting man the other day. A maulvi, but unlike the mullahs you have seen. He is educated, intelligent, knows a lot about the world. He said strange things – that Islam is under attack; that all over the world a conspiracy is going on to finish off Muslims.'

Rabeya looks amusedly at him, then stretches her hand to grab his flowing hair. 'You have always been a little crazy. Now you have gone completely, completely mad. And you get to know loonies like you only. You mad fellow.' She pulls his head to her side. Caught off guard, he loses his balance; his head falls into her lap. Only for a few moments, but that is enough for him to breathe in her smell – body talc, hair oil and the lost fragrance of Paankhali. She pushes his head away. While getting up, his face brushes her chest.

'Oh, you hurt me, Rabee, but I love that very much.'

'You… you are impossible!'

She opens a little plastic lunch box and holds it before him.

'What's this?'

'Grilled fish – no bones in it.' She layers it with blobs of sauce from a plastic pouch.

'Fish without bones? Does that rich man order such stuff from America?'

'I made it for him, stupid! He ate some of it and asked me to take home the rest.'

'And what's this, some kind of pickle, sharp-tasting?'

'This is sauce, green chilli sauce, paagal!'

'Rabee, I like it when you shout at me. When we are married, when I get home in the evening, will you scold me like this?'

'Marry a sloth bear, ha!'

Jamal holds her arm. 'Whatever you say, you know no man on Earth loves you more.' He puts his arm around her and pulls her close, clamping her in his tight grip. She does not resist. His chin on her head, her face pressed against his chest, she breathes fast. The hot air fires him up. He feels her breasts, their warmth transmitting into his body, his soul. She feels hot. *Am I running a fever?* Rabeya's not sure.

The cool air from the canal blows like a reminder of their delta, takes them back to the point where more and more tributaries merge into the Rupsa before it widens out, before the Sundarbans beckon and the river turns into the sea. And their excitement over the giant steamer on its way from Dhaka, waiting at Mongla Port every Thursday for the final lap to Khulna. Every week, it completes the same trajectory – Dhaka, Barisal, Khulna. The fishing boats come back with a rich haul of shrimp. The bustling Daulatpur Bazaar with its many smells of spices, dried fish and new clothes, the hooting of a launch…

All the sights and sounds and smells from another life now work up a desire, a deep longing. He clasps her face in his hands and kisses her. They remain like that, their lips locked, for a long, long time. For infinity.

7
Sunday Guest

When the doorbell rings, Arijit knows it's Nandita. Since morning, he has been a little tense, perhaps apprehensive, too. Would she be able to find the place, coming all the way from Hauz Khas in the heart of South Delhi?

She stands at the door. 'This place of yours, Arijit, is simply amazing. Completely out of this world.' She beams at him.

The tall, broad-shouldered girl with the big laugh comes back from his Paris days. When he was going through a difficult time in his life, she stood by him, brought him out of the dark pit. Without Nandita beside him, he would have slid down the tunnel. And Piu? Another stray child from a dysfunctional home.

Did he reciprocate all that?

Their eyes meet. Her face flooded with a warm smile, she is effusive as usual. Only, age has left its marks on her. Perhaps not age but a disinterest, weariness. The once-chiselled body is now cushioned by flab. She is worn out, battle-weary. The vivacious young woman striding down the cultural landscape of Paris, chasing news, interviewing artists and filmmakers, has receded. The person at his door has a frazzled, defeated look about her. The forehead wrinkles, the bags under her eyes and the streaks of grey in her hair tell him of the years since they last met. But she is still Nandita. The eyes glint, her smile infectious.

He walks down the couple of steps from his front door to welcome her in. As usual, she is carrying flowers and some foodstuff. Out of habit, Arijit gives her a hug. Her head rests on his chest for a few moments.

'You're still very handsome, Arijit.' Nandita laughs. She puts down the food basket on the dining table and gives him the chrysanthemums. 'I had no idea about this place.' She looks around the living room, peeps into his study, then walks onto the balcony. The farm at a distance – a smooth, green carpet from here – catches her eye. The canal – a surprise. 'So, you live on the river, Arijit? This is your Seine.' She has started liking the place. 'Does the lean river have a name?' She looks at him curiously.

'This is the Hindon Canal. Before this city came up, it watered the farm fields.'

She looks around – watching life in the other towers of Blue Lotus Grove. In the block across the lawn, some of the floors are still unoccupied; on the others, families have settled down. In a penthouse, guests have arrived, and children are dancing to stereo music. Two sound boxes stand on opposite ends of the terrace beside pot palms. A woman in jeans and a red top joins the children, shaking a leg and swinging. She clicks her fingers to the beat of the song to cheer them on. The other women and men clap. But the music, laughter – nothing travels this far. From here, the terrace carnival is nothing more than a pantomime show.

'All alone, without knowing anybody here, how do you manage everything?' Nandita looks at him.

'To begin with, it was a little difficult – depending on canned food or eating in the club. No one to talk to at home.' He gestures towards the kitchen. '…has changed everything.'

Nandita lowers her voice. 'Did you find her through some agency? Or someone recommended?'

'Came on her own. A slum dweller… lives on the margins.' He turns to make sure that their words have not reached the kitchen above the noise of dishes and cooking. 'Unsafe, exposed to danger… that kind of life.'

Still new to the place, the residents have gathered on the central lawn to explore, get to know each other a little more. Some women are playing badminton. At the other end of the lawn, a cricket match is on. The only sound coming up to the tenth-floor balcony is the muted wild roars as the ball flies over the ground for a big six.

'The design of the estate, the redbrick clubhouse – it's all very English, isn't it?' She points to another tower.

'I'm told the architect for the project has modelled it on Merchant Square, Paddington.'

'How did you discover this place?'

'Actually, it discovered me.' Arijit laughs. Sitting on the sofa across a glass-top coffee table, he tells her how Neeraj Gupta, a lowly official in the embassy in Paris, brought him here. 'Everything here is very new; in fact, this city is still in the making. When I go for my morning walk, I see new structures coming up over what was farmland until the other day.'

Rita steps out of the kitchen carrying a large tray. She nervously bows to Nandita and places the tray on the coffee table, removing the newspaper. Arranges around the table the teapot, two sparkling white, gold-rimmed cups on similar plates, milk, the sugar cube bowl and a plate of spring rolls. Little pots of mint chutney and chilli sauce next to the rolls. Neatly folded serviettes tucked under the cutlery.

Nandita watches the way she has placed everything on

the table. 'You are an expert. How nicely you have arranged everything!' She sounds friendly, warm. 'What's your name?'

Rita stands there, smiling nervously. Hesitant, unsure about the first guest in Kaku's house. Until the guest had arrived, she was in complete command. Now – well, she does not know.

'Rita knows quite a lot about food,' Arijit says, introducing the girl.

Nandita makes the tea, puts a roll on a plate. 'I can make that out from the way she has served tea.' She gives Rita a smile and bites into the roll. 'Mmm. Delicious! Where did you learn all this, Rita? It's better than what any Delhi restaurant would offer.'

Rita smiles back, regaining her place in the house. 'From my father.' She walks into the kitchen.

Arijit watches Nandita – busy smearing chutney around a roll. She was a part of his life, pulling him out of the rubble, counselling him, travelling with him, sharing his bed, taking charge of his daughter.

'Why did you leave Paris? You're so much a part of that city.' His eyes are meeting hers the way they have not for a very long time. The gutsy young woman, full of life, bursting with energy, now looks old, flagging.

'That place is for young people. An old woman, I had no choice but to quit.' She laughs. Perhaps she has read Arijit's mind.

She scrutinizes the man – someone in his early fifties, not a day older. His partly grey hair actually lends him a new dignity. His fair skin has tanned a shade. They were close, lived together for a while. Strange. How long ago was all that? She has lost count of the years.

'When you were all over television about the energy agreement, I sent Piu an email. Told her about the strong opposition to the agreement in India. "Why are they doing such a stupid thing?" she wrote back, upset. Piu is every bit your daughter.'

She holds his gaze, then looks away. Arijit knows she is trying to reconcile, figure out everything that has happened, everything that hasn't. Their brief life together. Is that time beckoning him? Both of them have turned the page, carried on with their lives, their togetherness tucked away in some distant corner.

Nandita – tall, slender, sharp-featured with a wave of light-brown hair – was so different from the woman sitting before him. He senses her struggle, effort not to walk back, relive the past. Meeting after many years, she does not want to recollect all that, put a burden on him.

Arijit smiles in quiet appreciation.

Nandita gets up, moves around the house, goes from room to room, admires his collection of books. Then stands at the kitchen door. Rita is busy scaling prawns in a plastic tray. With a pair of scissors, she cleans the crustaceans, trimming off the wiry claws, wobbly legs. She smiles, welcoming Nandita.

'Kaku told me to make something special for you. Let me see if I can serve you a dish you have not had before.' Rita has already overcome the initial tension, uncertainty around the guest. The woman, she guesses, is special to Kaku.

Nandita watches with interest the elaborate preparation for *something special*. In a pot are about two dozen finger-sized prawns – beheaded, scaled. The ingredients are kept in little glass bowls. Rita picks up from a basket four coconuts – cleaned of fibre.

'See, they are young coconuts, not fully ripe, not yet woody, the heart still soft.' She holds one for Nandita to examine. With a sharp cutter, she expertly slices the top off each one, pours the water into two glasses. And offers Nandita one. 'It's sweet.'

Nandita takes a small sip, then puts the glass down. Rita squeezes some tomato and chilli sauce into the pot of prawns, then lemon juice, a paste of ginger, garlic and cumin, a pinch of tasting salt, a few slices of dry plum. Then she pours a little bit of coconut water. While the prawns marinate, she puts a saucepan half-filled with water on the stove. On a tray, she has already kept a cup of fine-grained, freshly washed basmati rice. When the water starts boiling, she pours in the rice and lowers the fire. 'I need half-boiled rice,' she explains.

'Rita, this is not cooking; you've got it down to a fine art,' Nandita says admiringly.

After a while, Rita puts half the prawns inside two coconuts. 'You want it hot or not so hot?'

'Not so hot.'

'Then one green chilli.' She throws one chilli into each of the coconuts.

Now she stops for a second, trying to remember the next step. Next, next… yes… She picks up the sliced-off tops and puts them back in place; the coconuts are whole again. With a practised hand, she goes about putting a strip of dough over the joints. This done, she pulls a heavy plastic bag from a cabinet. What she brings out of it are chunks of soft earth dug out from the bank of the canal.

'Yuck! What are you doing with that slush?' Nandita frowns, fearing that in her excitement to do something special, the girl might be making a mess. She cannot hide her disgust.

'Just see.' Rita's smile has not faded.

First, she tightly ties each coconut with iron wire. The end of the wire turns into a hook so one can hang the fruit on a peg or carry it like a bag. Then she goes about plastering the coconuts with mud.

Nandita has not noticed the tandoor oven in a corner. It's a modern one – steel body, a lid on top – not the traditional clay tandoor they gathered around on her father's farm as children. Charcoal pieces are already smouldering inside the sleek cylindrical one.

Rita carefully places the mud-plastered coconuts in the belly of the glowing oven and stokes up the fire by fanning it from below. The iron hooks stick out above the lid.

After some time, she pulls out the coconuts – burnt, dazzling red.

Nandita smiles. 'They're like brick.'

In the other two coconuts, Rita puts the half-boiled rice along with the remaining prawns. And a few drops of screwpine essence from a little bottle. She repeats the whole process all over again.

The table is laid impeccably. Fine china artfully arranged over the white, embroidered tablecloth, brightly coloured petunias in a vase at the centre. Next to it, a bottle of wine looks benignly from the ice bucket at its connoisseurs. Nandita knows Arijit had very little to do with all this.

Their eyes meet, and she sees the guest has started liking her. By now, Rita knows she is not just an old acquaintance…

'I'm not sure if you will like the food, madam.' There is a touch of apprehension in her voice.

'I am dying to eat everything you've made. You said you learnt cooking from your father. And he?'

'He worked for a sahib from America. Radolf Sahib was mad about food.'

'Here – in Delhi?'

'No. In our place—'

'Your place?'

'Near Ranchi.'

'That American lived in your village?'

'Madam, he was a crazy man.'

Bemused, Nandita keeps looking at her.

'Let me go get the food.' Her steps hasten.

Arijit pours wine into two glasses. Delicately holding the stemmed glasses, they clink and *cheers*. Nandita takes a sip.

There is movement in the kitchen, the sound of crockery.

'Rita, are you done?' Nandita raises her voice. 'I'm hungry.'

'In a minute, Didi.' Both of them are surprised at how *madam* has turned into an intimate, informal *didi*. They know something is pulling them closer.

Looking at the spread on the table, Arijit fills their glasses again. Fried rice, roasted mushrooms, fish fry. A rich, appetizing smell floats around, hinting at some unknown festivity.

Nandita bites into a fry. 'Ooh, Rita, gorgeous! Mmm. Which fish is this?'

'Didi, bhetki.' The girl smiles. The approval from the first guest in the house is crucial to her survival.

'Great!'

Rita places two bone china bowls in the middle of the table. Her special dishes. Everything inside the coconuts – coconut meat, prawn, the other ingredients – has melded into a rich paste, emitting a mouthwatering aroma. In the other bowl, the rice has soaked in everything – marinade, the oil from the coconut.

Arijit takes a spoon of the prawn-in-coconut curry, mixes it with rice. 'Wonderful, Rita. I have never tasted anything like this, neither here nor abroad. What is it called?'

'Kaku, this is prawn-coconut korma.'

'And the other dish – with rice?'

'That's prawn-coconut kachchi.'

Rita puts a spoon of kachchi on Nandita's plate. 'When my

father made this dish for Radolf Sahib, he said no one in America had any idea about such gorgeous food.'

'That Sahib was lucky – as are we.' Nandita smiles.

For dessert, Rita serves ginger pudding with custard sauce. Then filter coffee.

Nandita observes the girl – lean, rickety, shoulder blades jutting out; unoiled rough hair carelessly tied in a big knot. Still, its jet-black exuberance casts a spell. The cheeks hollow, the forlorn look on her face traces the potholed road that goes to a faraway place. The large eyes are a reminder of some lost river somewhere. They are sad, their language deeper than she can decipher. Nandita is certain this girl is not from Ranchi, not from within the framework of a familiar world.

Rita quietly places the coffee jug and milk on a side table – this time in the study. She feels awkward after so much praise.

She turns to Arijit.

'Kaku, work in the kitchen is over. Should I go now?'

Is she reading too much into the situation, seeing herself as a kind of intrusion? Nandita looks at her.

'Do you work somewhere else?'

Rita is a little surprised. She shakes her head, no.

Nandita makes the coffee. 'I'll leave in a while. Why don't you come with me? I want to take a look at the market here.'

'I… you want me to come with you to the market?' She is puzzled, almost shocked by something so unexpected.

'Yes, we will go in my car, look around and see if we get something interesting for us.'

Rita laughs incredulously. She never expected the Sunday guest to be so caring, so generous.

'Kaku cannot buy what you need, right?' Nandita says in a friendly voice.

Rita smiles, embarrassed by the guest's gesture. No one has been this kind to her in a long, long time.

8
Shame

From inside the gate of Chancellor Club, Arijit notices the small crowd near the guardroom.

Back from his morning walk, he came here to talk to a fellow walker who is in a hurry to sell his car. Relaxed in a cane armchair, he listened to the man across the patio table on the smooth lawn. Arijit resents talking while on his walk, so they decided to meet at the club later.

'My son bought me the Honda City two years ago,' the neighbour said. 'He had come from America to see us. Now I am going to join them. He has a lovely wife and two children; bought a house in Des Moines and wants his parents to see his success.' He laughed genially. 'I have hardly used the car.'

Arijit looked at him keenly. In his early sixties, the man was happy with the world, grateful for everything he has got. That contentment was visible in everything about him.

'You don't worry about the price. Give me just half the money it takes to buy the car now.' He smiled, pressing Arijit's hand. 'I am in a hurry; I don't want to talk to the car dealers.'

They decided to go for a drive in the afternoon. Arijit shook hands with him and moved towards the club's wicker gate.

He watches the melee at the entrance. A handful of maids are shouting, gesticulating at each other. Among them is Rita. Some men – car washers, servants, scrap buyers – are amusedly watching them, their ugly fight.

One woman, refused entry by the Gurkha guard, is hurling the most colourful abuses at the others. 'In the rich people's homes, whoring comes first, brooming later, and these sluts love that,' she screams.

The men laugh. A ragpicker gaping at the woman actually starts drooling. Wah, a woman mouthing obscenities!

'They work not in kitchens but fuck factories.'

A sweeper bares his red, swollen gums in glee.

'The randis don't just do the dishes but soap the men's balls as well.' Seized by a paroxysm, she is gasping for breath.

'Oye, be careful,' a leering plumber cautions, more with relish than any intention to stop the hysterical woman.

'Chalo, chalo, hato.' Ram Bahadur Chhetri swings his baton in the air. 'No racket, no crowding at the gate.' He mildly pushes a car washer, then turns to the abusive woman. 'I will talk to the people in that apartment. If they say yes, only then will I let you in. They have gone out. Come tomorrow.'

But the woman is like an animal outside the slaughterhouse. Fear of denial, exclusion, the claws of competition – everything is pushing her to the edge. The dread of losing out has driven her mad. She pulls her hair, rubs her watery eyes. Her nostrils flare. Tears and mucus smear her face. Suddenly, she spots Rita making an entry in the register at the security post. Like a hungry predator, she sets on her.

'This Bangladeshi hooker tarts around, lifting her legs even to dogs. And she has got the best job here using a fake name.'

Now they are really close.

'The impure, beef-eating Muslim! And I cannot look for a job?' She wipes the snot in the flat of her hand, trembling in agitation.

'Don't say bad things about me!' Rita flares up.

The other woman pushes her back. She looks menacing. 'What else? Am I one of those horny men that I put you on my lap? You… you illegal *border crosser*!'

Insulted, angry, Rita pulls the abusive woman by the hair and slaps her hard across the face. Then once again. Thin, short, the woman tries to fight back, grabbing Rita's face and scratching her.

The lazy men enjoy the spectacle, making mild, indulgent protests. But they do not intervene. Two women fighting – they laugh, look at each other, savouring the scene. Titillated, they bite their lips.

'Bandh karo!' Chhetri shouts, rushing back from the booth after answering an intercom call. He separates the two and pushes the foul-mouthed woman away. She hobbles before falling down. Sitting on her haunches, she starts howling, striking her forehead.

Chhetri looks at Rita. In the scuffle, her clothes got ripped, baring much of her back. The men lap up the chunk of skin with deep red scratches. So much of a woman's flesh – living, blood oozing!

'Haramzade, bhago yahaan se!' Chhetri roars, breaking into cuss words. 'Bastards, get the hell out of here!' he shouts again. He raps the ragpicker on the knees. 'I'm going to shoot,' he threatens, jerking the rifle on his back. The crowd disperses. He takes Rita into the guardroom and opens a cupboard. After a bit of searching around, he pulls out a grimy, moth-eaten shawl and wraps it around her.

The girl looks strange in the frayed, threadbare maroon shawl. She comes out of the guardroom and smiles gratefully at him before walking away.

Going back to his apartment, Arijit feels uneasy, as if he has been caught in a shady deal, an illegal transaction. The foul-mouthed woman's abuses are buzzing in his ear: *Bangladeshi... illegal border crosser...* Like an assault, like hammer strokes smashing up the lid over a dark pit of illicit activity.

Disturbed, he moves to the balcony and looks at the spread of farmland – deep, diminutive from this distance. The dense vegetation offers a glimpse into a vanishing way of life. Rough-hewn farmers with their sunburnt, sturdy wives and children have always lived close to the earth. The irrigation canal flows quietly into the distant fields; the developers will take time to get there.

Arijit turns to the other end of the balcony, and the shantytown festers. So 'Rita' is a nom de guerre, a cover for hiding? Things are coming unstuck, the mystery unravelling. Her thick East Bengal accent had made him suspect what the wild woman's filthy words just now confirmed. She is an illegal immigrant from Bangladesh. He remembers an afternoon she stayed back after her work was over. From the study, he went to a bedroom to look for his blood pressure medicine. In one corner of the adjacent balcony, she was quietly offering her prayers, facing what she thought to be west. Her legs folded under, head covered with her dupatta, she bowed deeply. He had come away to let her have her secret.

Does she know he was a witness to her humiliation, the stripping of her honour, her undressing by a lurid mob? And still, he did not step out of the veil of decency to come to her rescue, to protect her. Was he scared of the mad woman's acid tongue smearing his impeccable reputation, drilling holes into the genteel veneer?

Impure beef-eating Muslim... illegal border crosser...

And here's her employer – a cultured patrician, eh? Actually a wimp, a hypocrite wearing a mask. A young woman bared, brought down. And he hid behind the trimmed hedge of the club's fencing lest the abusive woman laugh and say, 'Look, this is what I have been saying,' her raw, reviling words reeking of garlic and red chilli.

9
Soldier of God

Lying on the little cot in the muggy tenement, Jamal fidgets. He hears noises – a television blaring somewhere, men arguing loudly. They get back from work and gather in the little bazaar around this time. Someone has an old television. It is carted on a trolley right into the centre of the evening. A DVD player has been rented for the night from a video shop to watch a new Hindi movie. The slum dwellers intermittently talk about politics, events, scandals in town and things they have seen or heard about during the day. The temple priest analyses political events for them. Knots of men and women around the television unwind by the end of the day. Normally, Jamal is part of the gathering, often serenading them with a Kishore Kumar song. This evening, he is in no mood to gossip and gaze at a tinsel siren singing and dancing in provocative clothes.

Listless in his damp cubbyhole, Jamal frets and fumes. He is distressed, sick at heart. Rabeya is ignoring him again; she has not met him for days, dismissed his messages and looked the other way when she saw him at Mausi's shop. *Clear out of my way,* she seems to be saying. The temperamental, fickle-minded Rabee is being pampered by the rich man, tall and handsome like those big feudal lords in the old Dhaka movies. The silver-haired sahib sparks a primitive bloodthirst in Jamal. He wants to knock him off, smash his head into a pulp. The zamindar has snared, spoilt the simple girl.

No, it's not his fault. Jamal can see that. She is changing colour like a chameleon. Snuggling up in the comfort of the rich man's apartment, the deceitful woman has completely erased him from her canvas. Now he is neither a shadow nor even a dot in her life. The man who once rowed her on the river and sang only for her is just a nobody, not even a speck of Paankhali's dust. He's much less than a lowly burr sticking to her sari. Hers is not a heart but a hard, dark, soulless rock! The heart of Munir Sheikh's daughter does not miss a single beat for Jamal.

The slimy rich! Jamal's mood darkens. Blood shoots from his head.

They cheat us, exploit us and take away our women.

The other day, he saw Rabeya going with a fat woman in a big, shiny car. What a car! It looked like a palace. The driver was behind the wheel, and they were talking and laughing in the back. Behind the raised windows, Rabeya looked so different. As if she were one of them.

If she really slips out of his life, he will one day hit the sahib on his head with an iron rod and keep hitting until he drops dead. The filthy rich! Then he will go away – the nowhere man on the road without a place to get to. Love has turned him into a madman, a murderer and the tramp of Runa Laila's song.

He is startled by a mild, measured knock on the door. Something strange about the single, stealthy tap. No one has come calling before. He has never had a visitor. Is it her then? The fickle woman regretting her folly? Her aloof arrogance? He is not sure. She has never been here. The rap feels suppressed, sinister.

'As-salaam alaikum, Jamal Bhai.' The steely, measured voice floats in along with a faint hint of attar. The flinty mullah.

'Alaikum as-salaam, Maulana Sahib,' Jamal says, watching the man look around cautiously before slipping into the hovel.

Jamal suddenly becomes conscious of the wretchedness of his existence, the dank odour inside the pit. 'I could never imagine an important man like you would step into this hellhole.'

'Don't you worry, brother. All over the world, they are conspiring to keep Muslims in poverty, to deny them what is their due, to make them rot in subhuman conditions. Have you seen the poultry vans on the road? In heavy traffic, the terrified birds forget to cry. We're living exactly like that.' The cultured politeness of his voice has peeled off a little. The raw red meat is now oozing blood. 'Allah has poured faith in our hearts and oil in the womb of our Earth…'

'Oil?'

'Not in your wretched Bangladesh, nor in this deplorable Hindustan, Bhai.' The mystery man sniggers. He is irritated by Jamal's interruption, his ignorance. 'Most of the oil is hidden under the Islamic land – the Arab world. The wily whites want to keep us poor and divided so they can plunder the oil from Allah's territory.' His voice does not rise, but its frosty sharpness lacerates Jamal.

Awestruck, he keeps looking at the ghostly silhouette. Somehow, in the presence of this man, he loses his way, his own argument. His grip over his own life slackens.

'You said the right thing, Maulana Sahib; the city rich take away everything we have.' He slaps the seat of a little stool he once made welding odd iron pieces at Akhtar's shop. 'Please have a seat.' He squats on the floor, facing the icy, fiery mullah.

In the wan yellow light of the lone electric bulb, the man looks like a creature from another planet – fierce, obsessively focused and still spectral. An apparition not of this Earth.

'Bangla Bhai, all over the world, Islam is under attack—'

'The rich, Maulana Sahib, the rich snatch away our dear ones with their currency notes...'

'The Jews, Christians and now the cunning Hindus – they are together targeting our faith.'

The sleek, scrawny man with sharp, glinting eyes is an enigma. His frail frame heightens the sense of his remoteness and aloof contempt for the ordinary. He casually unzips the black bag in which he carried his laptop the other day, and with a cultivated disinterest, pours its contents on the floor. He lets the bag lie in the dust, in the undispersed damp.

Jamal gawks at the thick bundles of five-hundred-rupee notes resting innocently in the dust. In the pallid light spilling from the bare bulb, Gandhi shines on the notes. The ascetic bald man of peace looks incongruous, out of place on the avenging rupee bills. So much money lying on the dirt! Unbelievable. So much! In Bangladesh, it will be a huge heap of takas. The cleric watches him silently, gives him time to grasp the reality of the money.

'Two lakh.' He looks quizzically at Jamal and waits. There is no response. Jamal's eyes pop out. 'I have never seen so much money, Maulana Sahib.' He is confused.

'Send it home to your parents; ask them to build a house. I'll give three lakh more.' His voice does not falter; it neither rises nor dips. He talks about money with a curious disdain. 'Those at home – mother, father, brothers, sisters – we must try to make them happy.'

Still stunned, Jamal keeps looking at his surreal guest. The rainmaker smiles benignly.

'You will start training from tomorrow. Every night, someone will come pick you up. And yes, be very careful with the money and about our project.'

Jamal looks at him vacantly.

'For the faithful, there is nothing more glorious than giving up their lives for Allah.' The mullah closes his eyes for a moment. 'It's an unequal war… they have unmanned planes to track us down, armoured vehicles, computer-programmed rockets. We have only our bodies and our faith.'

Jamal wavers between the five-hundred-rupee notes and the horrid images the ghostly man's words have conjured up – of an extraordinary war in which human bodies will whoosh like rockets.

'I hope you get the meaning of our war right.' The man scowls at him. 'From this moment, you're Allah's soldier. There is no retreat, no deviation from this path. You go up blazing, faith fighter. Fierce. Fearsome. Unafraid. And if you have doubts, if Satan creeps into your mind, teasing you to be a traitor, then the death you die will be terrible. You will die slowly, burning in hellfire – not in one go, but a little at a time.' The visitor glares at him.

In the dark, Jamal tosses and turns on his narrow, wobbly cot. The pungent smell of the burning mosquito coil fills the cubbyhole. Something is tormenting him. Deep within. He did not go out to eat. He didn't feel hungry. After the unrelenting maulana left, he switched off the light and lay down. He now oscillates between restless sleep and uneasy wakefulness for the remains of the night. His mind in limbo, Jamal travels to another day. In Khulna – before he crossed the border.

When he reaches the shrine of Khanjan Ali, the fair is in full flow. Hundreds of people from faraway places are milling around the ground. The makeshift stalls on either side of the street buzz with business. It is the full moon in March. Winter is over, summer still away. The wind blowing across the fields renews the memory of the mystic who came to the deltaic land from far-off Persia six centuries ago.

Jamal stands quietly on the landing stairs to the lake. The still water shimmers in the soft moonlight. The noise of the crowd dissolves into the serenity of the lake. Goats bleat somewhere nearby. Left by those whose prayers have been answered, the pathetic creatures wag their short tails, caught between the chaotic fair and their uncertain future.

Somewhere in the middle of the lake, a huge splash deepens the dread of the dark water – the penumbra of many fables about its relentless hunger. Are the abominable ones asking for more sacrifice? No doubt they resent the melee on the fairground. Jamal laughs. A man throws a hen into the water, hoping one of the loathsome reptiles will bother to accept the offering. If it does, that will be a good omen. Once in a while, a bather loses a limb to the abhorrent creatures. 'That's God's way of punishing the sinners for their evil deeds.' Jamal turns. The old man standing behind him is grinning.

The melody is suddenly ecstasy; it's abandon. The zakirs have just raised the pitch of their singing. Jamal walks down the steps into the water to perform ablutions. He washes his face, sprays a little water on his head. He's going to join the zakirs. Until day breaks, they will be singing of man's submission to God, of the beauty of a faith in which everyone has a little space – man, crocodiles, goats, hens… the resplendent moon.

How long ago was the full moon of ardour and adoration? The shimmying waves of the lake? Jamal frets in fever and fear. Fear of forgetting the zakirs' songs, tales of Khanjan Ali. His own past.

10
Homecoming

Arijit was busy packing his large collection of books and attending dinners before leaving Berlin. It was difficult – four breakfasts during the course of one morning, three lunches and cocktails starting early in the evening. The German foreign office hosted a luncheon, the Dean of the diplomatic corps in Berlin – the Nigerian ambassador being the most senior envoy – gave a dinner party, and invitations were still pouring in from the Indian community.

Arijit knew the situation was still not bad; Europe more formal and easier to manage. Had it been an Asian country – Nepal, Pakistan or Sri Lanka – things would have gotten completely out of hand. He remembered the moments of leave-taking from all the foreign capitals – Jakarta, Islamabad, Paris. It had been a long time on the road, from one diplomatic mission to another with two intervals – a couple of years on deputation to the Power and Energy Ministry in Delhi as a joint secretary and a few years at the UN as a senior official. He could have continued at the UN, dividing his time between New York and Geneva, but his affinity had always been bilateral, for matters between two countries. The air inside the gargantuan UN headquarters was suffocating. What relieved his utter sense of loss in the rigidly formal maze were little chats with known–unknown people in the basement café and the serenity of the East River below.

His original plan was to spend a month with his daughter in New York before returning to Delhi. An associate professor of history at Rutgers University, Piu is an acclaimed scholar of South Asian art and liberal traditions. Her husband, Joy, teaches macroeconomics at Columbia. But unsettling all his plans, a call came from the Prime Minister's Office. The PM's principal secretary on the line: 'Rush back to Delhi, Boss wants to see you… seems urgent.'

Arijit took the next available flight. He met the PM at his residence late in the evening.

'This energy agreement with the US is crucial; where we stand thirty-forty years from now will depend on how well we bargain today.' The PM paused, choosing his next words carefully. Arijit waited uncertainly, not knowing what the big man was going to say. 'You must move to Washington as my special envoy.'

So Arijit rushed to D.C. and plunged headlong into the whirlpool of energy politics. He studied the history of similar agreements and profiled the lobbyists and think tank members. Very often, he went to bed when day was breaking. He was the first to enter the chancery at 2107 Mass Avenue and the last to leave late in the evening. Over the course of the day, he would go to meet a prominent member of the Republican caucus or a leading light of Brookings.

In the embassy, he had set up his own office. Often, he met journalists from the *Washington Post* and *New York Times* and, of course the correspondents of Indian newspapers. It took him no time to realize that there were many centres of power in D.C., each one of them extremely important.

The ambassador called him home for a drink one evening. He drove to 2700 Macomb Street – a wooded house at the end of a road.

They were old friends. Sipping Sutherland single malt with chicken tikka, they watched the Indian television network for a while. Then the ambassador picked up the remote to mute the television. 'You have done well so far; they are happy in South Block. But there are two big hurdles – the environment lobby here and the commies back home. Both are very powerful, very obstinate.'

Arijit held long sessions with the intelligence man in the embassy to learn more about the groups opposing the deal. He cultivated a prominent member of RAND Corporation, made friends in the White House, built a team of lobbyists to help clinch the deal. The most enthusiastic among them was a successful Indian businessman, a Republican fundraiser. Satwant Singh came to the embassy one afternoon in his gleaming limousine.

'Suppose the deal happens?' He looked into Arijit's face. Close. Menacing.

'We will have a drink together and listen to Ravi Shankar.'

'Chhaddo ji!' Singh's face contorted in disgust, contempt. 'Sitar and shehnai! The sleek folk in Delhi don't know anything else. Gal karo, Ambassador Sahib, gal karo. Talk sense.' The rusticity from the rough edges of life a generation ago resurfaced. He thumped the desk, discarding the thinly veiled gentility. 'From this evening onwards, my hotels will start entertaining everybody who matters here.'

'A Delhi street will be named after you.' Arijit laughed, indulging the hotelier's *talk-sense* ambition. He decided to play along.

'That's better.' The tall, hefty man hunched forward, his elbows almost edging out Arijit's across the desk. His silk tie flapped. He saw the envoy from the corner of his eye, pinned him down, then broke into a laugh – loud, volatile. Like the yaps of a hungry hound.

'Will you, Ambassador Sahib, will you recommend me for an award? I, the son of a Jat farmer from Punjab, on the annual honours list! Receiving one of the highest civilian awards of the land from the President of India in the high-domed Ashoka Hall of the Rashtrapati Bhavan…' His voice trailed off dreamily. 'That picture, framed in gilt, will hang in the lobby of every hotel I own.' Singh pressed his arm, his handlebar moustache – sharp, like the claws of a sea crab – too intimidating.

'Your efforts will definitely be appreciated,' Arijit said evasively.

'Done, Basu Sahib, done. Every bit of bump will be washed away with the choicest Bordeaux and Scotch.' He laughed, then his voice suddenly dropped. 'I will play an excellent host, ha ha,' he guffawed.

Despite some rough rides, unforeseen hurdles, counter-lobbying, the deal was successfully concluded. Arijit flew back to Delhi to report to the prime minister every minute detail of the agreement. The government happy, he returned to tell his American counterpart that the treaty could be inked any time now. Apart from attending a few parties in diplomatic circles, Arijit had nothing else to do. He did not forget to tell a senior official in South Block about Singh's hospitality offensive. What next? The question began to bother him.

One afternoon, Piu came with Bubka from New York.

'Baba, you are a celebrity! Like a star cricketer in India. Television channels and newspapers are full of you,' Piu gushed excitedly from the door. 'Joy has gone to Berkeley for a seminar, so we took the train from Penn.'

She asked Bubka to touch Arijit's feet. 'Tell Dadu what you felt when we saw him on CNN.'

'Dadu, you looked like a Brazilian soccer coach. Oh, yeah, my best friend Tim said that.'

They all laughed.

Arijit took Bubka in his arms and kissed his head, running his fingers through his hair. Playfully, he rolled a towel into a ball and kicked it to the other end of the room. Bubka ran after it.

'Really, Baba, we saw you very often on TV.' Piu was out of breath. 'Joy recorded some of your interviews.' A proud daughter, she was going back to the days when, as a child, she had watched her father making powerful volleys on the tennis court. 'I'm getting calls from friends in India… newspapers splashed your pictures. Niru Pishi called from Calcutta. One reporter from a Bengali newspaper went to talk to her, asked her to recollect your early life, what she felt about her brother's work. Wow! Your sister was on cloud nine.'

'It's all over, Piu. I'm out of it. The big bosses from Delhi will descend over D.C. in a while. I need some rest.'

'Baba, there's an excellent opportunity for you. One university here is looking for someone who can offer courses in South Asian affairs, not just an academic but someone with real experience, an expert. Can I send your CV to them?'

He asked for some time.

Most of his adult life, he had lived abroad. After two years at Cambridge, he had returned home to take the civil service examination. Among the first ten on the merit list, he opted for Foreign Service. He was twenty-four. Since then, he had been taking up residence in one world capital after another across the continents – Asia, America, Europe. But for a few years in Delhi, he had hardly lived in his country. A successful career, enviable reputation… but a man without roots, without memories of home…

Suddenly, a deep longing overpowered him. It was a moment of crisis. He was seized by an urge to discover who he really was.

But Piu would not listen. She wanted him to stay with them for some time.

'All my life, I have met you only on vacations. We never lived under the same roof even for a month,' she complained. 'Now that you are free, let's all live together. Bubka will finally know what a grandfather is.' She got sentimental.

But something had already begun to impel him. The vignettes from a life lived long ago. Fragments of memories flew around, pulling him to the past. Did he have a life before he put on the diplomat's suit? The butterflies tempted him beyond the hedges, deeper into the woods. Monsoon clouds, sad, wet days in the rain. It was all a haze now. Something chased him – not so much his memory as the lack of it.

Packing up a few things, he took the flight one afternoon. The seasoned, astute diplomat did something on impulse after a long time. The last time, it had been a disaster. But a widower, his only child well settled, he could not care less. Nothing held him back.

His friends and colleagues were happy seeing him in Delhi. They threw parties and hosted dinners. When they met at one such party, the foreign minister asked if he was ready to take on another challenging assignment, this time to Central Asia. One of those countries liberated after the collapse of the Soviet Empire had become strategically important for New Delhi. They needed an experienced man to carefully handle the relations. Arijit politely declined.

'Sir, I'm on a journey to my roots,' he said, smiling in deference.

'That's good. But whenever you feel like working again, do see me,' the minister said.

A friend living overseas had a house in posh Defence Colony. 'Please move in.' He sounded enthusiastic on the phone. 'I'm telling my brother to make the arrangements.'

So, Arijit began to live among the city's rich. Looking at the fancy cars parked outside every house, he got some idea about the new affluence in the big cities. There was a garish flavour of wealth around the place. The car showrooms, boutiques for designer couture, jazzy jewellery stores – all sure signs of a change that had happened in his absence. In every street, the graceful, balconied houses were being razed to give way to glass-and-steel structures. What struck him most was the disappearance of the stodgy Ambassador from the roads. So much a symbol of Nehru's aspiration for self-reliance, the frumpy old car had given way to smart Japanese and Korean beauties.

Still undecided, one morning he took a flight to Calcutta to see his sister. Stewardesses in smart red skirts moved daintily along the aisle, handing soft drinks and breakfast trays. The private airlines, which had taken to the skies in the years after economic liberalization, had brought in a new culture. He thought of the days when the government-owned Indian Airlines had an absolute monopoly – flights delayed to accommodate a late-arriving politician, unfriendly air hostesses who would grimace if asked for another cup of coffee.

Calcutta, however, was as it had been forty years ago – untouched by changes the economic reform had brought elsewhere. Niru-di, his elder sister, cried in happiness seeing him. Her hero. She could not hold back her tears.

'Buro, I thought I would not see you again! You go round the world, and here, in our father's house, you set foot after… after how many years?' She wiped her face with the end of her sari.

Nirupama had chaperoned her brother all through his childhood. The proud sister was protective, possessive of the bright boy, keeping a watchful eye on him until he left for Cambridge. Her only regret – she did not get a chance to find the right bride for him.

Neighbours came to meet him. Children asked for autographs, their parents sought his blessings so they could do well in life. Cameras clicked. He had no choice but to eat a large number of milk sweets – sandesh, chom chom, rasmalai, raj bhog. Thick, sweetened yogurt. Niru-di cooked hilsa in mustard sauce.

In the evening, he went to the Bengal Club with an old friend. A few others came to meet him. They explained that after long years of communist rule, the enviable industrial base of Bengal had turned into a rust belt. A revival was not possible.

Arijit was disappointed seeing, hearing about the decline of Calcutta, the second city of the British Empire. He had many fond memories of growing up in the Ballygunge Palace mansion. As a child, he had rushed to the giant marquee where the community Durga Puja was celebrated for five days at the peak of autumn, supported Mohun Bagan in a big match against East Bengal. Calcutta was a boisterous business centre. A vibrant city. Now it was hobbling, its economy stagnant.

He had a secret hope of settling down in the city of his birth, among his old friends, giving lectures here and there. That did not seem possible after what he had seen and heard. The natural impulses of a society, the vitality of a culture, had been stifled by the doctrinaire politics of the commissars. No, he could not reconcile all this with the image of a traditional, tolerant society he always had in his mind.

The next morning, Arijit took a black-and-yellow taxi to the airport.

11
Chandani Mahal

He walks down the long flight of stairs into another life. The ferry is taking him away from the familiar world of success and failure, loss and gain, fulfilment and denial. Jamal… Jamal… the name loses its validity this side of the river. It's another country – unknown, undiscovered. He is a dervish on a journey to the land of faith. Of love and abandon. Surrender and sublimation.

Across the river is an altogether different affair. The sharp, pungent smell of mangrove-palm leaves on the boats still lingers in the air. The tottering three-wheeled cycle-vans have gained a new pace now that they are fitted with cheap AB-SIFANG engines. In the teashops, laid-back men sip black tea with a squirt of lemon and talk of Nosimon, the wonder engine. If the striped giant prawns sustain the economy, the country rides on Nosimon – a retired policeman's wisecrack raises a wave of laughter. Nosimon – is it a derivative of the Arabic *naseem*, early morning breeze? Story writers down the ages have called a beautiful woman Naseemunissa, for she is as delicate and soothing as the cool wind at dawn.

He gets up and gives the shop owner a coin. Walks down the dirt to another river – this one much leaner, narrower. He carefully crosses the wobbly wood-and-bamboo bridge.

'Is this Chandani Mahal? The Bauls live here?'

'I don't know about them. But yes, this is Chandani Mahal.'

In a hurry, the man walks away.

From here, the land falls away to the lake. More like a swamp than a lake, weed and hyacinths cover most of it. One-legged date palms, palmyra trees girdle the water. The rich-green rice paddies exult in the descending sun. Having grazed enough, a cow relaxes on the grass, chewing her cud. She rubs her back against a coconut tree. At the end of the field, the house stands on a mound – bare, raw, without a boundary wall.

Jamal carefully walks down the narrow, raised strip of land between the swamp and the paddy. He sees a man singing with his eyes closed:

The strange mynah
Flits in and out
Of the cage deep inside.
Had I caught the bird I would chain no doubt
To my mind her two feet…

His flowing ochre robe flapping in the wind, long hair blowing, the man sings to the tune of the string instrument cradled against his chest. Those around the courtyard play tambourines, cymbals, keep time by clapping.

Jamal sits in a corner of the veranda, cross-legged. On the mildewed brick wall, he sees a poster:

Maij Bhandari Festival, Chittagong, 5 April
Gathering of Bauls and Fakirs

The song over, the man sits beside him. His face shimmers like a placid lake in the moonlight.

'Life is unwanted tension, boy? A burden one can do without?' His eyes glint in an impenetrable mystery. 'Do you feel drawn to our way of life? The life of a mystic, a mendicant who has made the road his home?'

'That's why I am here. To live the song – to be what the song is all about.'

The man laughs, pushing away his unruly, long hair.

Sadik Rahman has lived an interesting life. In his youth, he sneaked into India and worked in a factory in Punjab. A restless man, he went to Lahore, giving the border guards a slip, and from there on, he went to Iran. After a fight between the immigrants and locals, he was thrown in jail along with a few others. One day, the authorities got tired of the inmates and asked them to leave the country at once. Back in Pakistan, with the help of a few friends, he raised a little money and came home. By then, he had lost interest in life and its relentless pursuit of success. He bought this place and built the Baul Group.

'When you get tired of life, living is difficult.' He moves closer to Jamal. 'Tell me, boy, what has gone wrong?'

'I rowed her, sang for her, loved her, and then… then my love flew away. Over the barbed wire. To that vast, limitless land – India. Now she knows big people. She has been foreigned. I want to join the Maij Bhandari sect; I want to live for a song.' Jamal looks at the others. Sitting around him, they are all listening. 'I want to be a Baul, going from place to place to sing at every bazaar and ferry ghat. People say I sing well. Let it be my life. Initiate me, Kaka.'

'You sang for that girl, and she ran away,' someone from the group quips. Others laugh. 'Sing for us; let's see what happens.' They roar with laughter.

Jamal thinks of a song. The lines coming to mind are all about moist love for the fickle-minded girl, not about the ardour of tracing the divine in signs all around you. He goes back to all the songs he has learnt, hummed – they're all about a gazelle-eyed girl's long hair, her thin lips, waves of lustrous smiles… But yes, a Baul sang at the Notun Bazaar ferry ghat sometime last month. It's coming back to him… *Haven't got another friend like you, oh God…*

He borrows the string instrument from Sadik Rahman, plays his fingers over the string, clears his throat, intoning:

I will not get another friend like you –
Oh, kind God

His voice rises and falls, the words elongate, the tune stretches. He plays the single-string instrument and travels to that day at the ferry ghat.

Don't leave me alone
Now that I have seen you –
Oh, kind God

By the time he has finished, every face is beaming with admiration. Wah wah, they say. Bhalo, chamatkar!

'The Baul's life is not easy.' Sadik Rahman sounds grim. 'The path we walk is potholed, full of nails and shards.' He pauses, runs his fingers through his long, grey hair. 'The intolerant hotheads have attacked our seats, thrown bombs to disrupt our gatherings.' He looks at Jamal, wants to know if he is already scared. 'In Chittagong, they beat up the Bauls, cut their long hair. They say the song-and-dance way to God is flawed, corrupted. It's un-

Islamic. Their way is flaming white, stern and inflexible; ours is full of fragrances and colours, like the lazy murmur of the river.' He curves his hand to show the rise and fall of water. He smiles wryly.

'Let them follow the blazing white path, and we take the road of songs and colours. What's the problem?' Jamal probes the man's craggy face for an answer.

Sadik Rahman laughs, more loudly than Jamal thinks he is capable of. 'If there was an answer to that, boy, the world would have been a beautiful place without war and hate.' The weather-beaten man scratches his chin through the tangled bush of beard. 'They say jihad is for the pure, songs are for the corrupted.' His head shakes, and his shoulder-length hair flaps in the breeze from the lake. He looks towards the swamp. His eyes widen. 'They are coming.' He turns to Jamal with a faint smile. 'See the pull of your song.' Between the water and the paddy, two hazy figures in white are tottering along the narrow ridge. Others look in that direction, too.

The white apparitions have now acquired distinct identities. Two women, Hindu widows, stand on the ground below the veranda. With folded hands, they greet Sadik Rahman. 'Namaskar, Dada. We heard someone sing – someone pouring his heart out. We could not stay back any longer,' the older of the two says.

'This boy is crazy, he wants to be a Baul, join the Maij Bhandari group. I was telling him about our harsh life, all your years on the road.'

'Don't scare him, Dada. If he sang the song we just heard, he will one day become a great Baul – the whole world will listen to him.'

Jamal wakes up with a start. A terrible thirst is choking him. His throat dry, he feels suffocated. This black hole in the shantytown cannot be his home tonight. And tomorrow? He begins training to avenge all the wrongs done to Muslims around the world. At faraway places, places whose names he can neither pronounce nor remember.

12
City of Mirrors

Frisked by a woman guard with a metal detector, Rita walks through the security scanner to follow Nandita inside Atlantic Mall. Her head spins. She has never seen anything like this before. The stairs move on their own, taking you from one floor to another. Up and down. Like the Ferris wheel in the Charak Mela near their village. The rolling stairs! The lemony smell, hushed noises, glass-walled shops, waiters in smart uniforms serving customers at little tables inside the beautiful tea shops, a machine making coffee frothy in a flash – it's a world she had no idea about.

She gapes at the men and women behind a transparent glass wall getting their hair cut, coloured, shampooed. They're sitting side by side. *Shame shame!* How can they do that?

Nandita gives her arm a tug. She moves away from the salon front, embarrassed. After walking around for a while, they stop at an apparel store. The moment they step in, a young woman greets Nandita with a smile.

From the shiny steel racks, she brings out dresses – salwar kameez, kurta churidar, tops, skirts, jackets – stuff people on television wear. Rita cannot think of herself in those expensive, fancy clothes. The saleswoman takes her to a changing room, holds the door open and gives her the new outfits.

'Close the door from the inside; try out the dress.' Seeing her hesitation and the nervous look on her face, the woman frowns. Her smile disappears. 'Be careful; don't spoil the new clothes.' Inside the closed box, mirrors facing her under the white, fluorescent lights, Rita dies in shame. Take off her clothes when so many people are moving around outside? She can hear the noise, the sound of sliding glass panels.

Shopping over, the two go to a purple restaurant where they're serving coffee and cake. They sit at a corner table. Rita has already started liking Nandita, who is not young or old but has a lot of personality. Everywhere she went, she commanded attention. Stood out. Is she Kaku's girlfriend? The question bothers her. Why don't they get married then? Both living separately in the same city, they spend unhappy days together; perhaps they meet only to go back to a time when they were close. When they were happy.

'Let me buy you a cell phone,' Nandita says, as if she has suddenly remembered something. 'I saw you using one. Is that yours?'

'No, Didi, I have borrowed it from someone.' Rita feels embarrassed.

'You return it.'

Minutes later, they are in a Samsung showroom. Nandita chooses a simple, cute model for her. 'For a connection, I need an address proof,' the shop assistant says. Nandita rummages in her purse and carelessly takes out some papers. Dwarfed by her imposing presence, the man obediently photocopies and returns them to her. He does not ask any more questions.

'Call me whenever you feel like.' Nandita smiles, giving Rita the phone. 'Didi will always take your calls.'

Rita is in awe of Nandita. The woman she met for the first

time a few hours ago seems like the gateway to another world. She is many things to her. She sipped wine, and after lunch, lit a cigarette. While talking to Kaku, she often held his arm, patted him on the shoulder. She is caring, affectionate and supremely confident. One feels comfortable, secure in her company.

Back home, Rita carefully tries out the kurta, then the loose, flowing salwar. She drapes the long scarf over her chest from the shoulders and stands before the plastic-framed mirror hanging from a bamboo pole in the middle of her hutch. She cannot believe her eyes! It's another woman, not her. She will never be able to wear it to work. People will laugh, the rickshaw-wallahs might wolf-whistle. And there are bound to be catcalls from the sweepers at Blue Lotus Grove.

Slowly, carefully, she takes off the dress. Looking at her bare body, she feels a little flesh over the craggy bones. She has put on some weight. Her parched breasts are now full of moisture. Like dark clouds over the river promising rain. Or is it pulp? Swelling to a new happiness. *A man should see me now.* She laughs.

She thinks of Jamal, the lovesick loony. Unknowingly, the memory of the day before Eid comes back. The first Eid after Abba moved into his new house with the younger woman, leaving them behind. Sun and clouds, laughter and tears… her old life… back when she was Rabeya.

He rows her on his little boat from the Notun Bazaar ferry ghat to Paankhali. At high tide, the Rupsa is lashing at its banks with a new fury. The dinghy tosses up and down. The dark blue waves from the estuary rush to push it back.

From my house not very far
Is the city of mirrors.
There lives my neighbour,
Oh ho, I haven't seen her ever…

Is that song about me? What does it mean – *city of mirrors*? For Rabeya, it's a riddle. She is listening, but still not.

Getting home to the prospect of a bleak Eid, her mind is elsewhere. Her mother's cousin who sells choi roots in Daulatpur Bazaar gave her fifty takas. If she buys some rice, very little of that money will be left. For the past few days, their neighbours have been making delicious dishes – vermicelli boiled in milk with sugar, cardamom and raisin, mutton biryani, fish pilau, beef bhuna curry… The aroma of rich food distresses her mother.

Thinking of Eid in privation, she moves to get out of the boat at Paankhali. And then comes the surprise. He pulls out of the hold a big, red-crested rooster and the hilsa hanging from a jute twine.

She shakes her head and turns to walk away.

He holds her hand.

'Tell your mother to make hilsa pilau and chicken biryani,' he pleads. Humble, disarming, he is hurt. 'Give them to your ma. Tell her I said Eid Mubarak.' He tries to smile.

'Oh, no. Please. Thank you. Thanks for the ride.'

Gnawed by her refusal, he screws up his face. 'Will you stomp over my good wishes on the eve of Eid?'

She stands there, transfixed.

'If you think I am too small a man to give you something, then I'm taking the fowl and fish to Amma. Let her shoo me away.'

He starts walking beside her.

'All right. I'll tell her about you.' She knows the presence of the obstinate man in the village will set tongues wagging. 'You win.' She laughs.

Jamal has always stood by her, tried to help her out. Tidying up her little hutch, she looks back, wanting to know why nothing has come out of all this. His arrival in this slum, she is sure, was no coincidence. He must have searched, hunted for her. There is a network of middlemen who serve as a link between the Bangladeshis in Indian cities and their families back home. Jamal perhaps had found out from them where she was and dropped anchor in Noahda.

But the man is crazy, an incurable romantic. You can listen to his love songs – songs of separation and tryst – and feel your heart melt. Something twinges inside. But… quite an eccentric man. Not someone a woman could think of as her husband.

'Rabeya… Rabee – are you in?' Startled by the voice, familiar yet distant, she remains rooted there instead of starting towards the door. *Calling me Rabee…* Still, she cannot quite place the man waiting outside.

'Rabeya, Shafiqul Alam from Khulna. Open the door.'

Shafiqul – the middleman. Unable to see her mother's suffering any more, scared by the uncertainty of two meals a day, she talked to the man in Daulatpur Bazaar when the prawn factory laid her off.

'Will you take me to India where I can work?'

The man looked icily at her, waited a few moments before

saying anything. 'India is a big country… Where exactly do you want to go? Calcutta, Delhi, Bombay?' He smirked.

'Wherever. Take me to Calcutta. I have heard about that place.'

Shafiqul sized her up – her urgency, hunger, vulnerability. He ran his fingers through his flowing beard, smiled, revealing his paan-stained teeth. 'I am taking five or six other girls to Delhi. Wages are high there, jobs easy to get.'

When she got home to announce her decision, her mother wept. Deserted by her husband, for the single woman this daughter was like a pillar of support. She shared her pain, humiliation, loneliness with Rabeya. They were like sisters, working together, talking of the days when things had been better. When there was a man taking care of them. But life had been tough with no steady income. Every morning was a doubtful start, a question mark on the next meal.

Her mother finally agreed. She sold the last bit of gold – her wedding ring – to pay Shafiqul. When he counted the last of the takas, the middleman smiled. 'There was a time when the son would go out and earn for the family. Now it's the daughter's turn.'

The memories washing over her, Rabeya opens the door.

'See what I have got for you.' The man hands her a salted hilsa in a plastic bag. 'Your mother bought the fish in Daulatpur Bazaar.'

When she first went to meet the middleman, an unknown fear pulled her back. In villages around Paankhali, people called him Shafiqul-the-Croc. The dalal, they said, would sell young, innocent village girls to the vice dens of Calcutta, Bombay, Delhi, smuggle them to Dubai to feed the lust of decrepit Arab sheikhs.

The man is smiling genially, standing in the doorway.

He comes in and sits on a rickety stool. 'And your brother, Bablu, he has sent you this.' He pulls out a music tape from a battered suitcase. A heavily made-up woman stares at Rabeya from the cassette cover. 'Baby Nazneen – the most popular singer since Runa Laila.' He grins.

Rabeya walks up to a little rack of bamboo strips in a corner, puts something on a cheap plate and returns. 'Please eat it. I will get you some water.'

Shafiqul looks at the stuff, bemused. 'What's this? It has a sweet smell.'

'Cake. I made it in the house where I work.'

'Good-good.'

She opens a tin trunk and brings out a packet.

'I bought the blanket for Ma.' She watches the man. He is picking up the crumbs from the plate. Croc has never revealed his crookedness to her, never done the things she heard people talking about in Paankhali.

'I help people do what they want to; I have never forced them into anything.' Shafiqul's betel-stained teeth emerge in an innocent grin. Perhaps he could gauge her thoughts. She laughs. True, he hasn't croced her.

Rabeya feels uneasy. 'Please tell Ma I am fine. The man I work for is kind.' Then she takes out a little purse from somewhere inside her clothes and counts the hundred-rupee notes. 'One thousand.' She hands him the money cautiously. 'Tell Ma not to worry about me.'

Croc counts the rupee notes again. 'One thousand rupees – that means I will give your mother twelve hundred takas, right?'

Rabeya quickly works out the money exchange rate at the border checkpoint. For a thousand rupees, she would get at least sixteen hundred takas.

Croc.

She keeps quiet. The man is the only channel she has to send a little money to her mother.

'Tell Ma that Bablu must not drop out of school.'

The man gets up, holding the suitcase. Rabeya notices that its broken handle has been replaced by a bunch of plastic cords. 'I have to meet a few others.' He takes a couple of steps to the door, then stops. 'Oh, yes, I almost forgot.' He comes back. 'This letter came months ago. Your mother cannot read English but somehow knows it's for you, from America.' He hands her an envelope with stars and stripes stamped over it.

13
Kala Pani

Nandita smiles. The pint-sized mango tree she put in a clay tub in one corner of the terrace proudly shows off its flowers from a few branches. A little cluster of mangoes, no bigger than mothballs, glistens in the early morning sun. The dew has given them an extra shine. She bends down by the tub and touches one – the size of her thumb but still a mango. Faded green and round, the fruit has tapered off to a sharply hooked point at the end.

Nandita spends the early morning hour among the plants. Since her return from Paris a few months ago, she has slowly raised the garden on the terrace. With a lot of care. She still writes about Indian literature and art in French newspapers and magazines. *Les Inrockuptibles* published her latest article on filmmaker Ritwik Ghatak. His humanism and intensity, his self-destructive instincts. Watching *Meghe Dhaka Tara* in the St. Stephen's College auditorium all those years ago had made her think. The old, grainy black-and-white film, part of the new-wave director's Partition trilogy, is about displacement and migration. In Paris, she saw his other films and wondered why the anarchically original director had never got his due from the world. The well-researched article was her personal tribute to the bohemian filmmaker who had practically hastened his death by reckless drinking.

French television channels interview her once in a while – about Indian cinema, new writers, promising artists. The crew of *Arte* came, set up cameras on the lawns for her take on Bollywood heroes – from Raj Kapoor and Amitabh Bachchan to Shah Rukh Khan. Neighbours were curious. They looked out from their balconies when Benedicte Meyssan, the director, followed her, cameras on, as she drove in. The critic–commentator caught in action.

But she is increasingly getting cut off from that world. Cinema – her passion. Journalism that put her on the road around Europe. Publishing that gave her both fame and a deeper understanding of India. None of that interests her any more. Emptiness assails her. After living a busy, boisterous life for twenty-five years in Europe, she is now seized by a strange sadness. Ennui lays her soul low.

In this house, she moves into wisps of anonymity and recedes from the familiar world, obliterating everything that has been her past. She has a deep desire to disappear into a shadowy, silent province of her own, across the barbed wire of known, familiar life and its conflicts and divisions.

In late winter, her terrace is blossoming. The little plants in terracotta pots are effervescent. The trees around the lawns in the backyard – jacaranda, flame, neem, cotton, laburnum – will blossom soon. Their long shadows play with the morning sun. She does not want to look beyond this.

'Nan, tea's up?'

Radhika stands in the doorway. She turned seventy-four in January. Thin, straight, she is active, surprisingly agile for her age. Potters around the house all the time. Looking at her mother, Nandita sometimes feels old. At fifty-two, she is already exhausted – fagged out. *My mother should have been a little older,* she quietly laughs.

'Let's have tea on the terrace.' Nandita gets up, gives Radhika the little mango and hurries across the hallway into the kitchen. The teapot, two cups, strainer, milk, sugar, biscuits – everything is neatly arranged on a tray. She does not know when her mother entered the kitchen and did all this. She takes the tray to the terrace and puts it on the wrought-iron table. Radhika follows her. They pull chairs out and sit facing each other.

'How is your backache, Nan?'

'Much better, Mom.'

Nandita hands Radhika her cup of tea.

'Perhaps you can go for a walk in the morning? The weather is lovely now.'

'I will, I will. Let me organize myself a little more. I'm thinking of going to a gym.'

Radhika looks at her daughter closely. Many years in Europe have given her fair skin an unfamiliar paleness. Always whimsical, unpredictable, this daughter of hers has never followed rules, preferring to live the life of her choice. While some of her friends went to either Oxford or Cambridge, Nandita opted for the Sorbonne for her master's, and later, a doctoral degree. In no time, she became part of Paris society, making friends among the writers, filmmakers, artists. She made a name as a journalist. And later in publishing. The newspapers here often carried write-ups about her in the weekend supplements.

'Are you in touch with your old friends over there?' Radhika says, gazing at her daughter. She wants to know something – without making it obvious.

'Some of them email.' Nandita knows what her mother is hinting at. The old woman is trying to find out. Pry open the past.

She takes her mother's hand in hers and gently squeezes it.

'What?' Radhika grins, embarrassed.

'Mom, you're cute.'

'Kala pani – the ocean, my mother used to say, would make a man a little crazy when he crossed it. She was not wrong.' Radhika laughs, unusually flippant. She sips her tea, peers at the little mango. Feels happy, surprisingly cheerful. 'By the way, where is the ambassador now? I read a lot about him in the papers last year. He was doing something in America. An agreement?'

'For new technology to make electricity, Mom. No power cuts in our home in a few years.'

'I won't live to see all that.' Radhika breathes deeply, breaks a ginger cookie and puts a bit in her mouth. Then another sip of tea. She relishes the moment – ginger cookies with tea. 'A handsome man; those days he was often on television.'

'We met a few times after he left Paris, then lost touch. I don't know where he is now.'

'Now you're home. You must settle down. It's never too late.'

Her mother's words bring back a world Nandita has decided to forget, a part of her left behind in Europe, lost forever.

14
Little Bombay

A wildcat strike at Charles de Gaulle Airport has sent the flight schedules haywire. All the flights are delayed. No one knows when things will get back to normal. A senior minister arrived from Delhi early in the morning. He is on his way to Havana to attend the G70 summit of the developing nations. Old Castro's way of keeping alive the Cold War.

The minister, not very familiar with the nitty-gritty of foreign affairs, is standing in for the foreign minister, who is busy at another international conference. In India, the conservatives are in power. Traditionally enthusiastic about Third World issues and a vocal supporter of Castro's cause, New Delhi's response to the Havana summit is lukewarm. The minister has come with only a handful of officials. None of them have any experience in summitry to help him.

Arijit has been asked by the foreign office to travel with the minister to Havana and assist him with drafting and other work at the summit. To make sure that the K-word does not sneak into any of the resolutions because of some shrewd manoeuvre by the recalcitrant neighbours.

'Why don't you get an assignment from that Calcutta paper to cover the event?' Arijit turned to Nandita with a glint in his eye.

She was in his office, hoping for some news. 'General Ashraf is also going; it might be interesting.'

The minister is vegetarian. And he does not trust any of the restaurants to protect his brahminical purity. So the Indian chef in the embassy prepares a rich curry of peas and paneer, dal and a dish of assorted vegetables for lunch.

The ambassador, in keeping with protocol, has to sit next to the minister at the dining table. From the look on his face, Nandita knows Arijit is not enjoying a single moment of it. He has not touched the food. She sits beside a woman officer from the minister's department in Paris. After lunch, Arijit tells the minister to rest for a while. It's going to be a long flight across the Atlantic. The old man, stranded due to the sudden strike and unsettled by the new continent, agrees.

Arijit drives Nandita to Rue du Faubourg-Saint-Denis and walks down what is a veritable Indian bazaar. The winding street is a whiff of India – women in silk saris, aromas of spices and curry floating around. And the little stalls on the sidewalk a throwback to Jaipur or Agra.

'This is our Little Bombay.' Nandita points to a man selling incense. Many years in the city, her fluent French, she is almost a Parisian now.

They walk into his favourite Pakistani restaurant. The owner greets Arijit, 'Adaab, Ambassador Sahib.' His family is actually from Lucknow. His parents migrated to Lahore after Partition. He hums old Bollywood songs all the time.

They order kebab and roomali roti with Chianti.

The man walks up to their table, his hands clasped. 'Ambassador Sahib, the lanes of Old Delhi come alive in the evening with the strain of ghazals and the rich smell of kebab. Mirza Ghalib still roams around the old havelis. Isn't it?'

The man, who has never been to Delhi, is full of such tales from the Walled City. In his imagination, he has recreated the evening life in the narrow lanes around the Jama Masjid, unmindful of changes that have swept through the areas around the grand Mughal mosque.

Even before they board the plane late in the evening, diplomatic protocol sees to it that Nandita gets separated from Arijit. A woman official from the French foreign office takes charge of the minister and his entourage, guiding them through the VIP entrance. Nandita, only an ordinary civilian, lines up for immigration and security along with the other economy-class passengers.

On the plane, Arijit sits next to the minister in business class, and Nandita, poor journo, in the rear. From her window seat, she watches the terminal. A tall, robust dictator from an African country, in his blazing military uniform, is being given a ceremonial send-off. There's busy movement on the tarmac around the aircraft. The airport is humming back to life after the lightning strike. Everyone is headed for Havana.

Minutes later, another head of state in his military uniform starts climbing the airstair. Less flamboyant than the African, the South Asian dictator has a shrewd look about him. Every inch an army chief in khaki, he seems somewhat incongruous among the clutter of carefully polished decorations and badges all over his uniform. General Ashraf of Pakistan greets a few who have recognized him before taking his seat.

Uncomfortable among unknown, tired passengers, Nandita

watches the harried stewardesses pacing up and down the aisle, mouthing apologies about the delay, chirping flight information, trying hard to keep their smiles on. A little edgy, uncertain of the mood around. Perhaps unnerved by the absolutely packed flight. The aircraft begins gliding over the Atlantic after a smooth take-off.

Drinks have somewhat soothed the harassment of a long day.

Nandita scribbles a few words on her business card and hands it to a stewardess. 'Will you please give it to General Ashraf in business class?' She watches the stewardess's traipsing figure and waits with bated breath. She has acted on impulse. Given the current border tensions between the two countries, it is unlikely that the general will talk to the representative of an Indian newspaper. She tries to concentrate on an article about Islam in *L'Express*.

The stewardess returns with the card and measures her up in a quick glance. 'You can see him right away.' A hint of admiration in her voice.

Walking down the aisle with her little Dictaphone in hand, Nandita thinks quickly about what to ask General Ashraf.

Surprised by her presence in the front, Arijit gives her a quizzical look. She points to the general. He nods mildly.

Even before she can say hello, the dictator pats the empty seat next to his. Nandita looks around. On a totally crammed flight, the seats around General Ashraf's are vacant. For the security of the military dictator?

'Tashrif rakhiye,' he says in chaste Urdu. A smile flickers. 'Aapka mizaaj kaisa hai?' Is this warmth natural? Or a way of preparing the ground to send a signal to New Delhi? A slight man by military standards, he seems weighed down by the stars and badges all over his khaki uniform. A pendant-like medal hangs from a chain around his neck, his country's highest honour. The bright red band on his peaked cap glares. The leaf-shaped golden braids on the visor, epaulettes and lines of medals and badges won for various campaigns adorning his chest – all this seems to have burdened the man, saddled him with too much responsibility. Away from the button line, above his name badge, is the insignia of a hawk.

'That's my paratrooper's badge.' General Ashraf has noticed her curiosity.

He looks normal, almost ordinary, when he takes off his peaked cap and holds it in his hand, revealing his greying hair. 'The weight of the cap…' He laughs meaningfully. She gazes at the red band, then at the golden braids forming a leaf.

'Ah, that – scrambled eggs!' The general laughs again, this time a little louder. 'Doesn't it resemble scrambled eggs?'

Nandita smiles, nodding her agreement. She feels comfortable and quickly thinks of her questions.

The dictator, who captured power in a bloodless coup a few years ago, is polite to a fault. Despite his decorations and the *weight* of his cap, he has a good sense of humour. His modest appearance is in sharp contrast to the flamboyant African giant flaunting the shining aiguillette. The Goliath's voice booms a few rows away. General Ashraf's unassuming manner makes him look like an unlikely junta boss. After the massive African, he seems like, well, an apology for a dictator. Or is he too shrewd to play his cards straight, to let others know who he really is?

'Farmaiye.' He smiles affably, asking her to shoot.

She tries to remember the issues: the recent lows, flashpoints between the two neighbours and the possibility of dialogue. The wily military boss, who has consolidated his position with a string of populist measures, is in a mood to talk. Perhaps he has sensed an opportunity to start a dialogue with the neighbours.

He listens to her minutely, then remains lost in his thoughts for a while. Suddenly, he flicks a smile at her. 'Dil mein ek khwahish hain,' he says, like a child asking for ice cream.

Nandita is confused, apprehensive, too, about the dictator's *desire*. A military man…

'I want to watch a cricket match in Delhi. That city can cheer for both Kapil Dev and Zaheer Abbas.'

On its way out, winter in Delhi usually gives a last bite in early February. Tonight, a sharp chill settles deep into the bones. On the other side of the glass windows, a thick fog floats around, very much like threads of cotton loosely tied together. Or an invading army of nomads from behind the Himalayan peaks?

Nandita hears her mother cough in her sleep. 'Rabb-ji, oh… Mata Rani…' Radhika mumbles, the words sticking in her throat, cough and sleep.

She walks down the hallway into her mother's room, stands beside her bed and watches the frail thing tucked up in a colourful Jaipuri quilt. Her lips quiver, and then she smiles broadly. Is Radhika dreaming? Nandita puts a hand on her mother's forehead and feels the wan warmth of old age on a foggy winter night.

'Pagli,' Radhika says without opening her eyes, a faint attempt at a laugh warming her voice. 'Is life a plaything?' She slides back into sleep.

Nandita returns to her room, switches on the room heater and reclines in an easy chair. She does not feel like sleeping again.

She lights a cigarette and picks up a book from the bedside table. One of the new novels a friend has sent from Paris – Clémence Boulouque's *Nuit Ouverte.* She finds the journey of Regina Jones captivating, starting from Berlin in 1935 and ending with the female rabbi's arrival at Auschwitz in 1944. A tale of courage and loneliness. She knew the writer. Like her, Clemence, too, worked as a journalist after earning a university degree.

The smell of the book's newness, the feel of its cover, the pull of Regina Jones – it all takes her back to those Paris days. When she was young. When she ruled the world around her. The broad-shouldered girl with light-brown hair had the will to win and did not have any back pain.

And Arijit was by her side.

'Do you remember the day we flew to Havana?' Nandita asked. Across the dining table in his apartment that Sunday afternoon, she had put him in the frame, wanting to probe, paring away the dust and cobwebs of the intervening years.

'The flash strike at the airport… our flight got delayed,' he recalled.

With Regina Jones's story on her chest, the 555 stubbed out in a terracotta ashtray and the marauding fog howling to break in past midnight, she thinks of Arijit as he recalled that flight, happy she was back in his life. An old, withering woman, huh! *Did he sigh, recollecting my vivacity back in the day, my Paris persona?*

Was Arijit really disappointed to discover her after so many years? But then… Arijit looked at her again.

'Time is a trickster, isn't it, Arijit?' Nandita said, guessing his thoughts. 'I cannot go back to my days in Paris.'

'That's right, Nan. Those days in Paris were the best time of my life, especially after what I had gone through. But we went in different directions. You started the publishing business, and I had to come back to Delhi. Oh, what a mistake!' He leaned back, closing his eyes.

'You know, Arijit, you always carry two things with ease: elegance and dignity.'

He put his hand on hers and squeezed it. 'I don't know. Everything I have planned in my life has gone horribly horribly wrong.'

'That's what life is all about. Arijit, in a sense, we are all puppets on a string; no, actually, we are victims of our circumstances.'

Arijit looked at her again. Like he had looked at the sensitive, intelligent woman talking animatedly about new French writing and the films of Ritwik Ghatak years ago. Was he recovering the lively young woman of Saint Germain's literary cafés?

She shook her head... Nah, no way of knowing.

15
Bridegroom

Nandita goes through her old telephone book, looking for a number. She last called Piu about a year ago. The energy agreement was in the air. Arijit was in the thick of it. They have not talked since. She turns the pages. In the age of digital diaries and smartphones, she still turns to the black calfskin diary, her name embossed on the cover, to contact an old friend.

There was a time when she was both a mother and an elder sister to Piu. Alone in her room in Beach Hanger House of Caterham School, the poor girl would be upset if Nandita did not call for a while. She always talked to Nandita first about her doubts and fears.

From Paris, she took the train to London to spend the weekend with Piu. They went to Chelsea, shopping around King's Road the whole evening. Then dinner at Chutney Mary. Piu relished the chaat and found the lobsters funny.

And now, Nandita is searching for her number.

She feels a deep attachment to the young university teacher who, until the other day, was her ward. It is urgent to reconnect with Piu, to talk to her and to know about her life. Nandita turns another yellowed page.

She looks out the window. The trees around the lawns look bare after shedding their leaves in winter. But the flower beds are in full blossom. The roses, dahlias, carnations are many shades of red. In the mellow sun, the flowers look a distant blaze. She wants to soak in a bit of the fire – its warmth, unruliness, its love for life. After a very long time, that fire to have her way is coming back. The recklessness of her youth.

Just when she had begun to give up, tell herself it's all over, a gust of wind has blown in, feeding the flickers. Or is it a soft, moist hue of new possibilities? Between this house and that apartment in Noahda, they could divide their time – city and suburb. The two of them together, for whatever of their lives is left. They will spend their time in each other's company, having intelligent conversations and admiring books, music and art. They will not socialize much; they will mostly keep to themselves and stay close, knowing and listening to one another.

Since she came back from Noahda, Nandita has been putting together little blocks in an attempt to make a whole, a picture that has long eluded her. A dream she pushed away years ago begins pressing against the windowpanes. Like the warm wind announcing the end of winter. The old days are coming back, displacing the dust and cobwebs of fugue. A feeling of wellness and fulfilment caresses her.

That Sunday was an accident. It happened without intimation, without her knowing about it.

'Our second-floor tenant has given notice,' Radhika says over morning tea on the terrace. 'The gentleman is leaving the country. Why don't you talk to Gupta-ji? We got this good family through him only.'

Her mother, Nandita knows, is recalling Neeraj Gupta's help in settling matters beyond her. The lowly officer in the Paris embassy years ago is the kind of man who has an answer to the most annoying problems. After retirement, Neeraj Gupta is now a director of a construction company.

She looks for Neeraj Gupta's number in her telephone book. Sometimes, she goes through it simply to see how her handwriting has changed over the years.

Nandita calls his mobile number.

'Gupta-ji, how are you?'

'Nandita? What a surprise!' The practical man, always ready to help, sounds cheerful.

She tells him about the need for a good tenant.

'You don't worry. You will get a good tenant, better than the last one. A senior Toyota executive is looking for an apartment to rent in Hauz Khas.'

That matter settled, they go back to the days in Paris, compare notes on the people they knew.

'You must have heard about Basu Sahib?' says Neeraj.

'No. What about him? Still in Washington?'

'Aarrey, nah, nah – he is back; he lives here now.'

'Really? Strange! I didn't know.'

'Call him. He will be happy—' Neeraj Gupta stops, careful not to go any further.

Nandita at last finds Piu's number. Her first instinct is to call her at once, but she resists the impulse. It must be night over there. She will talk to Piu when she is home on a Sunday morning, playing with her child or listening to old Bollywood songs.

But it's the maid – scared, emaciated, the deep, dark waves of a river in her large eyes – who has burrowed into the uncharted reserves of empathy somewhere in his heart. Her vulnerability and exposure to the extremities of urban life have tapped the well of humanity inside the Cambridge man. For him, she is a challenge, a test of his ideals and values. In the apartment for a few hours, she could make that out. He wants to help her and give her protection. But does not know how.

And the girl – she calls herself Rita – is not just a poor, pathetic thing. There are layers and layers, and there are knots in her life. First, she is not Rita; Nandita knows for sure. Nor is she from Ranchi. From her accent and gawky ways, she knows it's probably another Bangladeshi working under an assumed name.

Still, she is more than an illegal immigrant working hard for a living. Her knowledge of Western cuisine points to another side of her. The spring rolls, soup, pudding – she could easily put a trained chef out of business. Her familiarity with dining etiquette… she has a connection, link to the world, has seen better days. The odd stray English words, phrases she unknowingly uses, are perfectly pronounced with a faint American accent. And the award-winning filmmaker.

When it comes to cooking, she assumes a different persona, a new authority that goes beyond her situation. With the pots and pans, spices, roots, leaves and stems in the kitchen, she is someone else. The one in command.

Whoever Rita is, she will continue to live with us, looking after us in our old age. My ward is my responsibility; her past will remain buried across some border. Left behind the barbed wires. Nandita laughs. Is she thinking, planning a little too fast, too far?

The garage's roller shutter opens noisily. From her corner in the first-floor living room, she knows Bharat is here – at ten on the dot.

Bharat Singh Bisht, a young man from the Kumaon Hills, came to work for the family as a boy. In her father's engineering firm, he ran errands, going to the bank to deposit money and checks, to the post office to send mail and to the government offices carrying files. When the firm changed hands after her father's death, Bharat had nowhere to go. He clung on to the family.

Her mother needed an attendant – someone who could take her to the doctor, to the neighbourhood temple, to the accountant's office. Bharat started driving her to all such places. He was many things rolled into one: driver, attendant, clerk and security guard.

Nandita hears steps up the stairs, feet shuffling outside the door.

'Come in, Bharat.'

'Namaste, madam.' He folds his hands and bows.

'I will go to the French Cultural Centre in the afternoon. In the evening, you take Mum to the Sai temple.'

'Yes, madam.' He stands in the doorway, his hands clasped, in awe of his late boss's daughter. The whimsical woman he does not fully understand. He smiles nervously – a sign of his humility, total obedience. After years of working for the family, he still hesitates to walk into the living room unless asked to. His life is guided by his fierce loyalty to this house.

'Bharat, come inside, sit here.' Nandita points to the ottoman.

Scandalized, he protests. Still scared and uncomfortable in the presence of the eccentric woman with unusual ways. An Indian and still not. The woman who drinks, smokes and wears shorts, easily hugs a man, holds him by his arm. She makes Bharat uneasy.

'Tell me one thing, Bharat.' Nandita tries to warm up to the young man whose presence she has rarely acknowledged before. 'Do you have parents back home? Brothers, sisters?'

16
Other Side of the Bay

In the morning, she looks worried, as if something has gone terribly, terribly wrong. She fears the past might be tumbling out of the closet. Like the walking dead in the fables, her secrets can come back to life, upsetting the careful arrangement.

Normally, she would hum some song. Chopping vegetables, making coffee, she croons absently. Her songs are mostly about the river life – ghats, boats, the first hint of sea.

No one has seen the other side of the bay
Be careful, oh my man, with your oar,
Row my little battered boat with care –
I say…

Arijit hears her singing, lost in a world of her own. Alone in the kitchen, she goes back to another place through the songs. That place, her past, keeps coming back in her lonely moments. Or is this her way of saying she is happy? Then the mood swings. She talks on the phone, laughing, shouting and picking up a fight. Today, she is quiet. In the middle of her work, she has actually made a quiet search of the kitchen – the cabinets, shelves, racks, behind the microwave, under the fridge. Nah, no trace of the envelope. Nowhere does she find the stars- and stripes-stamped piece of stationery. Has she lost it somewhere else? At the Blue Lotus Grove gate where the security men make an entry every time a housemaid comes in? No, she clearly remembers she brought the envelope here and kept it on the kitchen trolley. After work, she wanted to take it to Ameena. Her cousin can read English a little.

She makes a cup of black coffee for Arijit and thoughtfully walks across the living room into the study. He raises his head from the computer and looks quizzically at her. She feels uneasy, looks away, unable to take the glare. 'Let me get you the medicine; I forgot.'

She hurries out of the room. Caught in the frame of his gaze, she felt exposed, pinned down. Breathes deeply before going back into the study with the little medicine box and a glass of water. 'Your BP pills.'

Arijit quietly swallows a tablet with a gulp of water.

He hesitates, then reluctantly pulls the envelope out of a drawer. 'Are you looking for this? I found it lying outside the front door.'

In a busy hand, someone had written the address with a thick sketch pen:

Ms Rabeya Sheikh
Paankhali Village, Sherpur Police Station
Khulna District, Bangladesh

On the bottom left corner is the sender's name:

Radolf McGirk
New York
United States

Holding the envelope, she stands facing him – can neither speak nor go away. This man, who has begun taking her into his care, now knows about the charade of Rita Das from Ranchi. He has seen through the carefully arranged falsehood.

'What happened? Are you upset about something?' Arijit sits back. 'You fear there could be some bad news in this letter?'

'Kaku, I lied to you, I lied about everything – my name, the place I come from… you can ask me to go, sack me.' Though she never had proper schooling, Rita can read her name on the envelope, the address. She is distressed, her eyes tearing up. 'No one wants to hire a Muslim maid; they say Bangladeshis are criminals, thieves. So we take new names, try to pick up Hindi as quickly as possible.'

Arijit looks at the girl wiping her tear-stained face with the back of her hand. A little comfort, a new sense of security has given her a touch of health. But the irregular lines of tears are paring away that feeling of assurance, of well-being. She is back on the other side of the barbed wire, exposed to the elements again.

'You live all alone here or is there someone else?'

'My cousin works in a beauty parlour. Rekha is a clever girl. She has learnt fast and is in demand. In her off-hours, she goes on house calls to the rich ladies who pay more. She no longer lives in the slum. She has rented a one-room flat in a nice neighbourhood.'

'Why can't you move into a flat like that?'

Arijit regrets his words; he knows she cannot afford the rent.

'Can you read this letter?' He changes the topic.

'I picked up a few English words from Radolf Sahib when my father worked for him. He would often say, "Oh, gosh," and grimace.' Rita smiles, even though her fear has not entirely receded. 'When angry, he would shout, "Damn it, goddamn it!

What's wrong with the generator?" I learnt to say "thank you, okay, how are you doing this morning, great!" And he told me not to call him *sahib*. "Call me Radolf, okay?" He would stress the point. But no, I can't read anything except my name.' She is already feeling better. Those happy days coming back to comfort her.

'You want me to read the letter for you?'

There is nothing much to read. Two photographs. In one, Rabeya and her brother are in a little country boat, looking at the spreading water, hints of a forest on the far side of the river; in the other, little Rabeya is catching fish with a hefty, bespectacled American in the shallows. Plodding in the roiled water, they hold two ends of a fishnet.

The film I made in Bangladesh won an award. Is Rabe in India now?
Love,
Radolf

'Was he like the usual filmmakers?' Arijit asks. 'Were there lots of people with him – cameramen, actors, technicians?'

'Oh, no, nothing like that. He had a couple of video cameras and a few other things. He had brought someone from Dhaka, and the rest he did all by himself. My father learnt a few things and became his assistant.'

'Where's your father now?'

Rita keeps mum, looking away.

Is the man dead? Arijit wonders if he has unknowingly hurt her.

She finally breaks her silence.

'He gave my mother talaq and married again. He lives

separately with his new bride. With the money from Sahib, he built a new house in Khulna town.'

The picture is getting clearer – why the girl risked crossing the border without papers. The happy moments of the days with the filmmaker have given way to worries about losing her job.

Arijit walks to his favourite spot on the balcony. Looking at the large spread of farmland, he thinks of the girl – her life, her rivers, her songs, her curiosity about the other side of the bay.

Is he getting enmeshed in the web of another story? He came home to renew his links to a life left behind long before, but now, in this boomtown, he is discovering another land without actually getting there.

17
River Life

When Arijit clicks open the inbox, he is, as usual, irritated by a large volume of mail from the Hindu supremacist outfits. Myopic, ill-informed, they inveigh against everyone: the government, judiciary, media, intelligentsia, civil society… in fact, modernity itself. Without any clarity about what they want, the revivalist groups see Muslim *appeasement* in everything.

Clearly, a network is active; some of the born-again Hindus have taken on fake personae by adopting high-flowing Sanskritized names – *Acharya Dharmendra Maharaj, Swami Maha Pragyan, Sadhvi Veda Mahima Mayee*. Some of the emails have come from North America. The expat's saffron dreams are even wilder, his sense of persecution more gnawing.

It takes Arijit a while to clean up the inbox.

In the crowd of junk mail, he spots an interesting name: Radolf McGirk.

Arijit is surprised. He did not expect a response within a day. He googled McGirk, and without much trouble, traced his website, email, phone numbers, office address – everything. A well-known documentary filmmaker, he has captured life in strange locales – Alaska, Siberia, Jaffna Peninsula, Bangladesh, Afghanistan.

In Bangladesh, he documented the river life: a wedding party and a man mauled by a tiger travelling on the same boat to town. Someone's celebrations mix up with another's battle for life. Folk singers and magicians board at one ghat to perform on the deck, only to get down at the next. His camera has unerringly captured the culture in all its nuances and the rivers in their lavish extravagance. The sensation at the jetty at the toot of a launch horn, the tea boy joking with passengers, closed paper mills on the banks seen from the deck, the cheerful bustle of factory workers from the big cities going home for Eid – everything sensitively documented by McGirk.

The filmmaker lived in the delta for a year. He met Munir Sheikh in Dhaka, where he cooked for an American diplomat. When he was transferred out of the country, the envoy passed the cook on to McGirk. Munir followed the filmmaker everywhere – on land and on the river. McGirk loved food and had a curious mind. The two men sat in the evening talking about the art of making smoked hilsa, grilling prawns stuffed inside bamboo. Munir also told the director about the strange, eccentric ways of the rivers, how they criss-cross each other on their way to the bay.

Over such sessions, McGirk entered the world of Bengali cuisine, and Munir learnt about film-making. They became a team – Sahib, the technician from Dhaka, Munir, and his two children. The chef doubled as an assistant. The cameras zoomed in on life on the water. Loaded trucks, passenger-packed buses, cattle herds, cycle vans – together they rode the ferry from one bank of the Padma to another.

The motley crew did the Khulna–Barisal–Dhaka route of the fabled steamer service. From the river into the sea, then another river… McGirk found the trajectory interesting. On another trip, they captured life in a fishing village on a river island. Far away from home, McGirk now had a new family – Munir and his two children. The little girl with large, dark eyes and a disarming smile was his favourite. They went on talking, telling each other stories. No one knew which language they spoke – the American's broken Bengali or Rabeya's handful of English words.

'The river is our language,' McGirk used to say.

Rabeya walked into the kitchen to help her father with preparations for a sumptuous dinner. Munir handed her a plate of fish fries. 'Take it to Sahib; it's time for his…' He made a drinking gesture. McGirk saw the girl tiptoe into his room, holding the plate carefully. She stood there, looking bemusedly at his Bourbon whisky bottle. Their eyes met. Hers sparkled in a smile. The next moment, she was sitting beside him, talking and laughing.

There were days when they did not go shooting. McGirk was busy editing and reviewing the work done so far. Then he would walk into the kitchen. The tall man in his T-shirt and knickers wanted to know how to make steamed hilsa, smeared with mustard paste, chopped green chilli and a dash of mustard oil, wrapped in a fresh banana leaf. 'Dig the wrap into the rice bowl. The rice is still steaming but no longer on fire,' Munir explained. 'Hilsa is a delicate fish; that much heat is enough.'

In turn, McGirk told them how to use olive oil or wine in preparing special dishes. Wide-eyed, Rabeya saw how Radolf seasoned fish with orange juice and butter. 'You can have fish without frying it,' he laughed. Rabeya learnt quite a few things from him.

'Munir made authentic Western dishes; I could see no difference,' McGirk recalls in his letter. Long after his return to America, the director is still in touch with his old chef and his children, sending them picture postcards and little gifts. He sent Munir a little money a couple of times. Then learnt about the man chucking his wife and children out for a younger woman. He is willing to help Rabeya.

McGirk has sent as attachments pictures of his life in Bangladesh – Rabeya holding Bablu's hand, the two children playing on the riverfront, a tiger traipsing deeper into the jungle, Munir catching fish with a net. Arijit peers over one picture in particular – Rabeya playfully dancing through the paddy, absorbed in her own happiness, her coarse cotton sari flying in the air.

How old is she? Arijit works out. *Perhaps twenty-three?* Much younger than Piu. He sends McGirk a reply, thanking him for the pictures.

'Rabe works for me; she seems to be enjoying the job,' Arijit writes.

After sending the mail, it strikes him he has admitted at least to one person that he has hired an undocumented immigrant to work in his kitchen. It's on record now.

He thinks of the man who, at the height of success, left his wife to take a new bride. For Munir Sheikh, working for the American meant both money and prestige. In the picture, he seems an affectionate, caring father. In that distressed land, the money the filmmaker gave him was more than what he would earn in a lifetime. Why did he divorce his wife? Was it the man's way of savouring his success?

Arijit is tempted to trace Munir Sheikh for answers to all these questions. But the chef is not McGirk, nor is his deltaic land America. Sitting in his study with the computer, it is not possible to dig out a man who has no digital footprints.

The doorbell rings. A salesman perhaps? The boy who irons clothes in the basement? Arijit walks to the front door, irked by the intrusion.

A tall, wiry man, a shock of untrimmed hair falling in his face, in frayed pants and a dirty shirt. He stands at a distance, as if after pressing the bell, he has backed away, unsure whether he should wait or go back.

'Yes?' Arijit cannot hide his irritation.

'Saab-ji… Rabeya works here?'

'What? What business do you have to come here and knock?'

'Sorry if I have disturbed you, sir. We are from the same place – Rabeya and I. I need to talk to her – it's urgent.'

'What's your name?'

'Saab-ji, Jamal. I work in a grille factory. I have been looking for her.' He looks distressed, not someone with murder on his mind, not a bad character, stalker or thug. He is speaking Hindi with a thick Bengali accent. 'Sorry, sir, a poor man in rags. I should not have knocked on your door. Please tell her, if she comes here, that Jamal is looking for her.' He shakes his head, pushing back the wave of dark, dusty hair, and goes away.

Arijit keeps looking at the way the man has retreated – in a hurry to leave but unsure. He glances at the lift, then hurries down the stairs.

Arijit returns inside and calls the guardroom at the gate. He is angry, upset. That lumpen at the door – an infringement. An interruption to his privacy.

'Yes, sir. Any problem?' Ram Bahadur Chhetri sounds worried.

'Just now a fellow came here. Seems to be loafing around without any work. Such tramps should not be allowed inside the complex.'

'Sir, he came with window grilles; a flat is being readied. He had no business to be at your door. From now on, I will send somebody to see that such workers do not loiter around. Sorry, sir. I'll not let him in again.'

'No, no. If he comes for work, that's all right. But such people should not move all around the complex.'

'Sahib, I can tell you something.'

'What?'

'This loafer *sees* the girl who works in your apartment. He often comes, waits outside the gate for her. I often see them walking down the street. Together – talking and laughing.'

'Oh.'

Arijit sits on a sofa. He flips through an old issue of *Foreign Affairs* and puts it down, unable to concentrate.

The picture on the computer screen comes back – the little girl dancing her way through a deep-green rice paddy. Then the lout from the grille factory. Chhetri's emphasis on 'sees' – a key word.

She needs to be saved. A young woman, with considerable talent, is floating around in the grime of a harsh life, exposed to the dangers of the city's dark crevices. Anything can happen to her. An easy, soft target.

The doorbell rings rapidly, once, twice, thrice. Her way. He hurries to the door. Rita stands there, shamefaced. She knows everything.

Arijit feels like shouting at her. That despicable man, Jamal or whatever, is a betrayal of everything he has planned, an invasion of the world he wants to build. He restrains himself, slowly goes back to the study. She tiptoes into the kitchen.

She comes with a cup of black coffee on a tray, a little shaky, her usual self-assurance missing. Normally, she walks in, puts one book over another to create space for the tray on the busy desk, asks what he would have for breakfast, lunch… suggests a dish when he's unable to think of anything. Now, she stands there in the doorway, unsure if she should come in.

Arijit takes the cup from her, waits for the fit of anger to pass. 'Who's that fellow?' he almost shouts.

'We are from the same place. He works in a factory.' She seems to have got back her voice. As if she could see the storm coming.

He looks at the girl, sees the tension gripping her. He hesitates but decides to talk. 'Tell me one thing – is there anything going on between the two of you, is something…'

Rita flicks a nervous smile. 'Kaku, he's an eccentric fellow. No woman can marry a madcap like him. Tomorrow is Eid, our festival. He is hosting a lunch. Came to invite me.'

18
Long-tressed Khairun

Rabeya gets up early – earlier than usual. The shantytown is yet to wake up to the familiar noises of a new day. It is still dark. She spots the wet, waning moon in a corner of the grey sky above the canal. One star still gleams, defying the hint of day. Is the same star looking down over their Paankhali village? On the way to the river ghat, is her mother also looking at the star still glimmering up above? She hurries to the common bathing area behind a cluster of shacks.

Untreated water gushes out of a tap. On a brick platform, men and women take their turns bathing. A rule has evolved: women bathe in the early hours of the morning. Men later. Women always come in groups – four or five of them together – to build a wall against peering men.

Today is Eid. Rabeya reaches the tap much before the first men have stirred out of their ratholes. Sitting under the tap, she bathes, letting the water cleanse her body inside the clothes. She lifts her wet clothes here and there for the water to touch, feel her skin, take away all the grime and soot of a migrant's life. She tears open the Sunsilk shampoo sachet and empties it on the crown of her head. She rolls up the thick, long hair and works the cascade of lavish foam into the unruly mop. The white extravagance of bubbles with an alluring fragrance turns her head into a surfy column. For the moment, she forgets the slum – its daily rot and fug, brutal air and a manic lurch to beastliness – and thinks of a quiet place where someone will take care of the young woman blossoming inside her. She picks up the slice of Lux from a plastic case and rubs it over her arms, lifts the maxi a little and lathers her legs. Then, looking furtively around, she pushes her hand further to soap her thighs and groin. She moves the soap bar around her neck, feels the foam in her underarms and lets the lather caress her bosom, thinking of the Lux beauties on television. She smiles. Her breasts are gaining mass once again. Like succulent mangoes in June. The past few months of stability, a touch of comfort, the old man's care – all that has stroked her to bloom, to become a woman again.

Water dripping from her hair, soothing floral smells of soap and shampoo protecting her against the putrid smell all around, she walks back to her box of a room. But at the moment, it's not suffocating. That fear of being choked under patches of plastic sheets does not bother her any more. Nor does the thought of the wobbly shanties coming down one night to bury her. It's cool, quiet now – the world at peace with itself. A soothing breeze from the canal slips in through unseen gaps in the shack's corrugated tin walls.

Rabeya opens her small, rusty trunk and takes out a handloom sari. Against the bright yellow background, the red flower motif shimmers. A man comes every other month selling things from Bangladesh – saris, DVDs of Dhaka movies, music tapes. She bought this Tangail sari from him.

Holding the sari under the light bulb, she pores over the design. The intricate needlework with golden zari lends weight, richness to the sari's borders. When she unfolds seven yards of fine fabric, an old, comforting smell fills the little room. It brings back life in Khulna: busy sari shops in Daulatpur Bazaar, mounds of vermicelli under the awnings, men returning home from the big cities of Dhaka, Khulna and Chittagong, crowded launches whistling to drop anchor. The warm aromas of rich food – biryani, zarda, semai, payesh – waft out of every kitchen in the village.

That's Eid.

Then, things were different. Abba was still her abba and hadn't taken a new bride. Her mother would get up early to cook fish, meat and sweet dishes. Happy but exhausted after so much cooking. After the men came back from the Eid congregation in the village square, the house would overflow with people.

Rabeya sprays talcum powder on her body before hooking the blouse and drawing a dot in the middle of her forehead. Nandita bought her a perfume. More than the fragrance, she loves the gold-and-glass container. Not real gold but golden. The feel of gold. She thinks of spraying on a little perfume, then changes her mind. *Nah. I will give it to Ameena; the beauty-parlour girl will love it.* She puts it in her purse.

Locking the door, she starts towards the main road. Her open hair, past her waist, occasionally flutters in the morning breeze. At Mausi's shop, she waits for a moment. Is she looking for him, half hoping to run into the loony somewhere, say Eid Mubarak? She did not take his call the other day. He looked for her everywhere and had to face Kaku's ire. She feels bad now. Thinking of the crazy man, his clumsy ways, her own dilemma – she gets confused.

Something has happened to him. A completely changed man, he talks of going away, not coming back from that *beautiful place*. Seems to have got money. A lot of it. Rabeya flags down a cycle rickshaw.

'Sector 8, Janata Flats,' she says importantly, climbing onto the back seat. The rickshaw-wallah stares at her confusedly but pedals on. A rickshaw ride had always been a luxury for her until she sat inside Didi's big car. You drown in the softness and cool hush of the car's back seat, in the filtered darkness and depth of comfort, inhaling a mild, musky fragrance. Nandita – that's her name. 'Call me Didi,' she said. Rabeya felt an inexplicable assurance in her presence. She called the other day. 'My car will pick you up; we are going to shop again.'

The rickshaw enters an enclave of low-cost, four-storey flats. Built by the government for the socially marginalized, plaster has peeled off their walls, exposing the bare brick in places. Seepage has softened the buildings here and there, leaving a trace of salt on some walls. Still, Sector 8 is a long way from the steamy shantytown. The blocks, built in regular order on either side of a road, have taken on a pattern. There are open spaces and green patches all around the colony. The rickshaw-wallah stares at her again. As if he is not sure where she belongs – to the slum or Sector 8.

After climbing three floors, Rabeya gasps before knocking on the door. Someone inside is humming:

Oh, see, here's our beautiful Khairun,
Waves of her long raven hair –
Through her smile does she croon?
Ah, the crazy land says, 'Dear…'

Rabeya laughs. Her cousin – mad about Kishore Kumar's hit

Hindi numbers – is singing Mumtaz's old Bengali song with a lot of emotion.

...waves of her long raven hair...

My sister has gone bonkers. Rabeya laughs, waiting. The door opens – it's another girl, not dear old Ameene from the cyclone-swept banks of the Rupsa.

She gawps at the fashionable young woman beaming at her. Is she the same cousin who, like her, worked at the prawn factory and crossed into India, bribing the border police at the Benapole checkpoint through the agent? Rabeya's eyes widen. She takes in faded jeans, a sleeveless yellow T-shirt and russet-coloured hair, mushroom-cut with side-swept bangs. Ameena laughs, noticing her bewilderment.

'Ameene, whatever has happened to you...'

'Shush! My name is Rekha. Haven't you seen her in movies? Siren Rekha dancing in the rain in a see-through white sari around the trees?' She hugs Rabeya, taking her inside.

Rabeya looks around the room – two armchairs on either side of a low glass-topped table, a sofa lining the wall. Superstar Amitabh Bachchan dominates the room from a wall.

'You are an entirely different girl, Ameene. Honestly, I could not recognize you at first. You look like those women in the apartments, those who speak English, walk dogs, drive big cars – not the Ameene from Paankhali.'

'If you try, you can do a lot, sister.' Ameena looks thoughtful. Her new look is a professional matter. 'I have so much demand from those fat women to massage their backs, remove their body hair and rid them of wrinkles that I do not work in the beauty parlour any more.' She is excited about the new possibilities and confident that she can do it. 'I am doing a course in beauty therapy. For that, I go to GK I every evening. When I am done, I will start my own parlour.'

Rabeya looks at her cousin incredulously. 'Really, Ameene, you will run the place? The boss lady, bah!'

'Oh! No Ameena, forget her. I'm Rekha. Rekha from Calcutta.'

'Rekha… Rekha from Calcutta,' Rabeya mimics her.

'Getting a shop is not easy. You need lots and lots of money. But Jimmy is helping me. The whole thing is his idea.'

'Jimmy? Who's Jimmy? What's Jimmy? Haven't heard about that.'

'You'll be hearing that name very often from now on, Bubu. He is my boyfriend; he loves me.'

Rabeya is both stunned and amused by her cousin's words. She holds her tight. How easily she could say *boyfriend!* Without batting an eyelid, without blushing a bit.

'That means you two…'

'Of course we'll marry soon.'

'Is he a nice man? Does he have a job? Where's he from?'

'Go slow, Bubu, I'm not running away.' Ameena laughs. 'He is a decent man from Kerala. I don't know where that place is. He says it's the most beautiful place on Earth – the sea, sand and coconut groves. Wherever, whatever – I don't care. Jimmy is an educated man, has a university degree. He came here for a job, then left it and opened a coaching centre. Coaching centre, you know? School children come in batches; one batch goes, and another comes in – boys and girls. He earns a lot—'

'So, he is like a schoolmaster?'

Interrupted, Ameena frowns. She is irritated.

'Not like Kalim Master of our village school. Listen first…'

'Sorry, don't be angry with me, Ameene… oh, sorry, Rekha.'

'That's better.' Ameena giggles.

'Last year, a rich man came with his son and told Jimmy, "Sir, my son is neither intelligent nor does he study. If you help him pass the Board exam, I will be grateful to you. I am a builder, and in Noahda, my business is growing. I need him to help me. But he must at least graduate school."'

Ameena goes inside and comes back with potato chips in a porcelain bowl. She puts it on the table and sits on the sofa, an arm around her cousin. Keen to tell her story.

'Jimmy is a smart man. He knows how to make a boy pass his exam. He gave that fat duffer both questions and answers and told him to mug them up. The boy not only passed, he actually scored over 60 per cent – that's first division! Happy, the builder is giving Jimmy at cost a ground-floor flat on the main street – in the front will be the coaching centre, and inside, my beauty business. And late in the evening, when there are no clients or students, we will sit before the television and talk.'

Rabeya is happy for her cousin but a little apprehensive, too. It's too good a story. She tries to doubt, sees flaws, frowns, then lowers her voice. 'What's a Jimmy? Is he Muslim, Christian or Hindu?'

'My foot!' Rekha sounds annoyed. 'Bangladeshi girls are going to America to marry white sahibs. If I could speak English well, I, too, would have left for America by now. What do you do? Sit on that weirdo's lap and rot in the slum? Is that life? Bubu, you should have written to that American to take you to his country. I'm sure he would be very happy to do that. Maybe it's not too late now.'

'Then why were you singing the Khairun song?' Rabeya says hesitantly.

Rekha thinks for a while, as if she, too, wants to know why the song keeps coming back. She clicks her fingers, taps her foot… more rapidly… one two three…

Oh, see, here's our beautiful Khairun,
Waves of her long raven hair –

She breaks into a laugh. 'Can you forget growing up in Paankhali? The beauty of the Rupsa?' She peers at her cousin for a while before looking away.

Rabeya notices the television in another corner of the room. Rekha walks into the kitchen and opens the fridge. She takes out a Coke and the ice bowl, puts two glasses on a tray and comes back with the measured elegance of a young, accomplished woman. Sitting in an armchair, she faces Rabeya and opens the bottle, pours the drink into the glasses, tipping ice cubes with finesse. Gives Rabeya a paper napkin to hold the glass.

'You've become a pukka memsahib.'

'I learnt a little bit about the sahibs' ways from you only.' Rekha picks up an old English film magazine from the table, flips through it and looks at her cousin. 'Bubu, never talk about what I have told you to any of the Bangladeshis here. Don't talk about me when you call home. We are our worst enemies. This is my last Eid with you all. But wherever I am, I will offer my prayer and make a special dish this day every year.'

She listens carefully as Rabeya tells her about the old man's kindness, Nandita's support, their trip to the mall and the phone.

'Didi wants to say something but is waiting; perhaps it's not yet time. She called the other day asking me to go to her place. "My driver will bring and drop you back," she said.'

'Stick with them, Rabee. It seems the old man and his

girlfriend, your Didi, are planning to get married, and you will be like their child since they cannot make babies so late, eh!' Rekha laughs naughtily. Then she turns serious. 'Leave that slum as soon as you can. That's hell.'

'Where did you get all this?' Rabeya points to the television, fridge, furniture.

'Oh, that's nothing. There's a fat woman who wants to be fashionable, look younger and get into jeans and tees again. So, I pump her bum almost every day and remove disgusting hair from all over her body. She gave me the old things when she bought trendy new stuff. The gross female will give me whatever I ask for. Without me, she has no hope.' Rekha laughs. 'The other day, she asked me to clean her up down there. "My husband is coming back from a long business trip. I want to give him a surprise." She smiled coquettishly. Bechara. I doubt that businessman will ever waste his precious drops on that fat pumpkin.' Rekha bursts out laughing. Wiping a tear from her face, the relentless girl struggles to rein in her freewheeling tongue. Her eyes widen, blood rushing to her face, and Rabeya wonders how easily this cousin of hers can say all that. 'Listen.' Rekha nudges her, as if she has just remembered something. 'Jimmy is telling me to move in with him.'

Rabeya is scandalized. 'Even before marriage?'

'So what? I go there often, and we are in bed together.' Rekha laughs. 'He teaches me a little bit of English. If we begin to live together, you can move in here. I'll talk to my landlord. Stick to Rita. Don't let anybody know that you're actually Rabeya. People here hate our kind of names, don't want Muslim tenants. They are good people otherwise.'

'But Kaku already knows my story.'

'How?'

'He went to Kaku's house looking for me.'

Rekha frowns, her nostrils flare. 'If you want to survive in this country, dump that joker; he's a good-for-nothing. Chuck him out of your life.'

'I try, but he keeps crawling back.'

'I'll tell him one of these days to forget about you.'

'You need not. It seems he's going away.'

'Where?'

'I don't know. He told me the other day that this is our last Eid together.'

'Perhaps he has got a job somewhere.'

Footsteps come up the stairs – rapid, heavy. Someone is humming an old tune:

O Lolita, tell him to go away –
I'm not coming to the ghat to fill my pitcher.
O Lolita...

Jamal. Both of them laugh.

Rekha opens the door. 'Eid Mubarak!' they greet each other.

'I could not recognize you – really. You look like those girls on television.'

'Dada, Bangladeshis need not always be in tatters; they don't have to look like scarecrows.'

He scowls.

Rekha knows she has been harsh and regrets her words. Should have been nice to him today. She moves a step forward, manages a smile. 'Unless I look a little trim and tidy, Dada, no beauty parlour will hire me.' She holds his hand.

'True, very true.' Jamal laughs, instantly forgiving. He hands two big shopping bags to Rabeya.

She looks into the bags. 'You have bought a lot of things.'

'Mutton and hilsa.' He grins like he has come home after winning a big match. 'One whole hind leg. I know the butcher; he kept it for me. And I got a two-kilo hilsa; it's from Diamond Harbour, good – of course good – but no match for the silvery fish from the Padma.' He flumps down in an armchair. Takes a swig of Coke from the bottle. The dainty glass, ice bowl and napkins – not for him, huh? 'The Padma hilsa is a class apart… out of the world. What taste, ah!' He makes a guttural sound of pleasure.

'Bloody rich Indians buy the best hilsa from Bangladesh. They pay any price – five hundred rupees, one thousand rupees a kilo; it goes to their kitchens, their restaurants.' His voice is rising.

'Cool down, Dada.' Rekha offers him a plate of colourful candies. He looks at her, then picks one up. 'Why did you take so much trouble? You have spent a lot. Whatever is available in our market should have been enough.'

'It's Eid! Has to be special.' He looks for something in his sling bag. Fishes out two nicely wrapped packets. 'Here are your gifts, ladies.' He looks at the packets and hands Rekha hers. 'Tell me if you like it or not.' Then he gives Rabeya the other one.

Rekha curiously unwraps her gift. 'Wow, it's a Ray-Ban, a genuine one! What have you done, Dada? It must have cost you at least three thousand rupees.'

'Let me see how a Bangladeshi girl looks when she has got the right stuff.' Obliging him, Rekha slips on the sunglasses and fakes a catwalk across the room. 'Thank you.' She beams.

'Our Ameena looks like a movie star! She is like Runa Laila.' Jamal chews a candy. 'Do you remember Runa Laila? The beautiful nightingale went to Bombay, and her songs were an instant hit. Lata and Asha knew they had met more than their match. The nasty sisters saw to it that Runa Laila could not do business in Bombay.'

But the girls are not listening. By now, Rabeya has unpacked her gift – a trendy watch with a golden band. She wears it, moves her wrist playfully and laughs. Ameena picks up her purse from the rack and holds it stylishly, like a model. With her arm locked into her cousin's, they ramp-walk across the room, then pretend to pose for a photo shoot.

'I am Rekha; this is my sister Rita. And Dada, you are Kishore Kumar. Now forget your rants and sing a song.'

Both girls laugh. Jamal grins awkwardly.

'I don't have time for your silly chatter, girls,' he says self-importantly. 'I have to go buy sweets. Rasgulla or rasmalai?'

'Rasmalai!' Rekha shouts. 'And mishti doi.'

He thinks for a while. 'Montu and his wife are on the way. They will do the cooking. You two can relax.'

He takes a few steps to the door, then turns back. Leaning against a wall, he closes his eyes as if he has forgotten something. Before the two cousins can make out anything, he starts crooning:

People say things.
That's what they do.
So why bother
And shed tears?

'Great! That's vintage Kishore Kumar.' Rekha claps. Jamal looks at Rabeya. She smiles in approval but quickly looks away.

When Jamal returns after an hour in the back seat of a rickshaw, his plans for the day begin to unfold. Apart from foodstuffs, he has brought a DVD player, a music system with speakers and tapes and CDs of Bengali film songs.

A boy from the electrician's shop follows him up the stairs. He busily connects the DVD player to the television and shows them how to insert a DVD. The music system sits on a stool, and the sound boxes are at two ends of the room. He bunches the wires together and rolls them into a knot behind the television.

'If there is a power cut, you can still see a movie,' the boy says, pointing to the inverter connected to a battery. 'The switchover is automatic, so you don't have to do anything.' He packs his tools into a little bag.

Jamal gives him a ten-rupee note. Happy, the boy bows a little. 'I'll come tomorrow morning to take the things back.'

Montu's wife, much older than Ameena and Rabeya, has already taken charge of the kitchen. Rich smells fill the flat – of onion, garlic, tomatoes, red chillies and ginger being ground together into a pulp. Rabeya has a strange feeling: a lavish meal is being served without her in the kitchen. For the first time, she is a guest.

'The doorman in the Connaught Place showroom,' Jamal turns to Rekha, 'would not let me in.' He looks at the others before recounting his exploits. 'The scoundrel thought I must be a vagabond. I shouted at him, showing my wallet. The idiot then slightly opened the door, as if still not sure. For a moment, I stood there, taking in the cool, nice inside of the shop.' He laughs. '*I'll come back another day to throw a bomb into this shit shop,* I wanted to tell the moustachioed fool.' Jamal looks grim.

Rabeya darts a puzzled look at her cousin.

By the time the food is ready, it is late afternoon. Jamal and Montu move the furniture to one side and place rugs on the floor around the room. Rekha places a paper plate before everyone. Montu's wife puts a slice of lemon, a teaspoon of salt and a green chilli in a corner of each plate. Her face beaded with sweat, she is still happy to have gotten the charge of the kitchen and the honour of cooking so much good food.

She first serves steamed white rice, dal and fried aubergine slices. 'Don't bother about your figure; eat well even if you put on a little weight,' Montu jokes with Rekha.

'I'll have two pieces of hilsa even if I turn into a pumpkin,' she laughs, rounding her hands into a pepo. Then she sings, swinging her head:

Oh, see, here's our beautiful Khairun,
Waves of her long raven hair

'That's good – our bobbed memsahib is singing about Khairun's long locks,' Jamal roars with a big laugh. The others laugh, too, with food in their mouths.

Rekha's body shakes with laughter. Taking out the thin bones from the piece of fish with her right hand, she pulls her short hair with the other. 'Next time you come, I'll have long tresses like Khairun,' she grins, tears coming to her eyes as she savours the happy moment.

'Now, prim-and-trimmed Khairun, please have one more piece of hilsa,' Montu's wife coaxes, overcoming her diffidence. 'This one is special – from the fish's back.'

The others laugh again. The focus is back on the food. Montu's wife serves fish curry, mutton korma, tomato-and-date chutney, and finally, sweets. From the stereo comes Runa Laila's bawdy folk song:

I have reddened my lips from chewing paan…

Montu is a new immigrant who is still struggling to settle down. He works at a fish stall and dreams of starting his own business one day. He looks happy after eating such a big meal. His wife first hesitates, then gorges on the food she herself has cooked with a generous use of mustard oil.

'Great feast, Jamal Bhai! I haven't eaten so much in a long time.' With his tummy bulging, Montu seems to be enjoying every bit of it.

'Take home some of the excess food, Montu-da,' Jamal says expansively. 'And you don't worry. I will help you set up your fish stall. It's easy – give the beat constable some money. The rat will never bother you. Don't you worry; I'll manage everything. Have fun.' He inserts another CD into the player.

'We are going to see a great film, *Manpura*. No song-and-dance scenes, no dhishum-dhishum filmy fights, and still, it's a huge hit, a record for Dhaka films. The simple, sad story of Sonai and Pori will touch everybody's heart. In Bombay, they can't make a film like this for they don't have a river island like Manpura.'

By now, the others are used to Jamal's tirades and ignore his railing against Bollywood.

The movie begins. The quiet tone, soft, slow cadence, misty smell of a life left behind across the border fill the room. Scattered all over the floor, they struggle to fight back tears, their eyes glued to the television. The border crossers.

Their faces beam over the blossoming of love on the river.

The story of intrigue and villainy troubles them. Tortured by the suffering of the innocent, tears flood their eyes as evil casts its dark shadow over the bare, elemental world of simple folk, devastating the lives of the young lovers. The exuberant river flows on, carrying Sonai's boat after Pori's death. His trust in the people around him throws into sharp relief the suffocating grip of the decadent feudal forces on village life. The movie takes them back to the land of mighty rivers, superstitions, dark instincts and malevolent powers.

There is an interval with commercials crowding in to spoil the mood. Jamal presses the pause button on the remote. They all want a break.

'Let's have tea,' Montu says. After Jamal's assurance, he has gained a new confidence, not the castaway any more. He will have his fish stall soon. He turns to his wife. 'Make some tea for us.' She springs up as if waiting for the demand.

Despite the tea break, they find it difficult to return from the river island, where Sonai talks to his mynah to beat his loneliness. The deltaic land, criss-crossed by scores of rivers, pulls them back. No one talks. Suddenly, surprising everyone, Jamal begins to sing:

We first met in April.
Got close in May
Now rains are coming.
I'm nervous, not knowing
What'll happen.

With his eyes closed, head leaning against a wall, Jamal goes back to the tune from the past, which keeps him going when the road gets tough. Troubled, Rabeya tries not to look at him. At the moment, he pours out his heart into the song:

We first met in April…

Montu's wife serves tea in paper glasses. Holding her glass, Rabeya pretends to look for something. She gets up and slowly steps out of the room. He is a good singer, has a rich voice, and above all, a sense of music. Evening is approaching, and still, it's not dark. With her arms on the balcony railing, she looks above the apartment blocks, tracing a flight of homebound birds in the confusion of crepuscular light.

The eccentric man's song is eddying around like the waves of a swollen Rupsa at the peak of the monsoon. It's uneasiness, it's gnawing pain.

Rabeya keeps standing, tea in hand, hunched over the railing, not wanting to return anywhere close to him. She does not know when her cousin has come and stood beside her. Ameena puts an arm around her.

'Bubu, don't cry. He's crazy, but he loves you; he is mad about you.'

19
Scent of Death

'Piu?' Nandita waits. She is sure the voice on the other end is familiar.

Has the old bond remained intact? Is she still the same Piu? Angry or upset that I've not called for a while? Or has something snapped? Nandita's ears prick for a hint, the feel of a sound – a mild noise in the room, a child crying, a car on the gravel.

'It's me. And you? Oh, you're – oh, no, it's a call from India. I thought—'

'Nandita.'

'Nan! What a surprise! I knew it was you, but... you're in Paris, and it's a call from India.'

'I have come back to Delhi. Everyone needs to get home one day, Piu.'

'Baba said the same thing before he took a flight to Delhi. Nan, I am very worried about him. What's he doing all alone over there? Can he look after himself?'

'We met a week ago. In fact, I was the first visitor to his new apartment. It's a nice place in the suburbs. He has adjusted well. Perhaps for the first time, he is taking an interest in things around him.'

'Noahda – that's the new city coming up outside Delhi? Across the Yamuna. I traced it on Google Maps.'

'Right. It's a quiet suburb, not crowded like Delhi.'

'I call him almost every Sunday. He talks of Chhetri, the security guard, and Rita, who works in the kitchen.'

'Oh, that girl is a genius. The stuff she makes is simply fabulous: prawns baked in coconut, ginger pudding with hot custard. She takes real good care of your dad.'

'I'm very relieved to know that. We were worried when he went back on a whim without any idea of life over there.'

'I think he was a little tired after long years of living overseas. The energy agreement sapped him. He wanted to live a quiet life, to be alone for a while.'

'You're right, Nan. He kind of got fagged out after all the hectic negotiations and lobbying and the media glare. For him, the negotiations in Washington were the toughest challenge of his career. He is now working on a book – about the energy scenario in South Asia.'

'Yes… I saw stacks of books and reports on power, energy sources and things like that in his study.'

A pause – Piu is perhaps thinking about something. Nandita counts the seconds. Perhaps she wants to say something, is making up her mind. She clears her throat.

'Nan, you're one friend he values – I know that,' she says, as if they're sitting across the table in a café. 'It's good that both of you are in Delhi. Good that there's someone who can give him some support, someone he depends on.' Piu talks like she is eager to confide something in her one-time mentor.

'Arijit is independent-minded; he has organized himself well,' Nandita says. 'He is not doing what retired diplomats usually do – seminars, talks, television, golf, newspaper articles. He is working on a book – that's sensible.' She tries to listen in to something, then smiles. 'I hear sounds – that's your child?'

'Yeah – Bubka. Joy is a great fan of that Russian pole-vaulter. Sergei Bubka – that's the name?'

'Perhaps.' Nandita waits, thinking if she should say something else. 'I have never met Joy. How time goes by! Do you remember our last meeting? I took you to London from Caterham. You were returning to India for a vacation. We shopped around King's Road in Chelsea and had dinner at an Indian restaurant.'

'Oh, yes. I found the big lobsters amusing. Before I left London for New York, I went back to that restaurant with friends. Chutney Mary. Right?'

'I don't remember after so many years.'

'Yes, Nan, I remember. When I first went to Caterham, I was miserable. You came for my birthday. You were a great support. You were more than a mother.'

'Piu.'

'Nan.'

There is silence again. No words flow into the line. Seconds tick away. Piu decides to speak again.

'Nan, I want to say something.'

'Yes.'

'Why do you live separately in the same city? Why don't you get married? I mean it. You two love each other, admire each other. After Mom went back to Bombay, Baba turned to you for emotional support. You meant a lot to him.'

'It's a little too late in the day, Piu. We are now old people; you can call us senior citizens.' Nandita laughs.

'It's not late; many people marry late. Marriage is a relationship, it's all about empathy. Why don't I talk to Baba?'

'I'd rather you didn't.'

When Piu says exactly what she wanted to hear, Nandita shrinks away. Doubts come rushing in. She is not so sure. An unreasonable fear. Still… a happiness seeps through her body. After a very long time, she feels good again.

'Piu, why don't you come here on holiday, all of you? We will have a nice get-together. Joy, Bubka, you – we will have fun. My family has a farm on the city's periphery. All of us will have a good time there.'

'We will come for your wedding.' Piu's voice is clear, decisive. She seems to have made up her mind. 'Nan,' she sounds serious, business-like, as if she has already thought about it, 'Baba is a successful diplomat but unhappy in his personal life. He is a man of rare sophistication, appalled by the crassness around him. I think that's why he has gone to the suburbs, shunning his friends in the city. You're one person who understands him. My mother was a left-wing anarchist; for her, he was the Establishment. Nan, you two will be happy together – I am sure.'

Nandita keeps sitting in her revolving chair. Her unseeing eyes survey random objects in her room. On one shelf of the bookcase are the French titles she brought out during her years in publishing.

Soon, she grew tired of it, felt she was moving around the same circle again and again. And she came back. Had the choice of staying back in Paris and marrying one of her many friends. She could have been part of that society forever. Why did she return then? Was it her way of telling Arijit that she would wait?

The Oxbridge man with patrician good looks became a benchmark for measuring everybody else. Whatever little time she had spent with him was an experience, a learning process. He was – still is – like no one else. After he left Paris and the distance grew, she had no expectations of coming back into his life.

When he was in Delhi on deputation to the Energy Ministry, he considered marriage. But she hastily stepped back. So soon after his wife's death, she could not move into the house shaded by mango and wood-apple trees.

She arrives in Delhi to condole his wife's death. Goes straight to his official residence – a colonial bungalow – on Pandara Road in the capital's power district. Lutyens' Bungalow Zone. Ministers, MPs, senior bureaucrats, judges – they all live here. From the gate, the car takes her on to the porch, skirting the front lawn.

The scent of death, like the smell of stale, wilted white flowers, lingers uneasily in the corners, under the mantelpiece – everywhere. The thin trail from the burning incense quivers before the mahogany-framed portrait. The coiling white wisp of solemn fragrance, soft jasmine garlands around the picture, tuberose sticks in two vases and the shadowy, uncertain thread of Ranjana's death cascade into each other.

Nandita notices a framed photograph on the mantelpiece – Arijit with Piu after a game of tennis, the wide-eyed little girl admiring the racquet in her father's powerful hand. Nandita glances back at the portrait on the wooden platform. Ranjana – earthy, strong, so full of life. Perhaps the picture dates back to the first effusion of marriage. An intense, irresistible presence – Ranjana is captivating in the picture.

An elderly woman steps out of the hallway with a glass of sherbet on a tray. Nandita politely refuses. Arijit's sister from Calcutta. She sits next to her and talks. Learning about Ranjana dying uncared for in a cramped little flat in Bombay, how Arijit brought her here and made arrangements for her treatment. Initially, she responded well to close medical attention, but the excesses of the past many years finally took their toll. Her liver had been so badly damaged it could not be reversed with treatment.

Arijit has gone to the airport to receive Piu. The girl is coming down from London.

'Please come again.' Arijit's sister comes out onto the porch when Nandita leaves, unable to face Ranjana's picture and sit there waiting for the dead woman's man.

The bohemian theatre activist has a more compelling presence in death than in life. No, Nandita cannot be the usurper of Ranjana's bed in that Raj-flavoured bungalow. The rebel woman said no to the proposition of being part maharani, part memsahib in the opulence of privilege. She cannot settle for the discard.

The suave diplomat did drop hints. She received a birthday card – months after her visit to that bungalow to condole Ranjana's death. It had a breathtaking view of the snow-crested Dhauladhar range of the Himalayas, a picture he had taken on an official visit to Palampur.

Don't you feel like living close to the sublime mountains?

He raised the old question before signing off. His way of reinstating her in his life.

No, not for the time being, she decided. The theatre activist, with her mutiny against the Establishment and her contempt for conformity, was still intimidating, bearing down on her. Now that she was dead, Ranjana was an overwhelming presence – troubling, taunting, beckoning to her all the time.

Nandita had started making news in Paris with her publications

– Indian classics translated into French. She dithered, delayed and finally decided not to come to Delhi and live close to the *sublime mountains*. After a few months, Arijit sent her a sketch from a visit to the Jaisalmer desert – a lonely man caught in a sandstorm. His own affair with the pastel pencil. The caption meant more than what it said: *Lost in the desert*.

She hesitated to leave Paris. Could not forget the man nor deny his presence in her life. It was a strange dilemma – she was caught between two worlds. In empty moments, snatches of their brief life together kept coming back.

20
Varadero

The first two days of the summit have been hectic. Speeches, resolutions, statements – she was busy typing and mailing her dispatches. The time difference between India and Cuba has made her hurry early in the morning; meeting the deadline is a challenge while reporting from the other end of the world. On the third morning, the minister loses interest in the proceedings.

India has always been a major player at such gatherings of Asian and African nations. The fact that the meeting is back in Latin America should have had a special meaning for New Delhi. Latinos have always enchanted India with their football, magical realism and revolutions. But the new conservative government in New Delhi has no taste for such socialist grandstanding. Hanuman is the only hero; they don't need any Ches. At the UN, in the politics of summitry, they count on Cuba's support. But for them, Castro is no iconic figure; the obdurate loner railing against American capitalism sits over the debris of a failed ideology.

'I don't give this little country much time; with the old man, it too will go,' says the wife of the Indian envoy. Nandita looks closely at her. The lunch on the lawns of the ambassador's residence is a welcome relief from unrelenting summit politics. Mandarins are good at taking cues from the masters they serve.

Nandita thinks of the craze for the Che T-shirts during her student days in Delhi. She spots Arijit in a huddle of officials.

The ambassador's wife walks up to her, trying to strike up a conversation. 'Is this your first visit to Havana?'

'That's right.'

'In India, people grow up reading about the heroics of Che and the Castro brothers. But they have no interest in the country. You know, outside the embassy, only two Indians live in Havana. Just two. They represent two Indian companies. Once in a while, communist leaders from Bengal and Kerala come. One big leader came here once for his cataract operation. Can you imagine? All the way from Calcutta to get your cataract removed in Havana!'

Nandita points to the young mango tree in one corner of the sprawling lawn. 'That's a reminder of India.'

The woman smiles. 'I brought the sapling from Hyderabad. The famous Banganapalle mango variety. It grew fast but bore no fruit.'

Arijit comes out of the cluster, picks up a mojito. Their eyes meet. He walks up to her. They talk, walking around the lawn. 'My only job now is to see that Pakistan does not insert *Kashmir* anywhere in the resolutions,' he laughs. 'The minister is going back tonight. I'm free all of tomorrow. Let's go somewhere.'

'Where are we off to?' Nandita asks as the car flows down the road, leaving the city behind.

'Varadero. The beach is beautiful.' Arijit is relaxed. After three days of endless drafting and negotiations, he is in a mood to unwind.

In blue jeans, sneakers and a T-shirt, he is a different man, not the Foreign Service mandarin. He surveys Nandita in a tank top and puts a soft arm around her. 'Less than three hours' drive from Havana, you'll love it – shallow waters and sandbanks.' The car hums down the asphalt under an azure sky. On either side, stretches of plantation flit away, but Nandita is not looking at any of that. Arijit has dropped his guard. He is talking more than ever before, even cracking jokes. The elegant, reserved man is suddenly full of light-hearted banter.

'The shadowy CIA agents went after Fidel's beard. Not after his life but facial hair, ha! Just imagine. They mixed chemicals in the seawater where he did scuba diving. A plot to make him shave ha ha... The spooks believed his appeal is in his beard. For women, he's another Christ. And years after the fall of the Soviet empire, El Jefe Máximo hosted more than a hundred heads of state, defying America, see.'

Varadero is bewitching. A generous spread of soft sand lazily moves into the water. The yachts of the super-rich are anchored off the coast. Extravagantly built to define ultimate luxury, they are like a statement of affluence on water.

'Most of them are owned by Americans.' Arijit gestures with his chin at the lavish liners. He has already slipped into swim trunks. 'Since the US economic embargo against Cuba continues, they book their passage through other countries. The Yanks find Cuba magical.' Nandita surveys the deluxe boats.

'At Hemingway House in Havana, someone told me that the old boatman is still alive; the master wrote *The Old Man and the Sea* around him.' She expectantly looks up at Arijit. Perhaps she half hopes that with his diplomatic contacts, it will not be difficult for him to trace the boatman and arrange a trip to his home.

Arijit laughs mischievously, appreciation in his eyes; Hemingway and the boatman are far from his mind. He looks at Nandita, dazzling in a blue bikini. He is more interested at the moment in her transformation than the rebel writer being accused of spying for the Soviets after his time in Spain reporting the Civil War for an American newspaper.

Nandita pouts in mock annoyance. She wants to have her say. 'American tourists rush to his cottage to get photographed with him.' She raises her voice a little and laughs. 'They won't mind throwing a hundred-dollar bill to take home the picture. It's an important souvenir for them.'

Leaning against a clump of coconut trees, they look around for more signs of contact between the forbidden island and the world. A girl stands outside a little restaurant, actually a bare, makeshift shack of reeds and wooden poles. She smiles, unable to take her eyes off Nandita. Nandita decides to stop by the shack for lunch.

The girl waves at her. Perhaps confused, she cannot figure them out – neither white nor black. With her limited knowledge of tourists, she cannot place them. Nandita smiles back.

The sounds of heavy footsteps in the sand and cavorting make her look around. A tall, bulky, bare-bodied man in shorts is rubbing some gel all over the big, bare breasts of his partner walking beside him. The woman, equally hefty but even taller, squeals with delight.

Nandita turns to Arijit. 'This is a topless beach,' he says in a low voice. She looks at the girl in the shack again, and she gives her a knowing smile. *There are many more of them trying more stupid, daft things. From my perch, I can see all that, and I know a lot more than you think I do,* she seems to be saying with her eyes. Indeed, more such couples walk past them, fondling and smooching each other. Instead of lying down on the sand for a sunbath or wading into the water, they, too, decide to walk.

After trudging some distance, they come to a craggy cliff layered with thick moss. Sand has given way to a jumble of rocks teetering back into the water. No tourists are around. The heavy, moist air heightens the sense of alienation. The smell of weed pushed back by the big waves stresses the strange feeling of being cut off and hemmed in by the ocean. There's a faint hint of rot in the wind.

'Arijit…' Nandita holds his arm.

Unknowingly, they have stopped.

'You're thinking about something, Nan?' He pulls her close.

'Yee-s… about the fancy ships. They bring fun crowds here to enter a dream, but they only go away – back to different places. The bubble is momentary. All that remains is the memory of a holiday – mementos and pictures for the album. I fear we're going to end up like those luxury boats. Our life is just a reminder of the campfire and a beer on the beach.'

He laughs, ruffling her hair. A while later, with his hands wrapped around her, Arijit buries his face between her breasts and then inhales deeply – the heat in her body, the crimson glow on the skin, the lustrous auburn hair for all the mystery swept into it, her eyes for the dreams she inhabits, the lips for all the unsaid words. He shakes his head. 'Our life, Nan, is neither a ship nor a holiday; we will live in our home for a long time.'

Arijit walks up to the protruding rock outcrop and leans against it. He tears off a leaf from the bush below, crushes it between his fingers and offers the pulp to Nandita. As she moves closer to take the leaf, he holds her gently, traps her between his legs and tightens his grip on her. He kisses her, full and hungry. Recovering from the shock of the comforting incursion, she responds fervently, giving up the last shred of resistance, and spreads herself over his chest like a perched bird spreading out its wings. The passion passes from one body to another. He runs his fingers through her hair while gently biting her neck.

Waves of electricity transmitting through the fevered contact, they move under the bush behind the rock. The smell of damp, shrub and ocean mix into a sense of expectation to fill them. Nandita feels as if they, too, are part of the ocean, creatures pushed ashore at high tide. On the leafy, wet sand, the two bodies twirl, twitch and make love in tune with the crashing waves.

That day has stayed with her all these years – intact, mothballed against decay, not even a single shred torn off. The moment she closes her eyes, it topples over – live, pulsating. She has not realized that all through the long separation, she has actually lived inside the orb of the man. Suddenly, unexpectedly, in a matter of weeks, retrieving him from the detritus of the past has become a possibility. It's late; not much of their lives is left. Still, five… ten… fifteen years… what's the harm?

Nandita calls Arijit's number.

'Good that we're talking.' He seems to have been waiting for her call. 'I wanted to talk to you about something. An American filmmaker has mailed me a lot of pictures about his time in Bangladesh, where he shot his documentary on what he calls river life. You will be surprised, quite a bit of it is about Rita. Her father worked for him. As a young girl, she was with him, running errands, helping him with cooking. Strange, isn't it?'

'I could figure she is not just another domestic help or migrant pushed into a city slum by poverty.' Nandita recollects her talk with Rita in the kitchen, then in the mall. 'Her stray English words are perfectly American, the way she says *barbecue, topping, sandwich*. It's in the American sense. I think we might still be able to rescue her from her situation.' Nandita waits.

'But she is…'

'We'll talk about all that on Saturday. You remember Naël Dubois, the French writer? He is here. I am throwing a small party at my place. Only a handful of people. You are coming, right?'

'Sure. I would like to meet Naël Dubois.'

'And one more thing,' Nandita ploughs on. 'Can I have Rita with me for the day? I need someone to help me in the kitchen. Honestly, I know so little about cooking.'

21
Fish-eating Tiger

The maulana knocks at the appointed time – ten minutes past midnight. Jamal is awake. Ready for the outing. They told him to take a light meal.

'Give me a minute,' he tells the spooky figure, opening the door. He hastily ties his trainer laces.

The man, he has learnt, is anything but a cleric. With degrees from two universities, he lived abroad, gave up a good job for what he calls the war of faith. *Jihad* – when he utters the word, his face contorts in acute pain, his soul in torment.

He lives under different names, changes cell phone numbers every week. At Akhtar's shop, Jamal once asked him for his number. 'You don't worry, Bangla Bhai,' the enigmatic man smiled with a glint in his eye. 'Whenever you think of me, I will call you.' The sharp eyes were like the calm surface of a lake on a winter night – icy, unperturbed.

His name is Anwar Hussain. At least in this area. He enquires about Jamal's family back in Bangladesh. 'Have they got the money, Bhai? Your parents, brother, sister?'

He scrutinizes Jamal, flinty eyes piercing deep into him for the slightest hint of doubt, dilemma. 'Good.' He smiles, perhaps reassured. 'I've heard a lot about your land, tch tch.' A touch of repressed irritation in his voice. 'They eat fish, a lot of sweets, sing and speak in a springy tongue.' Anwar's mood suddenly changes.

He laughs genially, in a forgiving mood. 'You people are soft, sentimental. Not like Afghans. Or Iraqis. You guys cannot kill the kafir with disdain. Fish and sandesh have mellowed you into a gooey lot.' He shakes his head in distress. The next moment, his mood changes. He smiles. 'Rivers and rains, rice and rhymes – Bhai, you've been rasgullaed. Ho ho ha ha…'

The mullah, like so many other things in life, is a puzzle, an intriguing question mark. So is Rabeya; he is ready to do anything for her. Anything. She knows that, and yet, she has slipped away. She could not love him. Why?

He comes out of his hole, no longer the pathetic, sentimental fool or an illegal Bangladeshi. No – tonight he is the Royal Bengal Tiger out of his lair. Yellow-and-black stripes, fleet-footed, a certain majesty about his movements – the king of the Sundarbans on the prowl. Going after the game. The royal hunt.

The maulana assesses him approvingly: trendy T-shirt, smartly cut hair, a silver chain around his neck, branded jeans and Reebok trainers. A man about town trying hard to make it big – a sales executive, a computer engineer. The appearance must not raise the slightest suspicion. No one should get a hint of what magma is smouldering inside him. It is fun time with fast food, new movies, dates, discoing, drinks – he is not the cordite from a hidden war zone.

They walk side by side, along the dirt, towards the highway. A grey Maruti van is almost invisible behind a giant billboard. The driver gets down, opens the door for Jamal. The grille-factory man, always at the receiving end, resigned to the oxyacetylene flames, heat, boils, is not used to such courtesies. Savouring his new importance, he climbs into the front seat. The driver gets in behind the wheel. Surprisingly, the maulana stays back. He waves Jamal off and turns hastily, vanishing into the dark.

After moving on to National Highway 24, the driver speeds up, humming a film song:

I've seen for the first time
Love in the eyes of my girl

The driver whistles, easy on the empty wide road. 'I am Sajid, Jamal Bhai.'

'Where are you from?'

'Azamgarh. I came to Delhi to do an IT course. Then met Anwar Sahib one day. He said jihad is the only job now.'

Jamal cannot see him well in the dark. *Jihad is the only job,* he repeats.

'For about a month, we will train intensely, six days a week.' Sajid turns to him. His eyes glow. The frivolous mood dissipates. The man speaks slowly, as if with much deliberation. 'A very important man has come from the other side of the border – Major Qureshi.'

'Border?' Jamal is confused. For a fleeting moment, he thinks of the Benapole border he crossed from Bangladesh.

'From Pakistan, Jamal Bhai. It's not easy to sneak in. The dogs of the Indian Army are on guard round the clock. But he has done it for us. He first went to Nepal, and from there, travelled to Delhi by road. He is our coach.'

Jamal thinks of the war memorials all around Khulna, commemorating those killed in the War of Liberation against the Pakistani junta in 1971. He grew up hearing stories of the Mukti Bahini guerrillas fighting the Pakistani troops in the swamps and rice paddies of Bangladesh. A major in the Pakistani army will train him now in what Anwar Hussain calls a new kind of warfare.

We are going to war to save a flower,
To see the smiling face of our mother

The song everybody hummed when he was a little boy. It was about the War of Liberation – *Mukti Juddho*. Who was the singer? Apple Mahmood? He does not remember any more.

The car turns off the highway, slowing down on a rugged, uneven road. After a while, it crawls through a maze of narrow lanes. The ghostly shades and chimneys of dead factories stand like imposing gravestones around the necropolis. They are staring down at the shadowy intruders. Sajid manoeuvres the car inside the hulk of one such factory.

They enter the mosque through a side door. Though from the outside the structure looks morbidly sepulchral, a corner room across the inner courtyard is humming with activity.

'Come, come, Bangla Bhai,' Anwar Hussain greets Jamal.

There are three other young men sitting stiffly, clearly new recruits for the offensive. They look nervous.

One man, unlike the others, sits in a chair – tall, flab-less, light-skinned. His brown eyes sparkle. He takes one sharp look at Jamal, as if seeing through his body, scanning his insides. He smiles – perhaps in approval. 'I am told that in Bangladesh, even the tiger loves fish; the big cat catches fish from the river and doesn't kill the poor villagers ha ha...' His body shakes with laughter. 'The Bengal tiger is actually a fish-eater, not man-eater. Is that so?' He roars in good humour. Others join him in scrutinizing Jamal. Major Altaf Qureshi, the feared officer of the

Pakistan Army. 'Like you have always hooked fish from the pond, you must hit the enemy with the same accuracy. Flawlessly, no slips, no misses. Islam is in danger.'

Jamal has not noticed the hawk-eyed cleric sitting in one corner. Almost hidden behind his white, flowing beard, the man's eyes burn in a piercing anger. His nostrils flare. Like blowpipes to make an ebbing fire flare.

'We don't have the warheads of the Indian Army; you boys are our missiles, our big guns.' The old mullah scratches his cheeks through the forest of white beard. 'We are in the middle of an uneven, skewed war. Christians, Jews, Hindus – they all have ganged up against us. Islam is under attack. The pork-eating Americans are drawing up designs on their computers to hunt down the heroes of jihad. All their cameras and computers have failed to trace them so far. Now we are hitting back. In America, it may not be easy to strike big for a second time, but in India, you can do it as many times as you wish. Hindus are clumsy, sloppy chutiyas; they have no brains except for making money.'

After the harangue, the mullah leads them into the prayer hall.

He clears his throat. Then raises his voice. 'This body of yours is meaningless; this life on Earth is only a vehicle to carry out Allah's work.' The words reverberate from the dome. He seems to have bathed in bubbles of fire. A man possessed. 'And to reach Paradise to meet him. That's the abode of the blessed – the dazzling damsels offering you wine, grapes and dates, the fountains tingling around, cockatoos strutting on gold bars. Sons, that is bliss, the end result of your good work here on Earth, that is *firdaus, jannat, behest*. By whatever name you call Paradise. Our faith is under attack, so don't live the life of an imbecile. Don't! Rise, give it back to the cunning Hindus. What do you want? Tell me that. Do you want to live like slaves? In humiliation? Harassed, shackled, tortured by their thuggish police? Or will you blaze away, burn yourself to meet Allah up above in Paradise? Ameen. Ameen. Ameen.'

His voice drops off. Silence prevails. The cleric is overwhelmed by the intensity of his own rhetoric. Repressed fire. Tired and exhilarated, moments later, his eyes flash again.

'Are you ready to die fighting the corrupt and the crooked? Or do you want to go on living, decrepit until disease and decay claim your moth-eaten body? Each one of you – say yes or no.'

The cleric's acid-dripping words create a tumult inside Jamal. The rich in the city have taken away Rabeya, not by force but through the snares of luxury and comfort. She wants to live like them, among them. *I am a poor man, I have no reason to live on, joining steel angles with lead and flames at the weld works.* He breathes deeply.

'No, I don't want to live any more,' he shouts, surprising himself. 'Give me a gun and tell me who. I will pump bullets straight into his chest.'

'Shabaash! Bengali hero, shabaash!' Major Qureshi is glowing.

Seeing Jamal spring into action, the other three recruits follow suit.

The army officer explains his plans: a senior minister is coming to the headquarters of the Central Industrial Police Force for their Foundation Day celebrations. That date is a month away. They need to shoot down the minister and the top men of the elite force.

'Go down fighting, killing as many of the bastards as possible.'

'Inshallah.'

Everyone looks at Jamal.

'I only want all that to happen tomorrow, maximum a week, not a month later.' He flares up first, before anybody else. 'May Allah help us. Pray for our success.'

'Ameen.' The old, bearded cleric closes his eyes, touching his chest.

'You are brave, Bangla Bhai.' Anwar Hussain smiles – proud that he has spotted and broken in this terrific colt.

22
INA Market

Rita waits outside Atlantic Mall. The spanking red-and-yellow McDonald's sign towers over her. Smartly dressed men and women walk in and out of the large glass doors. Every time the door opens, a draught of cool air splashes her face. It's not hot yet – only the end of February. The sun is still soft, does not sear you.

Nandita called yesterday. Her chauffeur is coming to take Rita to her place. She is hosting a party this evening. Kaku will also be there.

Rita looks very different in the chic kurta churidar Nandita bought her from this mall. Looking at herself in the mirror in her pigeonhole, she had laughed. *It's another woman!* No different from the girls who live in those apartments and come to the mall to shop, to meet their boyfriends.

Mall! Ew! What a dirty word in Bengali! But here, it's a different world, part of the spume-swaying life. *I could be a resident of the happy street! With Didi and Kaku in a loving home, cooking for them, taking care of their needs.* Rita unknowingly smiles. *I can complete the story – of lovers, lost and lonely, coming together again, ending estrangement and distress.*

She looks at her watch to check if the driver chap is being late. The band shines like gold. And the luminous off-white dial – why, that's a studded pearl! She blows on the face of the Titan to clean imaginary dust off. Beautiful! Jamal was so extravagant with the gifts! Bechara! A good man who doesn't know the basic rules of life. He crossed the border and came to Delhi but still lives in Khulna, rowing his little boat from one ghat to another. Never learnt how to adjust to changes. He loves her. He loves her more than he can say but is clueless about how to make her happy. Everybody caught in a maze tries to come out of it. Only he gets more and more entangled in the web, moving deeper into the puzzle. He wants to take on everyone, wage war every day.

A young man waves at her from a distance. The driver. He drove Didi and her to the mall that Sunday.

When they talked on the phone, Nandita told her about the party. 'Your kaku will also be here in the evening.' Rita feels a strong sense of loyalty to Nandita, wants to cling to her. Didi gave all the instructions: wear the new clothes, pack a change, wait at the mall, buy some spices and vegetables. The driver knows the market.

'Have you been waiting long?' Bharat Singh sounds apologetic. 'Bad traffic – the morning peak hour.'

He walks alongside Rita towards the underground car park.

She watches the man: tall, lean, light-skinned… a nice fellow. The first day he drove Didi and her, he was like an obedient shadow following the boss silently. A little scared. Today, he is a different man – better dressed, talking, trying hard to impress her. And surer about himself. He looks at her, his gaze lingering on her face. Not a sneaky, greedy stare but honest adulation.

'When I saw you from a distance, I thought it was someone else,' he smiles. 'You look very different now.'

'Why, did I look like a hag the other day?' She relishes the first appreciation from a man of the new woman she wants to be. Her transformation has been noticed. Unlike Rekha, she has no need to bob her hair, wear jeans and tight sleeveless tops. She is very fond of her long tresses. This morning, she did her hair in the style of Kabori, the undisputed queen of Dhallywood.

Dhallywood – a funny word she first heard from Jamal. 'They have Bollywood in Bombay, we have Dhallywood in Dhaka. They have Amitabh Bachchan, we have Razzak. Are we any less – actor to actor, heroine to heroine?' The crazy fellow would get worked up facing an imaginary adversary.

Bharat Singh gallantly opens the door for her. Rita hesitates – the door to the passenger seat. With Nandita, she sat in the rear. She pauses for a moment.

'It's a long way from here. I thought we could talk.' Bharat Singh has noticed her wavering. 'I can tell you about the big buildings on the way. But you can sit in the back as well.'

'I will sit in the front.' She gamely climbs into the front seat. 'From here, I can see things better.' Sitting so close to the windscreen, steering wheel, little Ganesha idol on the dashboard, she is thrilled. 'Everything is so close!' Rita laughs, unable to hold back her excitement. 'The road is right below you.'

Bharat smiles. He buckles up, then tries to catch her eye. She is looking around, absorbed in the scenes on the road through the tinted glass. He mildly taps on her arm. 'You, too.' He points to her seat belt.

'What?' She looks dismissive seeing him point to his seat belt. The belt tied around the man makes no sense to her.

'It's to your side; pull it.'

She pulls the belt a little, then lets it swish back and starts giggling. The man feels awkward, not knowing what to do.

'Am I a bolting calf that you want to tether me?' She bursts into a big laugh again, her body breaking into waves, tears filling her eyes.

Bharat stretches his arm to help her belt up. While pulling the belt, his hand brushes against her breast, just for the spark of a second. The soft feel of her bosom lingers. He starts the engine, trying to look serious.

'If the cops see you in the front without the belt, they will slap a fine – five hundred rupees.'

Her eyes widen, thinking of the amount for such a small thing. Unable to figure the crime of not fastening the stupid belt, she laughs again.

'The police are something you laugh about?' He gives a puzzled look.

'No. The money you mentioned. F-i-v-e huuundrreed!'

'Then—'

'I'll give them fifty and say don't give me a receipt, baba.' She grins disarmingly.

The car zooms along a lonely road, then goes over a bridge. Bharat slows down, takes his right hand off the wheel to touch his forehead and chest and bows his head. Rita notices his gesture of reverence. Her eyebrows knit into a question mark.

'Yamuna-ji, the holiest river after Ganga-ji.' Bharat's voice has a touch of adoration. She looks out curiously for a view of the river. A lean flow of water meanders through shrubs and overgrowth, interrupted by hyacinths and heavy silt. Fat, lazy water buffaloes graze around the patches of farming.

'River, you call this a river, eh?' Her voice betrays contempt.

'What else?'

'If you only saw the river flowing by our village, the large steamers hooting away—' She stops abruptly, realizing her mistake. In an unguarded moment, she was about to give away everything.

'Where is your village? Which river?' Bharat asks playfully. 'Are you from Bombay or Goa?'

'From Calcutta. Have you never heard of that place where people bathe in the Ganga?' Her father once made the trip with Radolf Sahib by launch. After he came back, for days he talked only about the big, bustling city – trams, Victoria Memorial and the Monument.

The car goes past a grand arch in the middle of wide lawns ringed by cast-iron chains. 'What's that?' Her eyes sparkle, her voice a mix of awe and curiosity.

'Haven't you been here before? That's India Gate.' He looks at her incredulously. 'People come here in the evening for ice cream. And on the morning of 26 January every year, heavy military pieces move down this road – tanks, rockets, big guns. Soldiers perform like acrobats on their motorcycles, on top of the tanks, and finally, the air show: the fighter jets fly in formation and swoop down to do a namaste. Everybody claps.' Like an ace shadowgrapher, his hands join momentarily, with the fingers taking strange shapes. Their silhouette on her lap in the sunlight through the driver's side window looks exactly like a skein. He grips the wheel again. She smiles.

'Do you also come for the show?'

'Yes, every year. I get a pass from a friend who is a peon in a government office.'

Bharat looks at Rita to see if she is impressed by his connections. This girl, he somehow knows, is his employer's favourite. If he could get her hand, both of them would move into one corner of the big house. Though not fair like the girls from the hills, she has an earthy charm and laughs beautifully. He drives carefully around India Gate.

He decides to gamble a little, get a bit bolder. 'Next year, you can come with me. I will get another pass for you.'

'Me? For the soldiers' parade? Nah, baba. I will die seeing those guns and rockets. I cannot see people fighting.'

A surge of pity wells up in his heart for the simple girl. 'All right, one evening we will come only for ice cream.'

She lets the matter pass without a yes or no.

Bharat enters the parking lot of a market and gives the key to an attendant. 'We will be back in thirty minutes.' He commands authority with his voice. Then he holds Rita's hand and pulls her through the snarl of cars into a maze of lanes and confusion of smells – spices, fruit, deep-fried snacks, flowers, herbs, huge turkeys squealing at shoppers…

'This is INA Market. Madam comes here often. You will not get anywhere else the stuff they sell here.'

Rita sees fat, fashionable women of every age and ethnicity moving around, carrying packets of purchases. She looks curiously at a group of black women – springy hair, large hoops dangling from their ears – busily moving from shop to shop, speaking in an unfamiliar tongue, neither Hindi nor English, not even Bangla. 'They are Africans.' Bharat taps on her shoulder. The two of them loiter, looking at the things displayed in the little shops. Didi has told her what to buy – some exotic vegetables, fruit and flowers.

In one shop, she finds some of the vegetables Radolf Sahib would have bought from Dhaka's Gulshan Market – parsley, thyme, asparagus, broccoli, red cabbage. She is happy to touch, smell them again. Then they buy flowers – lilies, orchids, dahlias, chrysanthemums and the classic roses.

Effortlessly carrying the shopping bags ballooning with purchases, Bharat stops at a Coke–Pepsi corner on the pavement. Taking a small sip of Fanta, she catches him stealing a glance at her; clearly, he has taken a liking to her. The man with light brown eyes.

'Who all are at home?' He takes a step closer.

'Nobody.'

'Mummy, papa?'

'Long dead.'

'Nobody else?'

'My sister is married.'

'Why did you leave home?'

'I could not live alone in that empty house any more.'

There is a pause. Perhaps he can not think of any more questions. Still – he decides to keep the chat going.

'You don't have a friend? A young man who can take care of you?'

'Looking for someone.' She laughs.

23
Kesariya Baalam

With the arrival of the first guests, the lawn comes alive. Tucked away in the backyard of the house, it is a secluded patch of smooth grass screened off by large trees – jacaranda, neem, cotton, laburnum. An engineer who built other people's houses, Anand Kapoor had planned his own meticulously. He made brilliant use of the land, keeping in mind the need for a patch of open space in Delhi's sweltering summer.

In one corner, a man in a black jacket and red tie over a long-sleeved white shirt is tending the bar under an awning. Nandita has hired him for the evening from a catering company. A couple in traditional Rajasthani attire is singing folk songs from the desert to the accompaniment of a string instrument and little drums:

Kesariya baalam avo nee
Padharo mhare des re

The string instrument meanders through the evening, the dholak beats move back and forth, and the woman's bronze voice melts into rich melody, welcoming a handsome prince, a pink turban around his head, to the land of his love. Unmindful of the happenings around the lawn, the husband-and-wife team is absorbed in the rise and fall of their music.

Cane armchairs are scattered over the downy grass. The party is like an intricate quilt – a comforting smell of alcohol, soft, pale lights, the occasional burst of laughter and haunting desert music all woven into it. The mild fragrance of plumerias from somewhere around mists the evening. Confused by the light, a cuckoo is warbling from its perch in a tree.

After introductions, the guests ease into small talk with their first drinks in hand. 'Though India has been making high-quality rum for one and a half centuries, the world now knows it for its superb wine,' Adelle Dupont, a French embassy official, tells Barry Wilson, a doctor from Iowa, working with UNICEF.

'Uh-huh. Why rum?' The doctor smiles.

'Aha, that's because of sugarcane! If you go to Kasauli in the hills for a holiday, you can see the first distillery the British set up in 1855.'

Michael Daggett, a development economist teaching at Delhi University, shares his Indian experience with the French writer Naël Dubois and his Indian girlfriend. 'Pondicherry is both an idea and an illusion, far removed from the real India.'

Arijit shakes hands with Mandira Singh, who introduces herself as a lifestyle journalist. 'Ask me who's dating whom, which marriages are under strain, who's breaking up – I will give you the latest updates, ha ha.'

'Fantastic. How do you know so much?' Arijit is both amused and awed by the society columnist's expertise.

'Why, that's my research area, I hold a PhD in city scandals, hee hee…'

Kojo Okoro, an African American poet from Los Angeles, is curious about the Rajasthani song, the colourful clothes of the artist couple and the string instrument. He asks Sonal Joshi, an upcoming artist, about 'Kesariya Baalam'. With his springy salt-and-pepper hair, white scruffy beard and striking print shirt, Kojo looks like a dervish.

His arm around Sonal, Kojo now stands before the low platform of the musician couple, following the movement of their fingers. He seems to have got into the inner rhythm of their desert song.

'Yaaah!' he exclaims, excited about his discovery of music from deep inside the sands. In no time, he is tapping his foot and waving his raised hands, imitating what he thinks is some form of Indian dance.

After a while, he turns to Sonal. 'A couple is singing, so a couple must dance.'

Sonal laughs, setting down her wine. Together, they try out a dance step or two. Looking at her partner's awkward body movements, she shakes her head.

'Look, I'm actually from Rajasthan. I know what kind of dance this music is for.' She goes up to the musicians, asks them to play an easy tune and twirls in a few complex circles.

'This is a wedding song,' Sonal tells Kojo.

'Ooh, ooh!' He is excited.

Then they dance again.

Bharat Singh stands at the front gate, welcoming the guests and escorting them to the lawn. In a flowing white kurta churidar, he is a man completely transformed. No longer the diffident, mute chauffeur but very much a scion of the rural aristocracy in old Hindi movies. Sensing the importance of the occasion, he has tied a turban around his head. When no one else is expected, he goes back to the lawn to assist the bartender.

Inside the house, Nandita calls Rita into her bedroom. Most of the food has come from a famous restaurant; Rita has made only the fish fry. And Nandita a salad. 'Have you finished? Good.' She hands her a new sari, still unpacked. 'I bought this silk for you.' 'I was in a sari shop the other day.' She looks her over. She holds Rita's hand and looks closely at her spice-stained fingers. The girl is reeking of onions, garlic and fish. Rita smiles. 'Take a shower and get ready. You have to serve.' Nandita pats her on the shoulder and hurries across the hallway and down the stairs.

When she walks down the lawn with a tray of kebab, Rita is nervous and unsure of herself. So many unfamiliar faces look up at her. Still, she moves around, serving appetizers to the guests. It takes Arijit a while to recognize her. The famished girl who slumped outside his door asking for a job. In the moss-coloured sari, with her open hair past the waist, she is an altogether different person. He senses admiration all around. With a measured smile, she goes from guest to guest, offering paper napkins, wooden cutlery and kebab.

Barry Wilson, the bespectacled American doctor, smiles warmly. He points to the green paste in a glass bowl on her tray.

'What's that?'

'Mint chutney.' The words come travelling a long distance.

He looks into her eyes while layering a piece of kebab with a spoonful of chutney. 'Kebab goes best with this?' he asks curiously.

She nods.

Mint chutney, mustard sauce, nutmeg, green chilli paste, cardamom, black pepper, bhetki fillet, lamb chop, wings – she heard about many such things from Radolf Sahib over those elaborate cooking sessions. Sahib was crazy about food.

'Anything else?' The guest laughs, keen to linger on the conversation.

'Onion rings, lemon.' She carefully picks up a clump of onion rings with a fork and puts them on his plate. Then a wedge of lemon.

'Thank you!'

'You're welcome.' She smiles, moving away.

Nandita watches the brief encounter while talking to Naël Dubois. Then she walks up to the American.

'Barry, Rita told you about mint chutney and onion rings. She forgot another thing.'

'What's that?' The doctor looks intrigued.

'Red chilli.'

'Oh, that's a conspiracy, Nan! No, actually, subversion. You're plotting against me, eh?'

Both of them laugh heartily.

'She is Rita? You said…?'

'Yes. She is like a daughter.'

'You have adopted her?'

'You can say that.'

Arijit is busy talking to Michael Daggart. The old socialist lives in a slum among migrant workers in the city's soft underbelly. He overhears fragments of the conversation between Nandita and Barry. *Like a daughter* – the words resonate in his ears. The buzz lingers before drowning in the conviviality of the evening.

The party shifts into a new gear. Mandira Singh spices it up with gossip about the Delhi elite – politicians, businessmen, socialites. Naël Dubois is impressed. 'I have met quite a few interesting people here,' he tells Nandita. The short man, with flowing silvery hair touching his shoulders, and a goatee, is a charmer. 'For the first time in six months, I could speak French with so many people together.' He moves on for a conversation with Arijit about South

Asia and its problems, India's fascinating rhythm in chaos. Then he discovers Rita.

'You… *la belle* Bengali, there is more to you than the world can see.' He takes her hand in his and smiles like a magician doing a vanishing act. Uncomfortable being so close to the strange man, Rita manages a smile. She thinks of the fakir from a faraway land people in their village said could have been God. His touch, she knows, is like rain purveying the essence of the skies.

'One day, I will come back to write your story.' He takes her in his arms.

What she senses is the man's goodness, not the exact meaning of his words. She runs back to Radolf's words at the end of any such exchange. She smiles, nodding. 'Thank you.'

One by one they all leave – happy and grateful.

'Good times end too quickly,' Kojo says, hugging Nandita. He leans in to hold her, then kisses her cheek. She walks him to the gate and waves as he gets into his car. When all the others are gone, Nandita walks up to the bar and returns with two glasses of red wine. Seeing her, Arijit pulls out a cane chair, and they sit facing each other. A thick smell of food, alcohol and happiness hangs around the place.

'It was a good crowd,' Arijit says.

'Everyone came. Dubois is a major influence in France now. He struggled very hard to earn his place. Now that people want to hear him and worship him, he is on the run, almost in hiding. He lives mostly in Pondicherry.'

'What was he telling Rita?'

'Nothing and a lot.' Nandita laughs. 'As a writer, he seems to have an extra eye – you may call it clairvoyance. He could see she was not an ordinary girl.'

24
Pigeon on the Rooftop

Jamal hears the stealthy knock at the door – by now familiar but never predictable. And yet, every time, it chills his blood, his heart beats like a drum. Measured, cautious – meant for him alone. There is always a furtive pause after the first secret knock. If the footsteps inside start towards the door, a second one will not come. Everything about the man is icily dark, both opaque and watermarked. Like a disquieting dream. The unreal man. The maulana slips in with the surreptitious silence of a feral cat. His steps are unhurried, discreet but very sure. He pulls up the wobbly stool and sits on its edge.

'Bangla Bhai, the date of your exam is getting closer.' He looks Jamal full in the face.

Jamal is frightened – can the man's flinty eyes exhume his Baul songs, the full moon at the Dargah of Khanjan Ali? Facing the enigmatic man, he stands – bare, exposed.

'Are you scared? Does your heart miss a beat often, any palpitation? Do you break a sweat thinking about dying?' He smiles. Contempt clouds his face.

Jamal has often wondered why he cannot get to call him by his name – Anwar Bhai, Anwar Hussain, Anwar Sahib… The man's frosty look, the rise and fall of his voice, his frozen fire – all that stops him, thwarts his desire to call him by his name. The mystery man has an irresistible pull. An inexplicable gravitas.

Jamal gets up from the cot and takes a step closer to the visitor. The man looks puzzled, betrays a sense of fright, just for a second. Jamal grips his arm, then presses it.

'Maulana Sahib, I wish it were tomorrow, not two weeks later. That bliss of death comes into my dreams. The glory ravishes me. No, it does not scare me, that big moment. It thrills me, calls me all the time.' He releases the man's arm. 'I have always been a worthless man – clumsy, casual. Now in death, I want to prove something. I want to say I have been misunderstood, grossly underestimated, very badly—'

He gets a lump in his throat. A pain, a wretchedness he did not feel a minute before. He feels queasy. Struggles to get over the distressed moment. 'I want to prove I can do something big with my life. That I am somebody…'

The maulana gets up, holds Jamal in a tight embrace. He breathes deeply.

'Shabaash, Bangla Bhai! I am really proud of you. When you go into action, think of the thousands of faithful being slaughtered in Kashmir, Afghanistan, Iraq, Chechnya. They want to humble, humiliate the children of Allah. Give them a black eye, bring down the tower of the infidels, spill their blood!' Anwar Hussain's icy eyes flare in rare anger.

He hands Jamal a bulging leather handbag. 'The remaining amount – *thr-ee la-akh*.' Jamal carelessly slips the bag into the heap of his bedding. Without any expression. As if he has not heard the amount the maulana stressed.

'Send it home through an agent in a day or two. And tell your parents to call you. They must not mention money but only say, "The bird has come home." That's the code. The bloody rats of Indian intelligence listen; they listen a hell of a lot.'

Jamal smiles briefly. 'Let's go then.'

The Maruti van whooshes through the night along the familiar route. The smooth, wide road, mostly empty but for the occasional truck.

'Akhtar was praising you.' The maulana now speaks normally, in a matter-of-fact voice. 'Because of you, his grille business has flourished. You are hard-working, efficient… you're honest. Today, Akhtar is getting big orders from the builders. Before you, he was nowhere.' Anwar Hussain puts an arm around him. It's unlike him – travelling with a welder's man in the same car, talking about the ordinary things of life, showing emotion. His tone almost down to earth. Has he dropped his guard? Or is there a compelling reason? 'The Army of Islam needs many more soldiers like you, Bangla Bhai.' He pats Jamal on the shoulder.

The van enters the same industrial estate; after zigzagging through the narrow streets, it slips into a ghostly factory shed.

Major Qureshi of the Pakistan Army moves around thoughtfully, like a theatre director during a rehearsal. Spotting Jamal and Anwar Hussain, he bends a little, then raises his hand to his chest in a casual salaam.

'Now everybody is here.' He is satisfied with the punctuality of his wards. 'What we are going to discuss now is the final assault. Every moment of that Sunday morning as it unfolds.'

Major Qureshi sits at a makeshift table – a rough plank on a foldaway steel frame. He switches on his laptop, and the cursor moves furiously across the screen. Jamal looks at the keen, intent faces around, as if the youngsters have gathered to see the last few overs of a thrilling cricket match, holding their breath, eyes glued to the television. Even without his uniform, the army officer looks distinguished, his air of self-importance pronounced. His imposing ways, obsessive sense of purpose.

'This is the Gypsy that you four will be riding that morning. It looks exactly like the vehicles the Central Reserve Police officials use – neither brand new nor too old.'

Jamal sees it zoom across the screen – truly the kind of Land Rover policemen drive around. This one is painted olive, the colour of the Indian Army and paramilitary forces.

'We have fitted it with a flasher on top to fool the security men at the entrance.' The Gypsy returns and stands still at the centre of the screen. The cursor pinpoints the red dome perched atop the sturdy jeep. 'The idiots might even salute you, taking you for their seniors, those uncircumcised behnchods.' His laughter drips acid. The stern, unrelenting look has fallen away. Jamal looks at his open mouth. At any moment, sparks can fly out of the dark pit.

'Of the four, one will be behind the wheel. The man in the front seat must have the look of a senior official. He in the uniform of a high-ranking commander, complete with the badges and stars.' Major Qureshi laughs self-indulgently, in appreciation of his knowledge of the Indian security forces.

Jamal watches him keenly – a phantom, laughing, cracking jokes without emotion. Not human.

'Oh, yes, the high-ranking official must wear expensive dark glasses. To impress, to hide.' He puts each one of them in a sharp frame, under severe scrutiny. His gaze pinches, sears. Drills holes. 'The other two in the rear.' 'The question is who will be the senior official in the front?'

'Who?' His voice rings out. He is dismissive, disparaging – surveying his four wards with contempt.

'In Pakistan, none of you would qualify even for a sepoy's job.' His face sinks in a dark frown. 'Jihad is a noble mission; it requires pinpoint accuracy, acrobatic bodies.' He sharpens his gaze. 'Chalo, for that Sunday morning, let our Bangla Bhai be the DIG of the fucking Central Reserve Police Force. Deputy inspector general! Kya baat hai! He has the height to justify his rank. Wow!'

Major Qureshi's flinty gaze rests on Jamal, one second, two, three… 'Congratulations, fish-fighter!' He roars, stretching a hand towards Jamal. 'Do bugger them well, son.'

The sudden recognition does not excite him. Means nothing. The attention, the army officer's dark humour, his contempt for Bangladesh – he finds it disconcerting. Still, he shakes hands with him.

'That morning, you're a quick, slippery eel, not a sloth lobster.' As usual, the military man is the first to admire his own humour.

'This is the highway – NH 24.' The cursor hovers over a wide, smooth dual carriageway. The army officer fiercely surveys every minute object on the screen. Like a falcon eying a wobbly chick from the sky. He turns to Jamal. 'You stop after crossing the Yamuna bridge. You're not in a hurry, no tension, look relaxed, easy. You have a fake walkie-talkie. You are talking into it, waiting for the order. When the minister gets close, your mobile phone will ring: *The pigeon on the rooftop* – Noorjahan singing.'

'Noorjahan?' One of the three boys – still very rustic, unused to city ways.

'Any female, son.' The major is irritated by the slow fool. 'Any fat whore who puts on lots of lipstick and make-up and sings those lilting Bombaiya talkie songs.' He looks sharply at the dimwit. 'It will be your ringtone – "*Kabutar-r-rr chhat par baithee hai… hai… haye Rama…*"' The major mimics a typical female singer from the sixties. 'Bombaiya tamasha – fun, frolic and films – that's Bombaai. And of course its famous Fuckland –

Kamathipura, eh? I spent a night or two there – with the evening begums… not bad. Not bad at all.'

He meets the stern gaze of the martinet maulvi. The fiery old man of the fedayeen sermon strokes his flowing white beard in disapproval. Major Qureshi's bawdy mood dissipates. He immediately looks apologetic about his reprobate evenings in Bombay's red-light district. He clears his throat, regains the no-nonsense tone.

'If you see the minister's motorcade coming from Delhi, follow it at a distance – say one kilometre. Look serious, businesslike, no panic. Most probably, the guards at the entry point will let you in. If they suspect something, stop you, then ram the car in, fire indiscriminately and throw grenades. Remember, the minister is your target.'

Major Qureshi lights a Dunhill, inhales deeply, licking his lips in satisfaction. Little clouds of smoke float around before merging into the overwhelming darkness.

'If things happen smoothly, walk towards the stage, shoot the minister first. It's easy to spot him, the Indian minister, corrupt cockroach… always in white dhoti kurta or kurta pyjama so he can scratch his aloos often.' He clicks open a folder, the familiar figure pops out: bald but for a thin hint of grey at the back. The no-nonsense tough man they see all the time on television. 'If you get him, the picture in tomorrow's papers will tell the truth – the big fucker died scratching his aloos, ha ha ha ha…' Qureshi wipes the saliva from the corner of his mouth. 'Hmmm. After him, the junior minister. Then the top officials in the front row – as many of them as possible. The veggie Hindus are bad fighters – shoot them in the chest; you can send one or two bullets into their assholes as well, ha! Don't get unnerved by the noise of the screaming siren. Keep your cool and shoot. Avenge the Muslim blood in Kashmir, in Gujarat.'

25
Shiva's Consort

Arijit's eyes linger on the computer screen for a while: the last chapter of his book is neatly arranged in even paragraphs. Hearing about it, publishers have started contacting him. Someone from a big publishing firm called him the other day, offering to bring out the book simultaneously in America, Britain and India. 'Please let us know if you need any editorial assistance,' the woman on the other end said. 'One of our editors can help you with the book.' He politely said no.

At the moment, he is preoccupied with what should go into the book's conclusion. A common energy pool to integrate South Asia as a region of hope? A policy to harness all resources for the revival of one of the poorest parts of the world? Arijit drums his fingers on the keyboard.

Interrupting his thoughts, the doorbell rings. Must be the milkman. The boy leaves a milk packet outside his door, and after pressing the bell, rushes down the corridor. Arijit hears the bell, the hurried footsteps, his full-throated shouts: *Dudh… doooodhhhh…* But has rarely met the boy.

Arijit opens the door reluctantly; he was in the right mood to write the conclusion.

'Sorry, I hope I haven't disturbed you.' She stands there – smiling, apologizing. Very familiar and yet…

It takes Arijit a few seconds to recognize the neighbour he often meets on the way back from his morning walk. The young woman in a trendy tee, sweatpants or gym shorts, hair wrapped in a bandana or simply tied back in a ponytail, the smell of sweat and sleep about her, waiting for the lift. Yes, Neha. Neha Arora – outside his door – in a new avatar.

She laughs, amused by his puzzlement.

In a flaming orange sari, a dab of deep, fiery sindoor across her forehead, she is a burning spire. The blood-red vermillion trail glares from the parting of her hair. Gold earrings dangle. The locket shines imperiously over her chest. Around it is another chain – the black-and-gold mangalsutra, the mark of a married woman. Gold bangles sparkle on her wrists. Neha holds a large, round copper tray – covered with a red napkin.

'You thought it's someone else?' She grins.

'What a surprise!' Arijit surveys her, the flames of her transformation. 'Honestly, it took me a while…'

'I've been to the temple. To pour milk on the Shiva linga. Today is Maha Shiva Ratri.'

She has been affected by the heavy incense in the air, incantation of Sanskrit hymns, the ritual bathing of the dark, granite phallus with milk by a crowd of devotees. That's how they pray for regeneration, male prowess. For fertility – of the womb and earth.

'Please come in.'

Neha hesitates, then steps in. 'I have got some prasad for you.' She places a plate of consecrated milk sweets, flowers and leaves on the dining table.

'Please have a seat. Let me give you something – some orange juice?'

'No, thank you. I am fasting. I will do puja at home before I break my fast.' She peeps into the kitchen. 'The girl who works in the kitchen… isn't she here?'

'Uh-uh, she won't be here before ten.'

'Ah, my maid says she is a genius, makes fabulous dishes?'

'I am very particular about my food; past the age when I could relish the spicy, oily stuff.'

Neha's mood changes from frivolous to thoughtful. 'Wish we could do something for you, sir. You're our hero.' She walks up to him, draws a tika on his forehead with vermillion, then leaves.

From the door, Arijit sees her walk down the corridor towards the lift, leaving a trail of incense and devoutness in the air. He walks onto the balcony, knowing he won't be able to write now. He has lost his train of thought. A young woman in a sparkling orange sari, blaze of vermilion on her forehead, back after making an oblation to a mythical phallus, looms over him.

Unsettled, Arijit stands at his favourite corner of the balcony, leaning on the railing. His eyes touch the distant farm. For him, the green acres have become a source of life, his anchor in this boomtown. A parallel life he has entered. He is a familiar figure on the farm now. Every morning, the rough-hewn farmers, their sunburnt wives and noisy children crowd around him. They take him into another world. That scene of busy farming is part of Noahda and still is not.

By now, he knows the names of some of the children – Mahipal, Chhotelal, Jagdish, Hari, Akhilesh… The farmers' wives take him for a holy man from some faraway place. A kind of faith healer. The moment he appears on the farm, they all unhesitatingly come forward, circle around him, some with their children in their arms. Without the ochre robes, beads, a tilak on the forehead – still a hoary Baba on the scene.

The day comes back with all its emotions and surprises.

'Baba, this son of mine had a fever last year.' Lakshmi shows him the boy's skinny, twisted leg. 'He walks with a limp, one leg weaker than the other.' Holding the child, the strong, crusty woman suddenly bursts into sobs. Tears clammy her face, melting away the last traces of her sturdiness. 'A farmer's son, Baba, he has a tough life ahead; he has to deal with the earth to get a good crop. If he limps, how will he work on the field?' Lakshmi begins wailing, clutching the boy to her. The other women empathize with her.

Arijit knows the child had a polio attack. He sits down with him on the ground and lifts his weak foot.

'I took him to our village doctor; he jabbed him six times. We spent a lot, but nothing happened; he still limps. When Raju was born, I gave out mithai for two days – a healthy, lively child – a boy. It was a great day in my life…'

She strikes her forehead.

Arijit claps, clicks his fingers, makes dog sounds to amuse the boy. The dark, bright-eyed boy stares at him. After some hesitation, he starts giggling. Arijit cajoles him to stretch his legs. He places his hand just before the toes of the boy's affected foot. 'Push it, Raju, push my hand away. Jor lagao – aur jor… Yes – try, try hard. Yesss – push it harder… shabaash!'

The farmer's boy, smell of earth all around him, warmth of hay and husk in his subconscious, shoves Arijit's hand two inches away, fighting his resistance, overcoming his polio-induced weakness.

Arijit smiles. 'Shabaash!' He gives the boy a mango candy. He pops it, grinning. His mother's face beams.

'His weak leg can be strong again. For that, he needs a lot of exercise. I will take him to a hospital one of these days. But don't, *don't* take him to your village doctor, and please, *no more jabs*. They can harm him.' Getting up, Arijit runs a hand through the boy's hair and mimics a tiger's roar. Both of them laugh. He remembers the first time he saw him – limping his way to the bullock cart with a clump of spring onions clutched to his chest.

Even before he knows it, Lakshmi falls at his feet, hitting her head on his toes again and again.

'Baba, save my son. The day you first came, I knew you were not an ordinary man; I knew Raju was going to be all right again.'

The other women back her. 'Baba, now that you're with us, our problems are over,' they say in a chorus, commiserating with Lakshmi. Her husband has by then rushed from the field. Flummoxed by the noise, he also touches Arijit's feet. 'Baba, make the boy walk like all the other boys. We're poor people. With a leg like that, our Raju has no chance; a loser, he won't be able to even pedal a rickshaw.'

The crowd of men, women and children follows him across the dirt up to the asphalt. Raju's father gives him a bunch of bitter gourds, picked straight from the field.

Arijit comes back from the balcony. The bell rings again – actually, it raises a storm. The river girl who cannot wait. He opens the door before returning to the study. The computer has gone into sleep mode. Automatically shut down. No, he cannot write any more. The conclusion will have to wait for another day. He picks up the day's *Times of India*. Spreading the paper on his desk, he turns the pages. Going through the news columns, he sees the ad – full page. A new residential development by Delhi's best-known builders.

Own an independent villa with lawns and a swimming pool
Booking amount only 2%
Hurry! Limited Offer!

Arijit sees the address. It is close to his place, in the same sector of Noahda. At the centre of the page is the artist's impression of the villa: a two-storey house built in the mock-colonial style with patches of garden around and a pool to beat the summer heat – the ultimate luxury in suburban life. He smiles.

He turns on the computer again. Closes the book file and opens the inbox to check his mail. At the bottom of a long line of propaganda emails, it waits unobtrusively: a letter with an attachment.

Bubka's happiness and excitement at getting a new football on his fifth birthday burst onto the computer screen. In the months since he last saw him, the soccer-crazy boy has grown bigger.

The next one is about the ritual bathing of the boy on a stool under a dogwood tree. Piu pours water over two gold and silver ornaments above her son's head. For the boy's smooth, prosperous journey through life. As a child, he, too, was bathed the same way by his mother under a mango tree in the backyard of their Calcutta house. How did Piu learn about the family tradition? She has hardly lived in Calcutta. Perhaps from Niru-di. Maybe there's a website talking about all this with accompanying videos.

Rita comes with his coffee. The smell of it fills the study. Holding the tray, she stands behind him, looking at the birthday pictures.

'Your grandson, Kaku?'

'Yes. Last week was his birthday.'

'He looks like you.'

Arijit is stunned. It has never occurred to him that Bubka bears a close resemblance to him. Seeing the photographs now, it suddenly strikes him that, as a little boy, he looked exactly like Bubka.

After finishing her work in the kitchen, Rita sits in a corner of the living room. Perhaps there is nothing more to dust this morning. The kitchen racks, cabinets, fridge, furniture in the living room – everything is spanking clean. She takes out of a plastic bag a few pieces of cloth – actually an old sari folded in the middle and the sides of cotton mosquito nets sandwiched within. Rolls of colourful threads and stitching needles have tumbled out of a little chocolate box. Arijit guesses that the wrap, when stitched and hemmed, will be the size of a small blanket. As of now, the odd ends of the mosquito nets are jutting out of the sari fold.

Threading the needle, she expertly sews through the cloth. After a while, she holds out the cloth to see if a design is coming out. From his desk, Arijit notices birds, fish, flowers on the canvas of the old sari.

'Where did you learn this kind of stitching?' Curious, he walks up to her.

'Kaku, no one has to learn this. In our village, every girl knows how to stitch a nakshi kantha. My mother did one for Radolf Sahib. In early winter, it's so cosy.'

He scrutinizes the red-and-blue flowers, neatly raised with coloured threads. Her needle speaks.

'What about the flat you were going to rent?'

'I have given the landlord two thousand rupees as an advance. I will move in next week.'

'That's better. Leave the shanty as soon as possible. It's not safe; anything can happen to you. Why don't you move into the flat tomorrow?'

'The man is getting some repairs done. It will take a few more days.'

'Why don't you tell them to do the repairs when you come to work? In the evening, you can go home to the flat. After all, you have a door to close; it is proper accommodation. Give me the man's number, and I'll speak to him.'

26
Saddamabad

The penthouse in the tower opposite Arijit's has a different look this morning. The good vibes of that Sunday afternoon are missing. The sprightly woman who danced with the children and kept time with the music is not home. Nor are her children. She has taken them on an outing. The relaxed, gala mood has given way to a grim, hush-hush air. Back from the gym, Abhay Singh showered. Now he is busily moving about the house to see that the arrangements are perfect. For the first time, some big people are coming home, and he's keen to make an impression. In a Levi's red tee and khaki pants, he takes a close look at the living space – fresh flowers in two cut-glass vases, copies of Jean-Louis Paire's *Why Hinduism Answers All My Questions* and Christian Rogers' *Hindu Temples: Victims of Mughal Vandalism* stacked up on a centre table. He'll gift them to his important guests.

On one wall is a painting of Lord Hanuman, enormously strong, fiercely ruthless in destroying the demons and also the very epitome of kindness, a symbol of unflinching loyalty. The artist has used an earthy red to bring to life the mighty monkey god. Every inch a hardcore member of the new-age faith brigade if you ignore the lustrous brush. Under the soft yellow light from above, Hanuman glows.

On another wall is a large portrait of Sadhu Bhanu Pratap Maharaj. With the knowledge acquired through long years of meditation in the upper ridges of the Himalayas, the maharaj is now back to 'rescue' the Hindus, who are fast turning into a minority in their own land. Badly beaten, beleaguered, the sloppy fellows are learning to fight back under Sadhu-ji. A few *disputed structures* were recently renovated into beautiful temples. *Traitors* have been given a clear choice: either pack up and go to the other side of the border or be *loyal* to their country, learn to cheer for India in a one-day cricket match with Natsikap. Do not celebrate the *enemy*'s victory with firecrackers. Always in simple ochre clothes with a benign smile, the maharaj now rules the core of this ancient land. His supporters – their numbers growing by the thousands every day – believe he will rule all over the land very soon. And that will be the real merger of the gods' domain with the king's jurisdiction.

Abhay hurriedly places a low table below the portrait and puts a flower vase on it. Standing before the renunciant ruler within the lavish frame, he pulls out a kerchief from his pocket and wipes the already clean portrait. Holds the perfumed hanky before his eyes to see if it has caught a little dust. Nothing, not a speck. He nods, feeling happy. His restaurant chain, Nawab of Avadh, is growing fast. After Goa and Ooty, he is going to set foot in Dubai and Sharjah, taking the total number of outlets to twenty-two. He is dreaming big – a five-star hotel in the Holy City, an obvious go-to once the magnificent temple of the Lord comes up there. His should be the first starred hotel at the Birthplace – if Sadhu-ji puts his hand on his head. Even a good kick up the arse would be lovely! He – an entirely self-made man. Abhay adoringly looks at his Patek Philippe with its dark-bluish crocodile leather band.

He moves his wrist a little to admire his latest acquisition. Time for the guests to arrive. He worries. *Let me take a quick look at the meeting room upstairs.*

About to run up the stairs, he stops and turns back. 'Has the food come from the restaurant?' he asks the liveried waiter working in the kitchen.

'Ji, sir.'

'Dessert?'

'Ice cream, gulab jamun, gajar ka halwa.'

'You remember the steps? Coffee with cookies when we first sit here.' He points to the sofa sets in the living space. 'When the meeting starts upstairs, serve beer with roasted cashews. As soon as we come down for lunch, start serving wine and whisky. Black Label today. Whatever they ask for… Paneer pakora and French fries with tartar sauce. And don't forget the gifts. The shawls, gift-wrapped, are on a tray in my office. When they are leaving, you hold the tray and I offer them… Remember, if there's any phone call – I am not home. *Okay*?' Tense, he wants to make sure nothing goes wrong.

As if he has suddenly remembered something, Abhay moves to the entrance. Seeing him, the security guard sitting on a stool outside the steel gate stands up in awe. 'Guests will be coming any moment now. First salute them, then namaste and show them in with courtesy. And *do not* allow anybody else, neither the neighbours nor Memsahib's friends. No mechanics, plumbers, metre-reading fuckers. *No nothing*!' The man, in his fake military uniform and with a horseshoe moustache, panics as Abhay suddenly raises his voice.

Everything is in perfect order upstairs. Cushioned armchairs are arranged around a long, oval table. A glorious image of the yet-to-be-built temple in the Holy City, as imagined by a devout artist, dominates the room. A comforting smell of jasmine soothes him.

The honour of chairing the meeting undoubtedly goes to Ajay Dikshit, who retired as deputy commissioner of police a few years ago. While posted in Kanpur, he earned a name as a no-nonsense, tough cop after a ruthless crackdown on the meat-eating hotheads in the distressed colonies of tannery workers. As host, Abhay sits next to him. Among the others are Hari Om Saksena, a district court lawyer, and Sharad Tiwari, chief reporter of the *Satyajeet* newspaper. The stocky man sitting somewhat obsequiously at the other end is Bhola Yadav. After greetings and polite weather-cricket talk, Dikshit turns to the journalist. 'Sharad is an excellent newsman; I've known him for a long time. His coverage of the Meerut riots was superb, completely unbiased, unlike the trash the English newspapers wrote.' The reporter namastes him, joining his hands with a mild bow. The cop raises his hand in acknowledgement. Others take note of the brief exchange. 'Let's hear from him first. Sharad…'

The reporter takes a quick look at the papers in a stick file on his lap. He clears his throat before starting. 'The unauthorized colony that sprawls on either side of the canal has grown rapidly over the past two-three years. In the beginning, all migrants lived together – Hindus and Muslims. There were only thirty-five Muslim families; being a fast-breeding lot, their numbers rose to about two hundred and fifty in a couple of years. Now they have completely monopolized the other side of the canal, encroaching on the land that actually belongs to the irrigation department of the UP government. My team has carefully gone through the voter list for the last elections in UP. There are exactly 2,456 voters registered there. The local legislator, a staunch supporter of the Wrestler, gives them protection. In a close contest, these votes – about two thousand five hundred – could be a decider.'

'This is dangerous – a mini-Pakistan in the making.' Saksena gets worked up. 'Their own township within this city. How could this happen?'

Sharad nods with a sardonic smile. 'Though officially the slum is still known as Rajiv Camp, they've started calling their part of the colony Saddamabad…'

'From Saddam Hussein!!' Dikshit explodes.

Unswayed, the reporter keeps his cool. 'I sent a reporter to the slum to collect more data on the pretext of doing a story about literacy. His findings are startling: the most preferred boy names are Saddam and Imran, and there are quite a few Gaddafis and Musharrafs as well. One or two simpletons called their sons Osama; sensing trouble, the elders told them to change it. There's not a single Azad or Kalam, not even an Azharuddin. The most popular girl name is Benazir. An average family has six children…'

'The circumcised bastards are raising a brand-new mosque, all marble and Italian tiles with Gulf money!' Feeling overborne by the biggies, he has been so far sitting uncomfortably. The sudden outburst gives Bhola Yadav a new confidence. He earns his place at the table. Though he lacks the reporter's refinement, he, too, keeps a close watch on the situation – he is the head of the area's Monkey Brigade. 'Strange-looking people are often seen there – Arabs, Turks, Chechens, black people from Africa; they wear bizarre clothes, no one can follow their foreign tongue.'

'All this has been going on, and we didn't know anything?' Abhay raises his eyebrows. The heat of the angry words has defied the cool hush of air conditioning. He turns to the others, half raising his hand. 'Another round of beer?' Abhay presses his cordless bell to call the waiter from downstairs.

'Nobody should be within earshot of what we will be discussing,' the policeman had told him on the phone. 'Not even a single word. Servants are chatterboxes.' Abhay kept that in mind and told his wife to take their two kids to the mall, do some shopping, have lunch at a KFC and see the Harry Potter movie at the multiplex. The waiter was sternly told not to come up the stairs *under any circumstances* unless he himself called him. '*Don't let anyone else come upstairs*,' he'd warned, darkening his voice.

'We must strike before it gets out of hand.' Dikshit sips his beer. 'This enclave of Bangladeshis, Pakistanis, Afghans, Turks and Nigerians is a hub of gunrunning, drugs, flesh trade and snooping. A haven for terrorists, spooks and agents. An ISI hotspot flush with boodle. Let's burn down this beehive.' The cop turns to the lawyer.

'As a first step, let complaints be lodged with the police about a few Hindu girls molested in that colony, about inflammatory CDs, booklets extolling jihad being unearthed from the dugouts of subversion,' Saksena says thoughtfully. 'A few reports can appear in the media about such incidents. We need not make a splash right now but… well… things you can reference later.' The lawyer smiles knowingly. Turning to the policeman, he says hesitantly, 'For the first time, we have a friendly judiciary, we need to act – soonest.' Dikshit nods in agreement, looking amused.

Sharad raises his head from the papers, his serious look unflappable. 'We need to make sure television cameras do not get there until it's all over. We have a group of like-minded patrakars on the major papers. The best thing is to make sure the media does not get to know about it until the next morning. And our people should be around to brief the reporters whenever they come. We need to position women with children in their arms, sobbing and talking about homes burnt, boys missing, a daughter assaulted.'

'Correct.' Dikshit applauds the reporter. 'Handling the media is very important. Good thing the TV channels are with us now.'

'I'll set up a crack team and start training from tomorrow itself.' Bhola Yadav sets out to explain his role in the bonfire. His importance as the area's vigilante boss is derived from the ravages wrought by his gang. 'Our real problem is a pack of liberal motherfuckers… er…' Noticing Saksena's disapproving frown, Bhola Yadav regrets his lack of restraint. 'There are a few university professors in the area who abuse us all the time. Activist arseholes. They appear on television often. Then this tall man who lives in the opposite block.' Bhola Yadav gestures with his chin towards Arijit's tower. 'He has hired a Bangladeshi maid; he behaves absurdly.'

Dikshit turns to Abhay. 'He's a big man. You've got to be very careful when handling such people.' Abhay looks serious, his voice cautious. 'If something happens to him, that will be news in the London papers. We will bring social pressure on him, make sure he leaves this place. Most probably, he will go away after some time.'

'Thik hai.' Bhola nods apologetically. 'Now what about the expenses?'

'You don't worry; I'll take care of all that.' Abhay's voice is reassuring. 'If I have Sadhu-ji's blessings, I am willing to make such sacrifices.' He looks at the others, hoping to evoke a little empathy.

'Sadhu Maharaj is going to campaign in Bihar for the Assembly elections this Saturday.' The hint of pride in Sharad's voice does not go unnoticed. 'I will be flying with him; nobody else on the plane but his personal secretary. He has promised me an exclusive interview. If you agree, I'll talk to him about the situation here and the response it calls for.'

'Of course. Definitely.' Dikshit beams. 'He needs to know.' Then he turns to Bhola. 'You come to my farm tomorrow evening. Together, we will go to recce Saddamabad.'

Abhay bows to the policeman in admiration. Alert, thinking ahead, the old cop did not ask the rowdy to come to his plush house in Sector 15A, Noahda's most exclusive enclave, but the forlorn farm beyond the city limits. He warms up to Bhola. 'You go ahead with your preparations. Don't worry about anything – food, booze, money, I'll take care of all that.'

The meeting over, Dikshit administers the oath of secrecy to them, invoking Bharat Mata. They swear on the Motherland that they will maintain maximum secrecy about the deliberations. That not a single word from this meeting will go out to the world. Suddenly seized with emotion, Dikshit says in a solemn, tremulous voice, 'We take the vow not to allow India to be raped by the impure again, partitioned a second time.' They follow him in a chorus.

27
Rendezvous

Rabeya waits at the point where Noahda's main street merges into the highway. She did not want to be seen with Jamal anywhere near Blue Lotus Grove. It's difficult to completely wipe him out of her life and also impossible to let him in. Someone stuck in the past, he lives in some corner of his own, uncomfortable with life itself. He rails against everything, everybody, but has not found a way out of his own predicament. Being with him is uneasiness. She took Ameena's advice and told him not to think of marriage, the two of them being together, living as man and wife. Surprised, shocked, unable to accept rejection, he walked away.

But something has snapped inside him. When they all gathered at Ameena's place for Eid, he behaved like he was another man. The end-of-the-world air around him felt heavy.

Is he setting out to discover a desolate island? Like the lonely young man in that movie? Is the crazy fellow leaving for a forlorn country from where no one returns? Is that place across the seas? She shakes her head.

Standing under a giant billboard at the elevation of the street onto the highway, she looks at her watch. It's uncomfortable – being alone at such an odd place, neither a market nor a bus stop. Passing motorists honk suggestively, autorickshaw drivers stare. Irritated, she regrets having said yes to this outing. *I should not have agreed, could have easily given some excuse.* Rabeya bites her lip. He pleaded, though.

'Perhaps we will not meet again in this life,' he said. She was troubled by that touch of finality in his voice, the way he had looked at her, everything about him. It was not sadness but the sense of an ending. He had waited for her on the old brick bridge, leaning against the decayed railing. 'We will not be together again.' Their eyes met, she struggled, unwilling to relent. He kept pleading until she finally gave in.

The interminable wait gets on her nerves. She is no longer a migrant worker cooking in people's homes for a living. Within a week, she is moving into the flat Ameena is vacating. And when the two elderly people begin living together, she will be a part of their life. Will Kaku and Didi have a proper wedding? Rites, rituals, exchange of thick tuberose garlands, celebrations… Or will they one day simply come under the same roof, slip into bed, wake up the next morning – amused, embarrassed? She pictures that scene. Can make out the two old lovers have suffered a lot. Many years ago, they knew each other, loved each other. Then strayed away. Now, troubled by loneliness, remorse, they want to stop living like islands. They will be together: Mr and Mrs – what? She does not know. But they will be living under her care, she their child, she who will look after them – no longer an undocumented migrant but very much part of a household. Then one day, she will marry a good man.

Rabeya laughs to herself. The American's voice still rings in her ears. His disarming smile, the honest, intent look on his face linger. She did not understand a single word of what he said except that he wanted to know about the right sauce for kebab. But she somehow knew he liked her, fell for her. 'You charmed that American doctor, Rita,' Nandita later said. 'He's interested in you.'

But… so is Bharat. Bharat Singh Bisht. What a name! Not Bengali, not like Nayan, Munir, Khokan, Debashish, Bablu. And Jamal? Sure, not like Jamal either. She suppresses a laugh.

Startled by a rough, screeching sound, she looks over her shoulder. Jamal pulls up, his blazing red Honda motorcycle still roaring like a wild beast. In a striped maroon shirt, dark blue trousers, hair neatly brushed back – bright young thing, not the lost soul living in another time, wallowing in the old Dhaka movies and their popular numbers.

'Sorry I am late.' The bike halts, grazing past her. A test of his riding skills? Or his new daring? Rabeya is clueless. 'I tried calling you. To say I would be late. The bloody builder's man held me up, pressing me for a new deadline for the order.' He smiles, gesturing for her to ride on the back.

Sitting behind him, Rabeya pulls out her Nokia handset from the purse. Yes, a missed call she did not notice. She holds his shoulder for support. The bike is comfortable for riding two-up. Her hair blowing in the strong wind, she covers her head with the long dupatta of her kurta churidar.

'Tell me, Rabee, is life all about deadlines? Does the Rupsa have a deadline for high tides, for the floods to whip the banks? Deadline for the river ha ha…'

The bike hums along the road. She tightens her grip on his shoulder. A mild fragrance of aftershave taps her nose. The man is changing – perhaps in preparation for his journey to another country.

'Where are we off to?'

'How long have you lived in this country? Two years?' He turns to look at her at a traffic light, raising his helmet slightly. 'Have you seen their Parliament, President's palace, Prime Minister's Office, their big hotels? No. Today, I will show you everything. The Red Fort, Jama Masjid, Connaught Place. Everything.'

The boatman of the Rupsa whizzes down National Highway 24 on his scorching bike. *Let him do well in the new land.* Rabeya breathes out a prayer. Does the slow, sentimental man have ambition? Some purpose in life?

He is confidently overtaking cars, dodging past other bikes, roaring ahead like a fierce footballer – doesn't all this signal a decisive new turn in his life?

'That's the Supreme Court, the highest court in this country.' He points to a domed structure with a sprawling lawn in front. Black-robed men and women move around busily. 'They try the innocent here, and the rich crooks party.' The angry Jamal once again.

Waiting at red lights, surging ahead at the green, changing lanes, taking turns, he keeps up the commentary. 'The ministers live in these nice white bungalows with lawns all around.' He nods towards the colonial structures. Rabeya wonders when he got to know the city so well.

'That's the Méridien.' He raises his chin at a tall tower at a five-point intersection. 'Delhi's rotten rich come to this hotel to eat, drink and dance.' He slows down, then pulls up, putting his foot on the kerb. 'Well, I can also take you inside the hotel and order dishes.'

'Inside that hotel? Arey baba, nah! I will be scared to death. Among those fashionable memsahibs, this darky, smelly hag!' She laughs.

'You're more beautiful than any of those fat women.' His voice is strangely calm, with no trace of his usual rancour. 'Your large eyes – they say more than all their words, Rabee.' He turns to face her, his voice moist. They are close, upfront, two pairs of eyes meeting, measuring each other. The words she knows evoke another life, a surge from the past. 'And your long hair – the colour of the Rupsa's dark water.' He stops, breathes in its scent deeply.

He kick-starts the bike. After about a kilometre, he points to a grand, circular structure. Rabeya has not seen anything like that before – so imposing, so extraordinary. 'That's the Parliament.' Jamal gestures towards the domed Corinthian edifice supported by round, regular pillars. 'That's where they meet – their corrupt ministers and thuggish leaders – to find ways to oppress the poor. One only needs a couple of bombs to blow up the factory of repression.'

Rabeya frowns. The pleasant feeling of a minute ago is gone. Such words frighten her. Is he the same man who rowed her, crooning love songs? Is he bitter now that he is going away, leaving her behind? Violence, revenge, bloodletting – never before has he talked in such brutal terms. Slow songs of love have given way to an acrid hate.

Evil has entered your soul, boatman of the Rupsa.

'What are you saying?' she says without hiding her disgust. 'Worms are nesting inside you, man.' She takes her hand off his shoulder. 'Can't you speak normally any more?'

'You're right. Something has gone wrong with me.' He thinks for a while. 'I should not have said all that. Sorry.' They go along Parliament Street. 'Let me buy you something from Connaught Place.' As though he were ashamed, he is keen to make amends.

'When did you get to know the city so well? You have never been out of the shantytown. That grille factory – that's the only place you knew.'

'Rabee, I am a little more than what you take me for.'

'Have you got a big job somewhere?' she probes.

'Where I am going is a beautiful place. You do not have the fear of losing out, being outsmarted.'

'You sound strange, an entirely different man, someone I have never known.'

He laughs.

'This is Connaught Place. People come here to have a good time. Unless you have been here, they say, you have not seen Delhi.' He laughs boyishly, his dark mood gone.

They walk side by side, looking in the shop windows from one end of an arcade to another. He has already slipped on a pair of sunglasses. The glasses – the colour of dark red pomegranates – give him an unfamiliar look, no longer the serenading lover, sighing for her.

Uniformed security guards stand at the doors. A smooth, sweet smell of affluence hangs around. Rabeya does not know when they have clasped hands, their sides touching. He walks casually, trying to stretch every moment as far as possible.

He pulls her by the hand. 'Let me buy you a camera. When you go with that lady here and there, you can take pictures of mountains, lakes, monuments.'

Even before she knows it, Rabeya is swept past the scrutiny of the guard and into the shop. It's another world – a cool hush with air conditioning, accented by a mint smell, men and women doing business in soft white light.

A bald, elderly man smiles from behind a low showcase – his eyes telling them they are welcome.

'We are going on a holiday. Need a camera.' Jamal lightly holds Rabeya.

The man smiles benignly. 'Of course you need a good camera to catch the big moments. I will give you the right one.'

He goes back, opens a large cupboard and pulls out a few cardboard boxes.

'These are all Japanese cameras – very easy to use but tough.' He shows them the features of every camera and explains how they work. Jamal fiddles with the cameras before choosing one. He hands it to her – a Nikon. By now, Rabeya has overcome her uneasiness. She looks through the viewfinder. The bald man seems so strange, like a creature from another planet. Then Jamal comes into view. Amused, he smiles.

'It's a fixed-price shop; no bargain allowed. But I will give you a little discount.' The man writes the bill and points to the cash counter.

The Nikon in hand, Jamal is in a jovial mood. Coming out of the shop, he buys soft drinks from a kiosk and takes the first picture – Rabeya leaning against a cast-iron pillar on the promenade, holding a Coke.

A tourist couple stops to look at their guidebook. They readily agree when Jamal asks them to take a shot. He runs back to Rabeya and poses for the picture, gently holding her. The white woman in a long skirt clicks twice from different angles. She laughs, handing back the camera.

Back on the motorcycle, Jamal negotiates the turns expertly. He whistles: *We first met in April…*

'This is better. I was really scared when you talked of bombs and all that.'

'Rabee, if you are by my side, perhaps I can still pull it off. We get lost, run off to such a place where no one knows us, they don't have any idea who we really are.'

He slows down, veers off the main road into a shaded lane between rows of bungalows for senior government officials. The neem and jamun trees on either side arch overhead. It is all quiet but for a pack of quarrelling maids who have gathered in the driveway of a bungalow after the morning chores.

Jamal puts the bike on the centre stand under a tree and faces Rabeya, his elbows on the seat and chin resting on his hand.

'Perhaps we can still make it. We go to another city – Bombay, Hyderabad, Bangalore. I drive a taxi. I – Pradeep Kumar, and you – and you Rani. We live quietly in a little corner of ours. I wear a cricketer's cap and grow a big moustache. No one will know even if they hunt for me.'

'Who are *they*?'

'That's a way of saying.'

'Saying what?'

'Starting a new life…'

'You were going to another country?'

'That's right, that's right. But – will I be happy there without you by my side? Together we can go to Nepal, return to Khulna and live our life quietly. If you say…'

A police escort car comes out of a bungalow, followed by a stodgy white Ambassador with a VIP flasher on top. A commando clutching his automatic weapon gives them a mean look – boy holding girl by arm under a tree.

'Behnchod!' The man in jungle fatigues hurls the obscenity before turning to the driver. 'The loafer has no other work in the world, eh?'

Jamal breaks into a cold sweat, waiting for the motorcade to pass, then kick-starts his bike. Rabeya sees his stricken face.

He does not speak until they reach the run-down, congested

Walled City. It is an altogether different world. Dilapidated ancient buildings, beggars swarming around, crowded narrow streets, a giant mosque overlooking a bustling bazaar, the odour of rot in the air – a picture of decay all around.

'Let's eat something.' Jamal seems to have got back his voice.

They walk down a narrow, busy street before entering an even narrower alley. The rich aroma of Mughlai food greets them.

'This is Karim's, the best place in Delhi for mutton dishes.' He is his usual self again.

Food comes – biryani and mutton korma. Rabeya has lost her appetite. She wants to go home. An uneasiness has crept into her.

'Let's go back.'

'Why? There's so much more to see. I'll now take you to the famous Red Fort.'

'I am not feeling well.'

They leave the place without finishing the food.

Walking down the street, he points out the grand mosque. 'That's the Jama Masjid. The Mughals built it hundreds of years ago. See, it still stands there majestically.'

They cross the road and walk across the plaza towards the Red Fort. 'From here, the Mughals ruled all over the country.'

'Let's go back. I have a splitting headache,' Rabeya pleads.

'Maybe it's the heat. Shall I buy you some medicine from the chemist's shop? Have a soda?'

'No, thanks. Please.'

Flying along Ring Road, an idea strikes him. He pulls up to the curb and makes a call from his phone.

'Chacha, adaab. Jamal this side.'

'Yes, beta. I was actually thinking of you. Good that you've called. Otherwise, I would not know what to do. My boss is very worried about the deadline. You have to finish the work by the end of this month. Or else, we will not be able to sell the flats.'

'Chacha, I am coming to your estate in an hour. A guest is with me. We will spend some time there. And please make arrangements for tea.'

'Sure, by all means. Welcome.'

Rabeya overhears most of it. He is determined to make an impression. That he is not a useless man, that he, too, knows people, has a little clout. She decides to let him have his way.

'I know a place – completely out of the world,' he says buoyantly. 'Beautiful apartments have come up by a lake, around deep woods. We can spend some time there before getting home?'

'Is that the place you are going to work?'

'Where I am going is far from that place. It'll be endless happiness over there.' He hums an old song, then turns to her – close, their faces almost touching. 'That lady really loves you, like a daughter, eh?'

'How do you know?'

'She has been to many places around the world. Next time she goes somewhere, you will be with her?'

Rabeya feels nervous. Has he probed, poked everything? He has never met Didi. 'Are you a burglar, eh? Steal your way into people's homes to listen in?'

'Ha ha ha ha… You can say that.' Jamal laughs, riding on.

When they reach the estate, Rabeya is awestruck. It is a magic land in the middle of wilderness. Off the highway, among lush farmlands, a developer has built dream homes for those weary of the city, its chaos and crowds.

At the gate, the caretaker welcomes them.

'Good, good,' the old man chuckles, looking slyly at Rabeya.

He pulls Jamal back by his hand. 'Have tea first. Then you can look around the place.'

They walk into the club to see there are no other guests. A liveried waiter comes and bows politely to Jamal, placing menus before them.

In a white long-sleeve shirt and black pants, his bow tie gives the man a distinctiveness that seems a little out of place here. Rabeya notices he is talking to Jamal respectfully. 'Residents will start moving in soon. We're planning a big bash for Diwali. Please come at that time.' The man's formal soft voice echoes in the empty dining hall.

After coffee with pakora and cocktail sandwiches, they come out of the club. 'You are our guests.' The waiter declined to bring the bill. Jamal left him a hundred-rupee tip.

Rabeya sees a couple of peacocks on a tree branch. They walk down the gravel towards the lake. On one side, there is a tennis court, the swimming pool a little distance away. On the other, a tiled canopy spreads out like a giant mushroom. Rabeya wonders if it's some kind of shelter from rain. 'People will do yoga under it as their guru looks on.' Jamal's arm snakes around her waist.

A cool breeze from the lake brings a hint of winter gone not so long ago. Rabeya feels better. The gate in the high wall is closed. A security guard surfaces from nowhere to open it.

They walk through the trees and reach the lake. A man is rowing a little boat at the far end. Empty concrete benches. Rich residents, home after many years overseas, will sit around the lake and meditate, reflecting on life's journey and nirvana. Yoga their way to peace, out of the illusion of Japanese lanterns and itsy-bitsy candles to the glow of moksha.

They walk past the benches and sit on the grass carpeted by dry leaves. Before them, the lake looms – like an enigma.

'It's like our Paankhali village, isn't it?' Rabeya smiles. She's happy being here.

'We will come here again. The oar in my hands, the boat will pull for the other bank. Then back again. Like the old days.' Jamal presses her to his chest; she does not resist. The next moment, he slips his fingers into her hair. She breathes deeply. His other hand moves inside her kurta, feeling the soft warmth of the tight breasts. Blood rushes to her face. Her hot breath scalding him, he kisses her like a hungry man devouring food after a long stretch of starvation.

There is a deep silence dissolving them.

'Rabee,' Jamal finally says, taking her hand in his. 'Don't you feel like going back to Paankhali?'

'Look!' She points to a big fish bobbing up. Then it goes down. Bubbles clutter the surface. They laugh.

It is almost dark. The herons around the lake make noises before flying away. The ducks clamour coming out of the water to nest. In the woods, mynahs and babblers are making a racket.

'This is a nice place.' Rabeya's face beams. Their eyes meet. 'We could have spent the whole day here.'

'We will come another…' His voice falters.

'This pond is not our Rupsa—'

'Nor the trees the Sundarbans.'

'Still, they are close to where we come from.'

'Let's go back then. Right now. Tonight.' He speaks urgently.

'Are you not going to another country?' she asks, confused.

Jamal keeps quiet.

28
Wrath of Hanuman

The doorbell keeps ringing – sharp, insistent. The interruption troubles Arijit. Salesmen often come, offering all sorts of things – slimming belts, encyclopaedias, movie tickets, news magazine subscriptions… An act of incursion, an infringement of his privacy.

He ignores the mad alarm for a minute, but when it doesn't stop, he lets out a sigh, cursing the intrusion, and angrily opens the door. A man is unhurriedly walking away – perhaps impatient with his delay. An envelope lies on the step to the front door. Is he from a courier company? Going away without getting the delivery receipt signed? Then he could've slipped it into the letterbox? But he left the stationery outside the door – perhaps an act of daring – to confront, intimidate him. Arijit looks in the direction of the retreating man – stocky, walking with a swagger, an air of insolence about him. Waiting for the lift, he looks back at Arijit's apartment to see if the missive has been noticed.

Arijit picks up the envelope and comes inside.

On top in longhand:

Om

Below the sacred mantra is a salutation to the warrior god:

Jai Shri Ram

This is the new fundamentalist war cry. The signs and symbols of Hindu chauvinism puzzle him. In recent years, some ultra-right outfits have launched a virulent campaign to organize the community on rabidly religious lines, challenging the country's liberal-secular culture. They have misappropriated the glyphs, gestures, sounds, sonority – actually the entire language of an ancient civilization. Om, for example. The first incantation of the Vedic people, it has been monopolized by the stormtroopers of ersatz Hinduism. Ram, the protagonist of the Ramayana, a Sanskrit epic, has been revered down the ages as a symbol of righteousness. Now, he is the blazing icon of militant Hindu revivalism.

Do they want to sign me up as a fully paid member of some Hindu brotherhood? He laughs to himself, opening the letter.

Dear Sir,
We have noticed with disgust how you pamper the Muslim woman who works in your house. Our ancient nation has faced repeated Muslim invasions in the past. Pseudo-secular leaders like Nehru allowed the Muslim traitors to stay back even after Partition. Now someone like you, a well-known, learned man, is feeding a snake. These loose women, who tart around town, are actually Pakistani agents.

You liberal behnchod, you are a traitor to our motherland. In the kingdom of Ram, you are an intruder like Ravana. Beware, Bengali motherfucker, cunt-licker of the impure, the mighty Hanuman is keeping watch! Don't you dare incur the wrath of Bajrangbali!

Three skull and crossbones symbols in a line below stare Arijit stark in the face.

The letter is unsigned, dark hate its only signature, the abominable lines claustrophobe. It starts in English, then trails off in Hindi. Perhaps the obscenities – vicious, acid-fire – could not be adequately expressed in a foreign language. Arijit feels giddy. A retching sensation seizes him. He didn't know he was under some kind of surveillance. Then, suddenly, anger sweeps through his body. An irresistible, reckless rage shakes him.

Who are these people? What right do they have to interfere with my life? An irrational anger, a desire to take on a shadowy antagonist seizes him, turning his mind into a muddle of incoherent thoughts.

Sir, you are our hero. Neha's words.

For a year, I did not know how day broke and evening descended. I crafted every word of the energy agreement. Liberal sister-fucker?

Without knowing why, Arijit calls his sister in Calcutta. It's urgent for him to talk to Nirupama.

'Niru-di, Buro here.'

'Are you coming to Calcutta, Buro? Do spend a few days with us. You know what? Someone from that music school called, asking for your address. This is their golden jubilee, they want to invite you. I remember you went there for some time to learn recitation of Tagore's poems. Sumita Sen, the history professor? I told you about her. She was also in that recitation class. Both of you would go together. Then you lost interest. You were a pukka Englishman. Did you learn jazz from that Anglo-Indian?' After saying so much in one go, Nirupama gasps for breath. Sapped by her many ailments, she is still excited to talk to her brother. 'Sumita teaches at Calcutta University. Biplab, her husband, died when their son was in school. That boy has settled down in London.'

'Niru-di, do you remember Dad had a servant – people called him Barrister Basu's shadow. What was his name?'

'Keramat Ali. Why suddenly – Keramat?'

'A man from Chittagong, he spoke in a strange tongue. We would laugh hearing his guttural noise. Ma said Keramat talked in ululation, huh?'

'Do you remember all that, Buro? Yes, everybody joked about Keramat. But Baba was very fond of him. He had come as a young boy. And always lived in our house. Never went home. Why do you remember him now?'

'Hmmm…'

'Without him, Barrister Basu could not move an inch. I forgot to tell you, Keramat died a few years ago.'

'Oh, I'm sorry. But tell me, did anybody ever – any of our neighbours, political parties, local clubs, any group – object to Keramat living with us?'

'Why should anybody bother? Keramat was part of our household and a favourite of the neighbours as well. He doubled as a herbal doctor, knew a little bit about herbs and roots. Many people came to him for back pain or a sprain. His massage and poultice worked for them.'

'That he was from another country, a Muslim – living in a Hindu home?'

'Baba gave him a hundred rupees and a day off for Eid. One hundred rupees those days was a lot of money, Buro. Ma gave him new clothes for Pujo. Keramat had no one back home. He was like one of us. He never grumbled, never gave us trouble; he did not want to go home.'

'Yes, of course, now I remember.'

'Buro, why don't you come down for the jubilee? Sumita will be there also. As a historian, she's well known.'

'Let me see.'

'I forgot to tell you, Buro, Parijat is now in Dehradun. Her husband was transferred there last month. Why don't you go to Dehradun and spend a few days with them? Tia will be very happy to see her uncle.'

'I cannot leave Delhi right now. Maybe after some time.'

29
Border Crossers

Seeing her on the landing, the man comes to the door. 'Aao, beti, aao.' He smiles. Rita sees a thin layer of cement on his greying hair, blobs of mortar on the sleeves of his kurta. 'Your sister called me in the morning. The flat is almost ready. You can move in the day after.'

The warmth of his greeting, calling her *daughter* – all very reassuring. She walks in. After a coat of paint and repairs, the flat now looks nice. The smell of paint, the sharp noise of the plumber's saw cutting the end of a pipe, the newness about the place gives her a sense of importance, of being welcome.

'I have called him to replace a leaking pipe in the bathroom.' A simple man with long years of struggle behind him, the landlord is working along with the plumber. 'There must not be any drip-drip.' He laughs, baring his gutka-stained teeth.

'My sister says you're like an uncle back home.'

'Beti, I believe in signs and signals.' The middle-aged man offers her an armchair. 'I am a labour contractor.' He sits on the edge of the bare bedstead – the mattress removed before painting. 'When your sister moved in, my business looked up after a long slump. With you also, I am sure my good luck will continue.'

Rita smiles demurely. Rekha practically gave her a script for the meeting. 'Bubu, not an extra word, just follow the lines,' she warned. In a hurry to join her man, the crazy girl left almost everything. The furniture. The Amitabh Bachchan poster – now rolled up on the side table.

The man points to the desert cooler fitted into a window.

'Your mother will live with you after some time?'

She is clueless about a mother joining her. He notices her puzzled look and laughs.

'The long summer months are coming. When it's very hot in the afternoon, she will need the cooler.'

Not knowing what to say, she nods in agreement.

'You think how I know about your family?' He gives her a quizzical look. 'Your sister told me everything.' He laughs. 'That will be nice – mother and daughter looking after each other until you get married. I say when your father recovers from his heart attack, bring him over for further treatment. My nephew works in AIIMS. That big hospital – you must have seen. It's the best in the country. He will help.'

It's futile to chase Rekha's lies, figure out all the stories she has spun. She keeps smiling with an occasional 'hmmm' and a 'haan-ji'.

'You need not worry, beti. Most of the other flat owners in Sector 8 are from my caste. We're Dalit. Oppressed. Whatever you call us. When the government built these flats, this was a godforsaken place. Robberies took place in daylight. We stood together and fought together. Today is another story. Everybody wants to come here. I'll tell them to look after you.' A new happiness fills Rita. The simple man has removed the distance, beti-ed her.

When she walks down the narrow, unpaved lane between the shops and hutments in the slum, Rabeya has a strange feeling. Her days in the shantytown are over. End of a chapter. No more open toilets or fighting for her turn on the bathing platform. The gut-wrenching stench from open drains will not sicken her any more. Fear of stepping on turds. Damp in the cubbyhole will not choke her again. No need to close her ears to the lewd remarks from drunken men. Never again will she have to roll up her sleeves and get into ugly fights with other women over little things.

She goes past Mausi's shop. The old woman is handing a matchbox and packet of bidis to a boy. 'Aarrey, Hema Malini, our heroine! Don't forget old Mausi now that you move with memsahibs in big motorcars, eh!' Scratching her head through the mat of black and silver hair, she laughs. 'After all, I have been the keeper of your secrets, naah?'

Rabeya stops, retraces a few steps and stands before the shop.

'It's nothing like that, Mausi. I'll never forget you.'

'Putli, too, now lives in a flat. Her madam's sister has bought them a shop in the market. She and her husband have started a business – glass bangles. She's hatching that phoren lady's egg. "If they get a baby with my help, what's wrong, Mausi?" she said.'

The old woman looks around warily, then lowers her voice. 'But what has happened to your hero? Did you have a fight? Is he chasing another woman – or jealous that you have seen better days, left him behind? He is not to be seen in the slum at all. People say he goes out late at night, comes back early in the morning. Is he going to those notorious kothis? Spending nights with the pink-and-purple girls? Hai, hai! Ram-ji!' Mausi moves forward, holds Rabeya's hand. 'Not a bad chap if you ask me. Laid-back yes – but good at heart. I say the two of you get married. As soon as you can.'

Coming back to her pit, she starts packing. When she opens the flimsy tin suitcase, an old smell of naphthalene assails her.

Among the few saris is the one her father bought her for Eid from New Market. That was her first and only visit to the snazzy shopping plaza in Khulna town. The visit to New Market, the steamer ride back home, the sari packet in hand – she was happy. That was before Munir Sheikh left his wife and two children for a younger woman. Before happiness disappeared from their home.

In a corner of the suitcase is a yo-yo Radolf Sahib gave her when he returned from the holidays. And a few photographs of their boat life – the picnic days she will never forget. Hidden under cheap storybooks is the camera Jamal bought her from Connaught Place. And the pictures. She carefully holds between her thumb and middle finger the one the white lady clicked; for a change, Jamal in a cheerful mood, his arm around her, not grumbling, not ranting against the whole world. In his new haircut, sunglasses, trendy clothes, he looks different, very much a city lad.

One more day, and everything will be behind her – the vapid slum, Jamal, the name Rabeya, her past across the border.

Suddenly it strikes her: everybody in her new life is a border crosser, from either side of the barbed wire. Arijit, Nandita, Piu and of course she herself. Far or near, big or small, they will be coming and going across some frontier, from one country to another, flying over continents to the other end of the world, some with passports and valid papers, and she – bribing the border police at the Benapole checkpoint to get on the train.

And Jamal?

Will she ever forget the times circled by his love songs and abandon back home in Khulna? Rabeya breathes deeply. He, too, once crossed the border but has stayed where he had come from – the banks of the Rupsa. Entranced, rooted, reluctant to do anything other than what he grew up doing – rowing on the river.

The boatman of the Rupsa. In fair weather or foul, with a breeze or against the storm, he would firmly hold the oar, not knowing how to let go of it.

On the darkest night of the sinister storm, he runs from the jetty in the pelting rain, cradling her burning body to his chest, looking for shelter. At the back of the workshop, Jamal sees the tin-roofed little cabin, a padlock on its door. He kicks the wobbly door open and puts her on a bare, rough cot. Amidst thunder and apocalyptic squall outside, he first removes the wet sari from her shivering body. Then he throws his own clothes away. Climbing on to the cot, he covers her hot body with his, taking her more and more into himself. 'Come, bulbul, come inside me, into my warmth. Let the storm blow away, then we will row home.'

She feels his skin pressed against hers, his warmth around her shivering body. Her face dug into his chest, two bodies twirling, souls merging into each other. She stops quivering as the heat from his member pushes away chills, fears of the foul night, comforting her to a new happiness.

30
Bruises

When he first hears his phone ring, it sounds like someone has raised a mad alarm somewhere in the building. A fire in another apartment? A man stuck in the lift? From this distance, Arijit cannot decipher the right meaning of the piercing shrieks. He fumbles, gropes for the watch. Only 4.15 a.m. Undecided, he goes back to sleep.

After a few minutes, the little thing bursts out crying again. From inside the chamber of forgetfulness, he hears muffled groans. Not a carefully downloaded ringtone comforting his senses but an ear-splitting scream.

Why should anyone call me at this unearthly hour? Is someone in trouble? Is the little phone clamouring to give out bad news? Death, distress, disaster? Niru-di from Calcutta? Is Nandita in danger? Her old mother suffering from asthma? Is it Piu then? Has something happened in New York?

Unable to face all the questions in his mind any more, Arijit takes the call.

'Kaku… they have… I am… er… in the police station.'

His heart is beating so fast he can hear the pounding. He gasps, breathes noisily. 'Why? What happened? Was there a fight in your slum?' Words stick in his throat.

'No. They picked up… people like us – outsiders.'

'What are they saying?'

'I don't know. There are quite a few of us here.'

'Let me see...'

Arijit jumps out of bed. Hurriedly wears a T-shirt, puts the wallet and car key in his pants pocket. He runs his hand through his hair. His face beaded with sweat, fingers sticky. Rushing out, he stops in the doorway. Where is he off to? He is not sure.

Still, he steps out of his apartment. Mad and yet scared. He almost runs to the lift, not sure if he is angry and with whom. The girl with large, dark eyes has not harmed anybody... He gets off the lift without knowing what to do, has no idea where the police station is, what to say even if he meets an officer there.

'Sahib, you are going for your walk? So early?' Ram Bahadur Chhetri on night duty at the gate.

'Someone is in trouble, Chhetri.' He thinks of the day the gallant Gurkha saved Rita from humiliation, from the shame of being stripped naked by a foul-mouthed woman, her bare skin lapped up by the greedy louts.

The young security guard looks away, listening to him, his eyes screwed up in pain.

'Will you please come with me to the police station, Chhetri?' Arijit pleads. Is he betraying impatience or nervousness? He has heard horror stories of torture in police custody. Newspapers talk of lock-up deaths. She is all the more vulnerable, not in a position to complain – a non-citizen, someone without credentials. He starts pacing up and down the driveway.

'Sahib, give me two minutes, I know someone in the police station.' Chhetri runs into the guardroom and makes a call on his mobile. Still talking, he comes out, making gestures with the other hand. Tension has gripped him, too. 'Okay, okay, I'll get there in half an hour… Tell your friend I will meet him.' Arijit overhears bits of his conversation with the invisible policeman.

Chhetri walks up to him. 'I have struck a deal – five thousand rupees, and they will let her walk out of the police station. No case, no investigation.' He looks up at Arijit, distressed like him. 'There is a special police unit for dealing with Bangladeshis; their office is some ten kilometres from here. She, the policeman said, is all right.'

'Let me come with you.' Arijit sounds anxious. 'We will go in my car.'

'Your presence will complicate matters, sir. The police are always scared of big people. You go home and catch some sleep. I will bring her back in an hour. You don't worry, Sahib, she will be fine.'

Arijit pulls out his wallet and gives Chhetri ten five-hundred-rupee notes. 'Will you need some more? You don't know…'

'No, sir. This is the money I will give them. You don't worry; she will be back in an hour.'

But Arijit does not go home. From the gate, he keeps looking in the direction the Gurkha has gone, riding his rickety, sputtering scooter. Then he begins pacing up and down the driveway. At one point, he walks past the street to the highway, tries to trace Chhetri's trail, watches the heavy trucks droning away, their headlights still on. A dog-like animal with sharp eyes and a bushy tail stops for a moment, gives him a mean look, then plunges into the jungle. A jackal, homing after a night-long hunt.

Residents of Blue Lotus Grove are going out for their morning walk, some alone, others with their spouses. Most of them ignore him. In the beginning, when he had just moved in, there was curiosity about the newsmaker. Strangers would walk up to him to greet him, shake hands, invite him to house parties, to a game of cards. A big man. Of late, he has noticed, they tend to avoid him. The air of disgust too visible.

An elderly couple crosses the gate. The woman, weighed down by her huge girth, walks with difficulty. She stares at Arijit and loudly says, 'We also treat our maid well, but making her a maharani? Never!'

Arijit hears the taunt. Similar insults fly in the corridors, in the club. A few more anonymous letters landed recently with the choicest abuses and insinuations. *The dirty old man screws the smelly Muslim whore in the lonely apartment* – one of them.

He does not care. At the moment, his only wish is to get the girl back – hungry, insecure, defenceless. No, she does not look famine-stricken any more. Her scared, expressive eyes say more than she actually can. The first touch of care, feel of assurance, a little bit of support has changed her. He can see hints of polish all around her, a new happiness. The craggy shoulder bones are smoothed up by a layer of flesh. The haggard scarecrow has been buffed into a new life. At Nandita's party, everyone looked at her admiringly – in that silk sari, her long, open hair past her waist, fluttering softly in the evening breeze.

Have they tortured her in the lock-up? Put her to the third degree? An undocumented immigrant working in this country without a valid permit, she is easy fodder. The police are notorious for corruption and brutality. Far too often, he reads in the papers about custody rapes.

She is to move into the newly rented flat today. A proper flat on a housing estate would be safe… until all of them go to live on the farm. Suddenly, an image unfolds before his eyes: a tender, young gourd, mutilated by rodents, thrown away by the farmers in the early morning plucking session. All night, the field rats made a feast of the healthy fruit, burrowing into it.

'Oh no!' Arijit cries out, clasping his face.

He feels awkward under the gaze of the early morning walkers. The familiar busy cars from the airlines, television studios and call centres come and go, picking up their staff. People have begun driving out of the complex. He knows the early lot – mostly doctors, teachers and businessmen. There is busy activity in the plaza inside the gate. Morning walkers gather in small groups. They look at the aloof, proud, patrician figure, standing at the elevated ground where the driveway meets the thoroughfare – forlorn, wrecked by his own misery. For them, it's an unusual sight.

He does not know how long he has been there, how many cars have whizzed past him. Then he sees a speck in the distance. From under the mandatory helmet of a two-wheeler rider emerges the face of the young Gurkha – honest, expressionless. Riding pillion is the outline of a woman, leaning on the rider. Closer, the helmeted face wears a Buddha smile, a look of not a win or loss but of one more job done.

Chhetri pulls up before him.

Arijit sees Rita as if through a curtain of thick fog. There are dark lines around her eyes. Blood has clotted over a cut on her left temple. He notices scratches on her arms. Her hair dishevelled, as though she has gone through a dust storm. Her clothes lined with dust, torn in a few places. She tries to cover her forehead with a handkerchief, noticing his gaze on the bruise.

He shakes his head.

'I am all right, Kaku.' She tries to smile. 'They did not do anything to me.'

Chhetri stands his scooter behind the guardroom and walks with her towards the lift. Arijit a few steps ahead, trying to follow their conversation. She is narrating how it all happened.

In the middle of the night, Rabeya woke up hearing heavy footsteps and hushed conversation. Someone asked in a thick, husky voice, 'Where are they?'

'They live right here; this is the Bangladeshi cluster.'

Rabeya recognized the voice. A Bangladeshi agent who collected protection money from the immigrants every month. The vulture had always stared at her with a greedy eye. The last time he knocked on her door, she had refused to pay him anything. 'You will know very soon who I am,' he threatened.

The men from the Special Cell huddled them into the back of a van. The agent shook hands with the officer and disappeared into the dark.

In the police station, there was no space to lock up so many people. A constable in khaki pushed them all into a room and closed the door from the outside. Sitting on the bare, dusty floor in the fluid yellow of a weak light bulb, Rabeya kept swatting mosquitoes. A rat grazed past her to the other end of the room. Over the closed door, there was a blue-and-red sign: *Delhi Police, Always with You.* The luminous words in Hindi glared at her.

The constable returned, demanding money.

'You behnchod Bangladeshis; bloody thugs, burgling, breaking in all the time. Give five thousand, each one of you, and go back to your shitholes. Otherwise, we will put you on a train and push you to the other side of the border.'

Frightened, not knowing what to do, Rabeya called Arijit.

Arijit reaches his apartment, his ears pinned back, keen not to miss out on their conversation all the while. He thanks Chhetri when he takes leave of them.

Once inside, a strange feeling seizes him. He sees the entire system conspiring to take revenge on him, as if they knew about his empathy for this girl, his weakness. The Special Cell men picked her up, dragged her to the seedy police station to teach him a lesson. To humiliate him.

He opens a wardrobe, takes out a neatly ironed pyjama and a bush shirt on a hanger. Hands her the clothes, steps into the bathroom, switches on the geyser and puts some Dettol in a plastic bucket. Then slowly opens the hot-water tap.

'Take a bath in Dettol water and wear fresh clothes.'

She protests, ashamed of his concern for her. 'Kaku, nothing happened to me. I am fine. I will make coffee for you, then go home.'

'Do as I tell you.' Authority returns to his voice.

He looks at the strange figure coming out of the bath. In the loose pyjama and bush shirt, she looks like a cloistered nun. He asks her to lie down and rest. She listens, knowing her protests won't make any sense.

In the kitchen, he heats milk in a pot and puts it in a glass. From the bar, he takes out the bottle of Napoleon brandy and pours some of it in the milk. He kneels beside the bed. 'Child, now please finish off the milk; it'll do you good.'

She must have fallen asleep. Opening her eyes, she sees the big man kneeling like a penitent atoning for the wrongs of a world he has no control over. Shame overtakes her, tears of embarrassment fill her eyes. She feels a strong hand under her nape, giving her support to get up. He holds the glass to her mouth. Taking it from his hand, she looks at him. Close. Is he struggling to hide tears?

The brandy helps her get over the trauma of the night. He wipes the thin white line over her upper lip with a napkin. After a long time, a very long time, she remembers her father. And cries.

Confused by her crying, Arijit fears something more terrible may have happened. A rage rises in him, then he calms down, knowing it's futile. He turns on the air conditioning and puts a blanket over her.

'Now you sleep.' She feels his hand over her forehead.

Minutes later, he returns with a first-aid box. After cleaning up the wound on her temple with a swab of cotton dipped in hot water, he applies a little ointment onto it and sticks a Band-Aid over the wound. By now, she is fast asleep, her head slipping off the white pillow. He carefully puts her head back on it and leaves the room, closing the door behind him.

31
Late Blossom

After the Qutab Minar, the city ends and the suburbs begin. From the back seat of the car, Arijit looks at Delhi's most prominent pre-Mughal landmark, then takes note of the changing landscape. The first hints of country are here, and still, the city somehow lingers on. On either side of the road run the high-walled, deeply wooded farmhouses of the rich and powerful. The nameplates at the gates are like a who's who – big businessmen, politicians, fashion designers, media barons, top lawyers. Bharat turns left into a narrow street. The farms of the privileged follow. Arijit recognizes many of them – ministers, members of Parliament, industrialists… He turns to Nandita.

'When you lived in Delhi, Mehrauli was a village.' She explains his unfamiliarity with the area. 'My father bought some land way back in the sixties; it was ridiculously cheap. When I first came here as a schoolgirl for the winter picnic, this was a dirt road. Coming here would be a problem if it rained.' She pulls at his arm. 'See.' A cow with her calf stands in the middle of the narrow street. Bharat brakes hard. Off-balance, Nandita holds Arijit's arm for support.

From the front seat, Rita looks amusedly at Bharat. 'Honk!' She laughs.

The two have been talking, laughing at something funny on

the road. A relationship is clearly in the making, and Arijit is curious. He can see that Rita is trying to bully the simple boy from the hills.

'In America, you can buy vegetables and jewellery from the same shop. Do you know that?' She looks at him dismissively, playing with the end of her long, braided hair.

'Why should anybody buy vegetables from a jeweller's shop?' Bharat finds the idea funny. 'I would rather buy vegetables first, come home, cook, eat, and then, in the evening, go buy jewellery.' He laughs. The quiet, submissive chauffeur, overawed by his boss, is enjoying the banter.

'You idiot! In that country, people don't have that kind of time.' She jabs a finger at his ribs.

Arijit watches the scene of infatuation, the onset of love. He turns to Nandita again. She suppresses a smile. The vivacious young journalist who had swayed him in Paris years ago winks back at times. The tall, broad-shouldered woman is now leaner, sharper than the Sunday guest in his home.

The car stops outside a large, heavy iron gate. Even before Bharat can honk, the security guard rushes forward to salute and bows deeply to Nandita. The gates rattle open.

The car pulls into the driveway and stops on the porch of a quaint mock-Tudor house with a gabled façade. The brick chimney at the back looms enigmatically. Evocative of the Raj era, the building casts its charm on Arijit.

A man is threshing ripe, golden wheat at one end of the courtyard. Holding sheaves of wheat in both hands, he bends to beat them against a framed wire-mesh board. A thin white dust of chaff rises, leaving a layer on his head. He rushes towards Nandita the moment he sees her.

'Bitiya, you're here after a long time.' His hands join. After doing a namaste to Arijit, he turns to Nandita again. 'Those days come back when Sahib was still around. There would be a feast here every Saturday.' His eyes moisten, the head shakes.

'Kirori Chacha, I am planning to live here for a while.' Nandita holds him by the arm.

A cow moos from her shed, looking at the scene of arrival. A boy drives a tractor from the field, kills the engine and busily unloads bundles of freshly mown grass. At the moment, the bulky cow shows no interest in the fodder.

'My son,' the old man says.

'I saw him when he was a child.' Nandita looks at the boy with mild affection.

A servant has already spread cane armchairs on the veranda.

Rita has disappeared inside the house. In no time, she returns holding a large tray – paneer pakora and chai. Looking at her, Nandita knows the girl is happy being here. On her face is the glow of new love.

'Rita, now you are in charge.' Nandita smiles. 'Don't make many dishes – one or two, bas. If you need anything, ask Bharat. He knows the village well; he will go buy things. Let him work a little.'

'Let's take a walk around the farm.' Arijit points Nandita to the crowd of trees across the courtyard. 'I heard about Mehrauli but really had no idea about farm fields so close to the city.'

After tea, they walk past the cowshed into the orchard. The sappy smell of ripening papayas greets them. The yellow fruit hang from spindly, low trees. After the papayas begins a forest of lemons – many varieties of them. Then mangoes and guavas.

Arijit does not know when he has held Nandita's hand. Shoulders touching, their bodies get closer. She breathes deeply. Her auburn hair flutters in the breeze.

For the first time in many years, a woman is becoming important to him again. It is different from casual contacts, social occasions. He puts his arm around her, then holds her, first a little tentative, then assuredly.

Arijit turns her towards him, the two faces very close. They can hear each other breathe. Something happens inside him. Her face cased between his gentle hands, he sees deep into her – the images and emotions of their life together rush back from the past. Without knowing, he takes her lips into his. One second. Two. Three… Then lets the moment go. A cuckoo somewhere sings enchantingly.

'It's spring.' Nandita laughs.

'And it's time to home.' Arijit laughs too.

A large, uprooted tree lies on the ground. A red-crested woodpecker is strutting over it. Its golden back shines in the mild morning sun.

'It fell in last year's storm,' Nandita says to fill the silence.

They sit on the bare trunk, upsetting the woodpecker.

'The same old feeling is coming back, Nan.' He gently holds her hand and gazes into the thick foliage all around. Dark green lemons hang from the low branches. A few have turned pale yellow.

'You stood by me, Nan, when I was going through hell. So far, I have only taken, borrowed from you.' He stops. It's quiet, a little cold among the trees. He lets her hand go. Tears a blade of grass and offers it to her. 'It's an old habit – taking things from you.'

She smiles.

He pauses again, hesitates, makes an effort to say more. 'Once more, I want to ask for something. Want to say something.'

His deep, bass voice sounds unusual when he pleads. He pulls her close.

'What?'

'I want to say our life is neither a ship nor a beer on the beach.' He laughs.

'And—'

'And your hand, Nan. Will you be my benefactor one more time?'

A calf strays into the orchard. Not interested in grazing, she springs around as if to announce the onset of some carnival. She looks at the elderly couple, then turns in another direction.

'Let's live together for whatever is left. Let's not count the years.'

He stretches his hand, fumbles for hers. Nandita's eyes glisten as they take his face in. Then she smiles, offering him hers.

32
Golden Jubilee

Arijit is busy with his research about polio. The debilitating disease leading to paralysis of muscles, almost eradicated everywhere else, still persists in a few pockets in India. One of the areas where the deadly virus attacks poor children is western UP, adjoining Noahda.

The campaign against polio has not been completely successful in such places because of old beliefs, ingrained superstitions. People still hesitate to give their children polio drops, fearing this will make them impotent. NGOs are working hard to win the battle against the disease. Now they are persuading religious leaders, gurus and imams to tell people from their exalted seats about the gains of polio drops. And remove the fear of emasculation.

Arijit goes on reading. He has gone through the websites of all the Delhi hospitals offering treatment for polio. One of them, though not among the very best, has a comprehensive physiotherapy programme for post-attack cases. Run by a missionary group, it is one of the oldest hospitals in the city. The site gives the names and addresses of the administrators and senior doctors. Arijit writes down the particulars of the director, Dr Babu Thomas.

It's late evening – nearly nine. He first hesitates, fiddles with the ballpoint and writing pad. A few moments later, he calls the number.

'Dr Thomas here.' The voice comes through with a distinct southern accent. Arijit first apologizes for calling so late, then talks about the farmer's son. 'I am ready to bear the expenses for the treatment, but I want the child cured.' Arijit is surprised by the urgency in his own voice.

'You are a good man, Mr Basu. Normally, people do not show so much concern for those outside their own circles.' Dr Thomas is interested in Raju's case. 'A physiotherapist from Germany is currently working with us. For us, the hospital is not a business; we are here to serve humanity. I am touched, Mr Basu, by your love for a fellow human being. Please bring the child the day after – say, around ten in the morning. Come to my office, I will be waiting for you. I will then take you to Dr Madeleine Graff.'

Arijit breathes deeply. A sense of satisfaction fills him; at least he is being of some use to someone. Looking at the people in Blue Lotus Grove, he sometimes feels out of place, alienated.

Why can't I be one of them, partying with Neha Arora, her husband and their friends? he often wonders. He is nothing but a stranger, sliding deeper and deeper into his own chasm. A misfit, the odd man out. If Raju walks without a limp, his young mother will smile again. That is something worth a try. His life in the boomtown will be justified: not just a morning walker but an active participant in their narrative.

He feels relieved, reassured after the phone call to Dr Thomas. Little Raju running around the farm, playing with the other children, going home and holding his mother's hand – the picture from the future fills him with peace, a deep sense of happiness.

With nothing else to do, he decides to check his email. Perhaps Piu has written to him? Nandita talked to her a few days after their visit to her farm. They will be here to attend the wedding. Will it be embarrassing – daughter, son-in-law, grandson at his wedding?

'It's very common,' Piu argued on the phone. The marriage will end his exile, help him settle down. He is finally coming home. And this will be his way of acknowledging Nandita in his life. At a very difficult moment – the disaster of his first marriage threatening his diplomatic career, putting a question mark on the future of his child – Nandita had stepped in, salvaged him and steadied his life. Without her, Piu would have been just another child from a dysfunctional home. Whatever remains of his life – five, ten, fifteen years – will be payback time, time for taking care of his new wife.

Two new emails wait for him in the inbox – from Radolf McGirk and Sumita Sen. He is curious to know why the history professor has written to him. Ever since Nirupama mentioned her, Sumita has been looming from the past. Like the smell of a bunch of old letters lying forgotten in a corner of the bookshelf. He vaguely remembers the thin girl, their neighbour's daughter in Ballygunge Palace, walking with him to the music school every weekend. Beside the bright, brilliant boy, she was diffident, uncertain. Beyond this, he has no memory of her, no recollection of the days in the recitation class.

He opens the mail. Only a few lines:

Perhaps you have heard about the golden jubilee of the music school both of us went to long ago. They persuaded me to head the celebrations committee. It is a strange feeling writing to someone I knew as a schoolgirl. Do you have any memory of those days, learning recitation and Rabindra Sangeet? We will be very happy to have you among us for a day or two. By the way, the music school has moved into its own building.

Arijit shakes his head from side to side. A lost world beckons to him, but he can no longer relate to it. He leans back in his chair.

Radolf has written about his plans to relocate to Melbourne. Tired of New York, its crowd, frenetic pace, he has decided to live in Australia and intends to do a documentary about the Aboriginals living on the island of Tasmania. But mostly to live a relaxed life in semi-retirement. He mentions an award his latest documentary has won at a film festival and wants to know if Munir Sheikh's daughter is willing to come to Australia.

I am keen to bear all her expenses and be her sponsor. Perhaps, after some training, she will be able to adjust to the new country. Who knows, maybe she can even find a suitable man willing to marry her? This is the new fad – marrying into new cultures.

He has sent a few more photographs as attachments.

Arijit laughs, rereading Radolf's mail. He does not know that Munir Sheikh's daughter has been reborn as Rita. That the little girl who became a member of the documentary filmmaker's ragtag crew, travelling by boat to distant places, is all set to play the perfect bride to Nandita's chauffeur, that good-looking boy from the hills. She will soon formally accept his hand. He and Nandita will go to the Andaman archipelago off the Indian coast for a quiet honeymoon, the younger couple to Ranikhet in the Kumaon Hills. Nandita has made all the arrangements, planned everything. The two newly married couples of different ages will be living on the farm – in the care of each other. Their wedding will be a quiet affair; only a handful of friends and family will attend the function in a medieval royal palace in Udaipur. Nandita's preparations have left no holes. No loose ends.

After a light dinner of steamed carrots and beans, and a sandwich, Arijit makes a cup of black coffee and returns to the desk with the laptop. He is taking one last look at his book on South Asia before sending it to the publishers.

Nandita calls. 'My mother wants to move in with my aunt in her cottage in the hills. She has already visited the place near Nainital. I told her to live with us on the farm, but she won't listen. She wants to be among the *old people*. My aunt has been living there for years. Mum has always liked the place.'

'Do you want me to talk to her? I should, right?'

'That will be very nice. When you were on television over the energy treaty, she would ask me about you.'

'What about Bharat and Rita? Have you thought about it all over again?'

'Nonsense. She is my daughter. I am marrying her to the best boy I could find.'

At such moments, Arijit likes Nandita the most, feels extremely proud of her. Her certitude, assuredness. No self-doubts. Once something is decided, she will not go back to thinking over it again.

'Of course they will marry first,' Nandita resumes. 'They will settle down in the farmhouse and take charge, only then can we proceed.' She laughs. The touch of flippancy in her voice sweeps away all his hesitation.

'I think I should talk to your mother, persuade her to live with us,' Arijit says thoughtfully.

This marriage of his is still incomprehensible. It is and is still not. His life is putting down new roots at a time when everything seems almost over. It's happening and yet has the feel of unreality. As if it were an event in someone else's life. After almost a quarter century of first meeting Nandita, he is going to have her at his side. For all time to come. His old new bride. His surreal marriage. He breathes deeply.

The famished girl, who has just moved into a proper flat, leaving the festering slum behind, will begin a new life.

Arijit goes to bed late – in the early hours of the morning.

33
Gold Pocket Watch

'Nan, come. Let's have tea.'

With the winter gone, asthma no longer bothers Radhika. A fit of coughing no longer makes her chest feel tight. The early morning sun on the terrace cheers her up. She feels a mild tremor in her hands, and at times, her head shakes a little. But in a moment of paroxysm, her chest does not rise and fall like bellows any more. Day does not slip away before afternoon is over.

Radhika looks at her daughter. Pagli! She has messed up her life. Almost. It's time for her to see the grandchildren married – they're coming back with the little ones in prams.

Oh, zaraa nach ke dikhao saade naal soneyo
Dasso ji sawaal soneyo, ehdi kyun chaal soneyo
Eh naara naara naara, eh…

She sings, clapping to keep time. Her head bobbing, Radhika taps her feet and giggles, amused by the sassy song: …*nach ke dikhao saade soneyo*… The toothless mouth opens in happiness. Her furrowed face reddens. She drums the table, and the vibration unsettles the tea tray. A little tea spills out of the pot.

'What are you singing, Mum?' Nandita pulls up a chair.

'Women in our family always sang and danced before a wedding.' Radhika pours the tea. 'All the women – old and young. At my wedding, both my grandmothers danced, all the aunts, cousins. The best was Rajkumari, my bhabhi.'

'Not if the bride is fifty plus. You crazy…'

Radhika still laughs, avoiding her daughter's glare. 'How can there be a marriage without the pandit tying a mauli to the bride's wrist?' She is in a flippant mood. 'Mama-ji and Mami-ji had fasted until they slipped all the red-and-cream bangles over my arms – up to the elbows, ha!' She glances at her daughter from the corner of her eye and grins. 'Ah, Nan.' Radhika breaks a ginger cookie into small pieces, puts one in her mouth, sips tea. 'My elder brother is no more, but Rajkumari will be here for your wedding. And both of us will dance.' Raising her hands, she imitates a dance move.

'Oh, Mum! You're impossible.' Nandita shakes her head, grimaces in annoyance but suppresses a smile. She stretches her hand, holds Radhika's.

When she returned from France – confused, clueless, an end-of-everything feeling troubling her – Radhika stood by her like an anchor, steadying her life, holding her from drifting away. Her father had died a few years ago. Alone, Radhika gave her what she needed most at that moment – a sense of family, security. She was the buoy, giving her shipwrecked daughter an idea of stability after turmoil, a reason to beach, recover. Red-flagging the dangers around.

In the morning, mother and daughter would spend some time together, talking about Nandita's old friends in Delhi, her father, their relatives. That support, recollection of small incidents, little insignificant things, going back to the past… all that helped Nandita adjust, move on. She slowly got her bearings.

Life here is coming to a close. Radhika looks around – the paintings on the walls, cane furniture, the trees towering over the house. After the initial years of struggle as a refugee family from Lahore, they moved into this house. First a single-storey modest building. Then her husband slowly built it up, adding the first floor, and after a few years, the second.

Nandita was born here. She grew up playing around the lawns. Radhika remembers taking her daughter to the gate early in the morning to wait for the school bus. In her neatly ironed school uniform, the girl looked bright; perhaps her intelligent eyes hinted she would not follow the furrow but chart out her own plan. Schoolbag on the back and a water bottle slung from the shoulder, she would ask many questions to which Radhika often didn't have an answer.

When Nandita got the scholarship and left for Paris to study at the Sorbonne, she thought it was a mere fad, that her daughter would be back by the end of the year. She had already made a list of prospective young men in their family circle.

The news of her daughter becoming a part of Paris society, making waves, had actually frightened her. For the family, the girl was practically lost. They felt proud whenever a Delhi newspaper or magazine carried Nandita's pictures along with a write-up on her. But they knew the girl would never come home, never be theirs again.

Then Nandita came back. Not the successful publisher setting new trends but a disillusioned, dejected woman in her fifties caught in a blind alley. The castaway. The assurance of Radhika's own measured, predictable life comforted her, arresting her slide into emptiness. Slowly, Nandita settled down, became part of this place again.

They had reached a stage in life when mother and daughter were tied together by old age: she seventy-four, Nandita fifty-two, secure in the thought that the two of them would spend their days together, looking at an indefinite, unremarkable future. They clung to each other, sharing their thoughts, their fears.

The news of Nandita getting engaged to the big man came as a surprise. Radhika is happy, but she is apprehensive as well. It's too good – the handsome diplomat, quite a big name. It scares her.

Between her husband's death and Nandita's return, she had suffered acute misery, the gnawing feeling of being the only soul in the big house. *Such a thing must not happen to Nan in my absence.* Radhika worried all the time. She still feels distressed thinking of those days when she woke up in a ghostly home, ate all alone, went to bed with no one to say goodnight to.

Marriage fills up the empty space. *Nan should be happy with that man. Not a Punjabi, still very tall. Whatever. I will send him the gold pocket watch with the hunter case and chain my father gave my husband at the time of our wedding. They can live happily on the Mehrauli farm. Bharat Singh and the Bengali maid – are they getting married, too? – will look after them. The girl will cook, clean, and Bharat drive them around. A good arrangement. I should not be the odd one out among them, the two romancing couples!*

Radhika laughs quietly. The little cottage in Nainital that her brother had built a few years before his death should be the perfect place for her. Rajkumari lives there. They were friends even before she became her bhabhi. They will spend their days in each other's company, old people with their tales of life left behind. But she will miss Nandita a lot – this morning hour of togetherness, her complaints, quarrels.

'Nan.' She holds her hand. 'Be a good wife to him… he is a good man. He, too, has suffered a lot.' Radhika pulls Nandita towards her, pressing her child to her old bosom. 'Nan, I am very happy for you. My grandmother used to say a woman has not lived her life if she has never been married.' Her voice cracks, the skinny hands shake. She struggles to hold back her tears. 'Take care of your man.'

34
Evil Glee

Walking home from the neighbourhood supermarket with a few things – his favourite brands of cheese, shaving cream, tea and cornflakes – Arijit notices a man riding his Bajaj scooter up and down the street in a tearing hurry. Hunched forward by a belly bulge, the stocky man seems to be everywhere at the same time.

When he left Blue Lotus Grove about an hour ago, Arijit noticed him talking to a cop outside the police van on duty, a constant buzz of radio messages coming despite frequent static. 'Alpha alpha… Roger that,' a tall officer with hennaed hair was shouting into his walkie-talkie. The Maruti Gypsy with wireless communications is now a police control room on the move. On the lee side of the vehicle, where the road sloped down into the lowland undergrowth, they were engrossed in some serious talk under a tree. The face seemed familiar, and yet, Arijit could not exactly recall it. Such a character ought to have been scared even of a policeman's shadow. He found it odd that the fellow had such a good rapport with the officer.

And now he is pulling up at a construction site where a group of men, shady characters going by their looks, seem to have been waiting for him. He talks to them first in a hushed tone, then gestures to them to move inside the raw structure. Arijit suddenly remembers – it is the man who dropped the threatening letter at his doorstep. He feels uneasy.

As he enters the apartment complex, Chhetri, as usual, salutes him at the gate. But the disarming smile of the simple hill boy is missing. He looks tense, as if troubled by a sense of foreboding. 'Saab-ji, something terrible is going to happen.'

Arijit frowns. His heart misses a beat. 'How do you know, Chhetri?'

'Sir, you sense it in the air.' The Gurkha's nostrils flare. 'I don't know what exactly but something very very bad.'

'Do we need to do something? Is she…' His voice trails off.

'I told her not to leave home in the evening. Inside her new flat, she is safe. You don't worry, sir. Only – don't go out. And please do not talk to anybody here about what I've just said.' For the first time, the guileless boy from the Himalayas looks troubled, scared.

'Has something really happened?'

'The pandit, who looks after the little temple in the slum, is missing. No trace of him. He used to tutor the children and talk of politics. Everyone in that slum was fond of him.'

Back home, Arijit makes himself a cup of black coffee. At the desk, he checks his mailbox. A young Foreign Service officer has written ardently about a cohesive, integrated South Asia coming out of the deep gloom of stasis. *I have heard about your book, sir, and look forward to it.* Arijit is comforted that his line of argument in the book has already made some resonance. He writes a polite reply to his junior colleague.

After early dinner, he walks up to the balcony, the corner from where he always looks at the farm, lean canal and shantytown – all indistinct watermarks. Now in the evening, nothing is visible except odd, spooky lights scattered around the sprawling slum. The sights and sounds of that life – laughs, cries, fights, singing, coos, sighs – nothing comes this far. He is happy she's no longer part of that life, its rawness and brutalities. In that little flat, safe, secure, until one day…

Suddenly, like a volcanic eruption, the slum leaps up in flames, defying the dark night. Deafening explosions and gunfire beat the distance to assail him like the obstreperous glee of evil. Though faint, cries and shrieks float in. Stunned, he stands there statuesque, unable to make sense of the apocalyptic scene unfolding before him. The stocky man frenetically moving around town on his scooter comes back – only now does that image assume ominous proportions. *Saab-ji, something terrible is going to happen* – Chhetri's words ricochet.

He hurries back into the study and picks up his phone. Calls the estate's security officer. It does not connect. Next, he tries an undersecretary in the home ministry. No luck. The lines seem jammed. He writes an email to Gupta only to see if the rest of the city has been spared this orgy of violence. It fails. The internet is down. It's now getting clearer: the demonic forces behind the unearthly conflagration are powerful enough to have got phone and internet connectivity disrupted. Undecided, Arijit still feels impelled to do something. He locks up his apartment and goes downstairs to find out what's going on.

Chhetri's shift over, two other guards are on duty. Tense, unnerved, they fail to recognize him. He goes to the security officer's room in the administrative wing; it's closed. Coming back, he sees a man standing in a corner of the corridor. 'May I help you, sir?' Polite, sincere, he comes forward. 'We haven't met before, but I have heard about you. Well, who doesn't know you in India? Everybody who reads newspapers, watches TV, keeps talking about you. I'm Abhay Singh. I live in the penthouse opposite your apartment.' He extends his hand. Arijit shakes it. 'I saw the horrible scene – fire, gunshots, explosions... Phones not working, internet down, so I came to look for him to know what is happening.' He points to the security officer's closed office. 'Are we safe?'

'Sir, what's happening there,' Abhay nods in the direction of the slum, 'is nothing less than 9/11. Heavily armed, masked gunmen came riding armoured vehicles and fanned into town. They had specific information about their targets. They moved into the building just two blocks away to kill a highly decorated, retired army general. Now his personal security guards are bravely fighting back. There's news of the terrorists using drones.' He shakes his head in distress, in disbelief. 'No one knows why telephone lines are down. But that's meaningless. Those foreign terrorists are using satellite phones.'

'What're our police doing? They should have taken charge of the situation by now.'

'Do you really think, sir, the pot-bellied, paan-chewing sloggers are any match for the agents of hell? Sir, eminent citizens like you are their prime targets. If they harm some big shots, that will cause a bigger sensation. Please go back to your flat and close the door. And don't talk to anyone about all this even if the phones are working again. Delhi is going to be like Beirut, like Baghdad.' Moved by his own evocation of horror, Abhay holds the older man's hand, walking him to the lift.

35
Italian Villa

Arijit gets up at five – a full half hour earlier than usual. Sitting at his desk in the study, he sharpens the pencils and puts them in a box. When he is through with the whole lot, he counts them – twenty. In a little handbag, he puts the pencil box first, then the spiral notebooks, erasers and toffees. He wants to make it a big moment for the farmers' children – the good news that Raju's polio-affected left foot can get back its strength. That the little boy need not walk with a limp any more.

Dr Madeleine Graff, an experienced physiotherapist from Bonn, is waiting for him at St. Andrew's Hospital in Old Delhi. He has talked to her. The doctor assured him that Raju would be like any other normal child of his age. No operation, no cut or tear. Only a few regular exercises. She will have four or five sessions with the boy, and his parents can sit in with him.

'I'll bring the child as many times as you want, and I myself will help him do the daily exercises,' Arijit told Dr Graff. 'I'm a retired man. I have all the time in the world. Doctor, you understand, Raju's parents are farmhands; they cannot even sign. And both of them work on the farm from morning till evening.'

He will drive Raju to St. Andrew's Hospital every morning. Across the ground from the main building, Dr Graff's physiotherapy unit is housed in a dilapidated red-brick arcade where the hospital had originally started in the second decade of the nineteenth century. Dr Thomas gave him a tour of the hospital premises.

At the gate, Chhetri greets him with the usual salute and broad smile. 'Saab-ji, I met the Special Cell officer the other day. He said your maid will not be harassed again. He understands her absence in the kitchen means problems for you. No one else to make your meals. He has given instructions.' The Gurkha laughs.

Some more good news. And anyway, Rita has already moved into the one-room flat. Beyond the police and shenanigans of touts and slum toughs. At the moment, however, his mind is full of Raju, the promise of his recovery, the red-brick wing of a Raj-era hospital in the old town, and of course Dr Graff. Holding the handbag tight, he walks faster, as though he were not on his morning walk but going to catch a train.

His strides lengthen to cover the distance as fast as possible. He breaks a sweat, his eyebrows moisten, the T-shirt gets wet. Normally, he would look at the new apartment blocks to spot fresh arrivals. Another family opting for the boomtown, another line of terracotta pots on a balcony sporting creepers, palms and periwinkles. At the moment, he sees nothing. He does not notice when the blocks have disappeared.

He is close to the dirt track. Barely a hundred yards. Obstructing the view of the farmland and its green vista, a giant billboard has come up. It stares him down, intimidating the trespasser. He did not notice the mammoth sign even yesterday.

Buy an Italian villa with lawn and swimming pool
Experience the taste of luxury
Booking amount only 2%
Hurry! Limited Offers!!

He has seen this ad before in the newspapers. Clearly, the project is coming up somewhere here. Has some agency put it up at this point to draw the attention of the Noahda gentry on their morning walk?

Past the show home on the garish flex board, Arijit gets off the road, and crossing the sidewalk and line of trees, takes the dirt track. There has been a hasty attempt to mend the path, make it smooth, motorable overnight. The small but deep ditch at the approach of the mud road is now filled up. In a great hurry, someone seems to have been working on a war footing to level the uneven track. A spread of brick here, thick layers of rubble there.

Indeed, a couple of vehicles – a sturdy Bolero and a mean Scorpio – gleam in the early morning sun at the end of the path, blocking the entry to the farm. Arijit walks past the imperious cars.

There is no trace of farming anywhere around. The entire periphery of the farm fields now barbed-wire fenced, the spread of winter opulence has a bare, shorn look. The mild sourness in the air from the tomato bushes has given way to the yucky odour of cement floating around. Masons and their helpers are busy raising a structure – perhaps a site office to supervise construction. The lush, lusty shine of the fields has turned into a sad grey. And the ripening crops wiped off the fields expose a bare emptiness that now scares Arijit. Rogue elephants seem to have trampled down the fat radishes, rotund cabbages and dark green spinach. Not elephants. Tuskers cannot do such a thorough job. Did warplanes carry out successive strikes all through the night? The verdant fields of life have a bombed-out, blazed look.

The farmers are gone.

A man in formal dark trousers and a white long-sleeved shirt stands at what used to be the entry to the farm, holding a couple of paper files. His maroon tie flaps in the wind blowing across the fields. Perhaps the project manager. Or his junior.

Arijit walks up to him. 'Excuse me.' His spirit ebbs. His trainers seem to be dipping into the soft earth. The man turns to him, taking in the early visitor. After considering everything, he flicks a smile. 'Good morning, sir.'

'I come here almost every day – well, it's part of my morning walk. I spend a little time watching the activity on the farm, the men and women picking up vegetables, scything fodder—'

'Sir, all that is over. It was illegal activity; those fellows did not own the land. The bastards were making a quick buck.'

'Then who owns the farm?'

The man, perhaps in his early thirties, makes an irritated noise, a gesture of disgust, and thinks for a while. Then decides to try patience, give persuasion a chance. He slips a business card into Arijit's hand. 'We are Delhi's leading builders – Debonair Lifestyle Facilitators. Debonair is building an eighty-storey commercial complex in Kuala Lumpur.' He nods towards the mauled farm. 'We purchased the land from the farmers at least five years ago. The fuckers were raising crops and making money – bloody cheats. Squatters. You will not see them again.'

'Do they live somewhere nearby, is there a village—'

'Didn't I say they were dirty shitters, cheats, farming without any legal right to the land?' His eyes narrow. He measures Arijit, a sudden apprehension seizing him. 'Are you into some NGO activity? Want to create problems for us?' He gets both angry and apprehensive.

Arijit disarms him with a smile. 'You are getting worked up needlessly, imagining things. Just listen to me.' He briefly tells him about Raju, his polio and why he is looking for him and his parents.

The man's voice softens. 'I am sorry, sir. Actually, I was in KL, looking after the project over there. The MD called me and said, "Vikas, I want you to take charge of the new project in Noahda." I rushed back.' He tries to size up Arijit, passes the files from one hand to another. Unable to figure out his interest in the farmers. The fucking polio story… he is probably making it up. What does he want really? Vikas looks troubled. 'Anyway, sir, they are a migrant community, take hold of empty land, raise a crop or two, then move away, looking for land elsewhere. They carry their homes on their backs, here today, gone tomorrow – always on the move. Once they leave a place, it's difficult to trace them.'

Arijit looks at the bag in his hand, then shakes his head. He does not know what to do with the sharpened pencils, scented erasers, spiral notebooks. The toffees. He looks at the far end of the farm where a young crop of wavering mustard stood until yesterday. Raju's earthy mother, her shiny silver anklet, tears flooding her face… Arijit starts backing up. No, there is no need to engage with the ambitious executive of Debonair Lifestyle Facilitators. He turns back.

'Sir.' The man is walking alongside. 'You are a little unusual. I have not met anyone like you. Sorry if I have offended you. Getting land from the farmers is the biggest problem now. You have read about incidents…'

Arijit stops. The young man comes close to him. 'Selling units is not my job; still, I can tell you it's a huge opportunity. Book a villa now, today! The price will appreciate within months. Perhaps you have children – book it for them. If you don't want property any more, still make an investment. The big business houses, the expats – everyone is going to line up to buy a villa here. You can sell it a year later and earn a good profit – your money coming back tenfold.'

Arijit smiles. The little gathering of farmers, their wives and children around him comes back. The boy's mother wept, calling him a magic man with a cure. He looks up at the executive, shakes his hand and walks away.

36
Big Story

Back from his morning walk, Arijit picks up the newspapers from the doorstep before opening the front door. Along with the four regular English dailies, he notices, there's a Hindi paper as well. Not a prominent one, at least he never heard about it in his years in Delhi. *Satyajeet Samachar.* Perhaps an ambitious businessman has started the paper with new money in the wake of reforms.

Curious, he opens the Hindi paper first. It's a promotional tactic for newspapers to distribute free copies, hoping some readers will migrate to them. The page-one anchor is an account of the surreal orgy of violence that happened the day before and still didn't.

Remote-Controlled Terror: An Exclusive
By Sharad Tiwari

With the use of hi-tech weapons, flair guns and remote-controlled missiles, terror unveiled a new face in a Delhi suburb when masked jihadis hit specific targets with clinical efficiency and perfect precision…

The following paragraphs recount, Arijit is surprised, exactly what Abhay Singh told him that ghostly night, without the slightest variation. A number of assailants were gunned down by the brave personal security guards of the general. It seems his neighbour and the reporter had access to the same script.

Intrigued by the news story, Arijit tries googling the incident. The only other report – a mere four paragraphs – appeared in a corner of a small newspaper's local page. Though preferred by the intelligentsia, it's way behind the market leaders in terms of circulation. And this report only mentions gang warfare, nothing more than that. Well-trained terrorists laid siege to this neighbourhood for hours, set fire to a shantytown, a heavy exchange of gunfire and explosions ripped off in the night – still not a single television network got any hint of it or sent their OB vans for live footage!

On impulse, he calls an additional secretary in the home ministry he knew when in Delhi. 'Swami, isn't it surprising the media has blacked out the incident in Noahda? It all happened right before my eyes,' he asks, disbelief in his voice. Chuckles come from the other end.

'That's no news for the media, sir. Wait for a little tiff between two cricketers or Bollywood stars and see how they splash it over the pages. Even wardrobe malfunctioning during a fashion show is bigger news than twenty people dying in a factory fire.'

Going through the other papers, looking for international news, he still cannot get over the questions bothering him: why didn't a single major paper cover the mad dance of violence? Why did terrorists set fire to the slum where only migrant workers live?

His phone pings with a new notification: *Watch tonight THE BIG STORY. Sensational exposé of WAR WITHIN.*

A half-hour programme on the blitzkrieg night presented by star anchor Agni Ghosh. Immensely popular, polemical, he thrives on controversies. Adored and abhorred in equal measure.

Arijit notes the timing. Though he rarely switches on the television, he decides to watch *THE BIG STORY*.

37
Swaps

...It's indeed a pleasant surprise to hear from you. Yes, I remember our weekend recitation classes. I would have loved to be among you all. But I am in the middle of something; it's not possible for me to take time off right now. When I'm in Calcutta next, I will definitely look for you. Niru-di says the girl who went to that music school with me is now a well-known historian. I've asked a bookshop here to get me some of your books.

Arijit reads the lines all over again, pauses, moves his index finger on the touchpad and then hits the send button. Gone – his reply to Sumita's invitation. Browsing over the large volume of mail in the inbox, he thinks of the strange happenings around him. Have they surprised, shocked him, left him gaping, unable to respond appropriately?

Last week, he was with Nandita on the farm. She wanted to know if everything was to his liking. Showed him their newly furnished bedroom. She had sought to create the ambience of the old English houses still surviving in the hill stations, with period furniture. He looked around, admiring an exquisitely carved, gilded mirror on the wall.

'Authentic Chippendale?'

She nodded.

On a mahogany cabinet sat a delicately designed porcelain bowl. He touched it, then turned to Nandita.

'Chelsea.' She smiled demurely.

Two chairs faced each other across a round Victorian table. The two of them would read deep into the night before going to bed. The chairs with cabriole legs and stretched S-shaped backs were a reminder of another time.

Nandita held his hand. He pulled her close, played with her auburn hair and bent his head to press a kiss on her lips. But somehow, the very next moment, his mood changed. He walked towards the door – aloof, withdrawn. He seemed to have remembered something more urgent than antique clocks and mirrors collected from the auction houses.

'Where will they live?' he asked, as if that was a more pressing matter.

She took him into a room down the corridor. Its windows opened onto the garden. Well-furnished, it was complete with a bed, dressing table, television, a gleaming white Hitachi air conditioner right below the ceiling. The smell of fresh paint hinted at things yet to happen. He pictured Rita living with her man in that room.

In the beginning, his own marriage did not mean much to him. Not built around expectations or a rush of emotions, not the onset of another journey. End of his loneliness – yes. Payback time for him? Undoubtedly. An act of recompense, a step to expatiate an old sense of guilt? His way of accepting, honouring the woman who stood by him in a difficult time? Yes, yes, of course. Honestly, nothing more than that.

There is an urgency now. He wants it to happen soon, sooner than scheduled. That image from two weeks ago keeps coming back – the girl back from the Special Cell with scratches, a bruised temple she was trying to hide with one hand. Whenever she appears in the doorway, he looks for fresh marks of brutality. On the farm, under Nandita's gaze, the girl will be safe. Alone, he is helpless. There is no way he can protect her. A soft, slow guppy stung by the mean, marauding sharks. Without Nandita, he cannot save the slender, clumsy fish.

It's a relief that she now lives in the one-room flat – out of that gangrened slum burnt down days after she moved out. Still… that wee-hour phone call comes back, chilling his heart. Chhetri says the Special Cell officer has come to know of her contacts. He has given instructions… That's actually eyewash, the clever policeman's way of sending a message. He should not be penalized for what has happened. The retired diplomat perhaps knows quite a few senior officers in the home ministry…

What's made the picture more disquieting is the ghostly spectacle of gang war with sectarian overtones that went on for hours the other day. Strangely, the temple priest missing just before the conflagration was later found dead, his body floating in the canal. He had refused to allow his temple to be desecrated as provocation to spark trouble. 'Saab-ji, what all happens in a city?' Chhetri looked at him quizzically.

He wants to throw a shield around her, insulate her from the hungry wolves.

The doorbell rings: he hears, he hears not. Absently walks towards the door. She stands there – shamefaced, crestfallen about everything that has happened. That has not happened. A moment goes by, two, then three… she comes in, bowed, unable to look up at him. Normally, she would greet him with a smile, ask about the dishes she made yesterday, talk about her plans for lunch. The girl walks into the kitchen, downcast, without saying a word.

She stands there, pretending to wash something in the sink. Then turns back to ask what she should cook. He sees a deep pallor on her face.

'What's wrong? Tell me.'

Her head sways feebly. 'I am all right.'

What troubles her? He looks at her, trying to figure it out. No doubt she is ill. Before she can say anything more, some kind of pain – or nausea? – seizes her. Holding the edge of the sink, she throws up. Looking at the sick, her face turns red in shame. He steps forward to hold her.

'Who did it? Tell me that. When did it happen?'

She hesitates, turns her face away and starts crying – in fear, in shame. He holds her arm, presses angrily, shakes the frail body.

'Tell me.' His voice rises.

'The police officer. The night we were picked up. He took me into a room, saying he needed to record my statement. And then…'

'Then – what?' he shouts.

'He… he closed the door.'

His first instinct is to call Nandita and talk about it. He is about to pick up his phone but stops. Unsure, not knowing if that would be the right thing to do. Will anybody buy her story, believe her?

He sits down on the sofa. The girl is going to get married in a month, move into her new home, be part of their household. Word spreads. Clouds, cobwebs of suspicion… An unreasonable anger shoots through his head. Arijit feels like running to the Special Cell to confront the police officer, hold him by the scruff. 'Why did you do that to her?' he would holler, grinding his teeth, his jaw clenched. His own words – mad, loud – surprise him. He feels embarrassed imagining himself shout.

Arijit breathes deeply. The surge of anger passes. Calm, down to earth, he faces the reality and its harshness. There could be no case for a crime against a migrant without a passport, a visa. After all, for a bribe of five thousand rupees, they let her off.

Rita comes with his morning coffee. Unsure, scared. Her eyes red, hair dishevelled… must have sobbed in the kitchen. He notices tear marks on her face. Not the usual talkative girl, humming a tune, chattering, fighting on the phone. Suddenly, he feels trapped, hemmed in, pushed into a pit.

The sound of mute weeping makes him look up. Now she cannot hold back her tears any more.

'Brute… that policeman.'

Her tears are coming down like rain. 'A girl in my situation…'

'What?'

'Would have ended her life…'

Can he do something for her, remove the dark shadows threatening a happy picture? Something comes to his mind. Taking a sip of coffee, he sits down on the floor, looking for the old newspapers stacked up under the table. He vaguely remembers… picks up a sheaf of bills, booklets, catalogues that came inserted in the newspapers.

Among the ads for television showrooms, Chinese restaurants, playschools and beauty salons, Noahda Medical Centre stands out. Now he reads it carefully: a hundred-bed hospital run by Dr Ajay Nagpal and Dr Anupama Nagpal. Evidently, an enterprising husband and wife team has started the venture. Not content with their earnings as doctors, they dreamt big. On his morning walk, Arijit has seen the hospital across the road from Blue Lotus Grove. Perhaps new in business, and still struggling, Dr Ajay

Nagpal has given his mobile number in the ad. As the owner of a new hospital, he cannot afford to be aloof and exclusive. He needs patients, a lot more of them.

Arijit calls the number. The Beatles's 'Yellow Submarine' is the caller tune. He listens for a few seconds.

'Dr Nagpal here.'

When Arijit introduces himself, the doctor warms up. 'Hello! Someone told me about you, sir. I was thinking of inviting you for a free check-up. Good you called.' A friendly voice. His clipped English hints at refinement, exposure to the world. Arijit briefly tells him about the problem and requests confidentiality.

'It's still at a very early stage; absolutely no hassles. A minor procedure. You can bring her to the hospital or just ask her to come on her own – I'm here.'

The doctor's words come as a relief. A reassurance. She has not lost her battle. Not yet. She still has a chance. Before she moves into the safety of the farm, the last traces of outrage in the migrant's life need to be removed. The dark spots, distortions, violations inside her body – all cleaned up. Tomorrow's bride cannot carry an illegitimate life within her.

He turns to her. 'The doctor says it's a simple thing – getting rid of your problem.' He smiles. 'It'll take just fifteen minutes. And yes, don't mention it to anyone.'

'Not even to Didi?'

'Not even to her.'

Waiting for the lift, Arijit sees two fashionable women coming from the other end of the corridor. Neha and her friend. He usually nods, smiles, waves whenever they meet – at the club, in the lobby waiting for the lift like this. Neha loves to talk; in less than a minute, she would tell him everything – about her business, terrorists from

Pakistan, new Bollywood movies, some fresh scandal in Blue Lotus Grove. She is one of the very few people in the complex he talks to. The other woman also looks familiar.

Neha is in a pair of faded jeans and a sleeveless yellow top, her friend in a skirt and a frilled shirt – they're out fun-shopping, out to have a good time. Both are sporting trendy sunglasses. Arijit remembers the morning Neha came home with offerings from the temple – in a fiery orange sari, vermilion blazing in the parting of her hair, an air of devoutness around her.

They see him, then the maid and look away. Did they exchange looks, suppress a laugh? Arijit is not sure. He can detect a faint hint of disgust on their faces. Neha starts talking on the phone. An excuse not to say hello.

The lift starts going down, then stops at the fifth floor, moves again. Stray words from her side of the conversation hit him like barbs. 'You must not lose your balance… yeah, yeah, that's like setting a monkey in a crystal room…'

He is not sure if this is a genuine call, or she is faking some phone talk to insinuate.

'Totally bizarre things are happening, yaar… Is this not funny?' she blurts out. Luckily, the lift reaches the ground floor. The two of them get out first. 'You have to draw a line somewhere.' Neha walks away, outraged, indignant, without waiting for the other woman to catch up.

A police officer raped a young woman in the lock-up weeks before her wedding. Was that not a *totally bizarre* thing to happen? Arijit absently clenches his fists.

'Kaku.' Rita hesitates. Perhaps she has sensed the tension in the air. 'It's just across the road. I know the hospital. Let me walk. You come in your car later?'

'No! You're coming in my car.' He is surprised by his obdurate, rising voice. 'You're not well.' He hurries towards the parking area.

Chhetri has seen him from his post. He rushes, pointing to his car. 'Saab-ji, the driver has gone out for tea. He'll be back in ten minutes.'

'Thanks, but there's no need for the driver. *I'll* drive.' The new obstinacy in his voice sounds unfamiliar to him. He holds the front door open for her. Rita is puzzled. She could not think of sitting in the passenger seat next to him. She looks at him helplessly. 'Get in,' he commands. The Gurkha looks amusedly at the scared girl, uncertain of her next step.

'Listen to Sahib,' he tells her. He laughs, seeing her discomfort.

'She is not well, so I am taking her to the doctor,' Arijit says, explaining the outing to the security guard. He gets behind the wheel and starts the engine.

Is this not funny? Neha's words whirl around in his head. Arijit accelerates even before getting out of the gate. Like a youngster, he honks impatiently.

You are our hero, she had said, giving him the leaves and petals, milk-and-sugar barfis. She had wished him a long life. The star of the energy agreement.

The hospital receptionist already knows about Arijit. Even before he asks for Dr Nagpal or gives his name, she gets up courteously to greet him. 'Take sir to Chairman's residence,' she tells an attendant. Turning to Arijit, she smiles. 'Chairman lives next door. He is waiting for you, sir.' Looking at Rita, she says, 'A senior doctor will see her in no time.'

A young nurse in her shining white uniform is walking across the reception area to another wing. The receptionist stops her. 'Take her to Dr Sudha Manchanda.' The nurse nods and goes back with Rita in the direction she came from.

The receptionist walks up to Arijit and whispers, 'Dr Manchanda is the head of our gynaecology department; she is very experienced.'

The attendant takes Arijit to the next building across the lawn through a side gate. The modest two-storey house with a manicured front lawn has a welcoming look. The receptionist must have called Dr Nagpal. He is waiting on the porch. 'Welcome, welcome, Mr Basu! It's a privilege to have you here.' They shake hands before entering a large, tastefully decorated living room.

'Sorry if I've upset your schedule,' Arijit says. 'I practically barged in…'

'No way!' The doctor sounds cheerful. 'If everyone is perfectly fine, the doctor is out of work.' He laughs. 'Who will see the doc without a fever or backache, huh?'

Arijit laughs, too, relieved by the doctor's warmth and friendliness. A reasonably good watercolour on one wall, Dhokra metalwork by tribal craftsmen on the mantelpiece, a hammock hung from the ceiling in one corner, cane and wood furniture – all this creates an ambience. 'You're lucky if you know a good doctor; you're particularly fortunate if that doctor has a good sense of humour,' Arijit says. Both of them burst out laughing.

'Honestly, Mr Basu, I don't get a chance to laugh too often. Work stress is killing me. About a week ago, you must have noticed, there was a massive fire in the slum around the canal. Perhaps you heard gunfire and bombs going off. Throughout the night, victims were rushed to our hospital with third-degree burns, bullet wounds, hit by bomb splinters. We managed to save a few lives, but most of them were brought in dead or too critical.'

'Yes. I heard it was another terror attack targeting some important people in the area.'

'Nonsense. Some twenty people died, most of them Muslims – either petty businessmen or workers. Terrorists mostly shoot and scoot; they do not remain on the scene, firing and lobbing bombs for two hours. The incident has the stamp of the new vigilante gangs who harass small traders in the name of cow protection. From the ashes of the slum fire, be very sure, sir, now terrorists will rise.' Having said so much in one breath, the doctor stops.

Arijit looks thoughtful. 'Didn't the police do anything?'

'The police are part of the gang. This place technically comes under UP.'

'Hello, Mr Basu, I am Anupama.' The doctor's beautiful wife shakes hands with him. He has already seen the couple's photograph on a book rack – the two skiing in the Swiss Alps in their younger days. She has not changed much since that holiday in Europe. He glances at the framed photograph again.

'Both of us were working in London. He was a surgeon in the NHS; I, a paediatrician, worked with a senior doctor. We were crazy about our half-term ski trip to the Swiss Alps.'

'Why did you come back?'

'That's an interesting question,' Anupama says, sitting opposite Arijit at the centre table. 'We also asked ourselves if going home would be a mistake, leaving behind our careers in London. Mr Basu, we actually wanted to do something, something more than doing well for ourselves. We wanted to build an institution. We talked to a few friends here; they promised help. The government gave us the land at a subsidized price. And we have built the hospital brick by brick over the past five years. A new heart unit is coming up soon.'

'That's really admirable. One look at the hospital, and I could sense its efficiency.'

A man comes in carrying a round brass tray. In a grey-blue safari suit, he looks different from a typical help. He bows to the guest before putting down the tray.

Arijit looks at the tray – a wine bottle, stemware and a cheeseboard. Arranging them neatly around the table, the man leaves quietly. Do the owners of the sleek hospital have a major-domo?

'At the peak of negotiations for the energy deal, we eagerly waited for every statement you made from Washington,' Ajay says. 'In the evening, we sat before the television and intensely debated whether you would be able to swing the deal.'

'My role as a negotiator was very limited.'

'You are being modest, Mr Basu. Everybody knows the Americans did not trust our politicians, but they actually listened to you.'

Anupama is pouring white wine into a stemmed glass when Ajay's phone rings. His face contorts. He looks tense.

'What? A bullet? The MLA's nephew? Rush him into the operation theatre. I am coming.' He turns to Arijit apologetically. 'I am sorry, Mr Basu. I have to attend to an emergency. The local legislator's nephew was hit by a bullet in a gang war somewhere outside the city. The bullet is stuck in his chest. I have to perform the operation. Please carry on. And the young lady is fine. The treatment is simple. They have done an ultrasound. She can go home in a while.' He smiles sadly at his wife and leaves in a hurry.

Anupama offers him the wine glass and pushes the cheeseboard across the table.

'One does not get the impression that such gang wars break out in this quiet suburb.' He takes a little sip.

'It's not in enclaves like this that such things happen. Fights start in the outlying areas, where land is a big issue. Farmers do not want to part with their land. For them, land is empowerment, their identity. Businesses are pressuring the government for more land. Then you have the builders. All this has made the place a real tinderbox.'

Anupama reclines on the sofa, holding her wine glass. Moments later, she puts down the glass and lights a cigarette, offers the 555 pack to him. He smiles, declining. 'Gave up long ago.'

'Arijit, how do you spend your time?' She takes a mild puff. 'I guess you are being flooded with offers – many people must want you to be with them. Think tanks, associations, clubs…'

'When I left D.C., I decided to run away from the spotlight – power, privilege, easy recognition, media. I wanted to be alone for a while. You can say I am in hiding. I have just finished a book on the energy situation in South Asia. That apart, I do not do anything.'

'That's quite natural… after hectic years in diplomacy.' She pauses, takes another puff, then moves to the edge of the sofa. 'We have an informal group of friends, people like us, liberal, enlightened professionals who have seen the world. Over the weekend, we party to unwind, beat the stress. And we swap partners. Why don't you join our gang?' She bends forward, her chin in her palm.

Arijit takes another sip of wine. 'How does it work?'

'For instance, I work with another paediatrician at his clinic, his wife works with Ajay in our hospital. They spend an evening in this house. There is good understanding; we are not cheating on anyone; no deception. These are decent people from different professions. Nitin Deshmukh is a senior executive in an automobile company. His wife, Shuvangi, is a fashion designer.

They have teamed up with an architect couple. Entry into our group is by invitation only. Why don't you come to our party next Saturday? Come with your partner. Let's get to know each other.'

'This is really interesting. I really had no idea how society has changed. But I am moving out of this place. My wife died long ago. All these years, I did not have time to think about myself. Now I am marrying my fiancée of many years and will settle down on a farm in Mehrauli. That's the other end of the city.'

'Congratulations, Arijit. She is that famous socialite from Paris, right? She created waves in France… I'm forgetting her name.'

'Do you know Nandita?' Arijit cannot help frowning.

'Oh, no. I read about her in a magazine gossip column.' She laughs. 'I've seen her pictures. She has stunning looks – perfect European features.' She takes a cracker with a slice of cheese. 'I think the two of you are perfectly cut out for our group. Piko Sondhi – he has just retired as air commodore. And his wife Blossom – she is an excellent polo player. You know, you two pairs match each other fabulously. Both sides will have fun.'

Anupama's words – frank, unhesitant, easy – are somehow nailed into his mind. The whole city by now knows about their marriage. And what else? Even before the wedding and planned honeymoon in the Andamans, here is an offer to join the swappers club. For half the day, Blossom will be his partner, huh.

'Hope I have not shocked you, Arijit.' Anupama holds his hand. 'I assume Nandita has always been outgoing. Had friends among artists, writers in Paris?' She smiles.

Arijit is puzzled. This beautiful young woman with a faint Mayfair accent is digging into their past like a Bollywood gossip columnist. 'What else do you know?'

'Are you upset? Sometimes I hear snide remarks about our

partner swapping. I don't give a damn! What the hell! Why should I bother? It's my life anyway. By the way, have you heard about the upcoming theatre festival in Mumbai? For one whole week at Prithvi Theatre in Juhu. They are dedicating it to Ranjana Mathur. Her friends and admirers have come together. I just remembered when you talked about her death.'

This woman is like a magic mirror reflecting his past, present, perhaps future also. The mention of his dead wife unsettles him. He has never been in contact with Ranjana's family, friends. He has no idea about her relatives any more.

'Honestly, how do you know so much?' He can't help a smile.

Anupama laughs. Her body shakes, the perfect teeth flash. 'I'm sorry, Arijit. I only told you what I read in a blog. I'm no private detective.' She laughs again. 'But… the poor maid… how did she come into such a state?' She bites her lower lip suggestively. Mischief in her voice.

Arijit senses danger but decides to give her a firm answer. 'She lives in a slum. The police picked her up along with some others – perhaps as part of a demolition drive. Or some fight among them. It happened in the police station.'

'This suburb is technically not part of Delhi. Scared of the activist groups and media, police in the city behave a little more responsibly.' Anupama quickly retracts. 'But in Noahda, the cops are brutes, hooligans in uniform. Your humanity saved the girl, Arijit. Often, in such cases, they have no choice but to commit suicide.'

Her phone chirps.

'Ajay! How bad is the case? Will he survive? Oh, god, what a relief! If anything went wrong, the goons would have set upon the hospital. The girl can go home now? Good. I'll tell Arijit. He is such a wonderful man.'

Getting up, he takes another look around the elegantly done up living space. On a round corner table, under the lampshade is the mounted picture of the couple against the backdrop of a snowy mountain peak. Next to it is another – a beaming young girl in her school uniform riding a black horse. He waits before the picture for a few seconds.

'Your daughter?'

'Yes. Pallavi. She is in a boarding school in Mussoorie.' Anupama touches the gilt-framed picture affectionately.

38
Mrs Verghese

The woman doctor with a kind face asks her to climb onto the bed. She has already slipped into a green apron. Rita lies down on her back, vaguely looking at the ceiling.

'Relax. Keep your child passage loose.' The doctor smiles. The clinical smell in the room fills her insides. The doctor grips her stomach, presses down, her hand moves lower. She feels for something below the layer of skin, deep inside her body. Then she asks the nurse for medical gloves.

'Fold your legs up.'

She obeys.

The doctor's left hand expertly stretches out the rim of her vagina while the other one tries to push open the passage. 'Keep the child passage open,' she keeps saying. 'Relax.' After burrowing into the dark chasm of her secret, the doctor walks up to the other end of the bed. Throws the gloves into a tray and comes close to the bed. With her bare hand, she touches Rita's forehead affectionately.

'It's a small thing, just like a boil. You can get up now.' She mentions a pill, and the nurse brings it with a glass of water. 'Swallow it.'

Rita gulps it down with a big sip of water. The doctor watches her. 'Good.' She beams at her. 'I'm giving you four more pills.'

Dr Manchanda puts a hand on her shoulder. 'Day after tomorrow, you push them in.'

Rita stares at the doctor blankly.

'I mean through the child passage – four tablets, one after another. Don't be scared. No pain, nothing. You can do it yourself; your mother or a sister can also help. You will start bleeding. That means end of your problem.' The doctor flashes a smile.

Rita nods uncertainly.

'Don't worry. The pills are like small buttons; they won't hurt.'

Listening to the doctor, Rita thinks of the day on the farm, Bharat's clumsy kisses in the newly painted room where he says they will sleep together at night. Beyond the sturdy gate of the farm, her past completely obliterated. On the downy grass carpeting the lawns, across the shadowy orchard, in the corridor along the rooms, she will have a new identity – Kaku's adopted daughter, Didi's favourite, Bharat's wife. The old couple will live in one part of the house, she with Bharat in another. Once a year, Kaku's daughter, Piu, will come with her husband and son.

She – no longer Rabeya, only Rita – indisputably, undoubtedly in charge of the household, shouting at the workforce, giving orders, fussed if Bharat is late in getting things from the market. The real boss.

One Sunday morning, when Kaku had gone to the club to meet someone, the landline rang. It went on ringing. The normally pleasant tone turned into an alarm, reverberating from all around the house. As if the call was absolutely urgent, coming to break big news.

With hesitation, she took the call.

'Hello,' she said nervously, unsure if she had done the right thing.

'You're the girl who helps Baba in the kitchen?' Piu sounded friendly. Her Bengali refined, like a television announcer's.

Rita felt confident, reassured. 'When are you coming?' she asked, reciprocating Piu's friendly tone.

'We will come in the winter when my son has his school vacation.'

'He is Bubka?'

'Right.'

'He looks like Kaku.'

'How do you know?'

'I saw his picture – playing with a football. On Kaku's computer.'

'You're clever, Rita.'

'I have a name for your son – Bengali name.'

'What?'

'Nayan.'

'What a nice name! *Nayan* means *eye*, right?'

'Yes.'

'I've heard you cook very well. But don't make deep-fried stuff for Baba, okay? Give him boiled vegetables, sprouts and salad. He should not eat too many cutlets. When I come, will you make prawn curry with coconut milk?'

Rita was amused. 'I will make prawn-in-coconut for you, hilsa in mustard sauce for your husband and chandrapuli for Bubka.'

'Ooh! Rita, don't say any more. Hilsa, ah! I feel like rushing to the airport.'

Rita laughed. 'Don't you get hilsa in America?'

'It's not easy. By the way, how do you make chandrapuli?'

'Mix fresh coconut shreddings into thickly boiled milk to make a paste. When the paste tightens a little more, let it cool and spread cardamom powder over it for flavour. Keep beating it. And make conch-shaped chandrapuli with a mould.'

'Wonderful, Rita, you are a genius! If you come to this country, you will be on television.'

For some reason, Rita's mind keeps going back to the conversation with Piu when the doctor gives her further instructions. She raises her hand, wanting to say something.

The doctor notices and bends down to her. 'You want to ask something?' She holds her arm.

'When I get married, will there be any problem? I mean, I can have my child, nah?'

'Yes, of course. There will be absolutely no problem.' The doctor sees a sparkling tear marking a trail. 'Come to me whenever you want to have a baby.' As if to dispel the heaviness in the air, the doctor taps on her shoulder. 'So you want to take good care of your personal hygiene, eh? It's all cleaned up down there.' She rolls her eyes, smiling playfully.

Rita looks embarrassed. 'My friend works in a beauty parlour…'

'I understand. Better be careful about all such things.'

Turning on her side, she looks at the calendar on the bedroom wall. Less than a month. And she and Bharat will live together as man and wife on the farm. Its high boundary wall, two feet of sharp, winding concertina over the rock wall, the heavy iron gate, the security guards holding guns, and Raja and Munna, the two mean-looking, fierce dogs sniffing around – all this, all this will be protection against intruders, against beastly policemen. Her past.

Honestly, she does not think much of Bharat. Her breath does not moisten imagining the scenes in the bedroom overlooking the garden. She is sure the handsome, mild-mannered man will be a good husband to her. And there is no chance of her secret spilling out. Her life will nestle under Didi's wing and Kaku's tall presence.

She does not quite understand why Kaku is so concerned about her. The day she returned from the police station, the man seemed offended, shocked, angry and helpless at the same time. Cleaning the bruise on her forehead with cotton wool, he was actually crying. A father she lost long ago. Abba before he left them for the new woman.

A question keeps coming to mind; it troubles her.

Why is he marrying Didi so late?

They like each other, share a lot. She can make out that long ago, when they knew each other in another country, they were very close. Perhaps this is his way of paying off an old debt? Didi stood by him when he was in a mess. Now he wants to say: *I remember everything*. But is there anything else?

She has a feeling this marriage is his way of protecting her, securing her future. Without a woman by his side, Kaku is helpless, cannot do much for her. She has overheard nasty remarks by some people in Blue Lotus Grove. When she waited for the lift the other day, an old woman came and stood beside her. 'So it's you? Your stink has charmed him? After seeing the world, he has come to adopt a street tart, huh?'

This morning, those two women glared at her. She could feel the intense hate through their dark glasses. Their distaste, disgust for him. She somehow knows that the two fashionable women and many like them in the other apartments want to hold him like a trophy. Adore him, talk, gossip about him. A proud possession. Their showpiece. But he has disappointed them all by parenting the maid from the slums. A big bore. But a few more weeks, and those women will not see the big man again. Gone. Out of sight. So will she.

Nobody in the apartment complex will get to know about the wooded farm, the riot of mynahs, bulbuls and woodpeckers, the squirrels slipping from a square of sunshine into a circle of shade and those richly hued, imperious peacocks making a special appearance on the treetops. Her battle against hunger, struggle to be taken as a human will be over. Forever. She has never been Rabeya really and she has no past, no shadows catching up with her. Like the annoying burr in the field behind their Paankhali village. She has no country and definitely no borders. All Rita needs is a little shelter. That farm will be her home, her country. There's nothing beyond its fortified walls.

She has kept the four tablets in a small glass jar. Will bleed out of trouble, the doctor said. She is now feeling sleepy, a little dizzy. Still, she does not want to sleep.

A mild knock on the door alerts her. Any such intrusion now fills her with dread, brings back the night of the police raid.

'Who's that?' Her throat is dry.

'Rekha, Rekha from Calcutta.' The tingling voice breaks into a big laugh.

'Rekha, Rekha from Calcutta,' she mimics. 'Rekha from Bombay, eh?'

Her cousin breezes in. In a brown pleated skirt and white top, mushroom haircut, she looks like a girl tumbling out of a television soap. 'I was in Blue Lotus Grove to give a massage to a fat woman. An old client. The Nepali guard at the gate said you had gone to the hospital.' From a handbag, she takes out a Tupperware tumbler and a McDonald's packet.

'Have some chicken soup.' Rekha walks into the kitchen and comes back with a bowl. She pours some soup into the bowl, sprinkles salt and pepper, stirs it with a spoon. She pulls the armchair close to the bed. 'This will help you.'

Rita takes a spoon of the soup. The cousins look at each other. Even without exchanging words, Rekha understands; she nods knowingly.

'Policemen are like hyenas.' Rekha holds her cousin.

Rita is about to take another spoonful from the bowl. She stops. Her heart throbs. Has the news spread? She looks at Rekha quizzically.

'It happened to many others. The day I heard about the police raid on the slum, I feared for you. I somehow felt something bad was happening to you.'

'Ameene, our marriage is just three weeks away. Didi has already ordered the gold ornaments – bangles, earrings, a necklace for me. If—'

'We grew up together. What I can guess, no one else will. Your sahib saw to it. After hearing from the security guard, I rushed to the hospital. They flatly denied anybody like you had been there.'

'Sometimes I feel like calling him Abba.'

'You have got back your father.'

'The night in the police station comes back in my sleep. I wake with a start, sweating. Another twenty days – but it seems such a distance, the wait so long.'

'You will be out of all this, Bubu. For your sahib, you're a daughter. It hurts him that he cannot look after you well.'

'But what happened just before my marriage is a bad sign – it does not augur well—'

'Every day, so many women are being raped in this city. Most of them keep mum; only a few speak up. It happened to me also.'

'When? You never told me!' Rita is shocked by the casual way her cousin speaks about the violation.

'I got a call from a client. When I reached her place, I found she was not there. "Her uncle is in hospital, she had to rush. But I will pay you for the visit," her husband said.'

And then the man was courteous. He asked her in and had her seated on the sofa. 'It's hot outside, let me give you something to drink.' He got her orange juice in a small glass. A little later, Rekha realized there was something more to the drink. She felt drowsy, her senses going to sleep. He gently led her into the bedroom, whispering sweet nothings in her ear. By the time she came to, everything was over. He was on the sofa, smoking and watching something on television – about the endangered grey parrots in the African forests.

She cried, shouted, smashed the glass on the floor. She threatened to tell his wife everything, go to the police.

'And he listened, as if amused by my fuming. He walked back into the bedroom. I heard him open a chest or something. Came with a nice leather wallet. "See." Wads of five-hundred-rupee notes winked at me. I had never seen so much money together. Still, I shouted. I felt cheated, humiliated by the rich man. "Here is five thousand, one hundred multiplied by fifty – money you cannot earn in a month." He ran his thumb over the crackling new notes. "It's for you. If you do something silly, no one will see you ever again. You will simply vanish." He was a strange man. Went back into the bedroom, returned and sat on the sofa, fiddling with the TV remote. Then he gave me more money.

Said, "Here's another five thousand." He did not touch me again. Spoke politely, asked me about my work.'

Rita listens to her cousin – scared, wide-eyed. 'Did you ever find out who called you in the first place? Was it his wife?'

'Of course it was her. An old client; I knew her voice.'

'And do you think the man would have harmed you…'

'It was not an empty threat. Such things are happening every day – someone disappearing forever.' Rekha presses her cousin's arm. 'Bubu, you keep quiet for another few weeks, and everything is behind you. And be careful about Jamal. In his stupidity, he can make a big mess.'

Rekha goes into the kitchen for a glass of water. After talking to her cousin, Rita feels a lot better. She sits up, energized, keen to know about her new life. Rekha comes back with a plate, unpacks the chicken burger and places it on a stool.

Rita looks at the food. 'I'll need good food the day after. Will you come in the morning to *push them in*?' She laughs, pointing to the glass jar on the table.

'Is this the medicine they gave you in the hospital?'

Rita explains how the pills work. She sees her cousin up close with a tell-me-about-you look on her face. Knowing they know, the cousins smile.

'We have been married for about a month.'

'Married! Sister, you're married, and I did not know about it?'

'If I missed anybody at the wedding, it's you, Bubu. But it happened like an accident. We didn't want to marry until winter. We were having fun… Then it happened.'

'What?'

'Jimmy has a distant aunt who lives somewhere in Delhi. She

came one Sunday morning unannounced and saw us still in bed. She threw a tantrum, so the wedding was hastily arranged. The two of us went to a church, met the priest, attended a couple of counselling sessions over the weekend.'

The marriage was a simple affair. Around three in the afternoon, they reached the church – she in a purple Rajshahi silk sari and Jimmy in a light blue suit. A handful of his friends, that aunt, her husband, and from Rekha's side, the woman who runs the beauty salon where she had worked until recently. The guests.

The aunt looked important, knowing she had saved the family an acute embarrassment. Jimmy's friends were simple people, laughing and joking among themselves. One of them had a guitar. They sang a Malayalam song:

Poomukha vathikkal
Sneham vidarthunna…

'Bas, only these four words I remember. The melody is haunting, but I cannot follow the song.' Rekha pours some more soup into the bowl for her cousin.

'Was that all?'

'The priest asked both of us to recite from a book. I felt murmurs in my heart when I said:

I promise to be true to you in good times and in bad
In sickness and health,
I will love you and honour you all the days of my life.

It was a strange feeling. I do not know which book it was, but the words keep coming back… *in good times and in bad.* After the ceremony was over, we went to a South Indian restaurant, and Jimmy ordered appam with stew, idli, uthappam, payasam. Honestly, I did not like it one bit. One of his friends turned to me and said, "When we come home, I am sure we will get fish for the main course and rasgulla for dessert." Another friend joked from across the table, "Jimmy, good you married a Bengali, not a Punjabi. Then we would have to dance Bhangra." They all laughed. His aunt listened, then shed her arrogance a little. "There is a lot in common between Malayalis and Bengalis – both eat fish and both are literarily inclined." My heart was pounding, fearing the aunt would ask me about Bengali writers and poets. But the party was soon over.'

'How is Jimmy, your husband? Is he a good man?' Rita looks up into her cousin's face.

'He's a very simple man. The first batch of students arrives at our door by eight in the morning. The last batch leaves by seven in the evening. We go out on Jimmy's scooter, eat at a restaurant, do a little shopping and come home. Then he plays the CDs of his native music. I cannot follow it at all. Worse, when he talks to his friends or relatives on the phone. He talks about me, but I cannot follow a word. I only hear *Rekha*. *Rekha* in the middle of a liquid flow of words. And when he sits alone by the window singing his favourite song in his native tongue, I get a hint.'

Rekha stops, thinking about something. 'Yes, by now I have learnt a line from that song:

Oru maathra veruthe ninachu poyi

Sometimes he holds me and sings that line. It's about me, but I don't know what it means. When I hear him sing the line, I start preparing for the next number in bed.'

She laughs.

Rita blushes. Her cousin has always been a straight talker. Her tongue holds back nothing. Unabashed, she rummages in her purse for something. 'Here – see.' She fishes out a business card:

Tresses

Beauty Care, Hairstyle and Treatment, Bridal Make-Up

Rekha Varghese

At the bottom is the salon address, then her phone number and email:

rekhavarghese21@gmail.com

'Why 21? Is it going to be your name? Like Khan, Haq, like Basu, you're Rekha 21, ha ha…'

'Uff! Sis, you're impossible. That's because I am twenty-one – forever twenty-one, ha ha. Also, it's my email. If you write me a letter on Gmail, you have to use that as my address.'

'And who's Vaarges? Why is vaargas? What does it mean – vaargis…' Rita struggles.

'Slowly, slowly.' Rekha laughs. The newly married girl is amused. Then pretends to be annoyed. 'Bubu, you need to say this name right. *Vaar-geese*. My husband's second name. So mine also. When an elderly woman calls me for a haircut appointment, she says, "Mrs Varghese, Dina Kakkar here." Oh, how much I love that! Mrs Varghese!'

She looks at her cousin. Rita sees a new pride, confidence all about her.

'Could you follow me?' Rekha nudges her a little.

'Yes, Mrs Varghese.'

39
Agni

The programme you have been waiting for with bated breath is finally here. One billion people of this country have the right to know what happened that fateful night in Noahda. Real India Television's chief editor and the country's most popular news anchor, Agni Ghosh, is here with the truth. In an atmosphere of distrust and doubt, motivated propaganda and fake news, Agni is coming with his armoury of facts, an array of clinching proofs and startling details. The wait is over. Here's your favourite show, THE BIG STORY, *with Agni.*

The announcer – tall, lithe, pixie-cut hair – has a sense of the situation. While looking pleasant, she has not smiled. The touch of black in her dress lends to the solemn mood.

Arijit takes another sip of black coffee. He is watching something on TV after a long time. A man in his early thirties, overdressed in an expensive suit and a striped, long tie, puffy hair specially done and face shining with make-up, Agni is conscious of his pre-eminent position, the primacy of his role as host. With special effects created by quartz lamps and Fresnel lenses, and echoes dramatizing the sense of apocalyptic imminence, he is regally presented at the centre of the top-billed show. On his right, around the majestic oval table, is a security expert who heads a think tank and a left-leaning academic who occasionally writes op-eds evoking India's robust plural past; and on Agni's left are two retired military officers from the Kingdom of Natsikap.

'What I have gathered about the night of Devil's Firework in the backyard of Delhi is a perfect recipe for a massive disaster.' Agni's voice rises an octave. 'In fact, a great Indian tragedy is just waiting to happen…' He looks serious, affected by grim foreboding, turns the pages in a folder. 'We've the exclusive footage of how it began.'

Obliterating the studio, the screen takes the viewer to the demonic night: masked terrorists, holding sophisticated machine guns, like astronauts in helmets and night vision goggles. Like computer-programmed toys. They jump out of armoured carriers in the middle of a forbidding ground and fan into the shantytown.

'The point to be noted here,' Agni's voice booms, 'such highly trained, elite corps of jihadis, airdropped by stealthy choppers somewhere outside the city, are certainly not meant for a strike on distressed hutments. Then how did the slum catch fire?' At this point, the anchor's voice rises to a crescendo. 'Then how did the slum catch fire howhowhow?' Here his words take on a sharp, sarcastic edge. 'Don't we have *no* government? Has the home ministry *done* on a holiday? Do the officers *suspend* the evil regime of Natsikap?' Excited, carried away by his own rhetoric, the anchor's syntax, grammar… everything starts falling. He malaprops in style. 'As per our investigation, the hovels had turned into an ammo depot. Deadly weapons and munitions smuggled out of Afghanistan and Iraq, Natsikap's gifts to terror cells in India, had found their way to Saddamabad. That night, when the *angels of death* hurriedly searched for hand grenades and rockets in the shanties, an accidental fire broke out. Quite a *view* innocent people died.'

He then turns to the security expert. 'Dr Tikku, you are an internationally acclaimed expert on geopolitics. What's your reading of the situation?'

The man clasps and unclasps his hands in concentration. 'Well, Agni, the whole of India is grateful to you for ripping off the veil over the terror syndicate. What you've just shown fits into the format of limited warfare. Natsikap knows it stands no chance in a direct conflict with India. So, it is financing such subversive activity inside this country. It's their proxy war. And this trend is going to get stronger.'

'Thank you, Dr Tikku. So this is a war inside the country, not on the border?' Agni looks pleased.

'Absolutely.'

The anchor then turns to the liberal academic. 'You're perhaps upset seeing truth come out, Professor Jha?'

'You mean *the* truth – right?' The academic chuckles.

The anchor throws up his hands dismissively.

'Yes, I'm upset, for I doubt if this is the whole truth.' The professor looks on like the studio is an extension of the classroom. 'How do we know those masked people you showed were real terrorists? You don't have any footage of the ammo depot catching fire. The hand of the cow vigilantes behind the fire cannot be ruled out—'

'Hhhhowww can you make such an irresponsible, absurd, *absorbent* statement on this popular show? This is unpatriotic, anti-India activity. Do you teach subversion to your students—'

'I do, for what is subversion today will be law tomorrow.' Jha laughs, knowing he has won this round.

'This is treason! You're indulging in seditious activity. Our soldiers are getting killed fighting the enemy on the border, and you're siding with those who do not wish India well?'

'A television anchor cannot decide what's good for the nation or who's doing more harm to India – cow vigilantes or the slum dwellers. We demand a judicial enquiry into the incident.'

Grieving the academic's demand for a probe, Agni shakes his head. 'In history, your type has been known as the fifth *claimants*.'

The professor flicks a smile, shaking his head in disapproval. 'You mean *fifth columnists*?'

Totally unflappable, the host turns to the other side, muttering, 'A sad day for India. Very sad…'

He glares at the retired military officers from Natsikap. 'So, this is the game the bosses in your country are playing?'

'This is India's internal matter; we've nothing to do with all this,' the two say almost in chorus. The suppressed sniggers on their faces are not entirely lost on the audience.

'Didn't I produce evidence of Natsikap's dark designs to bleed India?' Agni is now roaring like a lion. 'If you did feed at the breast as a baby, face us upfront. You slimy jackals!' He dramatically thrusts the folder at them. Overtaken by emotion, his body shakes, eyes water.

As if terrified by the aggression, the two decorated army officers pathetically cower to save themselves from the flying missile. A TV anchor does what the government bed-wets even to think of – makes Natsikap duck for defence.

Wonderful, Agni's incendiary show! His fantastic pyrotechnics. Arijit laughs before switching off the television.

40
Wedding Ring

When Arijit comes out of the gate, it's still dark. The heavy-duty trucks on the highway have their headlights on. From this distance, they look like prehistoric animals, gigantic, burdened by their immensity. Weighted down by massive cargo, the sixteen-wheelers groan.

Since Rita's wee-hour call from the police station, he sleeps fretfully, keeps waking up around three in the morning. A fear grips him. He picks up the phone to see if there has been a missed call.

The street going past the new buildings to the highway is still not visible. He looks back at Blue Lotus Grove – the giant behemoth of tall apartment towers, snug in the depth of sleep. This place has been his home for a while. And now, it's time to move out, leave for another address.

Arijit hesitates, then sets out, taking long strides down the driveway.

Fluorescent street lights have failed to dispel the lingering night, its uncertainties and ghoulish impenetrability. Lumps of black – like tarred seeds of cottonwood trees in summer – float around with a hint of the sinister. He walks faster to leave behind the new structures of human habitation – Mayfair Apartments, Kensington Gardens, Regent's Park… As if the swanky mock-English developments are staking him out.

Past the buildings, he turns his eyes towards what used to be acres of farmland with extravagant crops. The cool breeze brought the rich smell of the earth's fertility. Until the other day. It now looks like a factory shed – huge quantities of iron rods neatly pyred, mountains of stacked-up cement bags sitting like the tomb of a lost way of life. Rollers and earthmovers parked in a corner like war-fatigued tanks. Men in mock-military uniforms from security agencies move around the place splashed by floodlights. Mounds of stone chips and sand have covered the area where yellow mustard flowers swung in the breeze.

He recoils from the scene of mutilation and turns away to walk even faster. As if he wants to deny the abomination, preparations to build fancy villas, *an exclusive range of properties* on once lavish farmlands. Where robust crops stood a fortnight back. He walks briskly past the last trace of boomtown and moves among the trees lining the highway. It's still cool, quiet here.

Suddenly, he hears piercing gunshots. The frost and ferocity of sharp fire immobilize him. He stands cramped, inert. His legs seem to be curling up under the weight of fear. Then retaliatory shooting follows and a stunning explosion like elemental thunder.

Rooted to the ground by the gun battle, Arijit struggles to regain control over his senses, overcoming the sudden numbness. Though his hands are shaking, he takes an uncertain step. Slowly, unsteadily, he gets out of the woods and climbs up the slope to the highway. The scene of the surreal shoot-out flares right across the road.

The mangled carapace of the bullet-ridden Innova hangs precariously between two trees after sliding off the road. Its rear has caught fire. Pulled by an unrelenting curiosity, he crosses the road. Thick smells of fresh blood – human flesh still pulsing with life – and gunpowder assail him. The man in the driver's seat is slumped to a side, one hand still on the steering. Three bodies lie on the ground, thrown out of the Innova by the impact of its fall – blood oozes from their heads.

He recognizes one of them – the tall, lean, lovelorn man who came to his house to invite Rita to his Eid party. Her shadowy lover. The grille factory worker who could not adjust to the world. Only, the long hair of the dejected lover has now been trimmed to combat-readiness. He had obviously jumped out of the car to fight back the crack commando team.

A little distance away, the tense dragoons are carrying a bleeding comrade into a vehicle. The man, still alive, is screaming, his olive uniform soaked in blood. The walkie-talkie in the police jeep is cackling hoarsely. A few curious bystanders have gathered – workers from a construction site, a milkman leaning against his bicycle.

'What are you doing here? Get lost.' The edgy commando, almost hysterical, shoves the milkman away. The man in uniform, Arijit notices, is trembling.

'They had plans to kill the home minister,' the commando tells Arijit in a gesture of deference. The man walks to the burning vehicle – alert, his Sten held tightly. 'We intercepted their calls and chased. When challenged, they fired at us.' He looks up at Arijit, perhaps for some appreciation. 'They were on a dry run.'

Suddenly, shrill sirens split the air. Police cars, fire engines, ambulances are rushing, their flashers flickering like fire.

Arijit crosses the road into the woods again. Before disappearing among the trees, he turns back, looking at the body lying on the ground – the tall, lanky fellow who came to his door, overawed, unsure of himself. While turning away, he sees another wave of vehicles zooming on the scene – OB vans of the television news channels.

Uneasiness creeps into him like an invisible insect. The grille-factory man's face comes back again and again. He stood there at his door, scared, humble, looking for the girl he loved. Was Rita trying to leave behind a clumsy, obsessive lover for a better life? Or had she closed the door on him because of his dangerous ways? That scene flashes back – Rita's face pressed against the grille, waiting to be spotted by the man working in an apartment in the opposite tower.

By the time he reaches the entrance of Blue Lotus Grove, news has spread. Small groups of sweepers, drivers, servants are talking excitedly about the incident.

'It's on television,' someone says.

Arijit looks for Chhetri, but he is nowhere around. He asks someone. 'He has gone home. Got a call from his uncle; his father is critical. He left this morning only,' the guard on duty says.

He looks around uneasily. Little knots of schoolchildren in their neatly ironed uniforms are waiting around the gate. Their mothers are busy talking about school, class teachers, new movies. One of them takes a call on her phone. Her carefully made eyebrows knit; her face contorts in shock. One hand moves up to her forehead. 'Oh my god!' she almost cries. 'Don't tell me... don't tell me!' She turns to another woman holding her son's hand. 'Do you know one of the terrorists killed just now was that crazy grille-wallah? He worked in our block only last week! Incredible!' She suddenly stops talking and looks sharply at Arijit from the corner of her eye. The other woman, too.

Unable to bear the glare he walks away.

Back in his apartment, Arijit picks up the *Times of India* and reclines in his armchair on the balcony. His favourite place in the house. Holding the paper, he looks at the farm in the distance. The paper with black coffee, his usual morning. She knows this. The leader, the views from the balcony, the noise of water in the kitchen sink, his moment to reflect – he cherishes all this. Still no trace…

It is rather unusual, unlike her. Rita knows how badly he needs black coffee at the moment. Strange. She wrote down a phone number on the kitchen calendar. He calls it – switched off. Is it then… the police cracking down on the terrorist's *moll*? Taken to the police station again? The rented flat in Sector 8 could not insulate her?

He pulls the front door shut and locks it before walking towards the lift.

Downstairs, he first turns towards the car park, then changes his mind. Better not to drive to Sector 8. He walks down the plaza towards the gate. The chief security officer is addressing his men.

'Point number one: *Do not* allow any unknown person inside. First, ask for the flat number. Call them on the intercom and see if the visitor is really expected. No suspicious objects must be allowed in. We are thinking of installing a walk-through metal detector at the gate. And *do not* allow any domestics, maids, servants, salesmen, junkmen without an ID.'

Arijit stops. His heart beats fast. The security officer makes a smart bow to him. Arijit walks up to him. 'In the morning, I did not see Chhetri at the gate. Someone said he has gone home?'

'Yes, sir. The poor boy had to rush home to Nepal; his father had a heart attack last night. But he won't get there before tomorrow.'

There is an air of efficiency about the man, a retired army officer working for a security agency.

'The new regulations have something to do with this morning's incident?'

'Sir, I fought in the 1971 Bangladesh War. I noticed that grille factory man. Had I got any hint of his evil designs, I would have shot him dead with my own pistol. Would not have allowed him to get that far. Anyway, from now on, no such characters will be able to sneak in. I'll be on the lookout.' He feels his pistol in its holster, tucked inside his uniform. He turns to Arijit with a new-found confidence. 'We are circulating a form about the domestics. We need their particulars – addresses, photographs, phone numbers, references… everything. We have to sanitize this place after what happened this morning.'

Arijit nods and walks down the driveway to the street. He stops a cycle rickshaw and climbs on. 'Sector 8,' he says briefly.

The drab, crumbling blocks of the four-storey buildings seem indifferent to what the high-rises are buzzing about. The place feels sad. Often, plaster has peeled off, baring brick; a balcony has collapsed somewhere. He climbs down from the rickshaw and moves into a block.

At the foot of the stairs, an old man is sitting on a string cot. Seeing the unusual visitor, he looks up curiously.

'Yes, sir. Is something the matter?'

'Does Rita live here?'

'She is on the third floor. Please walk up and turn left. Number fifteen. And you, sir?'

'Rita works in my house. She did not turn up this morning, so I came to see if she is all right.'

'You are a kind man, sir. I worked in a doctor's clinic for

twenty years. Three months ago, he threw me out for my eyesight was failing. But that was only an excuse. The real reason? He wanted a pretty woman to be his clinic assistant, not a grey-haired old man. A fashionable young thing – part of the furniture, eh?'

Arijit listens, stands there even after the old man has finished. 'Let me see if she is in.' He starts going up the stairs.

'She must be there – maybe a headache or fever. I am like her local guardian; she calls me Chacha.'

He stands outside the door after knocking twice. A minute passes, no response. Then two more. Perhaps she is sleeping. He decides to wait. Her phone is still switched off. He tries the door again, this time a little harder. It opens. It was not closed from the inside. He hesitantly walks in. No trace of the girl.

'Rita, are you in?' he shouts, looking inside the flat. No response.

There is shuffling up the stairs. 'Isn't she there? Beti, where are you?' The man stands behind him. Everything in the little flat is as it was. The television, wall hanging, Amitabh Bachchan poster, but no sign of Rita. On the small, rickety table, there are a couple of women's magazines – back issues. In its drawer is a pale envelope with the postal stamps of the United States. He looks for a letter, some note inside. What comes out is a photograph – a bearded American, flabby because of his new tropical lifestyle, and a bright-eyed little girl. He puts the envelope back in the drawer; then on second thoughts, slips it into his trouser pocket.

'She must have gone somewhere – to a shop or maybe to see a friend.' The old man tries to explain her absence. 'I will tell Beti you came looking for her.' He comes down the stairs with Arijit and walks him up to the road. 'Sir, nobody living in those high-rise apartments would bother to come down to see what happened to a maid. I will send her to your house.'

Coming back on a rickshaw jerking along the potholed road, he can see what has happened. She ran away. The moment she got to know about the encounter, she did not waste a single second. If she locked up her flat, that might have raised suspicion. Questions would have been asked. *I'm still around,* she seems to be telling the neighbours. Did not carry any luggage either. Simply walked away.

Where has she gone? Is she going home across the border? To another city? Or is she hiding somewhere around, waiting for the confusion to clear? That, he guesses, would be unlikely.

Exhausted, he goes into the kitchen to make himself a cup of coffee. Looking for the Nescafe container, he notices a cardboard box wrapped in glossy paper. He does not remember what came in that flat, wide container – tea bags, dry fruit? He opens the box carefully. Inside, he discovers her territory – a couple of Bengali novels published from Dhaka, music tapes and Bubka's photograph. She had asked for his grandson's picture after she saw on his computer the ones Piu had mailed him. She had started stitching a nakshi kantha for the boy.

Arijit leaves the kitchen without making coffee. He sits beside the telephone and calls Nandita on the landline.

'Nandita.'

'I was going to call you. The interior decorator is asking that before the painters and carpenters leave, if we would like to take another look at the house? You can meet her and make sure everything is to your liking.'

'Whatever you decide is fine with me.'

'Still, a visit to the farm before we move in, to see the furniture, décor, the overall ambience.'

He feels fatigued. Colour, furniture, décor – he tries hard to suppress his irritation.

'I wanted to tell you something. Something happened.'

'What?'

'Rita is gone. No trace of her. She did not come to work this morning. I went to her place; it's empty. Her neighbours do not know anything.'

'Hmmm. I see. Bharat has gone on leave for a couple of days. I suppose the two of them are gallivanting. You don't worry. I called Rita in the morning. Her phone was switched off. I know they are together, having fun at some water park or picnic spot. I will call Bharat. He cannot dare switch off his phone.' She laughs.

Arijit feels relieved. Reassured. He has not thought about that possibility. He tells Nandita about the encounter on the highway. 'I am a little unsettled. It almost happened before my eyes.'

'That's what urban life is going to be – living with terror, the underworld. Let's spend a day on the farm. You will feel better.'

'All right. I'll be there tomorrow afternoon. On the way, I need to stop at a market to buy something.'

'What?'

'A wedding ring for you.'

'Such things are not important, Arijit. All I want is some quiet time together. Undisturbed, uninterrupted time. We will take long walks early in the morning, work in the field to grow vegetables, do our reading and listen to music. Already, society journalists are after me. They want exclusive pictures of our wedding, want to write about it. I said sorry.'

'Good. I am sick and tired of the media – probing newspaper guys, intruding television cameras. Those months before the energy deal… they made my life difficult. All the time calling, peering, speculating – ugh!' He breathes out his disgust.

Relieved that Rita is probably having a nice time somewhere around the city with her fiancé, that she has not been picked up again for questioning, for another round of police brutality, he sits down at the desk with his laptop.

His landline rings. From the number flashing on the screen, he can make out his sister is calling from Calcutta.

'Buro, I saw you in a dream last night. You seemed to be in some trouble. Don't know why I am worrying so much about you. Is everything fine?'

'I am good, Niru-di. Please don't worry. How is your asthma? Is it under control?'

'Much better. You said you would come. The souvenir they brought out for the music school's golden jubilee has a nice write-up on you. And also, your picture. By the way, Sumita Sen has left Calcutta University. She is going to Boston to teach there. I am forgetting which university. A single woman, Sumita has no bindings.'

Arijit wonders if he should tell his older sister about his marriage. If Niru-di gets to know about his marriage from someone else or a Bengali newspaper, she will be disappointed. No point in holding it back.

'Niru-di, I want to tell you something.'

'What?' Her voice wavers in apprehension. In expectation.

'I knew someone in Paris. When Ranjana came back to Bombay and Piu was very young, she helped me in many ways. Without her support, it would have been difficult for me to bring up Piu. She now lives in Delhi. I am marrying her.'

'Is she Bengali?'

'No.'

'Is it that tall Punjabi woman? Her name… Nandini… oh, yes, I remember. Nandita.'

'How do you know?'

'She came to your Delhi house after Ranjana's death. This is really good news, Buro. You two should be happy. Loneliness is a terrible thing, more so when you are getting old.'

'There will be no ceremonies, no reception. Our wedding is going to be a very private affair.'

'That's better. When I think about you, Buro, I often cry quietly. Such a big name, so much fame, but you have lived almost a bachelor's life. Come home with your bride. Show her the house where our parents, grandparents lived, where we grew up.'

'We will come, definitely.'

'I have still kept Ma's gold necklace. Our grandmother put it around her neck when she stepped into her new home as a bride. It is my turn now to give it to Nandita. Ranjana was a rebel; she would have none of it. Now give me a chance…'

Arijit can make out his sister's voice is choking.

'Niru-di, we will come and spend a few days with all of you.'

'One more thing, Buro. I told you Parijat – we call her Tia – and her husband, Shantanu, now live in Dehradun. Tia has never seen you. Why don't you spend a weekend with them? Dehradun is not very far from Delhi.'

After talking to his sister, Arijit sits quietly for a while. An image appears before him – a large, boughy tree, its branches holding each other in close embrace. That's family. There's no escape; it catches up with you. He thinks of Sumita Sen teaching history in Boston. Did Niru-di have an expectation that he would look back on the days at the music school and think of Sumita as his life partner?

The doorbell rings. He wonders who it could be. Is it Rita then? Back after a little fun with her lover?

He opens the door eagerly. A girl, Rita's age, stands hesitantly. Smartly dressed in pants and a sleeveless top, large sunglasses covering much of her face, she is very much like her. In a way.

Without waiting for him to ask her in, she comes close. 'I am Rita's cousin.' Her suppressed, secretive voice hints at an urgency to say something – something that can be said only in confidence, behind closed doors.

'Come in,' he holds the door open. 'Please.'

The girl is more confident than Rita, more familiar with the ways of the world. She sits on the sofa across the centre table from him.

'I know how much you have done for Rita; you have been more than a father to her.' She has taken off her sunglasses. Arijit can make out that, despite the light brown tinge of her bobbed hair, carefully shaped eyebrows, hippie beads around her neck, she is very much Rita's cousin. The similarities are unmistakable.

'That fellow called Rita moments before he was gunned down. Though she had nothing to do with him, no relationship, he had bothered her, pursued her for a long time. Once in a while, she had to stop and talk, take his phone calls.'

'How did he get to know her?'

'He was from our place – Khulna, on the other side of the border. When she heard the gunshots on the phone, she knew what was happening. She was scared, knew the police would be chasing her first thing in the morning. She rushed to my place. She was in real danger. Since I have married a local man, I have been maintaining some distance from her. I run a beauty parlour. I told her to go sit in the salon as though she were a client. My husband was still asleep. I cropped her hair, plucked her eyebrows.

She began to look different, almost like a boy. I gave her a pair of my pants and a shirt. She was another person in her new clothes. She asked me to tell you not to look for her, not to enquire. If you talk about her absence, that will raise an alarm. Otherwise, no one will notice that a maid is missing.'

The girl is silent – only looking at him, around the room. She has nothing more to say. Hands chained in her lap, she keeps sitting. It takes him a while to understand the full import of what she has just said.

'How did you come here? I did not get a call from the security.'

'I came to give beauty treatment to a client.'

'Is Rita going back to Bangladesh?'

'She did not tell me anything. She fears, well that's my hunch, that because of her, you might be in trouble, too. She does not want that to happen.'

'That fellow was into crimes?'

'He was a very lazy, sloppy chap. Good-for-nothing type. When my sister turned him down, I think he took to the dangerous ways to prove himself.' She gets up, slips on her sunglasses and picks up her purse. 'Sir, I have never met you, I have told you nothing. You do not know me.' She takes off her glasses again, wipes her eyes with a neatly folded handkerchief. 'The slightest hint, little noise – and my marriage will be in trouble.'

She waits uneasily for a few moments, then leaves.

41
Live Telecast

After a brisk thirty-minute workout, Nandita leaves the gym. She does not want to look fat and fatigued on her wedding day. Even the handful of guests coming for the ceremony must not say that the tired, paunchy woman has grabbed the still-handsome former diplomat using her guile and old French connections. She smiles. However much she tries to deny it, her mind is still full of it – marriage, their new life on the farm.

For about a month now, she has been coming to the neighbourhood gym. Early in the morning, she walks the short distance from home to be the first on the treadmill. While going back, she nods, smiles, helloes to the familiar faces on the street. She has known some of them since her childhood. In a few days, she will leave this posh enclave again. Her mother will go to Nainital to live with her aunt in the quaint little cottage. And she on the farm. With Arijit, Rita and Bharat.

Where the street turns, she waves at an elderly man, a retired army officer. Surprisingly, he gives her an icy look. She is shocked. The decorated brigadier was her father's friend, used to come to their house for card parties before Diwali. She cannot fathom his indifference, the contempt in his eyes.

The unreasoned hostility in the elderly man's eyes troubles her. The stout, moustachioed army officer with a big laugh used to say, 'So, when will you teach me a little French?' Weeks before

Diwali, her father called friends and neighbours for the evening card games. A little late in the evening, they would all come, one after another, with their decked-up wives in tow. They played cards with a little money, sipping whisky with chicken tikka, roasted cashews and almonds. Their better halves, red wine or gin and tonic. The brigadier was at the centre of such gatherings. Whenever she came home, she brought a bottle of Bordeaux wine from Paris for him. The man now walks away, glaring at her.

Thinking about the brigadier's strange behaviour, Nandita walks along. She sees a woman opening her car door. She works in a bank. Nandita meets her every day on her way back from the gym around this time; they always talk for a minute or two. She is interested in new writing and films. Often asks Nandita about the upcoming French writers, movies, Depardieu jokes. 'When young, he was more bear than man – is that true?' Both of them would laugh. She is putting her purse, laptop bag and the day's newspaper on the back seat when Nandita waves – hesitantly after the brigadier's hostility. The woman stands holding the car door, looking more puzzled than concerned.

'What all have they written about you in *Indian Courier* today? Such awful crap!'

'About me?' Nandita looks absolutely stunned. 'Have they bitched about our wedding?'

'It's not the lifestyle supplements but the front page. The paper says you have terror links! What nonsense! Such shoddy, irresponsible journalism!'

'Me? Terror?' Nandita cannot hide her puzzlement. 'What's happening to the newspapers?' She sounds resentful.

'My husband reads the papers in the morning, and I, over lunch in the office. He read out the report in the *Courier.* He was shocked, fuming about irresponsible reporting.'

'Let me go home and read it first.'

Nandita can not see the connection… she having terror links. She breathes fast.

The *Courier* front page story links her to terror. The brigadier, her father's friend, walked away giving her an icy look. Now things are falling into place.

In her confusion, Nandita forgets to take leave of the neighbour. She almost starts running.

Waiting at the entrance for someone to open the gate, she sees an OB van parked on her side of the street. A reporter holding a microphone runs towards her, with the cameraman following close behind. Angry, irritated, she shoos them away, cautioning the girl not to infringe on her privacy.

Undeterred, the reporter, looking sleepy and shabby, positions herself before the camera, a little distance away from the gate. 'This is the house where everything began… Jamal alias Sultan came here regularly. Strange characters gathered at midnight…'

Nandita hears the girl's loud, theatrical bytes. Her first instinct is to run back and push the drooling reporter away. Excited about *breaking* news, she is getting hysterical.

Perhaps there's a question from the anchor in the studio. She waits, looks vacantly, narrows her eyes to grasp what the anchor wants to know.

'Yes, Sanjay, we talked to some of the neighbours. They saw suspicious-looking characters moving in and out of the house. She is well connected, divides her time between India and Europe. A kind of celebrity. The neighbours did not dare raise a question. They saw VVIPs, powerful people going in. Sanjay—'

Angry, humiliated, Nandita runs up the stairs to lock herself in her room.

'Madam.' Bharat on the landing. 'Two men from Delhi Police are here.' He points to the hall downstairs.

What was silly, irresponsible reporting by a little-known television channel now looms as a full-blown crisis. A scandal. Police officers are waiting for her. She just cannot make sense of it. *Why are they after me*? she feels like screaming out. A lump in her throat holds back the words. Suddenly, she feels choked. Tears come out.

'Madam.' Bharat notices her moment of crisis. He wants to do something. Be of help but does not know how. She looks up at him.

'I sent them tea and biscuits.'

She smiles. 'Good.' She walks down the stairs.

'Madam.' Bharat again.

Nandita turns back and looks up at him. For the first time, the humble, overawed chauffeur is talking to her without being asked to.

'Would it be better to call Basu Sahib? Talk to him first before talking to the policemen?'

Nandita waits on the step, gives it a thought, then walks into the hall.

Two hefty, tall men – not in uniform – sit patiently around the low table, finishing their tea. Seeing her, both of them get up.

'Yes?'

'Madam, we are from the ATF of Delhi Police.'

'What's ATF?'

'Anti-Terrorist Force.'

'I just cannot make out what's happening. First, I was told one newspaper wrote something about my links to a terror gang. Is this how you investigate? Don't you have any common sense?

Now one television channel is going live from outside my gate. Tell me who put out this story. On what basis?'

The two policemen remain unperturbed in the face of her rage. After she is through, one of them speaks.

'We have got some evidence. We have not come to any conclusion. Not yet. It's just a lead. You have to come with us to the office of the intelligence wing. If you cooperate, that would be good for you.'

'If I don't come?'

'Then we will arrest you.'

'Arrest me! On what grounds? Who do you think you are?' She does not realize that she has actually started screaming.

'Madam, please listen to me,' the older of the two says. This is not a brusque cop's command. His tone has a touch of pleading. 'We know everything about you. A visit to our Chanakyapuri office does not implicate you. Other officers are waiting. You can explain everything. Maybe we are on the wrong track. The thread is misleading. We don't have to tell you how difficult fighting terror is.'

'What about them – going live from here? Why did you leak unfounded suspicions to the media? What about the damage they have already done to my reputation?'

The man cranes his neck to look out the window at the TV crew. He laughs.

'Madam, they are a headache all of us have to live with. Perhaps by the evening, they will sing a different tune. If you want, you can come in your car. We will follow you in our Gypsy.'

42
Trial

Arijit is getting used to packaged food from the mall again. Now that nobody comes to work in the kitchen, he pours milk from a carton into a bowl of cornflakes, then eats an apple or some grapes. Makes a mug of black coffee and settles down at the dining table with the *Times of India*. More than the girl's delicious dishes, he misses her presence. The clanging of crockery in the sink. Her fights on the phone. Her buzzing around the house. Sitting on the floor with the nakshi kantha in progress. With her, the house came alive.

Along the corridors of Blue Lotus Grove, news travels fast. Now that they know the girl does not come any more, the level of hostility has gone down. No more snide remarks, insinuations. Hate mail has also stopped. No fresh anonymous letters swearing by Bajrangbali. Luckily, no one has seen the real reason for Rita's disappearance. Her connection to the slain terrorist. His neighbours think Arijit has given her the sack sensing their resentment. The other day, one housewife sent pancakes in a casserole.

He is reading the edit page when his cell phone twangs. Neeraj Gupta.

'Sir, what all is happening? This is an outrage!' The normally cool, mild-mannered man is shouting. He is agitated.

'Why, what happened?'

'Are you not watching television? All the news channels have broken their scheduled programming to focus on Nandita's house. They are saying horrible things. You must talk to someone in the home ministry. I think the police are making mischief. I am talking to some friends. But one call from you should be enough.'

Arijit looks for the television remote and hurriedly switches on an English news channel. They are broadcasting live from outside Nandita's house. A girl in shabby jeans and a clumsy top, barely twenty, is *breaking news* for the viewers:

> *This socialite, who has excellent contacts in important circles, is in the crosshairs of terror. The Anti-Terrorist Force sleuths stumbled on a minefield of information about the terror trail to her door. Jamal alias Sultan, the leader of the terror gang gunned down by the ATF commandos, called her minutes before the encounter. Prasun…*

The camera focuses on the anchor in the studio. Next to Prasun sits a bald man with a goatee. Arijit recognizes him – a retired chief of the Intelligence Bureau.

'What you are saying, Poonam, is absolutely sensational. A high-society woman, well connected, has close links with the terrorists. What is happening inside the house? Is any search going on? Are there others, people behind her?' The anchor in his salt-and-pepper beard tries to look serious.

'I tried to talk to Nandita Kapoor when she came back from the health club after her morning workout. She reacted violently, chasing me away…'

'We are showing the exclusive footage of Nandita Kapoor chasing away our reporter. The first scene of the drama that has since unfolded.'

The camera pans to Nandita reacting angrily, turning to tell the reporter not to follow her. All over the screen, Nandita in a tracksuit, Reebok trainers – again and again.

'Why did she react so menacingly? Mr Raghavan, you have *huge* experience in intelligence gathering, surveillance. What do you think of her reaction – let us see it again… Look at her – turning to intimidate, threaten our reporter.'

Nandita across the screen telling the reporter not to infringe on her privacy. Prasun clears his throat.

'Mr Raghavan?'

'I think she is upset by the media exposé. Obviously, she did not expect the truth to tumble out.' The former supersleuth smirks.

'Let us go back to the theatre of action – the house in Delhi's posh Hauz Khas enclave. Poonam, what is the mood like in the neighbourhood?'

'A while ago, I tried to enter the house to take a look at the lawn where those late-night parties happened, where dubious characters from Nigeria and Malaysia gathered. But a family retainer shouted at me and rattled the gate close.'

The camera closes in on Bharat locking the gate.

'Poonam, who is that man – a family member, a security guard or a muscleman?' Prasun flashes an insinuating smile.

The anchor is now going back to the encounter scene on the highway. All across the screen, the bullet-riddled Innova burning after the explosion, lifeless, blood-smeared bodies, three men lying on the ground below the car and the driver slumped to a side, a hand still on the wheel.

'Highly placed sources told us that the four were on a recce before the planned Sunday morning attack. Had they not been killed by the ATF commandos, they would have turned the headquarters of the Central Industrial Police Force into an inferno.'

Arijit is sweating. He feels suffocated. Unable to think clearly, he calls Nandita on her mobile. The phone is switched off. He calls the landline; it keeps ringing. No one takes the call. He gets up, dazed, and walks into the bedroom to change. He must rush to Nandita's side.

The television reporter raises her voice, overcome by a sudden paroxysm. 'Nandita Kapoor, the socialite suspected of deep terror links, is driving out of her house. She looks grim, sullen. Declined to talk—'

The camera captures the horde of television reporters and their assistants. Some of them shout questions into the car. Nandita, wearing large sunglasses, a newspaper between her hands, sits stoically in the back seat as Bharat dodges past the crowd of television crew and curious onlookers.

He switches off the television. His mobile rings.

'Arijit, Swami here.' An additional secretary in the home ministry. His old friend.

'Swami, I feel devastated. Our wedding is less than a month away.'

'I think something has gone terribly wrong somewhere. The police are pursuing the wrong lead. But how did the phone calls happen?'

'That fellow was a welder; worked in a grille-making shop. He used to put grilles on windows and balconies in new apartments in our area. Nandita met him at my place only, offered him work in her house. That's how he called her cell number; could have visited her place as well. How could she guess the chap would turn out to be a terrorist?'

'Right. I am sure the police will find out the truth very soon. What the channels are doing is disgusting.'

Arijit keeps quiet. The headline before a news bulletin on television flashes back:

The Masterminds at the Midnight Party

'Swami, can they say just about anything on television without verifying, cross-checking?'

'In the evening prime time, they rule this country. These three or four news anchors take over from the government. We are helpless.'

When Arijit arrives, the place has already taken on the air of a street cricket match. The entire area is crowded with people from the television networks, newspaper reporters, neighbours. The OB vans have lined up on the street. A couple of vendors are selling peanuts and popcorn. A group is talking agitatedly outside the gate. He recognizes one of them, Ishita – she works for an NGO. She steps forward, greeting him.

'We are all outraged by the media overkill, their attempt at character assassination. We are planning a sit-in at India Gate. The twenty-four-hour channels are the biggest menace. A few weeks ago, they did a so-called sting on a hapless schoolteacher and went on air claiming she was forcing the girls in her class into prostitution! Isn't it just horrible?'

Arijit feels a whiff of fresh air from the south. Everybody has not been carried away by the deluge on television. Nandita still has friends. They want to form a human chain and keep a candlelight vigil around India Gate to protest media irresponsibility. He feels better – recovering from the sense of being swamped.

'Where is Nandita? Is she in?' he asks.

'As usual, the police are harassing an innocent citizen. Their senior officers selectively briefed the media to prepare the ground for interrogating her. They let loose the pack on her to cover their failure. The would-be terrorists were training with their handler from across the border, and the police knew nothing!' Ishita works herself up.

Suddenly, there is a murmur of excitement from the other end of the street. *She is back, she is back* – the chant rises like a wave above the noise of the diesel generator sets of the OB vans. The television reporters run towards the car.

Surrounded on all sides by the hungry reporters, Bharat pulls up at the gate. Nandita gets out of the car. Arijit jostles with the crowd to get closer. Their eyes meet. It's a different Nandita – the dour, obdurate woman who once moved about Paris in search of her own meaning is now shaken, sapped. *Does she still have a lot of fight left in her?* Arijit wants to ask.

He knows she is ready for a fight. Takes her hand into his, presses it to give her support but lets it go lest the cameras catch the clasp of hands. With the reporters encircling her, he recedes into the background.

Did the police ask you about your terror connections?
How did the Bangladeshi terrorist Jamal get your mobile number?
Police are hinting you met some of the terror masterminds abroad?

'Who said that? Unless you apologize, I will sue you in a court of law. I hope you have the guts to stand by what you just said.' Nandita flares up.

Another reporter nudges the questioner. 'Keep quiet, yaar. Let me ask…' There is confusion, reporters pushing each other.

'Well, I am willing to answer your questions on two conditions: you will ask *sensible* questions and you *behave responsibly*.' Nandita takes charge.

There is an uproar of excitement. *The PC, the PC… Call the studio…* Within a minute, the screen of every reporter's Blackberry flashes the questions sent by the studios.

'I *mean* it when I say you must not make wild allegations. Let us sit somewhere and talk. I will answer all your questions.' She walks towards the hall on the ground floor.

'Ma'am, you are going live!' Excited, Poonam flashes a triumphant look, her hand almost touching Nandita's. She is now beaming. Other reporters have already begun treating her with respect. 'Prasun said I am getting a promotion,' she tells another girl. 'Yaar, I've not eaten anything since morning. Throw me a fag.' She smiles cutely.

Nandita smiles back at her. She calls Bharat to open the hall and bring more chairs and stools for the reporters. She mutters something to Ishita in an aside and turns to the reporters. 'Please, come inside.'

Ishita holds Arijit's arm and pulls him to a side. 'Wait upstairs. Nandita does not want you to be another victim of the media.'

Sitting all alone in the upstairs living room, Arijit surfs the channels. A maid comes with a cup of coffee. He enquires about Nandita's mother.

'She is on a sedative – sleeping.' The woman waits for a minute. 'After watching television for a while in the morning, the old lady complained of palpitation in the heart. She could not take it any more. We called in a doctor.'

Every studio is gripped by excitement. Uday is anchoring the sell-out show on another TV channel. Arijit senses the change in the air. The sleuth in the morning has made way for a woman activist as an expert. A sign of hope? Arijit is still not sure.

Her Side of The Story – the programme title emerges on the screen. Another channel roars: *She Speaks Out*. The viciousness of the morning is gone.

'In a few minutes, Nandita Kapoor, the well-known cultural personality, will explain her role. After building a career in publishing in France, Nandita returned to India a year ago. She published many Indian novels and short-story collections in French translation. She counts many celebrated French writers and artists among her friends.' Uday holds aloft a short-story collection by Munshi Premchand translated into French. Flips through the pages, then puts it on the desk. The camera zooms in for a moment on the legendary writer's picture on the back cover.

'In 2007, she won a prestigious French award in recognition of her achievements in the fields of art and literature. We talked to Nandita's friend and activist Ishita Bhatnagar. She accused the police of messing up the investigation and victimizing Nandita without any basis.'

The camera pans on Ishita among the activists and intellectuals holding *Friends-of-Nandita* placards. 'Since the police had no case against Nandita, they planted stories in the media.' Ishita raises her decibel level with every sentence while the others in the group put up clenched fists in a sign of solidarity.

'The police clearly passed on unverified information to the media to malign Nandita,' the woman activist in the studio angrily chimes in.

Uday wears a grim look. 'Eminent French writer Naël Dubois has deplored police harassment as a witch-hunt. Speaking to BBC from Pondicherry, the iconic writer said, "An innocent person is being unnecessarily hounded."'

Next, Nandita under sharp focus: slightly unsettled but very determined. The tall, daring journalist who chased news in Europe years ago is back. She sits – intent, intense, her arms folded on the table. The work of an artist friend, now very famous, on the wall behind her serves as a backdrop. A forest of microphones with the tags of the news channels does not leave enough space even for a glass of water on the table. They are all targeted at her. The reporters – noisy, excited – are all over the room. Nandita clasps her hands, looks at the microphones with channel names in English, Hindi, Gurmukhi, Bengali, Malayalam, Telugu, Tamil…

'Yes.' She signals the proceedings to start. She looks hurt but prepared to fight on.

It is as if Poonam is on a cue. 'Jamal alias Sultan, the Bangladeshi terrorist, made a call to your number moments before the shoot-out. How did you get to know him?'

'He was an employee in someone's welding workshop. I met him at a friend's place, where he came to put grilles around a balcony. I asked him to do some work for me also. And I gave him my address, my telephone numbers – both landline and mobile.

He came to this house at least a dozen times to redo our terrace. You can go up the stairs and take a look at the terrace. He was a smart talker, he chatted. We gave him tea, a couple of times food also. I mostly paid him cash, gave him a cheque once. Tell me what's wrong with all this. I did not know he would become a terrorist one day or that there was another side to his character. Do you check the antecedents of a man before you buy vegetables from him or take a ride in his tuk-tuk? I misplaced the phone, that's why he often called but there's no response.'

'Ma'am, this is Rakesh from Capital TV. Why should a terrorist call someone's number minutes before he died unless he had to say something very urgent, crucial to that person?'

'From whatever I have read in the papers, I got the impression that the gang was surprised, suddenly challenged by the police. He did not know he was going to die, if you are hinting that his intention was to pass on some code or secret to an accomplice. If you get a call from an auto mechanic or plumber early in the morning, do you expect him to tell you something urgent, crucial?'

'Ms Kapoor, I am Deepika Ghosh from Newsline. Isn't it strange that the dreaded terrorist came to this house day after day, and still, you had no inkling of what he was up to? He worked, he chatted, had his lunch and beverage also, and you want us to believe you had absolutely no idea about who he was?' Deepika laughs viciously.

'I worked in the media for a long time. And still, I had no inkling of my colleagues' unprofessionalism. I had no idea that they would write, broadcast unverified things on the basis of information from dubious sources.'

There is a hush in the hall. The reporters look at each other. But Poonam is not one to give up a fight so easily. The perky reporter moves forward. 'What about the midnight parties of the masterminds in this house?'

Nandita looks the reporter full in the face. Barely out of her teens, she could not care less. She stares back at Nandita.

'I can read out the guest list of the party here about a month ago, but I am holding it back. I want the channels, including yours, to apologize immediately. Otherwise, I will serve legal notices on each one of them.'

The intrepid fighter of the Paris streets Arijit knew steps out of the past. *La femme indienne*, a favourite of the writers, artists, left-wing activists, is back. The show is over, and yet, a perceived audience demand for an encore is met by a television channel.

'Here's an interesting turn to the unfolding terror story. Mandira Singh, the lifestyle journalist from the *Rajdhani Times*, is talking to Capital TV's Paromita Banerjee. She attended the *late-night* party hosted by Nandita Kapoor. This is a Capital TV exclusive. Remember, this is the first time a TV channel has explored the party angle, shed new light on what happened on the lawns of the house in exclusive Hauz Khas. Mandira…'

Arijit recognizes Mandira, who entertained them with the latest gossip about the Delhi elite towards the end of the party.

'Mandira, do you remember the other guests who attended the party?'

'I am quite amused, Paromita, by what has been said since morning on television. No one seems to have tried to fact-check.'

'The neighbours told us they saw suspicious characters…'

'Who are these *neighbours*? You did not interview the neighbours on camera. It was just hearsay. Among those who gathered on the lawns were a well-known French writer, a doctor from the US working in India, an African American poet, a former Indian diplomat and myself. There were no terror masterminds either from Nigeria or Malaysia.' Mandira laughs, clearly finding the allegations funny.

'There should be an enquiry into the blatant police attempt to implicate an innocent citizen in a terror case. With the police turning vindictive, no one is safe,' the woman activist screams from the studio.

The last question seems to have been asked.

43
Nymphomaniac

Walking up the road that winds around the mountain to Mussoorie, Arijit stops to look at the cloudy peaks. At one point, the road enters a forested area – quietly dark, secluded. From here, the view is breathtaking. Sublime mountain ranges on all sides – Shivalik, Chamba, Dhanaulti, Haathi Pao. Haathi Pao – what a name! Elephant feet. It evokes wilderness. Either the peaks from this distance look like the sturdy legs of a tusker, or that's the preferred route for elephant hordes.

The upper reaches of the Himalayas, shrouded in mist, appear to be part of the cloud kingdom. The occasional cold wind blows from across the mountain range with hints of a snowy region not very far from here. He walks on. Since the morning he got off the train to spend a few days with his niece, he has kept coming to the point where the hills take over from the plains. He walks the whole day. The town has a quaint, colonial flavour. Its Raj-era bungalows, century-old churches, the central vista, bakeries – all a reminder of a time when Europeans preferred the Doon Valley to the sweltering heat of Delhi.

Before going back to America, he decided to stay away from Blue Lotus Grove, from everything that had been his life for almost a year now. He called Parijat one morning to say he was on the way. She could not believe it at first. 'Mama, are you really coming down then? Great! Ma called from Calcutta, but I thought… well, it's too good to be true.'

Parijat and Shantanu came to the train station to receive him. They had ideas – a trip to a wildlife sanctuary, a night out in a log cabin, picnics, a party in his honour. Arijit told them he would like to spend some alone time before going back to the busy life of New York. They listened.

In the morning, they have tea on the front lawn of the bungalow. Parijat's two-year-old daughter Bulbul toddles around, picking up yellow leaves from the ground. Bagha, the pampered German Shepherd, sits on his haunches, keeping a sharp eye on the child. If a crow lands on the lawn, he lets out a reluctant half-bark to scare it away.

'Mama, isn't it strange we've never met in all these years? I only saw you on television, read about you in the newspapers.' Parijat pours tea from the pot into a large cup, puts a plate of cake rusks next to it. Perhaps the same age as Piu, she is gushing with energy – simple, ordinary. She keeps talking to Bagha alternately in Bengali and English, runs after Bulbul, gives orders to a handful of helpers. And still a sprightly girl from a South Calcutta neighbourhood.

Calling him *Mama,* she touches a chord. The family has grown, spread its branches, only he has not taken note of it. Ma-ma. Mother's brother. Simple two syllables, suggesting strong kinship, close blood. And he did not even know there was someone who could call him *mama*.

'When Ma called and said, "Tia, Buro will spend a few days with you all," I had a strange feeling.' Parijat mists up.

'Ah, that's why I decided to return. I was always rushing from place to place. I didn't know anything about my family.'

Arijit gets up, hurries down the gravel to draw level with Bulbul. He takes her in his arms. 'Look, look – *juju*.' He points to a grasshopper in the hedges. The child follows the direction of his pointed finger, then giggles. 'Hee-hee.' In the excitement of discovering the insect, she clutches Arijit's cheeks.

Perhaps I will not meet them again – Parijat, Bulbul, Shantanu. He kisses the child on her head.

After a light breakfast, he goes for a walk. It's not his usual morning walk – brisk, busy with a clear-cut trajectory in mind. Here, it's aimless rambling around town. He has no point to reach, no target to meet. Out on his walk, he keeps reading the nameplates of the elegant bungalows along Aketa Avenue: Peace Centre, Blessed Home, Shanti Sadan… The rich from the big cities have come to live in the cool quiet of the foothills. Some of them do not live here – they have built fancy houses and gone back to chase success, power, fame… He comes to the end of the street where the big houses give way to acres of dark, thick tea plantations.

Soon he reaches a Catholic church. Built in a distinct Italian style, it has the features of Renaissance architecture. He goes inside. A tall, plump European, evidently a professor, is telling a group of youngsters about the history of the church. They are taking notes. Their eyes meet. Arijit nods.

'Hello, I'm Professor Giovanni from Florence. These are my students at the Florence Academy of Art.'

He points to the group of young men and women with notebooks in hand.

'I am sorry. I did not know you're working here.' Arijit turns to leave.

'No problem. Please join us. Perhaps you will find our work interesting.'

Someone who loves talking about things close to his heart, Giovanni goes back to the days during the Second World War when an Italian prisoner in British custody turned out to be an accomplished painter. At the request of the parish priest, the English officers allowed Nino La Civita to do the frescos in the church.

'Now we are trying to restore the paintings, though we are not prisoners,' Giovanni laughs.

Arijit tells him about some of the oldest churches in the hills, built in the middle of the nineteenth century after the Europeans began settling down in Mussoorie.

Taking leave of the professor and his students, he walks down Convent Road along Parade Ground – the town's central vista. Across the sprawling ground, he sits at a roadside café and orders coffee and a patty. 'Make it strong. And no sugar,' he tells the kiosk owner.

Refreshed after the coffee, he roams around aimlessly, thinking how everything came to an abrupt end. The edifice of a quiet life, built with the utmost care by Nandita, came crashing down all of a sudden. He and Nandita, Rita and that boy – all of them living in different parts of the quaint mock-Tudor house in the midst of farmland, away from the stings and punches of the world outside – that picture was shattered. For no fault of theirs. A life of close companionship eluded them. The events of a single day ruined what had promised to be a good ending to a long story.

Nandita fought back and absolved herself in the war of optics. On prime time television. Viewers' sympathies were with her. The next morning, the newspapers turned her into a new hero. She was lionized by the edit writers. Her phone kept ringing in support, in sympathy. They talked of her courage to stand her ground in the face of an avalanche.

But the dark insinuations, accusations had ravaged Nandita. In no time, pits of the reactionary right flared up to consume her. Also, her lies. She was troubled by them. In the TV battle, she never mentioned Rita. That the cell phone the girl used had been actually bought by her in her own name. Facing the barbs from the television reporters, she said the phone had been misplaced, completely screening the undocumented immigrant. Investigators recovered the call records but could not trace the instrument. The sleuths were convinced that Nandita had run into a terrorist by sheer accident.

Despite the media about-turn, commiseration of the liberals, the prime-time blitz had cast its shadow over her. The indelible ink marks grew within her.

The city's well-entrenched packs of the religious right, their dreaded IT cell, made a late rally. They determined to demolish her totally. Write-ups appeared on social media about a *nymphomaniac socialite's brush with law*. There was a demonstration by the women's wing of a far-right outfit led by a sadhvi in orange outside her house. They demanded her arrest, that her passport be revoked, a thorough investigation into her role in the whole affair. Her inbox was bombarded by hate mail, obscene sketches. They unleashed on the internet a vicious *love-a-terrorist-if-he's-handsome* campaign with innuendoes that Nandita called Jamal home not just for some grille work. *A French artist or a fedayeen terrorist – for a good fuck it's the same*. On social media, they relentlessly carried on their malicious propaganda. Highly sexed younger female bodies with her face superimposed on them appeared on these platforms. #ArrestNanditaKapoor trended on Twitter. WhatsApp messages flew thick. Some of the women from South Delhi's rich families – leading lights of the city's party circuit – were at the forefront of the war of calumny. *Love jihad*, they taunted.

Early one morning, she came – unexpected, unannounced. Arijit noticed the car key in her hand.

'You drove all the way? Where's Bharat?'

'Bharat does not come so early. Besides, I wanted to be alone.'

He scrutinized her. In a blue salwar kameez, she looked much younger. Must have shed quite a bit of weight in the gym. She had been preparing for their wedding. The bride getting ready for the ring ceremony. For a few Sanskrit mantras.

Arijit pared through her appearance for a hint of turmoil inside. She had driven from Hauz Khas to Noahda, not even called before coming. Was she being troubled, tormented by something more than right-wing calumny? He poured black coffee from his Thermos into two cups.

Sitting across the low table, he looked closely at Nandita.

'I don't think our marriage is possible,' she said suddenly, without so much as a hint or a prelude.

He was stunned. 'What are you saying?'

'Luckily, they did not touch you. They could not discover Rita either. Arijit, I am feeling dirty. Debased. Neighbours give me strange looks. Shopkeepers talk of terror the moment I walk in. As if I am the kingpin of a terrorist plot. They think I got away because of my connections, because I was smarter than the television reporters. There is a bad odour about me that won't go in a while.'

Arijit counselled her not to rush to a decision. 'Let's postpone it for a while,' he said. 'We are too close to the unfortunate incidents. Besides, there's a right wing in every society. We need not give them too much importance.'

'Arijit, if you only read what all they are still writing… it drips acid. In their blogs, on Twitter, on Facebook… I am a fiend. A voluptuous, sex-hungry woman making love to a terrorist on the terrace. A witch casting spells on men for sex. I… I'm completely devastated. I just cannot…' She broke down. He went over to her side, his old new bride. Held her, pressed her close. But Nandita had already made up her mind.

'What about going abroad after marriage and living in some corner of the Earth?' Arijit turned to Nandita, his arm around her. 'I can teach somewhere, be a consultant.'

She shook her head. All that had happened since the first newspaper reports had sapped her. Stripped her bare. She had been left bereft, broken. The emails, blogs, tweets, texts pushed her to the verge of a nervous breakdown. She had long sessions with a counsellor to cope with the turmoil inside.

'As lovers, we are star-crossed.' Nandita tried to laugh. 'It's our destiny not to be together.' A friend runs an NGO somewhere in Rajasthan, trying to raise awareness against social evils like child marriage and female infanticide. She came to see her after watching the TV battle. Offered Nandita work. 'Come to Rajasthan, see what we're doing. If it interests you, I will put you in charge of a new project,' the friend said. Nandita had decided to go to the arid desert region to see if she could fit in there.

'No news of Rita?' she asked.

'No. I think she has gone back to her country.'

'Poor girl. Not in her luck either, to have a happy married life.' Nandita glanced down at the empty coffee mugs.

Then she looked up. Their eyes met. 'I hope you will forgive me, Arijit.' She cried, holding him, her head resting on his chest.

Her deep breath, rapid, hot, caused a sensation in him. He tightened his arms around Nandita and kissed her fervently, as if that was his way of holding her back, making her change her mind. With one soulful kiss.

'I'll be waiting for you, Nan – always. Maybe we will run into each other somewhere a while later.' Arijit pressed himself against her.

She smiled wanly.

With that, Arijit knew, a sense of finality had set in.

Seeing off Nandita at the gate, Arijit walked down the road. He tried not to look at the buildings on either side, Noahda Medical Centre, new apartment blocks, middle-class homes with creepers and palms on the balconies. He ignored the Italian villas coming up on the farm fields. Taking long strides, he moved into the woods along the highway and reached the spot from where he had heard the gunshots. Crushing dry leaves and twigs under his feet, he climbed onto the highway and looked at the site of the battle, where the Innova, hung precariously between two trees, had caught fire. The bark of the tree trunk had a thick, black coat – burnt by the madness of that night.

That black of the burn has left a layer inside me as well? Arijit shrugged. He did not notice the police Gypsy parked behind the trees a little distance away. A policeman was watching him suspiciously from its window. Were they expecting the next batch of jihadis to come take a vow of revenge here, between the blackened trees?

'This is where all that happened?'

The policeman looked strangely at him. He climbed out of the Gypsy.

'I live over there.' Arijit pointed to the high-rise towers over the woods. 'I came to see—'

'There is nothing to see.' The man in khaki was gruff. He tore off a piece of blackened bark and offered it to Arijit. 'Except this.'

On his way back, Arijit peeped into the security officer's booth. The retired army officer greeted him as usual. 'Good morning, sir. May I be of any help?' A war veteran, he was courteous to a fault.

'Any news of Chhetri? How is his father?'

'No, sir. To tell you the truth, most probably he will not come back. The bastards are like that. He must have found another job at a higher salary somewhere.'

Arijit walked slowly towards his block and waited in the lobby for the lift. A young man came forward and stood close.

'Excuse me, sir. We never met, but I know you.'

A handsome man in his early thirties. Arijit tried to recall if he had ever seen him somewhere. 'Mr Basu, my name is Rakesh – Neha's husband.' Arijit noticed a pained look on his face. 'Are you leaving this place? The estate manager was saying.'

Arijit glanced at him.

'I mean if I can be of any help… Sir, Neha is very sorry… she feels miserable. She respects you a lot.'

Arijit shook his head and laughed. 'Oh, no. Does she still go for her morning run?'

When he opened the door to his apartment, emptiness assailed him.

He made black coffee and filled the Thermos. He would be drinking it for a long time. That Sunday came back in all its details: the house thick with the aroma of rich food, Nandita at the doorstep smiling pleasantly, their recollection of life together years ago. Her visit gave his life a sudden turn, hints of happiness. This morning, she came to close that chapter, to remind him that ordinary humans must not dare defy the invisible circle around them. After she drove off, he went back to the spot where the demon-anarch had unleashed his fury in obstreperous joy.

Now loneliness tormented him again; he craved a little conversation, big laughs. Every few minutes, he had an expectation: the doorbell would ring, his bride back, smiling demurely like a little girl in the doorway. 'All that was a joke.' Nan would put a hand on his shoulder. He hid his face in his arms on the desk. The apartment began to scare him.

Just then, Piu called.

'Baba, I told you after so many years you would not be able to adjust…' Her voice rose on the phone. 'There's a lot you can do here. The university is still willing to take you.'

He told her he would be in New York within a fortnight.

The day before he got on the train to Dehradun, the doorbell indeed rang – Rita's usual time.

Is she back then? He hurried to the door.

A young woman, stronger, older than Rita, stood outside the door. Arijit looked at her –hair criss-crossed by highlights, deep-red lipstick, a touch of rouge on the cheeks; he caught a whiff of some cheap perfume in the air.

'Sir, I am Jessica. An English couple used to live here, in F Block. I cooked for them. Their work over, they have returned home. I am looking for a job.' She paused, fiddled nervously with her purse and smiled. 'I know their way of cooking – steaming, grilling. I can bartend,' she said with a touch of pride. 'I know how to serve drinks. Someone told me you need help in the kitchen.'

'No, I am leaving this place. I don't need anybody.'

The woman looked disappointed. She smacked her lips, then

smiled, raising her sharp eyebrows. 'I cook for parties also. If there is a weekend party in your house, please contact me.' She fished out a chit of paper with her name and mobile number typed on it.

Looking back on the morning Nandita knocked on his door – shattered, storm-swept – he now knows she had not slept the whole night. The marks of struggle were visible, though he had missed them back then. She was ripped apart by a dilemma before she could make up her mind and drive to Noahda. Why did she put an end to everything? Was it because she was tormented by the hostile WhatsApp campaign, poison texts? Vilified by the party animals? Or was there a deeper, gloomier reason? Did she feel her marriage now would fulfil only one part of the promise?

He will never know.

44
Passionflowers

'Strong coffee, no sugar, right?' The kiosk owner smiles. He tells a boy to dust the wooden bench as a special gesture. 'A hot patty, sir?' Without waiting for an answer, he puts one on the grill. 'The whole day you walk around. Are you looking for something?' The man comes out of the kiosk.

'Looking for something?' Arijit repeats, unsure if that really is the purpose.

'Sahib, I mean a good property. I thought you have come to settle down here.'

'Property? Oh, no. I'm going back tomorrow.'

'Tomorrow?' The man looks disappointed. 'Sir, whenever you come to Dehradun, please do not forget to stop by my stall. And tomorrow, before you leave, do come for a cup of coffee. On the house.' He joins his hands in a namaste.

Finishing his coffee, Arijit gets up. Touched by the man's warmth, he waits for a few seconds. *Am I looking for something?* He carefully weighs the question, every word, letter in the sentence. 'Sure, whenever I am in town, I'll come here for a coffee.' He looks around, pauses undecidedly. 'I like this place very much.'

Taking long strides as usual, without a destination in mind, he walks down Convent Road towards the church. By the side of the road, a bazaar has come up. Sprightly Tibetan girls in their colourful clothes are selling handbags, jackets, jeans. At one end, a man is selling noodles and momos. Arijit stops without knowing why.

Looking at the wares, he wonders if he can buy something for Parijat – a handbag or an umbrella. Undecided, he walks on.

'*Saab-jiii! Saab-jiiii…*'

At first, Arijit ignores the shrill cry. He hears footsteps behind him – rapid, urgent, someone running to catch up with him. It's a familiar voice… and still… Arijit turns. Ram Bahadur Chhetri. After running quite some distance the Gurkha is out of breath. When he finally draws level with Arijit, Chhetri is red-faced, gasping.

'I saw you from a distance, Sahib. I had no doubt it was you.' He laughs, his face flushed.

'Chhetri! What a surprise! Didn't you go home to see your ailing father?' Arijit steps down from the pavement.

The Gurkha walks alongside. For a minute or two, he keeps quiet, panting. 'I have a lot to tell you, sir. Please come with me.' He almost pulls his hand.

Arijit does not resist as Chhetri guides him into a quiet street. On either side, elegant houses nestle among large, shadowy trees. On the driveways, big cars gleam.

'This is Vasant Vihar,' Chhetri says, noticing Arijit's curiosity. 'The colony of the super-rich.'

'Do you live here, on this street?' Arijit sounds doubtful.

Chhetri nods. 'I am the caretaker of a house; the owner lives abroad. Actually, my uncle is the caretaker, but I do the job.'

After about a hundred yards, Chhetri stops and walks down the driveway to the gate of a yellowish bungalow. There is something evocative about the house – the front veranda, long terrace, opulent shaddocks hanging from the branches of a dark green tree. Not the most spectacular house in the enclave but visually soothing.

This house welcomes neither a prospective buyer nor a tenant.

The terse, rude notice above the letterbox seems to have been prompted by onlookers' interest in the property.

Chhetri artfully pushes his hand through a gap and opens the gate from the inside.

'Please come in, sir.' He holds the gate open.

They walk down a side veranda into the backyard.

'See, who's here! Uma, are you in?'

Arijit hears the shuffling of feet, the noise of footsteps. As if someone is hesitating to come out. Then the door opens.

A girl in cheap jeans and a long-sleeved shirt steps out. Her short, straight hair brushed like a boy's. Looking at the visitor, she feels uncomfortable, abashed. A sense of shame is pulling her down. She wants to run away. Unable to face him, she lowers her eyes, searching the ground for something.

She looks very different – shorn, shrivelled. A rain-drenched bird. Still, he knows her. Like the new name, this is another edition of her.

'Rita! What're you doing here?'

She waits. Her lips quiver. She struggles, but words fail her. Keeps standing there – caught in a web of silence, her eyes flooded with tears.

'Kaku, I never thought I will see you again.' She tries to smile.

It has been less than a month, but she looks so unfamiliar.

They take him inside the house. Through a carpeted hallway, he is ushered into the large, lavishly decorated drawing room. A sweet, raw smell of timber comes from the mahogany furniture. A wall-mounted tiger-head trophy glares at him. After a while, Rita – now Uma – goes back to make coffee.

Chhetri pulls an ottoman and sits close to his sofa.

'Early in the morning, even before night was over, I would go to a dairy across the highway to buy milk,' he recounts, sensing that the sahib would be keen to know the whole story.

'I was returning on my scooter when I saw it happen before my eyes. The police jeep overtook the badmashes' Gypsy and asked them to stop. They opened fire instead. Then a hail of bullets from the police jeep. The bandits' car swerved, hitting the trees. The moment I saw the crazy fellow tumble out of the car clutching his chest, I knew what it meant. I forgot the milk, went straight to her place, woke her up and told her everything.'

Sleepy, scared, she was undecided. 'You must run away; that police officer will come back for you, now he has got an excuse,' he told her. Confused, not knowing what to do, she started crying. 'Let me talk to Kaku and Didi,' she insisted. But Chhetri knew in a situation like this a gentleman could not help her. He knew he would have to do something to save the girl from landing up in the police lock-up again.

'Saab-ji, I alone could help her. So I said, "Let's run away. I will do for you what a husband can do."'

Arijit scrutinizes the young man closely, as though he were putting him under a magnifying glass. The Gurkha, not yet twenty-five, means every word he says. Honest, earnest, he is explaining his role, recalling everything that has turned so many lives upside down.

Hustled by the man who had once covered her shame with a moth-eaten shawl, she hurriedly put into a bag only a few things and left with him. He told her not to lock the door. 'Let your neighbours think you're around.'

From there, they went to her cousin's beauty parlour. While Chhetri waited outside, she went in and talked to Rekha about her need for a new look, to hoodwink the police. When she came back after a good half-hour, even he had difficulty recognizing her. She looked like a boy.

'I knew going to a bus terminus or railway station would be risky. So I trusted my old rusty Bajaj.' Chhetri laughs. 'As if we were having fun, boy and girl, I slipped on my old sunglasses and rode like a loafer – casually, a laid-back couple stopping at a tea–samosa shop, at another place for sugarcane juice. I did not overspeed.'

Chhetri is no longer turning to him for approval of everything they had done. He is seized by an urgency to complete the tale.

Arijit cannot believe that the young man sitting before him is capable of such quick decision-making, can move out of the straitjacket to do such an unusual thing. That he would take such risks, plunge into uncertainties for this girl. The scene of Rita's ugly fight with another maid comes back – her kurta ripped off, baring much of live skin. While the sweepers, servants, drivers were relishing the young woman's bare back, Chhetri gallantly stepped in to save her *shame*. Did he secretly love the girl? The grille-man's rival for her hand?

'Chhetri, when you went to her flat after seeing the encounter, had you already made up your mind that you would bring her here, take shelter with your uncle?'

'Sahib, I did not know anything. When I saw that grille-wallah coming out of the car, I did not even know he was a terrorist or a scoundrel. He was always a troublesome chap who bothered Uma a lot. I knew I had to do something right then. Otherwise, the policeman from the Special Cell would come back for her. She was so helpless that I had no choice; I had to do this. I did not have time to think what would happen to me. When her cousin was busy giving her a makeover, I rushed back to the apartment complex, told the security officer I was going home to Nepal, that my father had had a heart attack. I borrowed a little money from him. Then I went to my quarters and took all the money I had saved and returned to the beauty parlour to pick her up.'

At one point, the police had set up a barrier on the road, stopping, checking cars. Cleverly, Chhetri pulled up right in front of a police vehicle parked by the roadside. He walked up to an officer on duty and asked for directions to a medical college. 'Go straight, after about ten kilometres, turn left from the intersection. You will see the campus.' The policeman looked sharply at him. His genial mood suddenly changed. 'Are you both students at that medical college?' the policeman asked suspiciously when he saw Rita out of the corner of his eye. 'My brother works there,' Chhetri said. 'Ha ha. Sahib, I knew about the medical college. I still asked, so there was no suspicion. Hah!'

Rabeya-alias-Rita-alias-Uma comes with coffee and a snack. A mixture of roasted peanuts, flattened rice and chickpeas garnished with chopped onion, coriander leaves, flavoured with a dash of lemon. She stands shamefacedly beside Chhetri, her husband of one month – like a bird that has shed its feathers.

Arijit thinks of the party on Nandita's lawn. In a Murshidabad silk sari, her long, dark hair imperiously flowing past the waist, she was the find of the evening. The American doctor looked for an excuse to talk to her, chat her up. Perhaps that was Nandita's way of giving her an idea of the good life, what she could get by leaving her own milieu behind.

Nandita's way! Arijit sighs. Was it also her way to call the grilleman home to persuade, talk him out of Rita's life? And invite the wrath of the South Delhi socialites? *Love jihad*. And here is the girl – sick, scared, with cropped hair, a moulting duck – uneasy in jeans and a shirt.

Uma looks confused, unsure of her emotions. Perhaps guilt troubles her for running away without telling those who did so much for her? Or is she happy that she managed her situation, keeping them out of the mess? Is she curious to know about Bharat?

'Kaku,' she says finally.

He looks at her.

'You will have lunch with us.'

She does not ask about Nandita. And he decides not to say anything that will make her uneasy in her husband's presence. She walks back to the kitchen.

'So, you have decided to live here, looking after the house?' He turns to Chhetri.

'No, Sahib. We are just waiting for our Australian visas. My cousin runs a little restaurant in Melbourne. It's popular among the Indians there. We will join him so he can expand his business.'

Arijit is stumped. He never thought the security guard at the gate could have ambitions outside the apartment complex, let alone the country.

'Have you got Indian passports?'

'We have already got our Nepalese passports. My uncle knows an agent in Kathmandu, who gets things done for a fee. For five lakh Nepalese rupees, he has promised both of us passports, visas and air tickets. The passports are already with my father in the village. Soon, we will go to Kathmandu for the visa interviews. The agent said he will get it done. 100 per cent pukka.' Chhetri laughs.

'Have you already given him the money?'

'My uncle has paid him three lakh; the remaining amount when he gives us the air tickets. His man will see us off at the airport.'

'Where did you get the money?'

'I had some savings. But mostly, it's Uma's money. I do not know how she saved so much.'

'How did she get the Nepalese passport?' he asks out of curiosity.

'Saab-ji, everything is possible. Now, she has a birth certificate, her name on the electoral rolls of our village, school-leaving certificate – everything. In Nepal, it is possible. In the passport, her name is Uma Bhandari.' The Gurkha laughs.

So Melbourne instead of the farmhouse? Not a bad proposition. He thinks of Uma's money. He never gave her that kind of money. Nor did he ever find anything stolen, missing from his house. Nandita would surely not have given her that much without telling him. Where did she get so much money? Arijit thinks about it. There could be only one source…

'Saab-ji, we will leave for Nepal next week, after my uncle comes back. She is still scared, wakes in the middle of the night with bad dreams. She fears the police might come back to hunt her down. That's why she does not want to wear a sari, does not oil or comb her hair. We have been living here for a month. She has never gone out, not even for a single moment.'

Arijit recalls how he thought it was his responsibility to help the girl – frail, fragile, easy fodder for a corrupt system. But his plans failed, ended in a disaster, turning lives upside down. Chhetri handled the issue simply, much better, in his own way. Where he failed, the Gurkha succeeded.

'Sahib, she is a good girl. And for her, you are like a father. Often, at night, she cries in her sleep, calling out to you.' Ram Bahadur Chhetri clasps his hands, smiles. 'Once we are in Australia, all her problems will be over.'

'And what will she do there?'

'Hearing about her cooking skills, my cousin said she will be an asset.'

The aroma from the kitchen wafts in. He knows the girl is making chicken curry.

Uma lays the table – cheap stainless-steel plates, bowls, tumblers, plastic mats. She has changed into a sari.

Arijit sits alone at the dining table. When he asks Chhetri to eat with him, he looks scandalized.

'Have a meal with you at the same table? Baap re!' His face flushes with embarrassment.

Dal, fried brinjal, a cauliflower-and-potato curry and chicken – deliciously cooked. The food reminds him of the days in the apartment. After lunch, they return to the drawing room. Uma goes back to the kitchen to make coffee.

'If you think you need more money, let me know,' he tells Chhetri in a low voice.

'Sir, you have done a lot for us. I will call after we reach Melbourne.'

He tells Chhetri about his decision to return to America.

'You are going to America? And that American sahib – Rado or whatever, Uma talks about him – he now lives in Australia. Isn't it strange?' Chhetri looks up at him.

Radolf McGirk, Arijit now remembers, talked about his plans to relocate to Australia in his last email. Perhaps one day, he will trace Munir Sheikh's daughter.

A silence falls. Arijit thinks of McGirk. Will he succeed in recovering the little girl with large black eyes he left behind in the cyclone-swept delta? Instead of a father, now she has her husband at her side.

Chhetri looks at him, puzzled, unsure if the sahib is offended by something he has said.

'Chhetri.' Arijit sits back.

'Ji, sir.'

'Tell me what happened to your wife's mobile? Is she still using it?'

'That phone, eh? Sahib, on the way to Dehradun, you come across a channel of the Ganga at Roorkee? Coming down from the hills, it's very fast, the waters roar. When we were on the bridge, Uma asked me to stop. She got down, walked up to the railing and threw something into the water. I thought it was a coin. Everybody tosses a coin into Ganga-ji. When I asked her what she had hurled into the river, she said, "My curse," and laughed, looking relieved.'

After finishing his coffee, Arijit gets up. It's late afternoon, time to go home. Uma comes with something neatly wrapped in a plastic carry bag.

'This is for Bubka,' she smiles, the glint back in her eyes.

He opens the packet.

The nakshi kantha she used to stitch after work in the kitchen. With intricate needlework, she has raised a design – clusters of passionflowers – her memories of the meadows on the banks of the Rupsa.

Acknowledgements

Written over seven years and spread around the world, *Border Crossers* has been made possible with the unreserved cooperation of many. I am entirely to blame if no record of all those who have helped me in many ways could be maintained. For someone who does not keep a journal, it is impossible to remember everyone who extended a hand somewhere during such a long trek. Still I wish to put down with gratitude every gesture of support by some Samaritan along the road. Without their help, the book would not have happened.

The writer Jad Adams carefully went through the manuscript and made important suggestions.

Former diplomat Deb Mukherjee patiently answered my questions and offered his views on many issues.

The novelist Paul Pickering assuredly discovered the book even when I was still tentative about approaching the publishing world.

Dr Karan Singh, noted scholar and former MP, shared with me his experiences in many areas.

Sonali Jindal, my editor at Hachette India, spotted *Border Crossers* within weeks, showing how a publishing house earns its distinctiveness. She carefully edited the manuscript, often adding value to it. Her colleague Ashutosh Sharma promptly responded when he first heard about my book and let the matter start. Vinita Nayar also carefully went through the book.

Anupama Manral and Dipanjali Chadha worked hard to put the finishing touches on the manuscript.

Hachette India Managing Director, Thomas Abraham's strong support and appreciation were inspiring.

In Dhaka, senior journalist Ataur Rahman helped me reach out to experts and some cultural activists during my research in Bangladesh.

Well-known Bangladeshi writer Anisul Hoque acquainted me with many cultural expressions of the country's core values and impulses, born out of the struggle against neocolonialism that culminated in the 1971 Bangladesh Liberation War.

Debashis Chakraborty guided me expertly during my fieldwork in Khulna.

Dr Naresh Dang, my friend and physician, would answer my questions with remarkable clarity and helped me with my research into the ways of medicine.

My old journalist friend Suresh Sukumaran took me through vignettes of fascinating Malayali culture.

Protiti Roy and Naman Gupta were the best audience one could ask for. They often made important points during our weekend Google meets for book reading.